# PACHYDERMS

# PACHYDERMS

## DANNY BUOY

**NAVIGATOR BOOKS**
SAN DIEGO, CALIFORNIA

# PACHYDERMS

Copyright © 2012, 2013 by Danny Buoy

**Navigator Books**

www.navigator-books.com

Copy Editor: Joyce M. Gilmour, EditingTLC (www.editingtlc.com)

Cover Art © 2013, Navigator Books

Library of Congress Number: 2001119256

ISBN-13: 978-0-9890026-6-0

Printed in the United States of America

*This book is dedicated to the only female who encouraged me to write it, Laura Feld Musaw, and to the only male who ever thanked me for serving there, Timmy McCaw.*

*Thank you to all who served in Viet Nam.*

Popular movies might offer a viewer some glimpse of the dirty little war called Vietnam, but none address the true reality of being a soldier during that war. *Pachyderms* is my story of being one soldier who underwent that experience.

Young and anxious for my first duty assignment following the beginning ritual of basic training, I was somewhat astounded to discover my first permanent duty post was a United States Army Aviation Unit in a nonexistent company. With inadequate training and overwhelming obstacles, my fellow soldiers and I embarked on creating the 312th Aviation Unit. We soon discovered "What the soldier sees (or hears) isn't what a soldier gets." Eventually we all were faced with an even tougher struggle—coming home to America.

# Part One

## *THE 312$^{TH}$ AVIATION COMPANY*

# PROLOGUE

---

*I DID NOT FALL*
*MY NAME IS NOT ON A WALL*
*I SERVED WITH THOSE WHO*
*GAVE THE LAST FULL MEASURE*
*TO GIVE THIS WORLD*
*ITS MOST REVERED TREASURE*
*NO I DID NOT FALL*
*MY NAME IS NOT ON A WALL*
*BUT WITH MY COMRADES I*
*GAVE MY ALL*
*AND SURVIVED TO LIVE THE TREASURE*
*OF THOSE WHO GAVE THE*
*LAST FULL MEASURE*

I received the above poem from Retired Sergeant Carl Copelet about a year after the movie *Platoon* was awarded the Oscar for best movie. During the year before its arrival, a fellow office worker hounded me to see the movie and to comment. I told the worker I didn't want to see the motion picture, but repeated pressure from her over a sixty-day time span weakened my resolve and I told her I had seen the movie. "Paula" knew I was a Vietnam Veteran.

"What did you think?" she asked.

"Not the war I was in, Paula."

"You're wrong," Paula protested. "You vets have been hiding the truth all these years; that's the way it really was!"

Memories of my initial reentry into civilian life following my tour of duty in South Vietnam, along with the subsequent decade, taught me about trying to change another person's mind concerning a "dirty little Asian War"; "that's the way it really was," stuck. When I read Carl Copelet's poem, I felt as though I had the single most important reason to tell my story, especially after seeing other movies such as *Deer Hunter*, *Apocalypse Now*, *Full Metal Jacket*, *Born on the Fourth of July*, and *Platoon*. None equated my experiences to what I had seen on film. I was in a helicopter company in Vietnam, didn't play Russian roulette or water-ski on any in-country river, never partook in an assault on a hamlet while a helicopter broadcast some opera, couldn't imagine shooting any fellow soldier to insure someone's ticket home, couldn't run through a jungle while firing an automatic weapon, and did not fly high because of some overdose of drugs.

*Pachyderms* represents what I experienced during my two-year hitch in the United States Army. Never again in my life will I be as close to men as I was in South Vietnam.

# CHAPTER 1

## COPE AND COOBY

Thirty-seven, maybe thirty-eight years-old, six-foot tall, the man was 40 pounds overweight. His worn fatigues needed to be replaced and his black army boots had not seen polish in some time. His collar rank plates and belt buckle were tarnished and his fine, ash-blond hair required a trim. A cigarette dangled from his mouth and ashes covered the GI-issued desk I was standing at, while two piercing light blue eyes sized me up. This specialist was not the regular army sort I had been used to dealing with in my total ninety-day career. Specialist 5th Class Carl Copelet wouldn't be appearing in any recruiting poster, but he did outrank me by five grades.

"What army school do you come from?" he gruffly asked.

"Advanced Infantry Training School, Fort Jackson, South Carolina."

"What did you say, Private?"

I watched as he crushed the last inch of his cigarette into an overflowing ashtray.

"Advanced Infantry Training School, Fort Jackson, South Carolina," I repeated.

"That's what I thought you said. Jesus Christ! Here we go again. Leave it to the army to send me a ground-pounding infantryman." The specialist didn't look pleased and I froze in place. I didn't know how to react and I felt greener than long grass about to be cut.

He rested one elbow on the desk and started to rub his lips, a gesture I interpreted as disgust. After thirty long seconds, he barked, "Can you type?"

"Yes-yeah-yes I can, Specialist, but I'm no whiz."

"Well, that's good. It's the only qualification you need as my *on-the-job* trainee down here at flight operations." He didn't ask any more questions, and I didn't either. I couldn't have anyway. I was just plain scared. The feeling intensified when he casually remarked, "Two of my last three on-the-job trainees didn't make it." I couldn't imagine getting farther down any ladder of success, and from that point I began to wonder if I'd ever see the top of the barrel from my current position beneath it.

He pointed to another military desk across from his own in the small office and told me to sit down. "Do an about face, Private," he ordered.

I pivoted the chair and faced a wall behind the desk.

"See all the forms stacked on those shelves?"

"Yes, Specialist, I do. There sure are a lot," I told him, gazing at a ten-foot section of shelving loaded with endless piles of paper.

"By the time I'm finished, you will know each one of those forms just like you know how to hold your dick when you piss." The graphic comment was his job description.

"But there are so many, Specialist!"

"You will memorize all of them!" The tone in his voice was quite clear. "Follow me," he ordered.

The E-5 led me throughout the flight operations center, commenting about its various functions. He introduced me to twenty men. "Give it time, grunt," he remarked. "For right now the coffeepot is over here and the piss tube is over there. The rest'll take time. Come on now; let's go see our flight line."

A few civilian months earlier, I was a spectator at the Offutt Air Force Base runway, south of my hometown, Omaha, Nebraska, when President Johnson toured the defense headquarters of the Strategic Air Command. This place was big, and it took up to thirty minutes to drive across part of it. When we got back to his office, the specialist began an overview of the 176th Aviation Battalion.

"Major Albert Frankel commands the 176th. He has four helicopter companies under his wing. The 312th will be his fifth. That will be your outfit. All you really need to know about Frankel is he can fly anything and can make anything fly." He paused for a moment, and repeated, "He can fly anything and make anything fly."

I listened intently, still feeling uncomfortable. The "two that didn't make it" crack was gnawing at me.

"There are three battalions here at Fort Benning, and all of them are in the First Aviation Group, commanded by Colonel John Fenson. He's known as the *Ace of Aviation*, and the boys at the Pentagon have authorized him to train fully deployable chopper units for service in the Vietnam theater of war. Fenson is damn good at it, Private, and I suspect he'll get his first star by the end of this year."

I had spent four hours that June day in 1966, trying to digest as much as possible from what the specialist was either telling me or showing me; his words, "fully deployable helicopter units for service in the Vietnam theater of war," hit me between the eyes. I felt like peeing in my pants. As I recall, it was at that moment I began to seek someone or something to blame.

"Deployable? Does this mean I am going to Nam?" When I had enlisted, less than 5% of the Armed Forces were involved in the police action, or so I wanted to believe. Vietnam happened to others, not to me. Lord how I wanted him to be wrong!

"All of the units in this battalion, and all of those under the command of Colonel Fenson, will be crossing the ocean and joining our forces in the Southeast Asian Theater of Operations," he casually replied.

I was stunned, feeling like someone had just notified me that my mother had died. This easily had to be the biggest snafu of my young military career.

The specialist must have noticed my concern for he put me to work immediately, giving me a handwritten form that needed to be typed. "You and I are going to find out right now just how much of a 'no whiz' you are on a typewriter," he cracked, adding, "the army does not tolerate any errors on its official paperwork."

I didn't know anything about the form he handed me. It did require intense concentration, and when I finished, all the specialist said was, "It's okay, but don't get the idea you're done, kid." He was not joking, and in the next three weeks, I typed more meaningless forms than small slices of nuts in a Skippy Peanut Butter jar, wondering if I was ever going to grasp everything I needed to learn. Although I hadn't forgotten about wanting to blame someone or something, I didn't acknowledge one very important thing that was happening: learning about Carl Copelet. He was the NCOIC (non-commissioned-officer-in-charge), and nobody screwed with him.

We shared little personal conversation, but even I knew that E-5 was not an impressive rank for someone with his talent. Coffeepot chitchat and lunchtime gossip suggested he was a twenty-year *lifer*, with a tour of duty in Korea and two tours of duty in Vietnam under his belt. Why wasn't he an E-7? It puzzled me. Scuttlebutt reported retirement, but not so much as one rumor surfaced. In a rare exchange, he joked, saying, "I have more time in grade than most have in the chow line."

At the start of my seventh week of training, Specialist Copelet surprised me.

"It's time for two things, Private Coobat," he said while standing in front of my desk. "The first is that we cut all this formality shit, like using specialist and private, when we talk."

"What do you want me to call you?"

"Anything but *specialist*."

"How about if I call you, Cope?"

"Why Cope?"

"Because it's what I do here with you!" I saw his lips resist the urge to release the regular grin.

"Fair enough. What do you want me to call you?"

"Your choice, Special — I mean, Cope."

"Okay if I call you Cooby?"

"Fair enough." I began to relax.

"Great! Now it's time I tell you why you've been beating those Underwood Typewriter keys, Cooby."

"You mean there is a reason?"

"All that paperwork is the *army way*, Cooby."

"But why so damn many, Special — I mean, Cope?"

"Pay." It was a one-word answer.

"Like in money?"

"Yup! Like in money."

"A big bonus at the end of the year?"

"No, Cooby, a monthly benefit, twelve times a year. All men who fly in aircraft get two big bennies: hazardous duty pay and flight pay. One hundred thirty bucks for enlisted, $260 big ones for officers."

"WOW!"

"Gets even better, Cooby. Congress authorizes more."

"More? Must have been in one of those middle page news stories I didn't read."

"Combat pay."

"Combat pay?"

"Sixty-five bucks for enlisted, $130 for officers. Plus, all of it is tax free if you serve in Vietnam."

"No wonder Fort Benning is bigger than Offutt AFB, back home in Omaha."

"You catch on fast, Cooby. But there is a catch."

"Figures! What is it?"

"Congress requires paperwork. Rule number one: document everything. Rule number two: no documentation, no pay. There are *no* exceptions."

"Never?"

"Right now, in our battalion, 216 enlisted men and 144 officers fall victim to rule one and rule two if there was no recordkeeping. That figure increases when your company materializes."

I didn't have to be Einstein to calculate the numbers. It was huge. I reported to the flight line at 7 A.M. and left at 6 P.M. daily. My file thirteen was crammed each day and I envied the civilian paper salesman who reaped a real cool income long before reducing forests became political. I secretly had it in for Specialist Copelet for not articulating rule number three: Do it right the first time, or do it over. He did warn me that "the army didn't tolerate any errors on any of its official paperwork." He didn't tell me the work was monotonous, exhausting, and prone to mistake-making.

There was one province where I could not reprehend the specialist, and it was in the traditional division between military personnel. The philosophy was brainwashed into me at basic training and tattooed on my memory during Advanced Infantry Training. Officers were as different from enlisted men as feudal lords were from serfs. The belief was backed by an Act of Congress. The farcical ideology filtered into army aviation paperwork, and I recognized it right off the bat.

If private peasant flew on an aircraft, he recorded the flight time on a form called, the Dash 12, signed it, and turned it into operations. At the end of the month, that name, along with the names of all other enlisted aviators, were checked off as "yes" or "no" on one pre-approved form, and dispatched to battalion finance authorizing hazardous duty and flight pay.

If Pontius Pilot flew, his reporting was trisected, dissected, bisected, and analyzed on the largest most tedious form in army aviation: The Department of Defense Form 759.

It favored a ledger sheet from an accountant's office, with vacant columns awaiting useless information requiring a ridiculous code as difficult to memorize as "Beethoven's Fifth Symphony"; enlisted personnel needed only "yes" or "no"; officer grade required, 30/06/66/CH-47A/Inst-Plt/3.0/ATLFX/N/A-N/C. Each ledger line was for each flight.

"Why the code?" I asked Cope one frustrating day.

"It's the *army way*, Cooby."

"It's unnecessary and stupid! We have one form for 216 enlisted men, and 144 individual forms for officers. All of the 145 forms do the same thing: request pay. It's stupid!"

"It isn't stupid, Cooby. Flight records are a part of the permanent records following a pilot wherever he goes."

I wasn't convinced. I repeated, "think it's stupid. A pilot may fly the aircraft, but enlisted make the aircraft fly." I swear he felt I was right, but he knew I still was wet behind my ears about the army way, and the strength behind the DOD 759 form. Neither of us knew it, but I had a lot to learn about the specialist in flight operations that nobody screwed with. I began to understand a few days later when I was given two sets of permanent flight records. They belonged to Captain Harold Patton and Chief Warrant Officer, Third Grade, James Harsh, two pilots assigned to the newly forming 312th Aviation Company — my outfit. The two men arrived to confirm there was an exception to every rule, even army rules. Each scrap of paper in the United States Army streamed through an unbreakable chain of command. If the communiqués originated at the Pentagon, and landed in the hands of a private, they had flowed through a series of channels including division, brigade, group, battalion, perhaps some other stops, and finally company level. The two officers came to see E-5 Copelet, and they were hand carrying their personal permanent flight records.

"Looking for Specialist Copelet," the senior ranking officer stated. The captain's shiny railroad bars, his crisp heavily starched fatigues, and the observably spit-polished boots placed him in direct conflict with an E-5 who wasn't going to appear in a recruiting poster. Patton was slight of build, maybe 5 foot 8 inches, sported a crewcut hairstyle, had deeply set black eyes arced by thick brows, and a swarthy complexion. "You him?"

"Same one. How can I help you?" Copelet answered. In all of my seven weeks with Cope, I can't recall him ever jumping to a position of attention when an officer walked into a room.

"Think you'll be looking for these." The captain took one folder from the warrant and handed two to Copelet. I noticed one folder to be an inch thick, the other, thicker. "Scuttlebutt says you're pretty good with those." Patton's sly smile suggested a smooth talker.

"Hunch suggests you're with the 312$^{th}$, and experience says two flyboys don't want interruptions in flight pay."

Cope accepted the two sets of records. He opened each one to glance at the top page, closed both, handed the records to me, and commented, "Some pretty impressive numbers! You aren't related to...?"

"No, but thanks for asking," Patton rebuffed a question he apparently had heard often.

"Your records will be in good hands with my OJT here at the 176$^{th}$," Cope reassured the captain.

"Rumor has it you're hanging up the stripes," the chief warrant finally spoke. James Harsh had a medium build, blue eyes, blond hair, a collegiate appearance, and looked as though he just returned from a photo session for GQ. He filled out his olive-drab fatigues very well, and I judged him, as well as his partner, to be in his late thirties.

"Found my dream home," Cope responded. "Tacoma-Seattle, right on the sound. After twenty years, I'm ready to take a menial civilian job and ease into semi-retirement, far away from all my bitches with the army."

"What gripes could you have?" Harsh asked. "We have it on very reliable authority you're the best in operations," the warrant deliberately complimented the specialist.

"Too many to list, Mr. Harsh."

"List one for us," the warrant suggested.

"Well, one would be this infantryman I'm training to be your flight operations clerk."

"Copelet, didn't we hear you say our records would be in good hands with him?" the captain reentered the dialogue. I sat there holding my first two sets of flight records.

"Your records are in good hands, but one of my biggest peeves in this man's army, one that has pissed me off for a lot of years, is why the army trains a man in one area and then turns around and puts him in another. I've seen it happen too many times," Copelet opened up.

"What have you seen, Copelet?" Harsh was not about to be put off.

"Some dumb first sergeant will reassign my OJT to the mess hall right after I finish training him," Copelet told both. I listened intently. I knew my prospects to find blame had just become a little more difficult.

"Want a crack at the solution?" Harsh fired a direct shot.

"Not following your drift, Mr. Harsh."

"Might...once you hear our offer."

"What offer?" Copelet's tone was skeptical.

"Copelet, when you opened our flight records and took a peek, you didn't look at name, rank, or serial number. You looked at only one thing: total flight hours," Harsh began, winking once at the captain and gaining an unspoken nod of approval. "With over 10,000 total flying hours, you knew we've been around, and you knew we have the contacts to get things done."

"I was impressed."

"Sign up for another two years, volunteer for a third tour with the 312th Aviation Company, and be promoted to E-6 immediately, with a real good shot at E-7," the chief warrant officer bluntly spelled out the *offer*.

Cope rubbed his chin, lit a cigarette, and took a drag, exhaling the smoke with, "Tempting, very tempting, but the Mrs. and I have already put down a substantial deposit."

"Payments come every month, Copelet," the warrant told the E-5 specialist. "They'd be a bit easier with retirement pay based on E-6 rank, maybe E-7. I'd give it some thought," the CW3 reiterated.

"So would I," the captain chimed in.

"Appreciate the offer, gentlemen, but my mind's made up. Twenty years at the flight operations shit has worn me out. I'm just too tired to take on two con artists like you as my flight operations officers."

"Who told you we're the flight operations officers?" Patton looked startled. "That's top-secret info!"

"Rumor has it my current commanding officer, Major Al Frankel, will be head cheese for your sister outfit, the 713$^{th}$ Transportation Company, but even I can't vouch for Robert Fang, the lieutenant colonel about to command the 312$^{th}$." Cope purposely slipped in even more information.

Harsh squirmed too, surprised at hearing an E-5 spout classified material, finally erupting like a pushed pimple. "Jesus Christ, Copelet! I suppose you know where the 312$^{th}$ is headed?"

"Bear Cat," the specialist casually answered. "About 40 miles south of Saigon. Big part of the command headquarters of the 5$^{th}$ Division. All of this is *off the record*, right?" Cope let the officers know he wasn't as dumb as he looked.

"Anything else?" a humbled captain inquired.

"Nothing spectacular other than your CH-47A Chinooks will be the first medium-sized helicopters at Benning." The rookie threw in a comment for fun.

I was just as surprised as the two officers. I had just learned I would deploy with these two strangers to a place called Bear Cat, 40 miles south of a city I had only read about. There could only be one more question, and Mr. Harsh asked it.

"When?"

"Depends."

"Depends? On what?" an anxious captain asked.

"On when the civilian company, Boeing-Vertol, releases the helicopters to the army," Copelet advised them, as well as me.

"Any guesses?" Mr. Harsh acknowledged Cope as someone in the know.

"Doesn't matter, Mr. Harsh. The 312$^{th}$ isn't equipped with all the personnel it needs, let alone the 713$^{th}$. You'll see for yourself tomorrow morning when you meet with the entire complement of officers and enlisted for the two outfits."

"How'd you find out about orientation? We were advised only yesterday." A humbled Harsh knew he had been had.

"Rumors. Rumors and scuttlebutt."

I saw Copelet crack another smile. It was the second in seven weeks.

# CHAPTER 2

## FIRST ORIENTATION

---

The following day, after a pensive night of soaking in the term, "Bear Cat," I zoomed in on seeking that someone to blame. Cope's work philosophy had just put my inner feelings on hold. I was headed for a place that had a specific name, and it was forty miles south of Saigon. "How soon?" was the question my mind would not stop asking.

Instead of boarding the one and only deuce-and-a-half-ton truck leaving the 176th company area for my OJT job at the flight line, I walked to the building where all members of the 312th Aviation Company and the 713th Transportation Company had been ordered to report.

The brief walk took less than 15 seconds. The building was across the street from the 176th mess hall, and located in one of six unused buildings compromising an idle company area. No one was in the deserted barracks when I arrived, so I sat down on one of the naked bunk beds filling the bottom floor, and hurried up to wait.

I must have asked myself a hundred times, "How soon?" in the thirty long minutes I spent alone.

Three men finally joined me, quietly taking seats on the stripped bunks. Five lonelier minutes passed until the awesome stillness was shattered by, "Ah-ten-hut."

The decorous recognition came from Captain Harold Patton, while Chief Warrant, 3rd Grade, James Harsh, officially held the barracks door open for Lieutenant Colonel Robert Fang.

"At ease," he announced. "Take a seat." Four enlisted men and two officers followed orders, and sat their butts down on the awaiting metal mattresses.

I was instantly reminded of Elmer Fudd, but this version wasn't a cartoon and nowhere near as cute. Robert Fang stood 5 feet 8 inches tall, was 75 pounds overweight, and wore stretched OD green fatigues appearing to have been knitted over his bulky body. The matching ball cap, which he did not remove, snugly topped a bean-like head, and emphasized bulging eyes. It was evident Robert Fang hadn't missed too many meals.

"Men, I'm Lew-Lieutenant Ker-Colonel Robert Fang, Jew-Junior, commanding officer of the 312$^{th}$ Aviation Company," the pudgy man stuttered opening remarks to his full complement of officers and enlisted: one captain, one warrant, one E-6 staff sergeant, and three private E-1s. "My 312$^{th}$ will be the first Chinook helicopter company trained at Benning for deployment in the Southeastern Asia Theater of War."

This was the second time I heard the word, "Chinook," and I didn't relish hearing again, the awful word, "deployment." What I heard in the next fifteen minutes didn't brighten my spirits at all. The colonel discoursed on a lengthy history of the helicopter in previous wartime usage, comparing the CH-47 to the power capabilities of an elephant. He went on to challenge his command to "rewrite the pages of aviation history," an idea making me question why I hadn't burned my draft card in the first place.

"With this equipment, and your help, men, I know I will turn the silver cluster on my ball cap into a well-deserved eagle." The pompous field grade officer concluded a fifteen-minute dissertation that shouldn't have taken any more than five. Not only did my ears tell me I wouldn't follow the man to a foxhole, my unbelieving eyes sensed there was something wrong with the scenario. Even my basic training unit had 150 officers and men.

Following a clumsy moment of silence, Captain Patton ascertained the address was complete, and yelled, "Ah-ten-hut," militarily, at least, stamping an approval signaling "first orientation" was over and the commander was about to leave the building. Three privates and a staff sergeant jumped to the required position of attention with one of them banging his head on the top portion of a bunk bed. Mr. Harsh encored the door performance, and within ten seconds four enlisted men were all that remained of "orientation."

The sergeant waited until the departing officers were out of sight, then left without uttering a sound, leaving three privates alone.

"Hi. I'm Hubert Frock from Atlanta," one of the other two introduced himself. He extended his hand.

"I'm Dan Coobat, from Omaha." I returned a handshake.

"How long have you been *attached* to the 176$^{th}$?" he asked.

"Almost two months," I answered. "You?"

"Both of us," Frock pointed to the third man, "have been here for nearly a month. He's Timmy Boremba."

"Nice to meet you, Tim." I offered my hand, receiving a timid return.

"You believe all this shit?" Frock queried.

"Don't follow your drift, Frock." I played along.

"All this crap about the 312th!"

"I don't understand, Frock. What do you mean?"

"One lieutenant colonel, one captain, one warrant, one sergeant, and three privates who are going to 'rewrite the pages of aviation history!' Give me a break!" the Atlantan elaborated.

"You must know the army by now, Frock. 'Hurry up and wait,'" I kind of joked.

"Hurry up and wait for what?" he shot back. "A barracks, an orderly room, a first sergeant — A company? We both came from Fort Polk Army Administration School, and do you think we were given typewriters when we arrived here? No, Sir! Not us! We were handed rakes and sickles. What's the army have you doing? Driving a dump truck?"

"I report to a flight line every day where I'm learning to record information on aircraft and pilots." I felt very uncertain about revealing anything more.

"One out of three ain't bad," he cynically remarked. "What administration school did you attend?"

"Didn't. Came from Advanced Infantry Training School, at Fort Jackson, South Carolina."

"And you're working as a clerk, Coobat?" he barked at me. "What's your military occupational specialty?"

"My MOS is 11 B 10, Light Weapons Infantry, Frock."

"Well, at least you're *pounding* something, grunt! Why they have you working on aviation forms?" His bewilderment was as obvious as my own.

"Beats me, Frock! Right now I'm OJT, specialist in flight operations."

"Let's go," the third private finally spoke up. "Don't want trouble."

"Relax, Timmy! Nobody's looking for us." Frock tried to calm a nervous private who kept peeking out the barracks's dirty windows. Nineteen, maybe twenty-years-old, fine blond hair, blue eyes covered with black rimmed glasses, Boremba appeared to have been born looking scared.

"No trouble!" Boremba stressed.

"Maybe he's right, Frock," I cut in. "Sooner or later we all have to report back to someplace, and I know a specialist down at the flight line who has a ton of paperwork for me," I interjected, seeing a weak but noticeable wink of approval coming from Boremba.

"Well, all right, Timmy," Frock caved in, "but we'll just be cutting more weeds," he added, leading the way out.

Once outside I felt the need to kick a tree, but there weren't any in the barren company area. I was frustrated and had been searching for someone to blame, but at that same time, I now felt this mysterious desire to be near the two men I had just met. Both were just like me, skeptical and very uncertain about the prospects of deploying to the Southeastern Asia Theater of War. Cope had been there two times, and something was compelling me to be around him.

"Want some brew?" I asked the specialist when I walked into our office that day. "First orientation is over."

"Sure do."

I grabbed his lukewarm, half-filled cup, picked up my own, and went to the place Cope showed me on my very first day under his wing: the Benning flight line coffeepot. The mixture tasted like it was 1/4 tire, 1/4 grounds, 1/4 water, and 1/4 JP-4 aircraft fuel. Surviving the first cup made me hooked for a lifetime.

"How far off was I?" Cope accepted his refilled cup.

"You had more to say in a few words than he did in his fifteen-minute speech."

"Told the three of you there'd be something to see." He glowed as he drank his coffee.

"I can't *vouch* for that man, either." I remembered his exact word.

"The lieutenant colonel?"

"Same one."

"Why, Cooby?"

"He used the pronouns, 'my and I,' all too many times in his lengthy address."

"That bother you?"

"Sure does, Cope."

"It's the army way, Cooby."

"So is being promoted to E-6," I blurted. "You given any thought to the offer?"

"None whatsoever!"

I sensed he was lying and said nothing more.

I prayed I was wrong.

# CHAPTER 3

## RULE NUMBER FOUR

---

After a two-month mental hiatus at the Benning flight line, I felt like a veteran operations specialist, but even I knew "I had Cope." The job kept my hands busy, as well as keeping my mind occupied, learning the ins and outs of all the documents needed in this job. I was obligated to Cope for his off-the-record lessons on rule numbers one and two: document everything, no documentation, no pay. I also was aware of how obliged I was to him for forcing me to use rule number three: do it right the first time or do it over. While I was learning everything necessary to do my best, I didn't have time to think about the when and why of Vietnam.

No one coerced me to find out about rule number four. It was there the day I entered the army, and was currently alive and well at the 176th Aviation Battalion.

When I began my military experience, I rode on a bus that took me from the Columbia, South Carolina Airport to the front gates of Fort Jackson. Up front the army post looked as though it belonged on the top ten list of frequently visited resort areas.

Georgia's version was no different.

Fort Benning was bigger than Jackson. *Stars and Stripes*, the weekly army newspaper, called it, "the largest military installation stateside." Located in the heart of Dixie, about ninety miles from Atlanta, the fort spread over about a fifty square mile area. A double lane highway paralleled the post on the last five miles of my journey, and I was mesmerized by bordering chain-link fence posts, passing by like phone poles on a rural country road. Every three hundred feet were posted signs warning: Military Property! Keep Out!

On the other side of the mesh wire barricade, I viewed a country club atmosphere, replete with lush trees, scattered small ponds, most with fountains, manicured green lawns, and shrubbery making a botanical garden appear to be second rate. Strategically placed billboards advertised: Home of the 5th Division, Home of the First Air Cavalry, Paratrooper

School. I didn't know it at the time, but one sign being constructed would read: Home of Army Aviation.

As my camouflage military bus turned to gain admittance, my eyes were taken by white portals serving as the entrance. These were no mere gates, and the access area was staffed with neatly garbed soldiers in crisp white uniforms.

Following the usual records check, the bus entered the complex and headed toward the command center. I expected to see something lavish, but the clearly visible Fort Benning Headquarters was more stirring than Tara in *Gone With The Wind*. Flagpoles lined the entire driveway leading toward it, and bright flowers exploded like colorful pages from a spring issue of *Better Homes and Gardens*; even the Georgia pine trees somehow appeared to be standing at attention.

The road lured my bus to a circular driveway directly in front of a most magnificent structure. In its nucleus stood the tallest flagpole, flying the largest flag I had ever seen. Beneath Old Glory, was a blue and gold banner symbolizing the colors of the army post. Fort Benning was inscribed in white stones at the base of the pole.

All was just an appetizer in comparison to the three-story, 100-foot-long, pillared white plantation house known as "The Fort Benning Headquarters." The building was as brilliant and clear as the diamond on the finger of a new bride.

One tiered, columned portico eased forward from the stunning building, and trapped a portion of the circular driveway underneath. Its top level was an open patio; the second level showcased an elegant balcony. The bottom level, canopied with a large chandelier, invited onlookers to a "slice of Dixie." I had ample time to soak in all the ambiance; Benning Drive, the road to the site, posted a five-mile-per-hour speed limit.

Six, four-story rectangular buildings provided the backdrop for a perfect scene: The 5<sup>th</sup> Division, Fifth Division Museum, Paratrooper Training School, First Air Cavalry Center, the Benning Visitor Site, and the USO/POST Exchange. All were equally spaced from one another, all were identical, all partook in an initial first glimpse, and all of the buildings had been situated behind, to the right or left of the plantation house, creating an image suggesting tribute.

I felt like taking a photograph: Fort Benning's upfront appeal was enchanting. I bought the postcard sometime later at the USO/Post Exchange.

Mine wasn't a Greyhound Bus, and its driver ignored an open invitation, turning at the intersection of Benning Drive and Benning Way. An invisible rider was onboard the whole time. His name was "Rule

Number Four," and I encountered him the instant I got off the bus and arrived at my first permanent duty assignment, the 176th Aviation Battalion, way out back, and far beyond the plantation house. My new home was one of eight hundred company areas built on the north forty.

Each, patterned after a city block, consisted of six painfully similar buildings. The first, second, fifth, and sixth were two-story barracks designed to accommodate approximately eighty men; the third and fourth were one-story structures, serving as mess hall and orderly room respectively.

All of the structures were in a perfect row; each was 30' x 60'. All of them had the same black roof and the exact amount of doors and windows; each was equally spaced from one another. Street signs and shoddy asphalt distinguished each set of six, demanding memorization as mandatory in finding home.

I felt very alone, much like I had felt earlier when I was greeted by the arms of *Mother Army* at Fort Jackson. I wanted to cry; rule number four wouldn't permit it. The first night at Benning was scary and my invisible friend offered little comfort.

The interior of one of the barracks was more depressing than being dropped off in the middle of all of them. How I ached to be in Omaha, and in a bedroom where I could shut a door. The simple desire was impossible on the second floor of my barracks where two rows of ten bunks paralleled each other like cold railroad tracks laid out in an open area. I didn't think I could feel much worse, but did the next day when Specialist Copelet delivered the deplorable knock-out punch. "Just why in the hell was an infantryman attached to an aviation battalion?"

By September of 1966, I was a six-month veteran of the United States Army. I reported to the flight line each day and returned to the bleak barracks each night. Saturday was a half-day of work; Sunday, a day off. Still, Benning life was as routine as 4800 identical buildings.

I learned to adapt, becoming grateful for the diversion of the flight line; mostly I began to understand the growing friendship forming with Carl Copelet. I just flat out liked him. I think he had the same opinion of me.

Cope didn't share big chunks of his personal life; he did release bits and pieces here and there. A listener was forced to construct the rest.

He married a Japanese girl, Reiko, sometime following one tour of duty in the East; they had three kids: one boy and two girls. Prior to the 176th, Cope was assigned to Fort Lewis, Washington. The couple loved the Northwest so much they eventually bought a home. Reiko agreed to stay until Cope's retirement. Boy did his eyes sparkle when he spoke of

Seattle/Tacoma, and the great fishing near the "sound." Cope relished smoked salmon.

During one rare moment, he confessed that his teenage daughter, Kathy, had been in four different grade schools, adding that Angie and Carl Jr., wouldn't be dragged about in the same way.

I knew he wanted to retire; from a lot of what he did not say, I guessed his Oriental wife, Reiko, was inclined toward waiting longer. He oftentimes brought up the gap between Occident and Orient, and I presumed she invited a promotion; E-5 wasn't a prestigious rank for a lifer. It plain ass stunk. While I was seeking someone to blame and a reason to run away, he was battling with staying in.

On the second Monday in September of 1966, I arrived at work three hours late. Cope was reviewing some aviation records with Captain Patton as I tried to sneak unnoticed past the two men.

"Where in the hell have you been?" Cope was terse, but he never yelled. "This better be really good, kid," the E-5 emphasized for Patton, the entire flight line, and me.

"It's Mon-Monday morning, Cope—I mean, Specialist." I slowly slipped into my office chair.

"Big deal; it was Monday morning last week."

"From now on, by order of Colonel Fenson, all training units are required to be at the parade field at 0430 hours for presentation of the colors," I managed to squeak out.

"That was at 4:30; it's 10 o'clock, and even a dumb E-5 like me knows it doesn't take five hours to salute a damned flag."

"Colonel Fang decided to march his men to the field," I started to explain.

"So what?"

"He got lost on the way to the field and on the return trip," I continued. "He had me carry the company flag; said I'd be representing the infantryman in aviation."

"And...?"

"We got back at 0650, about twenty minutes after the one truck leaves for the flight line," I answered him.

"So how'd you get here?"

"I had to walk, Specialist."

"Christ, Cooby. Haven't you ever heard of a phone?"

"Look, Cope," I snarled back. "I was ordered to march to a field, to carry a flag, to march back, and finished most of the morning marching down here. Isn't that what infantry is all about?" I was tired, hungry, and pissed.

"What does being in the infantry have to do with being late for work?"

"Infantrymen are ground pounders and grunts, right? I did both this morning getting down here, Cope."

"Situation normal, all fouled up," he growled. "See what I mean?" he asked the captain.

"Not exactly," Patton seemed amused.

"Remember me telling you and Mr. Harsh about my peeve, the biggest snafu in the army?"

"You said training a man in one area, then reassigning him to another, really pisses you off."

"I won't have my clerk working as an infantryman when we deploy overseas!"

"What did you say, Copelet?" A grin formed on Patton's face.

"Won't have anybody fuck with my clerk when we deploy, Captain. Pardon my French."

"Welcome to the 312th Aviation Company, Sergeant, E-6." Patton offered a congratulatory handshake.

I sat there stunned giving some thought to an invisible friend, rule number four: "What you see (and hear), is not at all what you get."

# CHAPTER 4

## FIRST FORMATION, FRIENDS,
## AND FAMILIAR RULE NUMBER FOUR

By the third Monday of September, 1966, I couldn't decide between being sorry over Cope's displaced retirement or being happy that he was my flight operations sergeant. What I knew was six short days following his promotion to Sergeant E-6, a 312th Aviation Company began to take shape.

The first sign came when Cope and I moved to a new office down a corridor from the 176th Aviation Battalion. It wasn't much of an improvement; metal wall lockers were used to sort out companies in the drab 30' x 60' building. The relocation, at best, was a statement to other units.

The second noticeable sign appeared during nonworking hours. Back at the barracks, I was teased about "the company that can't fly," or "a unit the army forgot." Those ribbings quit shortly after Cope pinned on sergeant's insignia.

Colonel Fenson's Monday morning presentation ritual was the third. Our first was attended by seven men; the most recent involved 100 men stumbling around in the dark on the vacant lot.

Nothing confirmed the impending changes more effectively than the 176th Aviation Battalion's public address system, on the first Sunday night in October of 1966. Rumors and gossip were held to be just that, until a crackling noise, followed by the sound of human breath blown into a microphone, and the two words, "testing, testing," was heard in the company area. A company's PA was an integral part of a soldier's life; all were awakened by it, counseled by it, informed by it, as well as bedded by it.

On that late October Sunday night, at about lights-out time, everyone in the 176th expected the regular crackle and four words: "testing, testing, attention, attention." I was one of about a hundred not quite willing to hear: "By order of Lieutenant Colonel Fang, personnel assigned to the

312$^{th}$ Aviation and the 713$^{th}$ Transportation Companies will convene in the 176$^{th}$ Battalion's ball field, tomorrow at 0830 hours, for a full company formation." The message was repeated.

I lay awake most of the night trying to avoid asking *why*. Nothing worked; just like everyone else, I had to wait and see.

When 0830 hours arrived, I found myself at the 176$^{th}$ area ball field, a routine lot situated between barracks. Its former resident did a "MacArthur fading act," letting the heavily trampled grass resemble a diamond; there were no fences, bleachers, or dugouts. A jeep had been backed over home plate; in its ass end, one large bullhorn stood at the ready. The makeshift podium offered anyone standing in it, an elevated platform, to face the ball field with the panoramic western Georgia sky as backdrop.

Of the 100-plus men loosely amassed on it, I knew five. Standing on either side of me, about ten feet left of third base, were Privates Boremba and Frock. Sergeant Copelet, Mr. Harsh, and Captain Patton were near the jeep milling around with other men.

At approximately 0845, the tallest of the men near the military vehicle, boarded its rear end, picked up the horn, and shouted, "Men, at ease!"

Only the megaphone had been standing at attention.

"I'm Sergeant Frank Turtz, First Sergeant of the 312$^{th}$ Aviation Company." He aimed the bullhorn. "Want to welcome ya'all to our first official company formation."

I squinted at the tall hunk blocking out a portion of the morning Georgia sun; sheer size made the jeep he stood in appear more like a kid's Red Flyer wagon. With Bowie, it was a knife; with Boone, a coonskin cap. With First Sergeant Frank Turtz, it was bulk. "That's one big fellow," Private Frock whispered to me.

"CO ain't here yet, so let me introduce the men with me, standing around this here jeep," he continued, using a free hand to retrieve a wedged piece of paper squeezed within the pocket of a stretched fatigue shirt.

"Lieutenant Colonel Robert Fang, Commanding Officer, 312$^{th}$..." he cut himself short, apparently realizing why the original start-up time had been delayed.

"Major Albert Frankel, Commanding Officer of the 713$^{th}$ Transportation Company," he read on. I hadn't met the man whom Cope termed as, "someone who could fly anything, and make anything fly," so I lowered my line of sight a notch to see who'd acknowledge the introduction.

After a moment of silence, someone shouted, "He's bringing Fang."

"Men," Turtz tried to recover, "he's bringin' the CO and ain't here yet either." I couldn't prevent a chuckle; neither could anyone else.

"Captain Shawn Jones, Operations Officer, 312th." He struggled, gambling on one out of three. Someone raised up a hand. Its owner did not wave an acknowledgment to the mustered men. Instead, the officer, a slim man, about 5' 10", wearing stiffly starched fatigues and an obvious frown, walked to the podium. He stood there, hands on hips, quietly glaring at the sergeant holding the bullhorn.

One uncomfortable moment later, Turtz noticed what all saw: the officer's collar insignia weren't railroad tracks. He instantly blared, "Men, Major Jones, Operations Officer, 312th Aviation Company." Without any apology, he continued on with more introductions of officers, including CW3 Harsh and Captain Patton. The repetitive marred preludes ceased to be hilarious, and I wondered whether the sergeant knew how to take notes; my speculations were conferred when he spoke in the megaphone to recognize Sergeant Clifford Foone, his counterpart E-7 for the sister 713th Transportation Company.

Foone was the "mutt" to Turtz's "Jeff." A small framed man, at best, 5 feet tall, ambled toward the jeep, stepped upon a crate, and vigorously waved his right hand at the men. His tiny physique was not complemented by an overweight problem, and became even more accentuated when onlookers noticed that the top of his head barely matched knee level of the upright Sergeant Turtz. He couldn't walk two blocks let alone fly a mile, I thought, recalling Frock's comment about "rewriting the pages of aviation history." I was headed to Vietnam and these two men would be top dogs in charge of all enlisted in both companies. The latter, with his monkey-like antics at the side of the jeep, could have been called a "baboon"; the former, with his imitations of a master of ceremonies: "flirts." As I stood in that fake ball field, I remembered William Bendix, and his signature phrase, "What a revoltin' development this is."

Just as Turtz was blasting, "Sergeant Carl Copelet...," he stopped his words in mid-sentence and yelled at the men, "Company. Ah-ten-hut!" The two commanding officers arrived. Sergeant Copelet, cigarette dangling from his mouth, waved anyway.

Boremba, Frock, and I, abreast of one another, came to a position of attention. Everyone else duplicated something similar; the mob more favored green recruits leaving the bus at boot camp.

In the few seconds after shouting the military salute, *Flirts* stumbled and fell upon *Baboon*, who hadn't left the side of the jeep. Ignoring the uncontrollable laughter, he stood up, brushed off some of the Georgia clay from his fatigues, and handed the bullhorn to Colonel Fang. Both men ignored any standard operational military greetings.

"I'm Lieutenant Colonel Fang, and I'm here to tell you the 312th and 713th aren't companies the army forgot, nor are they the companies that can't fly." Instant applause erupted from a horde that took in three privates who were standing near third base. A second burst exploded when he announced, "Major Albert Frankel, Commanding Officer of our sister unit, the 713th Transportation Company." I was applauding too; this delivery was unlike the orientation devoid of esprit.

I became curious about the major that Copelet knew. He looked about forty-two, was slim and in shape, and didn't wear a ball cap. His exposed head revealed neatly trimmed graying crewcut hair; his way of nodding to the assembly reminded me of an English professor I had in college. Major Frankel challenged my expectations of the aviator. A pipe was the only thing missing from my first impression. Cope told me later that he smoked one.

Once the applause subsided, the colonel commenced with an address giving meaning to "the Lord giveth and the Lord taketh away." The great beginning didn't have a middle, and I feared, no end. Even Frock murmured, "suppose he'll speak about 'rewriting the pages of aviation history,' just about the time we're all dismissed to go cut some more weeds." I couldn't have agreed more; if my mother were there, she'd have said, "morale: she just flew out the window."

While the colonel rambled on about the inception of the cargo helicopter, I was gladly distracted by the group of men formerly huddled around the jeep. The men, including the two majors, had massed on the asphalt street dividing the 176th area ball field from other routine sets of six buildings. Everyone, except the colonel, saw the impolite behavior. *Baboon* and *Flirts* kept gesturing toward the company area on the other side of the street.

Five minutes passed. Sergeant *Flirts* broke away from the huddle and meandered to the jeep, purposely disrupting the formation to deliver an urgent message to the colonel. Fang put down the bullhorn, did an about face, and stared across the tarred road. He did another about face moments later, then announced, "Men, the home of the 312th and the 713th is across the street."

There were six army structures across the street. Each was 30' x 60', painted yellow. Two were one-story; four were two-story. All of them were vacant.

"Looks like the career as weed cutter is over, Frock," I remarked to the Georgian.

"None too soon, Coobat," he responded.

"Rather cut weeds." Boremba's curt statement was very accurate. Those six buildings had been vacated for a long time. "Run down" didn't come close to describing them, and "work" was a polite term for the monumental, ball-busting task of resurrecting real estate the army forgot.

The detail began immediately; everyone was relieved of previous duties. Our first day was consumed by merely removing debris; the bonfire, a blaze almost screwed up by a buffoon who wasn't adept at igniting fires, was held in the 176th Company ball field.

Within a week, be it ever so routine, the two sister companies had a home; Frock, Boremba, and Coobat berthed on the second floor of the fifth in the row of six. The three of us E-1s, along with all other low-ranking men, were overwhelmed by the tons of materials that flowed to the 312th and 713th. All of us knew about "hurrying up to wait"; what was occurring was happening all too fast.

"Their fault," Boremba would remark each night just before lights out.

"You mean Turtz and Foone for 'finding this palace'?" Frock usually joked.

"Wrong. This happened because Copelet was promoted," I'd argue.

"Their fault," Boremba persisted.

Frock always fell asleep first; Boremba and I weren't far behind. Everybody in the two companies had been taken to the point of exhaustion by the hastened pace.

By November of 1966, Boremba and Frock had their hands full of personnel files and orderly room paperwork; down at the flight line, the Boeing Vertol Company handed over fourteen CH-47A helicopters to the brand new unit.

Trucks, jeeps, equipment, supplies, and men poured into the two companies like water gushing from a burst dam. Boremba wouldn't relinquish his "their fault" theory and I held onto my "Copelet promotion" view; Frock remained neutral. Rule four was present for all to see.

On a fall day in November, the three of us decided to escape the fracas; noon on a Saturday ended duty time, and the USO/PX beckoned. Although we had to walk, I convinced my buddies imitating infantry would pay off.

"Chicago burger." The two words issued from this Land of Lincoln man as easily as the chirp of a small bird. For the first time, Tim Boremba was not sporting a scared look.

"Timmy, they don't grow Chicago hamburgers in Georgia." Frock skipped along, "Don't care what the PX has. Anything is better than mess hall chow, right, Cooby?" Frock started to use Copelet's nickname.

"Right, Frock." Even I had shelved blame-searching.

"Chicago burger," Boremba repeated. He still resisted a smile.

The USO/PX didn't disappoint any of us; it was as big and brilliantly white as I had remembered. The complex had everything a soldier wanted but couldn't afford. We spent an hour in the PX gazing at civilian products unusable to male recruits about-to-be deployed. This "up front" version of Benning was a combination of two buildings joined by a cleverly designed, glassed-in restaurant/bullshit stopover.

After hearing, "Chicago burger," one more time, Frock said, "Let's get something to eat," and within minutes, a waitress took our order for three Cokes, two hot dogs, one hamburger, and three fries.

"They're ours," Boremba whispered, just as the waitress left.

"Who's ours?" the curious Georgian asked.

"They're ours," the Illinois transplant repeated, trying to disguise a gesture pointing at the next table.

Frock and I leaned forward to hear more; the private placed one finger on his lips, quietly indicating that we should eavesdrop.

"Shor is a big 'un, Austeen," the large black man told his companion. My eyes caught sight of two white specks in a deeply black face scanning the restaurant. The metal E-7 insignia on his ball cap told me he outranked me. "They's got nuttin' like this in Augusta." The big man struggled with the camouflage ascot strangling his neck.

"Ain't seen anything like it, Towie," the other man agreed, as he too surveyed the huge facility.

"Dat PX is sumthin else, Sargint Austeen." The E-7 wiped his mouth with his hand.

"Closest I've seen was in Germany." Austeen's ball cap was pinned with a single hashmark over an eagle. It was one less than Towie's, indicating E-6. His headgear was too large. So were the fatigues, which draped over his frail frame. "More coffee, Towie?" he asked while shoving aside the leftovers from the meal.

"Shor." Towie flagged the waitress.

Just as the server refilled their cups, Austeen asked, "How we going to handle it, Towie?"

"You means da flight physicals?"

"Towie, none of the men in our platoons are being paid hazardous duty or flight pay, and they won't until battalion finance gets a copy of their current flight physicals. It's as simple as that."

"Not's my fault we ain't got 'em yet, Sargint Austeen. Betcha a new sargint in operashuns is holding 'em up. What's his name?"

"Copelet, but why would he be holding them up?"

"Doesn't matter, Austeen; Firs things Monday, youz and meez are gonna sees Top 'bout it."

"Why don't we just go see Sergeant Copelet?"

"'Cauz Turtz is Top, and he's gots more muscle."

"Maybe you're right, Towie; Turtz is first sergeant."

"I knows I's right, Austeen; now let's beat feet and checks out dat PX."

Both men got up and left, ignoring a huge sign stating: "IT'S YOUR PX: KEEP IT CLEAN." Our six eyeballs trailed the men until they were out of sight, and just then our waitress arrived with our order.

"What'd you make of that?" Frock began devouring a hot dog.

"Trouble," Boremba immediately remarked.

"You worried, Cooby?"

"No, Frock, I'm not."

"Trouble," Boremba repeated.

"No trouble at all, Timmy."

"Why you so sure, Cooby?" Frock was more interested in his foot-long hot dog.

"Because Copelet didn't break any rules, Frock."

"What rules?"

"Rule number one and rule number two."

"What's rule number one, Cooby?" The Georgian delayed taking another bite.

"Document everything."

"And rule number two, Cooby?"

"No documentation, no pay." I started to eat my dog.

"Trouble," Boremba emphasized a third time.

"So why don't the two sergeants just fix it, Cooby?" Frock had stopped eating altogether. Boremba just kept on.

"Haven't heard about rule three, Frock?" I took a sip of my Coca-Cola.

"Wait a minute." Frock sounded perplexed. "These two sergeants didn't get the right documentation, and the net result is no pay for the enlisted men. They don't want to ante up and want to shift the guilt to Copelet. Am I right thus far, Cooby?"

"So far, so good."

"What the heck is rule three?"

"Do it right, or do it over."

"Well, now that's all cleared up, did you at least like your Chicago burger, Timmy?"

"Coke was great."

Two privates finished their food, and three privates toured the post exchange. Nothing more was said about the eavesdropping. We spent as much time away from the company area as possible. I couldn't help but think about it, both that Saturday and the following Sunday.

When Monday rolled around, Cope greeted me with, "The captain's going to the orderly room; you and I are going with him."

"What for, Cope?" I instantly recalled the weekend.

"You'll see when we get there. Get in the backseat of my Ford LTD. We'll be out shortly."

I didn't say one word on the ride back to the company area. All I knew was I didn't feel like getting out of the car when it parked.

"May I help you, Sir?" Frock asked the officer as the three of us entered. I winked; he couldn't wink back.

"Here to see the CO, Private; Sergeant Copelet is here to see the First Sergeant."

"Who shall I say is asking, Sir?" Frock's militarily correct courtesy was at its best.

"Captain Harold Patton, Flight Operations."

Frock picked up the phone while I gazed around. I had been in the orderly room, but only when it was being resurrected. A middle wall halving the building prominently displayed: "Commanding Officer"; the sign was intimidating. Eight desks, four each in two rows, created a liberal aisle. Frock's was nearest the door; Boremba's across the aisle and adjacent to the first sergeant's. Two men were visiting Top. One was Towie; the other, Austeen. Turtz, along with his two visitors, had their eyes locked on Sergeant Copelet.

The resulting quiet in the room was obvious; only the repetitive sound of Boremba's typewriter disturbed it; as if on cue, Colonel Fang emerged from his walled barricade.

"Ah-ten-hut," the captain assumed lead role. Everyone else assumed the standard military position, even the E-6 from operations.

"Sir, Captain Patton is present as ordered and requests permission to speak with the commander."

"Permission granted." Fang returned the salute, acting as if he were on a stage and recruits were being instructed in proper military greetings. "Come in, Captain," he said. The two officers retreated to the enclave behind the wall.

Just as soon as the CO's office door closed, Sergeants Towie and Austeen began to leave, walking past Copelet and me with their eyes looking downward. "How's things going at operations?" Master Sergeant Turtz greeted the new E-6. "By the way, congratulations on the promotion." He motioned for us to join him.

"Thanks, Top." Cope sat down; I did the same. "Guess I can say we're hanging in there."

"That's great; anything I can do to help?" The big man looked even bigger less than five feet away.

"Well, Top, I have a problem with this clerk who's been assigned to operations." Hearing "deployment" wasn't great; having Cope say, "clerk and problem," in the same sentence, somehow seemed worse. Boremba's typing was becoming incessant.

"Is he screwing up?" Turtz immediately locked his eyes on me.

"Oh no, Top! Nothing like that. Coobat's a fine clerk, but he's OJT in operations, with an 11 B 10 MOS, and..."

"And you don't want the first sergeant assigning him someplace else when we deploy." Turtz spoke Cope's thoughts.

"It's been a peeve of mine for years, Top."

"You have nothing to worry about, Sergeant Copelet; my clerk has already typed the 'Request For MOS Change,' and I have the paperwork in my desk. I've been on this one right from the start." Boremba's noisemaking came to an instant halt. "Can you have Coobat report to me Friday, just after morning mess hall?"

"He'll be there, Top. Thanks."

Cope and I left and went outside to await the captain. We silently smoked while leaning against his auto. Within five minutes, Captain Patton exited the orderly room.

"Have any luck, Captain?" Cope asked the officer getting into the passenger side of his car.

"The son-of-a-bitch doesn't care about anything but his 'introduction party,' being hosted by brigade. You?"

"I struck out too."

"What makes you so sure, Sergeant Copelet?"

"Turtz's nervous clerk stopped typing the minute he said the paperwork was in his desk. That and the colonel."

"You don't like Colonel Fang?"

"Reminds me of Elmer Fudd, with all due respect, Sir." The comment was the first I heard from Cope where he called an officer, *Sir*.

"Yeah! Elmer Fudd, the flying dud." Both men chuckled; so did I. "How about you, Cooby? What'd you think about all the doings?"

"Well, Sir, all I know is what you see, what you hear, and what you expect in the army, is *not* what you get."

I spent the rest of the week expecting and waiting for Friday to come and go as quickly as possible.

# CHAPTER 5

## PAST AND PRESENT

---

Eight days after Boremba found out Benning didn't grow Chicago burgers, the two of us woke up to an empty barracks. Our second floor suite in the fifth building of six, making up our company area was vacant. Frock secured a weekend pass to Atlanta, our other roommates were either on duty or gone as well, and Timmy and I planned on doing something we hadn't done in a long time: go to church. It was Sunday.

"We're gonna be late," I yelled down the stairs; at the bottom were three doors. One was the exit, another an entry to the lower floor barracks. The third was the entrance to the latrine facilities.

Don't think Boremba heard me; I wouldn't have heard his yell twenty minutes earlier while I was luxuriating privately in a community shower. God, it felt terrific to not have to wait in line.

Within twenty minutes, he had buckled the belt on his one pair of civilian pants and was casually walking down the stairs. I darted.

"If my ma knew this was the first time I was going to mass in such a long time, she wouldn't talk to me for a week."

"Me too."

"Assumption is the only Bohemian National Parish in Omaha, Tim. We observe all old customs, like singing the traditional religious hymns, and putting on a yearly Czech Festival. Assumption Church is a block and a half up the hill from my ma's house. We always walked."

"Mine's Polish."

"Mary Coobat goes to church every day, Tim."

"Helen Boremba too."

"Wouldn't it be great if our two moms could meet some day?"

"Never happen."

"You're probably right, Timmy; Mary Coobat wouldn't leave Omaha if somebody gave her an all-expense paid trip to the Vatican."

"Helen Boremba, either."

"You don't talk much, do you, Tim?"

"Nothing to say."

"Something bothering you?"

"Turtz."

"Don't talk to me about him."

"Don't want to."

"Remember his telling me to be there after mess hall on Friday?"

"What he do to you?"

"Duty roster."

"He put you on it because you stopped typing?"

"You're on it."

"I'm on it?"

"Yes."

"Why, Tim?"

"Figures."

"As in money?"

"That's right."

We kept walking. Boremba kept silent. I had some time to soak in what he was waiting to say. After about one block, I asked, "He wants my hazardous duty pay, doesn't he?" Boremba knew I was an 11 B 10, infantryman, authorized to receive it; he also knew my present on-the-job training didn't delete the monetary provision.

"Flight pay too."

"Both?"

The chill in the Sunday morning Georgia air seemed somehow colder. My Friday meet with Sergeant Turtz was less than honest at best. He suggested a method to preserve both allocations while still allowing me to work in flight operations. "Just accept the monthly allotment and I'll overlook and fix the rest," Turtz elaborated. My Catholic past spelled deceit, and I said so. The sergeant's last comment was, "You just might be persuaded to change your thinking."

"Yes, both."

I didn't want to hear that affirmation but he already told me I was on the duty roster, so I asked, "How often?"

"Tuesdays and Thursdays."

"Guard duty on Tuesday, kitchen police, Thursday?"

"Other way around."

"For how long, Tim?"

"Turtz didn't say."

"Until I crack." We finished the walk to the interdenominational church without saying another word.

The church wasn't Czech National or Polish Traditional; it was a routine 30' x 60' building. A steeple had been added to the front of the structure; on it, the Star of David shared space with a cross. Inside, "one size fits all" replicated its interfaith purpose. Two godforsaken sinners duplicated all the rituals, but my mind was not hellbent on having a religious experience; don't think Boremba's was either.

Following the service, I asked Tim if he wanted to join me at the USO/PX for coffee and a roll.

"One Coke," he answered.

As we walked toward the complex, I asked Timmy if he wanted to take another walk.

"Where?"

"Down to the flight line."

"Why?"

"Got some typing to do. Has to be done before I get to work Monday morning, Tim."

"Who for?" he asked me.

"Mr. Harsh needs an updated DD Form 759 on the colonel; seems like my last one had an unacceptable error. He's going to take it to Fort Rucker, have it enlarged, and present it to the CO at Fang's welcoming brigade party. Won't have any time tomorrow morning."

"Can't go."

"Why not, Tim?"

"Duty roster."

"You've got Sunday detail too?" I didn't want to be reminded. "Blame" was more than enough, dubious details on a mandatory work schedule, alarming, and I was about to trek down to a flight line on a day off. Worse, the nontalkative Boremba wasn't about to be a shoulder.

"Turtz's orders." The two words were quite succinct.

I ate my roll and drank my coffee; Boremba sipped on his Coke. "Mellow Yellow" played on the public address, and neither of us knew about any possible significance. Before we parted company, we stopped at the exchange where I did buy the picture perfect postcard of the plantation house.

When I began my walk, I prayed I would get lost, but too many familiar guideposts kept me on course. Fort Benning, for all practical reasons, was dead on Sunday. As I walked, I found my gait picking up the "hup-two-three-four" cadence so regular on Monday mornings:

Harsh and Turtz! Harsh and Turtz.

Whatever I do, I'm lost in a search.

My own quick pace, memories of Assumption Church, and a far better place lulled me back to the start of 1966.

I was center stage, Omaha Civic Auditorium; Father Don McNeil, Dean of the College of Arts, Creighton University, was conferring my bachelor's degree in English. I ached to see my mother's face again, the way it appeared that commencement night. I was the only one of nine children to grant her wish: a college degree in the family.

Why I had chosen English was never so clear to me as it became during my two-hour sabbatical. I chose English because it was easy, and because it kept me in school. A 1-Y deferment prevented my draft number from being called. How secure I felt one year earlier. I had escaped the Bay of Pigs fiasco and was free to snub what was appearing in every living room across the country. Vietnam had been one middle page news story I neglected to read.

Harsh and Turtz! Harsh and Turtz.

Whatever I do, I'm lost in a search.

I would have given a month's pay to meet Sergeant Tom Verzal that Sunday on that journey. He was the recruiting sergeant who promised everything when I enlisted. How well I remembered going to the U.S. Post Office, the building where my late father worked, to sign up. It was tough going there; I saw my dad's office while climbing the steps to the upper level. All four branches of the military were represented.

"Army needs college graduates, and with the background you have in English, communications school, Fort Augusta, Georgia is the place for you. Just sign here," he told me. "Following six weeks of basic and an immediate six more of advanced training, the army guarantees you a spot at officer candidate school, Fort Augusta, Georgia."

After hearing a litany of other promises, I signed my name on the dotted line. The next day my mother told me: "Verzal translated from the old Bohemian means, 'squeaky.'"

I found out how literal her translation was at 3:30 A.M., on the 25th day of March, 1966. My chariot led me to Echo-Nine-Two (E-9-2), Fort Jackson, South Carolina. I was given one pillow, one blanket, and the bottom half of a metal bunk bed.

One hour later I was introduced to the United States Army.

"Get your butts out of bed, you worthless pieces of shit," the determined man yelled over and over. While he screamed he used a nightstick to beat the insides of an empty garbage can. For special effects, he pushed over an occupied bunk bed.

"I don't allow civilian crap in my barracks, so strip it off, you pansies, and I mean NOW! You can burn it, send it home, or throw it away; just get it out of here," the buck sergeant emphasized. In two minutes, all but one man in that barracks was buck ass naked; each was scrambling to conceal any semblance of a past.

"Seems I have your attention, boys!" The fully clothed man addressed about sixty men in their birthday suits. "I think we can now *try*," he underscored the word, "to attempt to make you look like soldiers." He pointed and yelled, "Fifty feet in front of the door is the factory that will make you green men...Move it!"

The simple walk forever changed my mind concerning any warm, hospitable, Southern atmosphere.

I put my first pair of green boxer shorts on backwards. I didn't care; I was cold. I felt the same way when issued a green t-shirt, green pants, green socks, and a green fatigue shirt. They were warm.

At 6 A.M., the army introduced me to the first half of an old benefit: "three hots and a cot." Hominy grits rubbed my teeth like sand; powdered milk helped wash the stuff past my craw. I understood instantly, the meaning of *mess* hall. No talking was permitted.

Phase II, introduction to the United States Army, began immediately after breakfast. All sixty men of E-9-2 were lined up, two abreast. I was in the first set of two, standing outside the front door of a uniquely small building. My partner and I waited until about 9 A.M. When we heard, "You're first," we entered. Inside were two adjacent chairs. The walls were mirrored. Neither of us could avoid watching the other being sheared. Once bald, we were exited from the rear door to experience feeling really humiliated and naked at the same time.

Ample time was granted to the clipped sheep to see one another prior to being herded to the nearest vacant lot, where certified practitioners, brandishing several long sterile needles, poked and punctured about seventy men, prearranged in ten rows of seven each. Two fainted. I found out I was allergic to penicillin. The good news was I forgot my serial number, requisite for entry into the E-9-2 mess hall, and meals thereafter. With all the medications flowing throughout my system, I most likely couldn't have eaten the army's cooked liver and onions. With the unknown schedule yet to come, I was very happy I didn't.

Harsh and Turtz! Harsh and Turtz.

Whatever I do, I'm lost in a search.

Five grueling hours lie ahead, the second half of the first day; each was loaded with physical activities, which were planned to awaken muscles none of the men knew about because they hadn't gotten much use previously. Can't say how many pushups I was required to do, nor could I calculate the number of miles our new outfit marched. At about three in the afternoon I was dog tired; by six, all of us wanted to lie down and die. None got the chance.

About 6 P.M., after a repeat serving of leftover liver and onions, our barracks's sergeant encored his early A.M. performance: "This place is filthy!" He banged away into the tin garbage can. "Get off those sorry groaning asses; you're going to make my barracks shine, and I mean inside and out."

Lights went out about 2 A.M.; came back on at 5 A.M. revelry, at which time the community latrine became less organized than a department store on Christmas Eve. At exactly 6 A.M., the members of E-9-2 were ordered to fall out and fall into some type of formation. What befell was just that. The buck sergeant was not amused and proved his displeasure by canceling breakfast. He immediately began physical training exercises. Dissenting opinions were altered with a swift sting from a baton.

Somewhere about 10 A.M., the recruits were granted the privilege of meeting the company commander of E-9-2 (Echo Company, Ninth Division, Second Battalion). The young man had an unusual name: Lieutenant Colonel B. Sergant. He was southern, had red hair, wore sunglasses, sported the rank of first lieutenant, looked bored, and his body English defined the difference between enlisted and officer grade. He walked among the prone privates struggling with pushups as though he were a plantation owner checking on slaves.

Why he stopped at my location, I don't know. What I remember was looking at very spit-shined boots not more than two inches from my face-down position.

"Got any schooling, boy?" he asked. I could hear the tap of his riding wand.

"Who, me?" I didn't look up.

"Stand up, you dumb shit! Don't you know enlisted men address officers as, *Sir*?" The training sergeant prodded me with his nightstick. "Stand up!" he yelled.

"Yes, I do...Sir." My eyes looked down; my ears listened to the tapping of a wand and the beating of a nightstick.

"How much real education do you have, boy?" His remark was condescending.

"College graduate...Sir." I knew I didn't want to be hit with a blow from a stick.

"Can you type, boy?"

"Yes...Sir...I can."

"Have this man report to the orderly room right away, Sergeant. That's an order!" The young officer saluted, and departed to his awaiting jeep. Thirty minutes later I was introduced to the other half of the story.

"If you want to make it to officer's candidate school, the records of E-9-2 will be the best Fort Jackson has ever seen. Do it my way, and both of us will be happy." This was my first introduction to an officer; my churning stomach told me I had serious problems with the Act of Congress declaring him a *gentleman*.

"Sir...I don't know anything about army..."

"You'll learn, Private; my orderly room clerk will teach you," he assured me, while pointing to a desk covered with enough paper to make the census look like a minor job. I hadn't met Copelet yet, but I learned about his pet peeve right at the start. The lieutenant's clerk had been in the battalion motor pool prior to his present assignment.

In the remaining 5½ weeks, I faked my way through a maze of paperwork, and with little help from a commanding officer and his clerk. Since there was no time to both train as a recruit and be a clerk, I was forced to forge my own documents; I even provided my own grades for graduation from Echo Nine Two, and was busy with finishing paperwork the day of the final parade ceremony.

"What's this, Sir?" First Lieutenant Sargent handed me an official-looking document. His job was done; E-9-2 had completed basic training.

"Your orders, Coobat; you're going home for a thirty-day leave."

"Sir, I'm assigned to go to Advanced Infantry Training."

I recalled Sergeant Verzal's promise: "Following six weeks of basic training and advanced infantry training, you will enter officer's candidate school at Fort Augusta, Georgia."

"Candidate school is fully booked; you report to battalion thirty days from now. You'll get new orders then."

I went home; when I returned, the army had assigned me to Delta Company, First Division, Second Battalion. It was an advanced infantry training unit, commanded by a captain. His name was Colonel B. Sargent. E-9-2's records had earned him a promotion, and I was in for an encore.

Harsh and Turtz! Harsh and Turtz.

Whatever I do, I'm lost in a search.

My flashback ended once I entered flight operations. A chief warrant officer and a first sergeant took precedence.

"Hi, Borque," I greeted the charge of quarters. His duty was to guard the empty premises, which no one would visit anyway.

"Hi, Cooby. What brings you down to paradise on Sunday?"

"A lousy period, Borque. The DD 759 Form I typed for our Colonel Fang had a period followed by a comma after 'Jr.' Harsh circled it in ink; says it's wrong. Wants a corrected version by 6:30 A.M."

"Why don't you just white it out?"

"Rule number three, Borque: Do it right or do it over."

"Sucks, doesn't it?" He grinned. "Don't worry about any invasions while I'm in charge."

I laughed at Borque's comment as I headed down the corridor of wall lockers toward the 312th's operations office. Who would even consider invading such a place? The equipment was old, the furniture was used, and the only purpose for the joint was to correctly record some useless information onto mountains of paper.

I sat at my desk and picked up the colonel's sacred DD 759; the inked circle irritated me as I reread Harsh's handwritten note: "Do it right the first time, or do it over. Have it corrected by early Monday morning."

I began work immediately, estimating the chore would take two hours; I hesitated at the header line, the spot where a period and a comma followed "Jr.," which had to be replaced with one comma only, scratch the period. I was an English major and knew a little bit about the punctuation correctness of abbreviations; this warrant was a pilot, what did he know? Halfway into the job, I was startled by a civilian, dressed in sport pants and a golf shirt. It was CW3 Harsh.

"What you doing here, Coobat?"

"Fixing the colonel's DD 759, Sir."

"What?" he seemed surprised.

"Sir, your note said, 'Have it corrected by early Monday morning.'" I handed it to him.

Mr. Harsh smiled as he read his own note, then walked behind where I was seated to examine what I had done so far. "See you omitted the period," he said.

"You're the boss, Sir."

"Saw the bike in the parking lot. Where'd you find an old Schwinn?"

"Bike belongs to the 176th; the charge of quarters used it to get here this morning, Sir."

Mr. Harsh reached over my shoulder and yanked the DD 759 from the typewriter. He crumpled it, and said, "You walked down here, didn't you, Coobat?"

"Excuse me, Sir!" I was pissed. "You have ruined my work, the work I'm doing for you; now I'll have to start all over again. It's your punctuation, your orders, and your requests that are incorrect!" I was mad as hell.

Without saying anything, the chief warrant then left the small office; he was carrying two cups of Benning Brew when he returned. "One's for you."

I took the offering wanting to throw it in his face; it was one thing to purge the page, another to crumple it in my face, and a third to do it on my day off. "Why'd you do that, Sir?" I was about ready to take a swing at him.

"We won't need it." He calmly sipped the muddy liquid. "And anytime you're ready to throw that punch, go ahead."

I took a sip, not knowing what to do; his diplomatic *throw-that-punch* remark was unexpected. The silence was deafening.

He eased over to the corner of my desk where he sat down, casually glancing at some paperwork. "I'm not the beast you think I am, Cooby...I can call you Cooby?" he asked.

"You can now...if you want to, Sir."

"Been an operations officer several times now, and I try to practice one policy with new clerks," he began. "I always refuse the first work requiring my signature; most of the time I've been right. Don't like to admit it, but in your case I was wrong. The colonel's 759 was perfectly correct."

"Yes, Sir! It was," I asserted myself. "Still have to prepare another, however."

"Not today, Cooby. I'm taking you back to the company area."

"What about the DD 759 you need, Sir?"

"I'll just use an older one."

"You sure, Sir? I can still do it." My anger had been allayed and I think I was beginning to like this man.

"Positive. Just let me find my pipe, and we're out of here."

I watched him move some papers on his desk, open a desk drawer or two, then find his missing pipe sitting next to the humidor on top of the file cabinet. "Got it," he said. "Now let's get you back to your day off."

We left the still office, said good-bye to Borque, and headed toward a sleek 1955 MG, parked alongside the bicycle. The little convertible was neat with a capital "N." It was red, the top was down, and I climbed aboard aching to feel as though the piece of civilian life was mine. It wasn't, but even privates can dream.

"Why'd you want that DD 759 anyway, Sir?" Don't think I cared anymore. An officer and a private were in a vintage car driving down Benning Way.

"Patton and me won't be in the office tomorrow. We're flying Major Jones to Fort Rucker. Fang was assigned there before the 312th and left some mementos. We're bringing them back. Going to present them at the welcoming brigade party, along with an enlarged copy of his last DD 759. I won't be seeing you until Tuesday."

"I owe you one, Sir. That should have been 'Patton and I won't be in the office tomorrow.'"

"Touché! I'll remember when I tangle with your obvious grammatical skills again."

"Couldn't resist, Mr. Harsh, but I won't be in operations on Tuesday. Seems I have KP that day."

"Does Major Jones know?"

"Can't say, Sir; I found out myself today. Guess I'm a Monday, Wednesday, Friday, and half-day Saturday clerk from now on."

"What happens on Thursday, Cooby?"

"Reliable authority tells me its guard duty."

"Who's the *reliable authority*?"

"First sergeant's duty roster clerk; we bunk together. Thanks for the ride, Sir."

"You're welcome, Private...I mean Coobat...Cooby. Wish today didn't happen, but do enjoy what's left of it."

As he drove away, I realized my ongoing quest for blame had eased up a bit; not only did I have Frock, Boremba, and Copelet to lean on, I now had Chief Warrant Officer Harsh. I rushed to the fifth building in the row of six, anxious to share my experience with the Illinois private. The barracks was as empty as it was when the two of us headed for church. I sat on my bunk and gazed out the window; the company area was similarly vacant. My Timex, the one civilian reminder of a previous life, said it was three in the afternoon; my stomach told me I hadn't eaten since morning. My conscience recalled I hadn't written home lately.

Halfway into my letter to Mom, I dozed off; Boremba was tapping my arm somewhere near 6 P.M.

"Wow!"

"Wow, what?" The private didn't realize he had awakened me from a dream. I was driving my own red MG, down Highway 275 in Omaha, Nebraska.

"The duty roster."

"Yeah, Tim." The interruption forced a reality check. "I know I'm on it; you gave me the good news this morning." As I sat up, I didn't want to remember anything other than one sleek red MG.

"You're off."

"Don't rub it in, Tim; I know I'm on...what'd you say?"

"You're off." He repeated the two words.

"I'm off? What happened?"

"Harsh called."

"Called who?"

"Turtz."

"Why?"

"Take you off."

"Anything else?" I was primed to believe a CW3 might be willing to sell a red MG.

"Your promotion."

"My promotion? I don't know anything about a promotion. To what?"

"PFC."

"Who's a private first class?" Riding in Harsh's car was becoming difficult to remember.

"You."

"Who told you that, Tim?"

"Turtz."

"Harsh requested a promotion for me?"

"Yes."

"Wow! Let's tell Frock."

"Can't."

I had forgotten the Georgian had a three-day pass. One glance at his wall locker reminded me why. Everybody in the company knew about Bunny and Frock; the other orderly clerk friend of mine had a picture pasted inside his footlocker. She was gorgeous, from Atlanta, and his fiancée; a mere look at her photograph incited envy from a viewer.

"When's he due back, Tim?"

"Later."

I didn't want to wait to share my news; then I realized I was sharing it with a terse private from Calumet City. How fond I had grown of him. His conversation consisted of brief comments; each of them, however, was concise, direct, to the point, and totally honest. Unlike the army, what I heard from Tim Boremba was what was; I didn't just like the man, I loved him. His company that night was more than sufficient.

Met with Frock the following morning in the chow line. Clerks always entered first, were lucky to find time for a noonday meal, and usually closed the mess hall at night. I was about to burst with my news when he said to Tim and me: "You can't believe the breakfast I had Sunday. Ma scrambled three fresh eggs, fried crisp bacon, made some hominy grits, and even baked biscuits and squeezed real orange juice. She let me sleep in until nine too," he exploded. "Bunny and me got in late Saturday night."

"Must be nice to have Atlanta only ninety miles away." I slid my tray on the rack. Omaha was 1500 miles from Benning; Calumet City, close to 1000.

"Went to Jazz Time, in underground Atlanta; danced all night long. Best 'Dixie' this side of the Mason-Dixon." The fond memory beamed from Frock's eyes.

"You look like you had a good time, Frock." His return grin confirmed my compliment. He was the only child of Mr. and Mrs. Hubert Frock, Sr. Frock's dad was a big shot with the Philadelphia Carpet Company, and Frock kept no secrets about someday working there as well. Like me, he chose the 1-Y deferment plan to avoid the draft; unlike me, he didn't have acceptable grades. Once, he confessed to me, that his dad said, "Not everyone is a Ramblin' Wreck, from Georgia Tech." He never spoke of school again; I understood that to mean his student deferment had elapsed. Just like mine.

I genuinely liked Frock; he had a heart as big as the State of Georgia. Boremba did too; he followed Frock like a baby puppy follows its mother.

The dazzling sparkle in Frock's eyes disappeared when cream chipped beef on toast was slopped on his food tray. Army *shit on a shingle* could churn the stomach of a statue.

"If my mother knew we're served this stuff, she'd be sitting on the White House steps, backed by every Southern Senator in the country." He shoved his tray aside.

"At least take some coffee," I urged him. I opted for the same choice. So did Boremba.

"Why do they keep serving crap everybody dumps into a garbage can?" He reluctantly poured a cup.

Tim and I encored his selection; we went to a mess hall table and silently sipped our coffees.

"I haven't told Bunny yet," Frock broke the silence.

"What do you mean, Frock?" I asked.

"Goddamn it, Cooby, I haven't told her yet!" he yelled at me.

Boremba stiffened; so did I. Frock didn't do outbursts.

"Told her what, Frock?" I hesitated to ask.

"That the 312th is going to Vietnam," he confessed. "I ain't told my folks either; they think I'm going to some new administration school, Cooby."

"Nobody knows?"

"I don't know how to tell them, Cooby; don't know what to say."

"Same with me," Boremba spoke up.

"You too, Tim?"

"Yes," he whispered.

"What are we supposed to say, Cooby? Tim and me aren't *English majors* like you!"

"There is no easy way, guys. One thing is for certain, however, you can't hide it forever."

"You mean we should say it up front?" Frock asked.

"Is there another way?" I didn't know what I was talking about. I hadn't told my own mother.

# CHAPTER 6

## 312<sup>th</sup> TRAINING

---

I had lingered a little too long in the mess hall that Monday morning listening to Frock worry aloud over what he, Boremba, and I didn't want to face. I remained so long, I nearly missed the one and only truck departing the company area for the flight line. On the ride down, I lulled over a lot of thoughts. Promotion and deletion from a duty roster surfaced immediately; something that did not surface was the asked for MOS change. What mostly topped my list concerned whether I could help figure a way for us to communicate a tough message back home to our families. The concept clouded all my thoughts and slowed most of my work efforts. When my duty time ended, I ached to brainstorm with Frock and Boremba. Vietnam was certain, and the relatives back home had a right to know.

I went straight to the second floor, fifth building in a row of six, the minute the dump truck that brought me to the flight line, returned me home. My friends weren't there, nor were they in the mess hall. I imagined both went AWOL, until a sinister companion, just before lights out, clued me in as to their whereabouts.

"Attention! Attention in the 312<sup>th</sup> and the 713<sup>th</sup> company area," the public address sounded. "Lieutenant Colonel Robert Fang has ordered all officers, all noncommissioned officers, and all administrative personnel to be present at a briefing in the 312<sup>th</sup> and 713<sup>th</sup>'s mess hall, at 0830 hours, tomorrow."

After hearing the announcement, I relaxed knowing Frock and Boremba were burning some midnight oil; I knew something was shaking when the two of them weren't present at reveille. They didn't appear in the mess hall for morning chow either; I went back to the barracks to await 0830. About 0815, I saw a familiar 1965 Ford LTD parked near the orderly room.

"Take you in for some coffee, PFC?" Copelet asked when I approached his car. Sergeants and specialists with a rank of E-5 or above could enter the hall at will; E-4s on down had to recite a memorized number to gain access, and only at prescribed times. I was an E-3.

"That'd be nice, Cope."

"Sorry for only two out of three, Cooby."

"Two out of three?"

"Harsh and I went for the duty roster, your promotion, and an MOS change." He tossed his cigarette butt aside.

"Should of guessed you were behind the scenes." I wasn't really too surprised, just better informed. "Thanks."

"Anytime, Cooby."

"What's this briefing all about, Cope?" We had entered the one-story building, poured the coffee, and sat down in a totally rearranged mess hall. The regular drab cafeteria had changed into a pseudo miniature auditorium. There was a podium of butted tables facing two parallel sets of tables, five in each row. Several men were present; so was the ugly division between officers and enlisted. Majors Frankel and Jones, Captain Patton, Mr. Harsh, and a few other officers occupied places on the militarily correct right; Sergeants Turtz, Foone, Towie, Austeen, and a few I didn't recognize were located on the enlisted left. We had chosen the proper side, and in the last table.

"Probably about training; most likely it will be..."

"Turtz!" Sergeant Foone shouted. The loud yell cut Cope short from answering my question; protocol was protocol. "I figured out what I'm going to do." The short first sergeant of the 713th Transportation Company stood up.

"What's that, Foone?" Turtz recognized his counterpart.

"Hit me like a punch from a pugilistic training stick."

"What did, Foone?" a confused Turtz asked on behalf of everyone present.

"The newspaper story about me in *Stars and Stripes*," he grinned.

"Newspaper story?"

"The one about me re-enlisting in the army." The E-7 grinned some more.

"Why would *Stars and Stripes* consider writing a story about a lifer re-upping for two more?" Turtz's chuckle was apparent on everyone's face.

"'Cause I'm going to do it in a Chinook, up in the sky." Foone dazzled the men, me included. The idea was rather unique.

"Well, I'll be goddamned, Foone."

"Think the colonel would administer the oath to me as we flew above Benning?"

"Probably ask Fenson to be the pilot." Turtz smiled. "We even have some college-stuff PFC to help with the story."

I cringed when I heard the remark; the first sergeant was referring to me, and I had already experienced some of his persuasive tactics.

My personal feelings did not curb the applause; everyone seated at the tables, both sides, stood up and toasted Foone with coffee cups. Cope and I joined in; after all, the idea was novel and *the army way*, as E-6 Copelet might remind me. When the commotion subsided, Frock, Boremba, and a third man entered the mess hall. Frock was carrying reams of paper; my Illinois buddy and the other man were lugging 5' x 4' posterboards. I had seen the *training charts* in the orderly room when I visited Sergeant Turtz; these report cards mapped the "Training In Progress," and "Completed Training" activities for each of the sister companies.

Just after Boremba and his helper leaned the visual aid cards against the makeshift podium, Major Frankel announced, "Ah-ten-hut." Lieutenant Colonel Robert Fang, Jr., came into the facility.

"At ease, as you were." He sauntered toward the center of attention, while waving both arms in gestures indicating that we should remain seated. Once at the podium, he motioned for a glass of water. Everyone stayed silent.

"I have some great news," he started. "Beginning Monday, following regular presentation of the colors, the 312th and the 713th will commence bivouac."

No one stood up and cheered. Bivouac meant giving up the luxuries found in second-story suites and exchanging them for backwoods living during simulated wartime activities.

"In addition," the colonel continued, "our sister units will undergo an IG. As you can see on the training charts," he pointed, "both are required prior to deployment."

Hearing the word, "bivouac," was like getting kicked in the ass; combining it with, "Inspector General," became, in effect, similar to inserting a foot and twisting it. An IG was all about crossed "t's" and dotted "i's"; the inspection was hated by both sides of the traditional division of men in the army.

"Guessed bivouac," Copelet nudged me. "Didn't figure on an IG." Blank stares were everywhere.

"Colonel Fenson, our brigade commander, has consented to assist us, men." The company commander continued to pierce the awesome silence. "He will pilot our lead aircraft above a parade of 312th and 713th vehicles crossing Benning Way. *Stars and Stripes* will be on hand to record the news-making event, and I anticipate an exclusive front page story," the colonel boasted. "Itineraries are available; we will deploy all fourteen aircraft and use every vehicle. Are there any questions, gentlemen?"

"Sir, have you been notified Boeing-Vertol has grounded eight of our fourteen aircraft?" Major Albert Frankel, *the one who could fly anything*, asked.

"Can they do that, Major Frankel?"

"Sir, Boeing-Vertol owns the aircraft until such time when they release them," the major spouted the rules.

I waited to hear, "Da-da-dats-all, folks"; instead, we all listened to prolonged silence. The flustered lieutenant colonel had been shot down and didn't seem to have a chute; when he finally spoke, he acknowledged what everyone knew.

"This means less than half of the 312$^{th}$ and 713$^{th}$ will undergo bivouac and IG."

"It's the *army way*," Frankel borrowed a phrase.

"To hell with *the army way*, Major," he stammered. "No one will cheat my company out of a front page news story. If we have six aircraft, that's what we'll fly. I can assure you, the six will fly over the biggest parade this post has ever seen. Colonel Fenson and I will lead it."

With that last statement, *Elmer Fudd* darted out of the building. No one shouted, "Ah-ten-hut"; no one evicted the assembly with, "Fall out." Everyone had been dazed by the outburst; even more so by the somber news.

I sat in place next to Cope; Frock and Boremba sat across from us in the next adjacent table, way in the back of the room. The four of us watched as sullen faces left the mess hall one by one.

"Orderly room," Boremba muttered.

"What's the rush?" Copelet asked. "Bet you're Colonel Ponderosa."

"Yes." Boremba's normally worried face sparked an ever so slight smile. I had told Cope about the one-lining man from Calumet City, as well as about a Southern friend from Georgia.

"That must make you the *president*." Cope glanced at Frock.

"Guess Cooby doesn't keep too many secrets from the guy he calls Cope," Frock responded. "Nice to meet ya, Sergeant Copelet."

The two men shook hands; then Cope asked Tim, "Why does Cooby call you, *Colonel Ponderosa?*"

"Joke."

"It's not a joke, Tim," Frock spoke up. "Our barracks's sergeant, Desoto, gave him that name. He says Boremba is like a skinny Hoss Cartwright from *Bonanza*, who carries a lot of weight but speaks softly."

"He give you the president's name, Frock?"

"Yeah! I'm supposed to remind him of Jefferson Davis who had too much authority during the confederate cause, Sergeant Copelet."

"Call me, Cope, Frock; you too, Boremba."

"Cooby tell you what Desoto calls him?" Frock grinned.

"No, he hasn't, Frock; Cooby must keep some secrets." The sergeant looked at me. "What does Desoto call you?"

"General." I exposed the term Frock would have spilled anyway.

"General?" Cope looked bewildered. "What on earth for?"

"Because I'm driven to the flight line every day in my own personal truck."

"A deuce and a half?" Cope laughed. "Does Desoto have names for everybody else?"

"Just us three," Frock informed him.

"Why do you think that is, Frock?"

"'Cause we're all clerks, exempt from the duty roster, and he can't hook us with dirty details...Cope." Frock said it the way it was; the power of rank defined "subordinate."

"Bother you, Frock?"

"Sticks and stones may break my bones, not names," the *prez* confidently rattled off. "Can I ask you a question, Ser... I mean, Cope?"

"Fire away."

"Think the 312th and 713th can undergo bivouac and an IG at the same time?"

Cope waited a minute before answering; I could sense he was searching for the right words to say. When he opened his mouth, he had six words to share: "In '66, yes; in '56, no."

"Why, Cope?" Frock asked for the three of us.

For a second time, Copelet didn't respond immediately. Before he did, he took a long deep breath then said: "There was no Vietnam in 1956, no Fenson looking for a first star, and no Fang anxious to pin an eagle on his collar."

Cope's answer was much too succinct, and we all knew it was true. I left the mess hall with him, realizing my blame list had grown. I felt a little like Dorothy from *The Wizard of Oz*; in my case the storm had yet to sweep me away. All I wanted to do was go home; I think Cope did too.

For the remaining week, we sullenly crated up everything needed but not nailed down; moving flight operations from a building to a field site in the boondocks was no easy task. When I realized Frock and Boremba had to do the same with an entire orderly room, I almost cheered up. Neither were happy on the eve of the move when I advised them Boeing-Vertol had grounded a ninth aircraft.

"Five out of fourteen aircraft!" the *prez* screamed at me that Sunday night. "I don't believe this shit."

"Not good," Ponderosa commented.

Both articulations were accurate. One-third of our outfit was headed to simulate the future; two-thirds were not. When lights out hit, I lay awake for most of the night. I felt the open stares of my sleepless buddies; like me, they were also searching the darkness for someone to blame.

No one in the company felt any better after the ritual Monday morning parade, and the depression during the first meal. I boarded the *general's* dump truck, and rode to the line. Cope was there when I arrived.

"Ready for the *Stars and Stripes* bivouac move story?" he cynically greeted me. He handed me an itinerary; the guide was fifteen pages thick. I didn't read it, but I was positive the last page credited any implied Sousa marches. "I'm in it; somewhere near the end. Got me down as, 'truck commander.'"

"I'm jealous. How come I'm not in the Fang Itinerary?"

"You are, Cooby, near the end, like me."

"As what, Cope?"

"Flight Operations NCOIC. Once I'm out of the building, you become 312$^{th}$ Flight Operations."

"Big deal. What am I supposed to do, load boxes on big trucks?"

"You'll be doing that once the move is complete; during the relocation you will monitor and record radio broadcasts between aircraft and ground vehicles." He explained my role in the exclusive Fort Benning news story.

"I don't have any experience using the radio, Cope."

"You will about four hours from now. Borque's here. He will help you out."

"It's the army way, right Cope?"

"Remind me to write your mother a letter, Cooby; want to tell her what a quick learner her son is," he joked.

"We'll both know about that four hours from now, won't we, Cope?"

"Three things before I play my bit part in the parade: first, monitor and record everything; second, memorize the bivouac map site over there on the wall; third, be sure to load everything on the truck. Prez and Ponderosa will be onboard; they'll help you."

Just as Cope was leaving, people from *Stars and Stripes* invaded the premises. From that moment on, the sun became a minor glow in comparison; anchoring the entourage was a stargazing Fenson and an eagle-chasing Fang.

"One more by the map, Sir..."

"How about the two of you together, Sirs..."

"Adjust your flight helmet, Sir..."

"I'll be at the Plantation House to snap a photograph of the lead aircraft, Colonel Fenson, Sir, just as you fly above the parade passing by Fort Benning Headquarters..."

"Nice touch, young man," the would-be general commended the newsman, then ordered, "Let's get the show on the road, Fang."

I think it took about fifteen minutes to acclimate to the dimly lit flight operations office, but as soon as Borque and I did, things began to pop.

"Battalion control, this is Lead Bird One, over," the flight operations radio squawked.

Borque snapped into action.

"Lead Bird One, this is battalion control, over."

"Battalion control, Lead Bird One; notify vehicle one five birds are taking flight, over."

"Lead Bird One, battalion control. Wilco, out."

I watched as Borque put one microphone down and picked up another, announcing, "Vehicle one, battalion control, over."

"Battalion control, vehicle one, over."

"Vehicle one, battalion control. Five birds taking off, over."

"Battalion control, vehicle one. Understood. Out."

"So that's how it works, Borque; guess I haven't paid too much attention to your work. Tell me, why two different microphones?"

"One frequency for aircraft; the other, land vehicles," he explained.

"Why two?" I asked him.

"Radio signals from above are easier to transmit than signals going across terrain." I was impressed, and quite aware of the experience Copelet left for the learning.

"Ground vehicles can't talk with aircraft, right?"

"That's why we have a battalion control."

Borque and I spent the next forty minutes relaying messages between the parade on the ground and the pilots flying above; can't say it actually happened, but I knew the moment when Lead Bird One flew over Fort Benning Headquarters. The recording process became as routine as well; Cope's method of teaching was indisputable.

Somewhere around 10 A.M., Borque and I heard an unusual radio transmission.

"Battalion control, Lead Bird One, over."

"Lead Bird One, battalion control, over."

Battalion control, Lead Bird One. Leaving flock. Advise Bird Two, over."

"Lead Bird One, battalion control. Copy. Out. Break. Lead Bird Two, battalion control, over."

"Battalion control, Lead Bird Two, over." I heard the voice of *the man who could fly anything.*

"Lead Bird Two, battalion control. Lead Bird One leaving flock. Lead Bird Two commands, over."

"Battalion control, Lead Bird Two. Understood. Out."

"What's that all about, Borque?" I asked my teacher.

"Fenson's calling it quits and coming home."

"Why?"

"Don't know, Cooby, but I'd bet Major Frankel knows."

His observation was correct. As it turned out, the *man who could fly anything, and make anything fly,* soon would be the man who could land anything as well. A Ch-47 was a double rotary helicopter with twice the lift ability of the UH-1D utility helicopter, an aircraft for which the bivouac site had been built. The downwind parented by one landing Chinook generated enough gale force winds to blow away an entire battalion. The bivouac site was a piece of cake in comparison.

Only one aircraft landed that *Stars and Stripes* day at the training area; all others were directed to return home. The week long, army-required exercise became nothing other than a "Humpty Dumpty routine," a detail requiring the men put back into place what had been blown down.

Frock and Boremba didn't unload their crated boxes; I didn't either. When the Inspector General's staff reviewed the debris, all became fully compliant with any official army rules and regulations.

Six-and-a-half days later, the returning one-third of the company found the latest edition of *Stars and Stripes* awaiting them on their individual bunks. Large photographs plastered the front page; each of the selected stories had its own captions:

### SERGEANT MAKES AVIATION HISTORY

Sergeant Clifford Foone raises his right arm while he takes the Oath of Re-Enlistment from Commanding Officer, Lt.Col. Robert Fang, Jr., while flying in a CH-47 over Fort Benning, Georgia. The Chinook aircraft was flown by Colonel John Fenson, the Commanding Officer, First Aviation Brigade. The E-8 is the only sergeant in army aviation history to re-enlist while flying in an aircraft. Hats off to the 312th Aviation Company.

**FENSON LEADS THE 312th TO A SUCCESSFUL BIVOUAC**

> The arm of Major General Hine Perez, Commanding General, Fort Benning, GA, is seen waving at the column of military vehicles parading in front of post headquarters. Above the convoy is a contingent of 312th Aviation Company aircraft. Col. John Fenson, Commanding Officer of the First Aviation Brigade, pilots the lead Chinook. Lt.Col. Robert Fang, Jr., Commanding Officer, 312th Aviation Company, copilots. As of this printing, the 312th has successfully passed inspection for deployment to Southeast Asia.

"Do you guys believe this crap?" Frock stared at his copy of *Stars and Stripes*.

"Big crock!" Boremba commented.

"And you, Cooby?" Frock asked. "What's the general have to say?"

"What the soldier sees, what the soldier hears, what the soldier expects—and now what the soldier reads—is not what the soldier gets."

# Part Two

## *DEPLOYMENT*

# CHAPTER 7

## DEPLOYABLE

---

The weekend following bivouac couldn't have been more depressing to one-third of the two companies that had been part of it; the other two-thirds found it difficult to sort between the real story and the propaganda read in *Stars and Stripes*. Rumors told of a 312th and 713th that didn't train. What made the scuttlebutt unbearable was twofold: it sprang from within the sister units, and it was all too true.

The prez, Ponderosa, and the general, tried to snub it by focusing on the upcoming 1966 holiday season. Two of us weren't very successful; Frock had an escape.

"I'm going to surprise Bunny on Christmas, you guys, by swinging a three-day pass," Frock informed us. "If I can do it, I'll repeat for it New Year's. Think you can persuade First Sergeant Turtz, Tim?"

"I'll try," Colonel Ponderosa answered. For Tim and me, a three-day pass meant two days of hopefully connecting air flights to Chicago or Omaha, and one real day of home time; Frock's destination was a mere two-hour ride to Atlanta. I envied him; I think Boremba did too. The holiday season of 1966 was to become the first time either one of us were not at home.

Frock was granted both wishes; Ponderosa and the general were relegated to the second floor of building five in a row of six. Our company area was not bedecked with red and green blinking lights; neither was the 176th or Fort Benning, Georgia. Both of us were given a half-day on Christmas Eve and all of Christmas Day off; the present was repeated on New Year's Eve and the first day of 1967. All fourteen Chinook helicopters had been grounded for "structural integrity"; still both the orderly room and the flight line remained open for business.

Timmy and I spent December 24, 1966, alone in our suite, pretending to write festive greetings home. On Christmas Day, we attended church and walked to the USO/PX, where the army tried to duplicate a traditional holiday dinner, with turkey and all the trimmings. Tim and I didn't feel like celebrating, although I ordered a hot dog with a Coke, and Tim got his

Chicago burger. We hardly touched our food, maybe eating a few chips that were a complementary side dish. We just sat and sipped our Cokes and appreciated each other's company. We repeated the same scenario on New Year's Eve and New Year's Day. Fort Benning's somber holiday season was not anywhere near "cheery and bright."

I ached for the second of January to arrive. When recorded reveille blasted throughout the company area at 5 A.M., I was eager to see Frock and engage in more than one-line phrases. The *president's* bunk was empty when I opened my eyes.

"Where's Frock?" I asked Colonel Ponderosa.

"Orderly room."

"Why?"

"Don't know."

"How come you're not there as well, Tim?"

"Don't know."

"What time did Frock wake up, Tim?"

"Early."

"Darn, I wanted to find out if he told Bunny about..."

"Attention! Attention in the company area," a familiar pest cut me off!

"What's this all about, Tim?" A shrug told me he didn't have a clue.

"By order of Lieutenant Colonel Robert Fang, Jr., CO, 312$^{th}$ Aviation Company, all personnel will assemble in the company street at 0800 hours," the PA announced.

"Any guesses, Tim?" The blank stare and a second shrug answered my inquiry. "Frock will fill us in; let's get over to the mess hall."

Frock wasn't there. After a somber breakfast, Boremba scurried off to the orderly room, and I waited, with about 500 other soldiers, in the company street.

At 8 A.M., on the morning of January 2, 1967, Lieutenant Colonel Robert Fang, Jr., addressed the two companies: "It is my duty and honor to announce, gentlemen, that as of January 2, 1967, the 312$^{th}$ Aviation Company and the 713$^{th}$ Transportation Company, are 'deployable for overseas duty.' Official orders have been cut. As of March 24, 1967, our new home will be in South Vietnam, where we shall serve as an assault support helicopter unit for the 5$^{th}$ Division."

No one rooted. I didn't. March 24 was my twenty-fifth birthday. Out of the corner of my eye I saw Timmy's already drooped shoulders sink an inch lower and I felt my own heart fall into my stomach.

"There will be a four-part relocation beginning with an advance party of about 15 officers and enlisted. This part one commences the last week of February. During the first week of March, fourteen fully staffed

Chinook aircraft will take off from Fort Benning; destination is San Francisco, California. There, they will board a U.S. Navy aircraft carrier bound for the South China Sea," the colonel coldly delivered one-half of the unwelcome message. One of the thoughts racing in my mind at the midway point was how fourteen helicopters, grounded for *structural integrity*, could miraculously become so healed they could fly across the continent to the Pacific Coast. Another was the realization I didn't need to search for blame. The *deployment* word I so feared now had a specific date attached to it.

"The third phase pertains to equipment allocation," Fang continued. "In the third week of March, everything not nailed down, will be loaded on flatbed railroad cars and shipped to another waiting U.S. naval transport on the West Coast; it too will be headed for South Vietnam. Remaining personnel will be transported to Air Force Star Lifters in the fourth and final phase of our deployment." He paused for a moment. "Everyone will be issued an emergency two-week leave. Dismissed." Fang returned to the inside of the orderly room, leaving everyone to stomach his ominous message.

The rest of January 2, 1967 dragged more slowly than all of December 24, 25, and 31, 1966, along with January 1, 1967. When the depressing workday ended, I tried to question Frock about what else he might know. The look on his face mirrored the sullen expression appearing on Boremba's.

"I should have told Bunny," he confessed. "I'm not only headed for Vietnam, I'm in the advance party."

"You're in phase one, Prez?"

"Fang, Jones, Frankel, Patton, Harsh, Turtz, Copelet, and me leave Fort Benning along with some other unnamed lucky stiffs in a 'Caribou' at the end of next month."

"Why you, Prez?"

"Hell, General, I don't know what a 'Caribou' is?"

"Don't worry, Prez; you'll find a way to tell her. If it will make you feel any better, I haven't written my ma yet."

"Me either," Ponderosa admitted.

"What do I tell her, that I've lied?"

"You tell her the same thing I tell my mother, Prez. The truth."

"Bunny is not going to like it!"

"Neither will my mother."

"Desoto wasn't too far off when he named you, *General,* and you, *Colonel.* I couldn't be in better company."

"We ain't doing too bad ourselves, Prez."

# CHAPTER 8

## OPERATION: MOVEMENT

---

Military life turned into a nagging anxiety after the announcement, both at flight operations and at the orderly room. Down at the line, all fourteen CH-47A aircraft seemed to suddenly pass structural integrity tests, and only rare "maintenance flights" needed documentation. While the 312th Aviation Company was winding down, a 312th Assault Support Helicopter Company was gearing up for the biggest training experience of its young existence.

Each night, Frock reported similar occurrences in the company area.

"Tell Cooby what Turtz did with his training charts, Ponderosa."

"Tossed 'em," Boremba relayed.

"He threw them away?"

"Yup!"

"Why?"

"Told Tim and me since we're fully deployable, they're no longer needed."

"*Fully deployable*," I snickered. "He should have said *fully deplorable*. What training? What IG? What bivouac?" I could have gone on with flight physicals, hazardous duty pay, machine gunner practice, and even my own MOS; I didn't. All of us knew the answer.

"Top sure spends a lot of time on coffee breaks, Cooby; the colonel doesn't even show up until 10 A.M., and always is gone by 3 P.M.

"Off my ass!" Boremba sounded relieved.

"All we do now is work on emergency leaves and spend the remaining time boxing and crating."

"Same-o at the line, Prez."

"You fellas want to go to the USO/PX tonight?"

Boremba nodded and I agreed. Three beers later Frock felt pretty relaxed; two beers later, I did too. A president and a general, however, were delightfully astonished at what a single beer could do for a one-lining

Colonel Ponderosa. He sang an entire verse of, "Mellow Yellow," never missing a beat; he was damn good too.

The activity proved popular, and we continued with it up to the night before Frock's emergency leave. Ponderosa had two beers, finished the entire song, and delighted the two of us.

"Got a deal for you two." Frock waited until Boremba finished.

"What's that, Prez?" I asked.

"Since you've thrown me this going away party, would my two buddies let me do the same when we meet again?"

We agreed; Colonel Ponderosa had a third beer, and we had to assist his return to the barracks. When Frock came back from leave, I requisitioned a jeep and asked Tim to join me in seeing Frock off.

"No trouble?" he questioned.

"What's the army going to do, Tim? Send us to Vietnam for borrowing a jeep?"

He reluctantly got in, and we drove to the flight line. All the assigned men slated for the advance party move were there along with one photogenic officer looking for a star. All had relatives present to say, "good-bye," all but Staff Sergeant Copelet. "Thanks for coming; you too, Ponderosa," the flight operations sergeant greeted us.

Cope was glad to see us but deflected any attention to himself by adding, "Looks like someone will have to pry the two apart." He pointed to the farewell of Frock and Bunny.

"He found a way, Tim," I told Boremba, who smiled in agreement as we watched the advance party board the turbo-prop aircraft in descending order of rank.

Just before entering the C-141, Frock turned to wave to a tearful Bunny and his parents, then yelled, "Remember the next reunion party is on me."

We watched the camouflage Caribou climb and disappear into the western Georgia sky; when it became an undetectable speck, I asked, "Want to come next week to the Chinook takeoff?"

"Guess so." He masked the choking, which was clogging his throat; for the first time, I saw tears in his eyes.

"I'll have to borrow another jeep."

"Going anyway." The colonel plagiarized my words.

The next week, the day before our leave, we were on our way to watch our aircraft begin part two of the move.

"Towie doesn't suspect a thing, Tim. Hell, if the guy can't find 40-plus flight physicals in a year, how the heck will our temporary first sergeant miss one jeep?"

"Won't," Boremba conceded truth, just as we arrived at the Fort Benning flight line.

There was a mob there, and it was led by Colonel Fenson and a retinue of suck-ups and *Stars and Stripes* reporters. I imagined the news story the following week.

"That guy really does want a star," I confided in Tim.

"Only one?" His terse comment defined the scenario.

By itself, the sight was great to photograph. Fourteen Chinook aircraft were revved up, and aching to slice into an anxious southern sky. When they did, I remarked to Boremba: "Farho should be taking this photograph."

"Who's Farho?"

"The *Stars and Stripes* news reporter who took pictures of Foone's re-enlistment and the 312th's bivouac."

"Why?"

"A snapshot like this would get him a promotion to the *Stars and Stripes* headquarters in Washington, DC."

"Is something," the one-liner summed up the view. Those aircraft formed a straight-line trail in the sky as they set out for San Francisco. It was militarily stirring.

"Our turn is next, Ponderosa."

"Home, first." Again he was right on; our time for the emergency leave and the unfinished business of telling our relatives was very close at hand.

A very gracious army provided the *hop* into Atlanta; the United Airlines flight to Chicago and to Omaha, wasn't free. On my layover, I met Ponderosa's sister, Bernadette, who had come to take him home. On my return flight, I met with Tim's entire family: mother, father, and sister.

"Tell them, Tim?" I asked the Illinois native once we were seated on the flight back to Atlanta.

"Yes."

"They're worried, aren't they?"

"Very."

"My family too; so am I. How about you?"

"Scared."

Boremba's comment pretty well described the feeling in the company area when we arrived. Everything was gone except the 450 plus men remaining to be transplanted; the 312th and the 713th didn't exist any longer in the United States. Our sister units were relegated again to leaning upon the 176th.

On the morning of March 20, 1967, a convoy of borrowed trucks filled the former company street. Eighteen men, each carrying issued and personal equipment in their duffel bags, were herded into twenty-five deuce and a half army vehicles. The destination was unknown.

Two hours later, the column parked on the tarmac of an air force base. Whistles were blown, commands were shouted, and the men in the trucks were directed to line up, three abreast. Once the order was executed, we gazed at the huge air force transports anxiously awaiting our boarding.

The massive aircraft were called Star Lifters; a mere glance dispelled any skepticism. The underside of one was somewhere near fifteen feet from the ground, and each had a wingspan defying description. The windowless transports were safely adjacent to one another; their rear ends were open and beckoning us to enter.

Bullhorns shouted the cue: "The first men will occupy the farthest internal seats." An aisle separated two rows of triple seating; 75 spaces on each side, 25 rows. There was ample room for a third insert. "Stow your gear at your feet," the harsh command blasted.

There was no, *hurry up and wait*, to this action; in fifteen minutes, 150 men each, were boarded into the three camouflage air force super transports. Within seconds, the noise of electrical motors whined and the tailgate closed; any exit was denied, and virtually all light eliminated. We faced the rear end of the aircraft with our feet resting on duffel bags; the design was not without purpose. Once the engines demonstrated thrust ability, hurling was prevented; so was speech between passengers. I could barely see Timmy, who sat next to me; I couldn't hear him or talk to him. The aircraft was not user-friendly, nor was it United Airlines. Cramping began early, and everyone aboard became grateful for winter fatigue apparel donned the day of an unusually cold spring day in Fort Benning, Georgia.

Eight hours later, the Star Lifter touched ground.

"Where?" Boremba asked when the incessant noise of jet engines abated.

"Don't know, Tim." I didn't, and both of us had to wait for the tailgate to open. We had landed at Ellendorf, AFB, in the 49th state; I could tell from the blue hue on Timmy's face, *Alaska*, was not a word he wanted to hear.

"Grab your gear and deplane in an orderly manner," the bullhorn blared.

Dazed, tired, hungry, and cold, the passengers were led to another convoy. This time it was air force buses, taking us to a contained reception area. The chain-link fence, the armed soldiers, and the guard dogs quite adequately spurned even the remotest thoughts of considering going AWOL.

"I hope your stay at Ellendorf will be a pleasant one," Sergeant Mart greeted us. "Your continuing flight, and phase two of *Operation Movement*, commences at 0900 hours tomorrow. On behalf of the United States Air Force, please enjoy your stay."

It was not too difficult to take in Ellendorf Air Force Base; Timmy and I were given a room to share that was much more like a Holiday Inn.

"Hot shower." He noticed the *civilian comforts*.

"Hot meal," I one-lined back. Our flight did not have stewardesses.

Neither of us were disappointed; Boremba luxuriated in a shower for twenty minutes, then joined me in a repast fit for kings. "The Navy got the gravy, and the Army got the beans, but the Air Force got everything else." We were unaware that the Marines got nothing.

The second phase of Operation Movement duplicated the first. We were airborne by 9 A.M., flying to an unknown place. Nine hours later we landed at Tempo AFB, Japan. Ellendorf was great; Tempo, better. I remember joking with Boremba, saying, "Even a condemned prisoner is granted one last wish."

By 10 A.M. the following morning, we were airborne and on the third leg of Operation Movement. At 7 P.M., March 23, 1967, the three big Star Lifters touched ground. Everyone anticipated more air force hospitality.

None occurred.

We landed at Long Binh, AFB, South Vietnam.

# CHAPTER 9

## WELCOME, VIETNAM

---

TWO unforgettable things hit me while I was in the belly of the Star Lifter as hydraulic motors opened its butt end. One was the rush of tropical heat engulfing the aircraft; the other was the stench that accompanied it.

"You're home, greenhorns," a rude military PA greeted us. "Line up, three abreast, and march to the column of trucks."

As at Benning, and unlike Ellendorf and Tempo, a readied convoy of trucks was awaiting. The 2½-ton vehicles were dust-covered and nakedly exposing the ribs which held canvas coverings. Within thirty minutes, the line of trucks was crossing the broad Long Binh runway with about 450 new arrivals on board. I stopped counting Star Lifters at forty-two, just as our caravan passed through an opening of seemingly never-ending chain-link fence. Our parade met an audience on the other side.

"I'm out of here, you sorry ass fuckers."

"Short time, mother, your turn now."

"Only fifteen days, you worthless sacks of shit."

No one in the column could avoid hearing the catcalls, which intensified anytime someone on board stood up to take off an obviously unneeded fatigue coat. I had my taste of *hurry up and wait,* but the longest fifteen minutes I ever spent in my life was in the back of that army truck crossing the Long Binh military complex. I was tired, hot, hungry, in very unfamiliar territory, and my welcoming fellow soldiers were jeering and laughing.

"Out of here, asshole."

"Your turn now, you fuckin' grunts."

The comments were plentiful, descriptive, and relentless. They persisted until our convoy reached the perimeter of the military installation. The barrier was a thirty-foot wall of earth, bulldozed into existence, capped with concertina wire, and extending as far as the eye could see in either direction. Gun emplacements, enclosed by sandbags, severed the ugly line of meshed barricade, every fifty feet.

"Hope you fuckin' make it out there, buttheads," was the last remark I heard when passing through a rare opening in the man-made fortification.

I wanted to close my eyes, click my boots, and go home.

Instead I got my first glimpse of Vietnam.

A totally barren area, maybe 500' perpendicular to the wall, existed on the other side of the dike. Something like oil saturated every inch of ground, making the defense look similar to a firebreak in a forest. This one was huge, and signs were posted everywhere, reading: "Minefields." A lot of unraveled barbed wire replaced remnants of choked growth.

Almost as suddenly as bleak nothingness appeared, green lush vegetation showed itself like grass growing alongside a sidewalk. It was thick and very much alive. The road we were on sliced it like a channel carved into Jell-O. On both sides of the path was a clearance of approximately 25 feet. I think I imagined DeMille's *The Ten Commandments*. No one knew about Agent Orange or the torching abilities of napalm, but we all visually observed the scorched aftermath.

Less than a half kilometer from Long Binh's perimeter, and only on one side of the cleared path, indigenous thatch-covered shanties vied for space among the road, one another, and the vegetation.

"Rosie's, Good Times, and Dong's Bar," were only a coloring of a few inciting primitive signs.

"Look at those shacks, Timmy."

"Sin sells."

How succinct Boremba was, I thought to myself. Who else but Colonel Ponderosa could aptly describe in two words what appeared to be happening outside the perimeter of the largest military complex in the world.

Four helicopters joined our motorcade; they shotgunned overhead. Everybody knew exactly what the steel rods were that pointed outside the body of each. Their presence did provide some consolation; no one in the column was armed. The UH-1Ds hawked above, two at the front of the convoy, and two in the rear. They matched our speed as we commenced to barrel down a virtual dust path made up of plain dirt and tons of ashes.

After a twenty-minute ride, the transport came to a halt. A message was relayed down the line of vehicles: "Piss stop." There were no objections; latrine utilities on board the Star Lifter consisted of an issued *pee tube*. Captain Flark, our vehicle commander, and one of the pilots not making the move with the Chinooks in phase two, stood alongside Tim and me at the nearest ditch. I had met Flark at the flight line. He hand delivered his flight records, and introduced himself by saying, "Harsh told me you do wonders with previous errors." With Cope's help we corrected a two-year long mistake netting the captain, beginning his second tour of Vietnam, about 75 more flight hours.

"Nobody's going to screw with us with those gunships hovering above," Captain Flark informed Cooby. He relieved himself. "The people who live here can see them too!"

"Sounds good, Captain; doesn't feel too reassuring." Flark was a lot like Cope and didn't place emphasis upon the standards of required military greetings. I found out I could respect any officer who was in the same boat as me, but handling a different oar. All of the awareness sprang from being around Carl Copelet.

"Follow me, Cooby." He buttoned his fly. "Want you to see something." Boremba trailed me like a puppy.

"Where we going, Flark?"

"Over there. See that group of Vietnamese by the side of the road?" He pointed to a single file line of mixed men and women not too far in front of our column. All of them were short, appeared skinny, and wore loose-fitting clothes and cone-shaped hats. Some were leaning upon hand-pulled carts, others against what appeared to be two large sacks. Most of the remaining squatted on the ground.

"Should we go nearer?"

"See the old one, Cooby? The one balancing her sacks with the stick on her shoulder?" Flark ignored my doubt.

"The one who looks about 65?"

"Hey, Mamasan," Flark yelled, motioning to the woman.

The old lady's face brightened, and she scurried toward us. Flark reached into his fatigue pocket and removed a pack of cigarettes; when he did, she liberated the load weighting her shoulder. She bowed a couple times, accepted the gift of cigarettes, vocalized a few screeching sounds, and smiled at the captain. Both Boremba and I noticed her blackened teeth. We backed away.

Flark bowed back at her, then said, "She's harmless."

The two new arrivals remained skeptical, but watched as the old woman retrieved what looked like a large green leaf from one of her sacks. She then wrapped her gift, fastening it with some type of slim vine, and placed her gift into her sack. When she finished, she bowed several times at the captain, and uttered more shrill sounds.

"Bet you can't lift those two sacks, Cooby," the captain challenged me.

I wasn't ready to accept his dare, but curiosity told me to try. "I may be cramped from the trip, but I'm not so old I can't lift what she can." I accepted the bet. When I began to straighten up, the ropes tightened, and the stick dug into my shoulder; I could not lift the containers.

I sheepishly replaced the stick and returned to Boremba's side, all the while listening to shrill, but discernable cackles of laughter. "How does she do it?" I asked. Both bewildered greenhorns observed the frail Vietnamese ease herself under her lever, lift the burden, and hurry away, almost skipping as she did.

"Coobat, you have just witnessed one of the strengths of these people; make sure you don't underestimate any of them," Flark warned, as whistles signaled the end of a piss break. Within minutes our convoy was moving forward.

"How long?" Boremba asked.

"Don't know, Tim," I imitated Boremba; a closed mouth and squinting eyes became a popular sport traveling along the man-made passageway burned into the vegetation.

Forty-five minutes later, the transport ceased forward motion and the shotgun helicopters vanished. When the dust settled, I stood up to take a look.

What I saw was a barricade of dirt, similar to the one we exited at Long Binh. It was bulldozed into place, topped with concertina wire, and extended endlessly on either side of the column. At its base, and perpendicular to it, was an area of barren land the length of a football field. Several posted signs cautioned: "Minefield." The trucks stopped at the only access I could see; above it was a stretched rope supporting a crude, but readable wooden plaque: "BEAR CAT! HOME OF THE FIFTH DIVISION."

It didn't take too long for the barbed entrance gates to open; when they did, our transport moved ahead. When my vehicle passed through, I saw sandbagged gun emplacements on each side. Soldiers clad in fatigue pants, boots, and a helmet manned them. They wore some sort of thick vest which didn't cover the upper portion of a body like a shirt does.

There was no Fenson trying to catch a star, nor a Fang chasing after an eagle, on the other side. Absent as well, were news reporters and photographic equipment; the arrival of a virgin company wasn't front-page material.

In attendance to greet us however, was sight and sound.

I noticed the color green instantly, but not the green of growth or the green of spring. It was the dusted hue of camouflage, as in tents, vehicles, headgear, and fatigues. Natural growth had been snuffed out of existence. Drab tents predominated; most were pitched on ground, some on platforms of wood. All failed at forming neat patterns, and all looked more like shade umbrellas rather than tents. Encircling each was a sandbag bunker, and in every collection, one building prevailed. It was one-story, wooden,

30' x 60', windowless, and louvered. There were a number of similar clusters in what I guessed to be an encampment perhaps three miles square.

Catcalls provided the background music for our arrival.

"Short time, fucker."

"Welcome to hell, shitface."

One shirtless soldier flipped us the bird with one hand, grabbed his crotch with the other, and yelled, "Bosebaugh's got your ass now, sucker." No one knew who Bosebaugh was.

Another used two hands to flip two birds while blaring, "I'm out of this stinkin' asshole, tomorrow, baby."

Our reception committee continued with the jeers as the column headed toward our final destination; all of them were unwanted, misunderstood, and relentless. At one point during the trek, as we passed by the Bear Cat runway, so proclaimed by another sign post, I hoped we had arrived; the catcalls sounded hateful. It didn't happen. The 3500' tarmac airstrip, filled with fixed wing aircraft on one side, and helicopters on the other, was not the new home of the 312th. I wished it were; it favored a miniature version of the flight line back at Benning. There was a defined runway, parked aircraft, one structure resembling a radio tower, and personnel scurrying about as though they knew what they were doing. As our convoy passed it, virtually everyone within sight took some time to mock the new arrivals.

Ten minutes into an unwelcome penetration of Bear Cat's interior, Boremba nudged me and exclaimed, "Look."

I wasn't in the best mood for more sights; the sounds we heard weren't appetizing, and I almost yelled back at him, shouting, "Look at what?"

"That," he pointed.

I turned my eyes to see what had attracted Boremba's attention, and couldn't believe what I saw. It was a sixty foot, yellow, mobile trailer home that exploded upon the greenless scene like the first crocus in a barren garden. The unusual oasis was fenced, manicured, and complete with a rock-lined driveway leading from its guarded front entry all the way to its perch-like position. Flags flew everywhere inside its boundaries, and they shared space with a few well-placed indigenous palm trees. Two matching yellow umbrellas stood at attention on the wooden deck constructed on one side, and although I couldn't see it, I knew a pool was somewhere near. A large, hand-painted sign proclaimed: "Major General Bosebaugh, Commanding General."

"If I didn't know better, Ponderosa, I'd swear I was fifteen miles south of Omaha, driving by the north forty of a rural Nebraska farm." From my perspective, in the back of a military deuce and a half, this sight ranked as one of the mysterious wonders of the world.

"Fink," Boremba summarized the obvious disparity, just as I recalled a hateful catcall: "Bosebaugh's got your ass now, sucker." The Calumet City native was keen at observing reality. He could look at or hear anything, dismiss all the nonessentials, and cut to the quick. He didn't say, "Rank has its privilege"; what he said was, "fink," and the word was poignant. Radar O'Reilly wasn't famous yet, but if he were, Colonel Ponderosa would have been named differently.

The two of us sat down in disgust, as did everybody on the transport; we waited for the inevitable.

Five short minutes later, our parade came to a halt. We had arrived at the 312$^{th}$ Aviation Company's new home. It was a flat corner of Bear Cat loaded with metal conex containers, heaped with piles of quiet canvas, cluttered with equipment, and all of it spread about as though it had been dumped. Six tents defied the word, *pitched*, and a few wooden platforms appeared to be a *work in progress*. One thing was obvious: the arrivals were given the potential for becoming a company.

"If it ain't the general and the Colonel Ponderosa," a familiar voiced sounded from somewhere alongside our truck. Tim and I jumped off and landed in two inches of dust. We knew nothing of a dry season, or a rainy season. Our duffel bags made bigger splashes.

"Frock." We started to shake hands but gave up; he hugged Tim as well.

"It's great to see you two." He smiled, exposing white teeth set off by a deep tan. "Didn't hear any Caribou. When did you guys land at the Bear Cat runway?" Frock asked.

"Rode by it, but didn't land there. The air force gave us a no frills hop to Long Binh. You land here?"

"Sure did. Wow, was I surprised!"

"Not much here, is there, Prez?"

"Was even less when I arrived."

"Where's our flight line?"

"Have to build one, General."

"From the looks of it we'll have to build a company."

"Fifteen men came over with the advance party. Ten were chiefs; the rest were Indians, Cooby."

Frock didn't have to say any more; the look on his face said it all. Five Indians couldn't possibly build a company for about 700 men. I expected the one-lining Boremba to say something like, "bivouac was better," but he too was stunned by the complete nothingness. An outfit about to "rewrite the pages of aviation history," was the same company that had to begin from ground zero.

"So where do we park our butts, Prez?"

"Follow me," he instructed, trying to ignore the forlorn look parading on the faces of the officers, NCOs, and everyone else. Attention getting whistles didn't blow, sullen officers just dragged their duffel bags into the midst of the helter skelter supplies and equipment, and the ranking cadre followed suit. One very evident fact was clear: some God awful force had sucked up everyone and dumped them in the midst of no man's land. There was no way to leave; no return flights.

Frock led Tim and me to a spot about fifty yards away. With limited choices, he had selected as his niche, an open space between two unpacked metal conex containers. Both had been somehow situated to one another, unlike the rest. The inventive Georgian had placed an army blanket over the two, creating a shading umbrella above the metal packing crates. In one box was a GI desk with a typewriter; apparently this was the current orderly room. In the other was a cot and his personal equipment. Scattered about both were the trappings of his office back at Benning.

"I swiped a couple of pneumatic mattresses from one of the containers," he told us. "You won't be sleeping on the ground your first night." Tim and I watched him remove from his home what he must have considered to be essential. From his perspective, we were green; from our own, we hadn't landed in *Kansas*. "Blow them up," he added.

While we were filling the air mattresses, Frock fidgeted with his box from home; between breaths, I asked, "What do we do for food?" Tim and I hadn't eaten since the sumptuous meal at Tempo, AFB, Japan.

"We go to one of those louvered buildings; it's borrowed until we build our own."

"When?" an anxious Boremba asked.

"In the morning, Tim."

"Tomorrow?" Boremba beat me to the punch.

"This isn't Benning, Colonel Ponderosa," Frock scolded the Illinois private. "The food ain't great, and neither is the quinine pill you'll take every Monday morning. Either one will give you the shits. Nobody warned me, so consider yourself lucky."

"Place is full of surprises, right, Prez?" I commented. I wasn't happy being nowhere, Boremba wasn't either; the prez masked his sentiments.

"There are some special ones," Frock told me. "Sit down, you two."

We followed his instructions, and watched as he fumbled around some more; he produced a round, fruitcake looking tin.

"Remember my promise back at Benning?" He handed me the tin. "Happy birthday, Cooby."

"We left on the 20$^{th}$; spent three days in the air, Prez. My birthday ain't until tomorrow, the 24$^{th}$."

"Sorry. You crossed the international dateline; you're a whole day later and a full year older, General. Open it."

I was stunned by the news but opened the tin. Inside were three cupcakes wrapped in wax paper, a Diamond matchbox, and something stuck to the bottom. "Where did these come from?"

"Bunny sent them to me, Cooby; light the candles."

"Think they melted, Prez." I showed him the interior of the tin.

"Then we'll use the matchsticks."

"Better marry that girl, Prez."

"I will...just as soon as I get out of this place. For right now, happy birthday." He handed me a two-week old cupcake with a lighted match, gave one to Boremba, and grabbed the last one for himself.

"Happy birthday, General," Boremba chimed in.

"Thanks, guys. I don't think I'll ever forget this, and I know I'll always remember the two of you," I told them, as I devoured my dry cake in two bites. "Be sure and tell Bunny 'thanks' from me, Prez."

"I will, Cooby, but I better fill the two of you in on a few bare essentials first. In thirty minutes, it will be very dark at Bear Cat, and I mean really dark. The urinal is the ditch; the shitter is behind that wall of 55-gallon barrels," he pointed. "It ain't much but it works. Just don't slide the butt on the wooden plank."

"Must be why they call this place, *Bare Cat*, Prez."

"It's more than what I had, Cooby...get some sleep now. Tomorrow is going to be one hell of a day for everyone...Oh!" he added, "use your army-issued blanket as a pillow. If you don't, you'll get up feeling like you slept on the ground." The president then placed the mattresses together and repeated, "Get some rest."

Boremba conked out immediately; Frock wasn't too far behind. I lay awake for a while. I was exhausted, covered with dirt, hot, scared, in a strange place, and the roof over my head was woolen; on top of it all, it was my 25$^{th}$ birthday, and Frock's description of the next day was, "going to be one hell of a day for everyone."

He wasn't wrong.

At 5 A.M., on the March 25, 1967, seventy howitzers delivered Bear Cat's version of reveille. The thunder shook the earth like a rare Nebraska earthquake.

"What the hell was that?" I damn near screamed. Timmy covered his face with his army blanket.

"It's wake-up call, guys; the 5th Division is calling."

"It sure works, Prez! I'm awake."

"You'll get used to it, Cooby. When the night patrol spots anything unusual, division replies with a volley or two," he explained.

"What's a night patrol, Prez? And just what's anything unusual?"

"Night patrol is the 24-hour guards who man machine-gun emplacements on top of the thirty foot wall of dirt circling this place. It's called *the berm*. 'Anything unusual' means activities on the other side."

"Any more neat surprises, Prez?"

"In about five minutes, a few helicopters will buzz over us to have a look at where the shells exploded; it's going to feel like they're going to land right on top of us. They won't."

"Where's the toilet?" Sudden diarrhea hit.

Frock pointed.

I ran. But it wasn't to a toilet, or a latrine. It was to a squalid, open cesspool.

Thirty minutes later, dawn lit up the 312th and 713th company area, and the impact of not waking up from a dream set in. The unusual reveille and the hedge hopping choppers achieved their intended effects; so did observing the other men, who like me, realized they weren't in Kansas.

While we all struggled for some semblance of identity, rumors became as common as the inches of dust no one could ignore; fear and confusion spread quickly. At about 7 A.M., a whistle blew and word was passed among the disorganized men that Colonel Fang would address his troops from atop one of the metal boxes. The one selected was appropriate; its backdrop was the stacked 55-gallon drums disguising the only fetid facility available to the new in-country arrivals.

The eagle-seeking officer was brought in a jeep flying a flag with two little stars on its front right fender. The vehicle backed up to the conex container, and the colonel used it as a stepping stone to climb atop. When he stood upright, he immediately began to speak. There was no fanfare, nothing to resemble military decorum, and little to reflect a sense of urgency.

"Welcome to our new home, men," he began. "The 5th will assist us as we get on our feet, and Major General Bosebaugh has personally promised his full cooperation and all of the equipment and materials required to build our 312th Assault Support Helicopter Company. This includes the use of adjacent company facilities and neighboring mess halls. The first meal we'll have at Bear Cat is available to us now in the louvered building across the way." Raising his arm, he pointed to the structure.

Fang didn't have to say another word; nor could he. Just as soon as *meal* was associated with *direction*, every man, save three, beat feet toward it. Colonel Boremba, President Frock, and General Coobat walked. I performed the green apple two-step on the way over.

"Make sure you eat something and drink something," Frock warned us. He and Ponderosa were helping me to the borrowed mess hall; I had expected to be helping him assist Timmy.

"Prez, I just deposited my guts in that thing called a toilet; not so sure I want any army cooking right now."

The smell inside the louvered building was so distinct even Tim remarked, "Can't eat."

"Guys, I'd cut off my left nut to get some home cooking right now, but my ma's eighteen thousand miles away. If you don't eat and drink something, you'll find yourself at the division aid station just like I did. Twice," he added.

"No doubt you ate this crap!" Shit on a shingle, Bear Cat style, was served with its own brand of stench.

"What I did was not eat, and not drink," Frock replied.

"I'm not convinced, Prez; this stuff not only smells, it stinks."

"Me either." Colonel Ponderosa sported a clear frown.

"Do it, or three or four hours from now, after steaming under Bear Cat's tropical sun, you'll be forced to swallow an APC, two quarts of water, and a salt pill," he forewarned.

"What's an APC, Prez?"

"All purpose capsule, kinda like aspirin. The medic, on my second trip, explained the real cure for this climate. He told me salt makes your body function like the radiator in a car. Salt makes you sweat. If you don't have any liquid, the body responds with heat stoke. All the iced tea, all the water, and all the food is loaded with salt."

"What about that quinine pill you mentioned?"

"There's a mosquito here that spreads sickness with a single bite. Quinine counteracts it. I've seen some of the dizzy guys with what's called encephalitis; I'd prefer to have the *shits*."

"Medic teach you that too, Prez?" Class One: Introduction to Bear Cat, was a work in progress.

"The medic, and your friend, Sergeant Copelet." He began to eat the SOS.

"I haven't seen Cope; thought for sure he'd greet us."

"Sergeant Copelet keeps pretty much to himself; mostly he is building platforms for tents and unpacking the stuff for operations." Frock chugged a huge gulp of tea. "Drink," he persuaded Tim and me.

The remaining members of the triumvirate followed suit; the experience was similar to having your mouth open while diving into the Pacific Ocean for the first time.

"Keep the t-shirts on; this sun scorches, and Walgreens ain't around the corner," Frock continued with more of Class One.

Five hours later, Colonel Ponderosa and General Coobat witnessed what Frock tried to explain and Mother Army hadn't. Thirty men collapsed from overexposure.

"How come Fang didn't get some help with this place?" We watched the men being carried off.

"Cooby, the 312th is here to support the 5th, not the other way around," he snapped. "Besides, Fang ain't around much; I've seen him three times since our C-141 landed."

"Where does he stay?"

"Certainly not here! Think a lieutenant colonel would hang around lowly enlisted personnel who live in a hovel?" His cynical question prefaced the next revealing crack: "He stays at the mellow yellow trailer park...the *Emerald City* — where Bosebaugh lives. If you passed the Bear Cat runway on your way here, you had to see it."

"Same-o, same-o." Tim Boremba did not say "rank has its privilege," but he summed up, in two words, the glaring gap.

The prez didn't say anything more: he didn't have to. He helped Tim and me sort through our belongings and attempt to establish some type of organization. Not much could be done. The net result was three men would be sharing a space under a blanket stretched between two empty metal containers, living conditions a little more improved over what most had.

At midday, the sound of another in-camp whistle heralded the noon meal. No one rushed, and everyone resisted the need to bend an elbow. Bear Cat liver and onions outdid Bear Cat SOS. During the *try-and-keep-your-stomach-walls-separate meal*, four sergeants made sure everyone knew Colonel Fang would address his troops at 1:30 P.M. Austeen, Towie, Foone, and Turtz did not eat. Like most, they drank prepared tea; like all, they had to wait for the scheduled talk. By 1:30 P.M., Bear Cat SOS, a quinine pill, and the searing sun had combined with Bear Cat liver and onions. There was a line of men waiting to use the one and only latrine; the rest dropped their pants at the closest ditch.

By 2:00 P.M., a mob had formed around the selected metal box with the unique backdrop.

"On this 25<sup>th</sup> day of March, 1967," Fang began his talk, "let me dispel doubts about the proud heritage our company brings to the 5<sup>th</sup> Division, and our assault support role to a great organization commanded by Major General Bosebaugh."

I listened, concentrating not so much on what he had to say, but on the gross difference between what I had either seen or heard from movies—the part about "following someone to hell"— and what I was observing. Colonel Fang was not a leader; rather, he was a pompous, overweight imitation of a man who just happened to have silver oak leaf clusters.

"Men, the general has offered all the supplies, water, food, and equipment at his disposal; I have accepted on the behalf of this organization. Our first priority will be the construction of a suitable home for the Executive Officer, Major Aron, and myself; I am confident you will accommodate our needs. In addition, work shall begin immediately on the mess hall and club for our officers; these facilities will be the talk of Bear Cat, as will our operations, our orderly room, and the maintenance office for our sister outfit, the 713<sup>th</sup> Transportation Company."

Almost 20% of the men had been felled by heat stroke or diarrhea, and virtually 100% had no place to sleep. This did not bother our commanding officer. I wanted to push his butt into one of the several ditches where several had defecated, praying he'd tread water; instead, I was forced to hear more priorities essential for the 312<sup>th</sup> Assault Support Helicopter Company. None concerned anything urgent.

"I will be billeting with the general," he ended. He left in the borrowed jeep, the one with a little red flag bearing two stars, which was flying on the right front fender.

When he departed, I felt as though Ramses had just made a surprise visit and instructed his Egyptian lieutenants to disperse among the slaves to assure: "So let it be written; so let it be done."

# CHAPTER 10

## THE BUILDING OF THE 312th

Only Lieutenant Colonel Fang escaped the ball-busting job of recreating a home for the 312th and the 713th; work began as soon as the jeep flying the flag with two stars on its right front fender left the site. By 3 P.M., one detail of fifty men did nothing other than unload vehicles coming from the 5th Division's seemingly endless stash of goodies. Lumber, portable generators, hammers, skill saws, sacks of concrete, tons of sand, shovels, screen wire, blister bags of water, kegs of nails, and a range of assorted tools and equipment were forced to find some place to coexist with previously dumped conex containers and approximately 450 crowded men.

First Sergeant Turtz wasted little time in forming a detail to begin immediate work on the commander's abode, and his desire for a louvered building that would become the officers' club and mess hall. Frock, Ponderosa, and I were assigned to work with Copelet, who had spearheaded the initial platforms that would someday revert into the first row of tents that comprised our new company. Copelet already had three made; six more were needed to complete officers' row. Nine 24' x 12' wooden framed floors were required. On our first afternoon at Bear Cat, everybody, except officers, hauled materials. Captain Patton and Mr. Harsh, advance party arrivals, supervised our work.

The same set-up operated for about 10 other details: 45 men, one NCO, and one or two supervisory officers. Not much progress passed during the second half of the first day in our new home; what did happen was disorganization, more confusion, and severe sunburns. No one in the 312th and 713th slept on his back the night of March 25, 1967.

When Bear Cat's version of reveille rocketed reality into the company's soul the following morning, all of the new arrivals were introduced to the unique happening that occurs when a burned face is scraped by a sharp razor and then rinsed with salted water. The sensual experience was encored by another serving of Bear Cat shit-on-a-single and immediately followed with pounding a lot of nails into wooden planks.

"Why?" I asked Cope the next day.

"Why what, Cooby?"

"Why do we raise the platform and set it on the spent howitzer shells?"

"You'll find out once the monsoon season hits," Cope answered.

"That much water?"

"Cooby, the worst Nebraska thunderstorm you've been in will be like a mere drizzle in comparison. When we're done with the nine platforms, then we dig a moat around each one of them."

"Another question," the supervising Mr. Harsh asked.

"Fire away, Mr. Harsh."

"How'd you guys keep cool on your last tour?"

"We started with showers," Cope smarted to the warrant.

The smile on CW3 Harsh's face couldn't be ignored; like everyone else, the Bear Cat sun had singed his face. When he opened his mouth, his white teeth appeared iridescent. "Not talking about the men, Cope, I'm wondering about hooches."

"We built them close to the showers," Cope reiterated.

"Pretty good, Cope," the warrant acknowledged the perseverance. "You know what I'm talking about. A green tent under this sun has the makings for a hot oven."

"Make you a deal, Mr. Harsh." Cope ceased pounding nails and eyeballed the chopper pilot.

"What kind of deal?"

"You talk, officer to officer, with Major Frankel, about real priorities around here, and I will give you the secret to keeping a green tent cooler."

"No dice, Cope; Fang's the commander. He makes the rules."

"Is true, Mr. Harsh, but while Fang's away, the men can play, so to speak. Frankel's in charge when Colonel Fang whiles away at the yellow trailer house."

"What makes you think Frankel would listen?"

"He was enlisted before he became an officer."

"Not my place, Sergeant Copelet." The warrant wiped some sweat from his brow.

Cope put down his hammer and walked to the finished platform where Harsh was seated. He too rubbed away some lingering beads of sweat, then sat down. "Mr. Harsh," he began, "we have 45 men tripping over one another in each of about ten projects; what we need is 45 projects with ten men in each. We have a lot to do, Sir." That was the first time I heard Sergeant Copelet address a superior officer with *Sir*.

"I know you're right, Copelet, but I'm a CW3, not an *officer and gentleman*; that kind of rule bending should come from someone with higher rank."

"You're also a man, just like the enlisted personnel here who don't have a place to sleep tonight. Frankel is one too," Sergeant Copelet emphasized.

CW3 Harsh sat there for a few moments, as if mulling over the simple suggestion. He fidgeted, wiped more sweat away, and eased himself into capitulating by asking, "You think Major Frankel would listen?"

"I know he will."

"I'll do it," the warrant caved in. "But only after you tell me the secret to keeping a tent cooler."

"It's so simple you'll laugh, Mr. Harsh," Cope teased.

"A deal is a deal, and I'm not laughing. What is the secret?" Harsh's impatience was rising faster than rank.

"A parachute."

"What?"

"A parachute," Cope repeated.

"If this is a joke played on me, Copelet, I am not at all amused."

Cope chuckled a bit at Mr. Harsh's reaction, waited for a few seconds, then reassured the skeptical warrant: "The use of a parachute is not a joke; actually it's a good idea and as I told you a simple one."

"I'm listening," the warrant said. So was every man in detail working with Sergeant Copelet.

"Your plans are to build nine platforms, right?"

"Those are the plans."

"When they're built, the next step is to erect a stick-like framework on which you'll drop a tent, right again?"

"Two by fours are more reliable than a pole and ropes," CW3 Harsh remarked.

"Yes they are," Cope agreed, "but if all you do is rest the tent on the frame and roll up the flaps for air movement, what you get is the same effect as a hot air balloon. Trapped hot air, with no place to go, radiates."

"How does a parachute help?"

"If you stretch it over your framework, like a ceiling, ventilate it a bit, the end result is an attic."

"Insulation," Boremba one-lined.

"Deal, Copelet; now where do I get the parachutes?"

"Ask Major Frankel," Cope told the warrant, as whistles blew signaling another unforgettable meal. When it was over, a new emphasis took hold in the 312th and 713th companies.

The new approach was subtle, not formally proclaimed, and was not intended to replace any of the commands of the absent Colonel Fang; it was a policy planned to complement what was required for the survival of about 500 men living in unacceptable conditions. Instead of a few projects that were overloaded with too many volunteers, forty were begun, with a sufficient labor force in each, to get a lot of jobs done. Everybody, including me, believed, *same-o, same-o*; no one initially acknowledged the light that began to shine in a very bleak atmosphere.

In addition to the orderly room, abode for the colonel, and the officers' club details, several more were added to the platform building detail; rows two, three, four, five, six, and seven were begun. Like officers' row, number one, each had nine wooden platforms on which nine tents would be set. All 63 matched the traditional military pattern.

Five groups of ten men each were designated, according to plan, to construct several acceptable latrine facilities. These outhouses were the brainchild of Sergeant Copelet, who shared his previous experiences with his new company. Cope's design was new to Bear Cat. While it looked like an outhouse, there were no holes dug into the ground. Each little building had two doors, ventilation near the roof, providing four *holes*, and had a trap door in the rear large enough to insert a half barrel, filled with fuel, and placed under each seat. At appropriate intervals, each container was to be removed, ignited, burned off, and reinserted. The idea was very simple; although it was no sophisticated bathroom, Cope's latrine was an improvement over the open ditch. The design was noted, and eventually duplicated and copied at Bear Cat.

I got detailed to work on shower facilities; none were available when the ensemble of personnel arrived. If it had not been for one man's *deal* with a warrant officer, none would have become available for God knows how long. One day under Bear Cat's sun generated indescribable body odor; two days under the Asian sky burner made peeling off a t-shirt a memorable experience with red blister badges of courage to prove it.

Cope devised a 3' x 4' x 8' wooden box and suspended it on telephone poles. "If the army can keep fuel in containers made of rubber, 30' x 4' x 30', we can use the same material to store water." He taught us how to over-flap to avert any leakage.

"How do you plan to get the water out?" I asked.

"Gravity." Cope's one-word answer reminded me of Timmy Boremba's ability to summarize. "Do you remember the times you needed gas for your Briggs and Stratton lawnmower, and the only place to get it was to siphon it from your old man's car?" He used hydraulic fuel lines, fastening the lower end with a clamp device resembling a clothespin.

"Eventually we'll have a concrete base; for right now a few muddy feet is better than nothing."

Twenty-five were made in eleven days; the number of outhouses increased as well. By the end of two weeks, a physical company had been formed. All of Colonel Fang's wishes were either completed or well underway, and each man had a billet, a cleaner outhouse, and a place where he could bathe. Officers' row allowed four men per tent; all others were eight. Frock and Boremba were placed in the first tent in the second row, close to the completed orderly room; I was given an eighth of the second tent in the second row. I wanted to bunk with my friends, but the military establishment assigned the first tent to clerical personnel, and my MOS remained light weapons infantry.

At the start of the third week, when everyone began to rest on their laurels, and forget why and where we were, I was still attached to one of Copelet's details. Boremba and I were stretching screen wire over the upper vent in one of Cope's outhouses as he nailed it in place. Warrant Officer Harsh came by to check on progress.

"One clerk, one infantryman, and one flight operations sergeant. The way I see it, you three guys aren't in the right MOS," the warrant joked.

"Strong backs; weak minds," Cope responded. "Can you hand me a few nails?"

Mr. Harsh bent down, picked up a few of the U-shaped nails Cope needed, and cracked, "Whatever happened to the guy with a pet peeve? Wasn't it about 'training a guy in one area then assigning him to another?'" Mr. Harsh's face flashed a broad grin.

Cope took the nails, hammered them into place attaching the screen, then smarted back with, "I'm sure you wrote the letter of protest to your congressman just after your first Bear Cat shower."

"The very first thing." Harsh rolled with the knock-out punch. "Glad we convinced you to come over."

"Not too sure I am, Mr. Harsh; tomorrow we begin work on our flight operations building." The news shook me back into reality; being in a helicopter company, in country, was about more than just hooches, latrines, and showers.

"None too soon, Cope; scuttlebutt says the carrier with our birds has docked at Vung Tau. You know what that means."

"Sure do! Those helicopters need a place to roost. Have any guesses as to how long before they're here?"

"I figure about a week; it'll take that long to get them off the carrier, flown to land, checked out, and make the trip to Bear Cat."

"Like I said, Mr. Harsh, none too soon."

"Right...but I didn't come to talk about that, Cope. I came to ask your advice."

"About what, Mr. Harsh?" Cope asked.

"My hooch."

"Tent loose, floor crooked?" Cope was the architect.

"No, nothing like that, Sergeant Copelet. It's about the interior...What's the best you've ever seen? I've been with Jones, Patton, and Thurgode since Rucker, and I want the best," Harsh explained his visit.

On that early April day of 1967, the temperature rose faster than the Bear Cat sun; our t-shirts had become part of our skin, and the looming arrival of our helicopters was indicative of the unknown. I suspected Sergeant Copelet was not too crazy about spearheading another project, similar to construction of an entire flight line facility. I wasn't too keen on the idea of more work either. I watched Cope put his hammer down, light a smoke, take a drag, and then undertake another teaching session.

"It'll cost you," was what he told the warrant.

"You mean like in another deal?"

"Sure."

"How come everything has to be some sort of deal?" Mr. Harsh didn't seem too pleased at the remark.

"Dealing and trading is a part of life; over here it's called *bartering*, an idea centuries old, Mr. Harsh."

"All I'm seeking is a plan for my hooch; one that'll make it the most efficient for the four of us. Why should I have to *deal* for a simple idea."

"If all you want is the plan, that's real easy. Best officer hooch I've seen was at Chu Chi. A CW2 divided his tent into three parts. On each end was a place for two of the residents; one on each side. In the middle third was a sort of communal area with a poker table. Lost one hell of a lot of money at that table." Cope divulged the plan.

"That wasn't so hard, now was it? Sounds exactly what I've been looking for. Thanks, Sarge."

"Anytime, Mr. Harsh." Cope sounded conciliatory. "Too bad you're not interested in the completed plan." Cope was quite skilled at teasing officers.

"What do you mean *completed plan*?" Harsh swallowed the bait.

"The air conditioner...that's what finished the hooch."

"Air conditioner? Where did your warrant buddy find an air conditioner?"

"Same place General Bosebaugh got the three hanging out the windows at his yellow trailer house."

"Where might that be?" a disbelieving warrant asked.

"Black market...course that's not the problem." Cope slipped a little more.

"What's that mean?" Harsh's question verified a real curiosity.

"Getting an air conditioner is easy; finding something powerful enough to run one is tough."

"Why not use the portable generators the 5$^{th}$ has?"

"Would take two to power one air conditioner; three if you wanted electric lights. The constant irritating noise would drive you nuts."

"So what's your solution?" Cope's hook had taken hold.

"A 25-K, diesel-powered generator."

"Army doesn't have that in its tactical and equipment roster, Cope."

"Air force does." Cope reeled in his catch.

"So what do we do?"

"Trade." I expected Boremba to utter the word.

"Trade with what?"

"Seems the air force has big generators and none of the little ones; it also seems we have the little ones and none of the big kind."

"Can we make a deal, Cope?" The green officer had been sucked in.

Cope took another drag from his Camel and gave Mr. Harsh one of those, "you know I've been around the block a couple of times" looks. Then said, "Just so happens my brother, in air force supply, is currently stationed at Long Binh. Got a letter from him a week ago. Twenty-five portable generators and some nonscheduled flights to the resort area near Vung Tau will net you a diesel-powered, 25-K generator."

"Where in the hell will I get 25 portables?" the novice to bartering asked.

"Trade," Cope mimicked Boremba again.

"With what, Cope? We've hardly been here a month and are lucky we got this far."

"Think again, Mr. Operations Officer. In a few weeks you will be able to dispatch our aircraft at your discretion. Now could it be possible there might be a general who could use a reliable method to secure civilian goodies every so often? Or just maybe there might be certain supply sergeants at the 5$^{th}$ who seek air travel into Saigon for whatever reason."

"I get it." A light finally flashed in Harsh's head. "One hand shakes another."

"More like scratching backs."

"Where do I start?"

"Tell Major Frankel you've come by a 25-K generator and need about 25 portables for the trade. Tell Major Thurgode as well; he'll know what to do in advance of its arrival," Cope spelled out the particulars.

"Anything else?"

"A deuce and a half, plus two guards."

"Tell you what, Cope. Since I'm faking it as a wheeler-dealer, and you're posing as a *Long Binh Connection*, how about we ask the clerk and infantryman to masquerade as the guards?"

"Sounds good to me; let me know when, Mr. Harsh."

The three of us observed Harsh skip away like a kid who had been told, it's recess. I expected some one-liner from Boremba and something profound from Copelet; instead, I heard him dismiss Boremba with, "Your work on my detail was needed; it's time for you to report to the orderly room. Cooby, we're going to start our flight operations center. Let's go have a look-see at the site."

"Our flight operations center and maintenance buildings will be the best ever, Cooby," Cope told me as we walked the 2000' distance to where one berm wall met another. "Nobody's going to change my mind. Our centers might have to conform to the traditional 30' x 60' structures outwardly, but inwardly they'll serve our needs. They'll have concrete floors too."

Back home in Nebraska, I had been in a few home projects when brothers got together to pour a new concrete sidewalk or driveway; grading, forming, and mixing the cement for two perpendicular slabs of concrete, 30' x 60', was a totally different story. The backbreaking job took three days and used every muscle in everyone's body. What was astounding was the end accomplishment forty men could create as long as someone was in charge that knew what he was doing. Cope was that man.

More incredible were the buildings he produced on the newly poured concrete.

The maintenance office was some piece of work. While it conformed to the standard operational procedures required by the 5th Division, and looked like other 30' x 60' structures at Bear Cat, there was a marked difference on the inside.

Cope organized the interior of the 713th Transportation Company's office to fit the needs of its purpose. It wasn't a *one size fits all* building, but a center designed to fill the requirements of a sister outfit whose function was to be the mortar and grease for the aviation company it supported. He split the inside into two sections. One-third was reserved to handle the disbursement of daily work assignments and any essential details. The building had four separate entrances: one on each side. Only one allowed flow-through traffic; the other three existed for emergency exit or private access. A huge counter blocked unnecessary visiting or loitering. Every activity occurring in the maintenance part of the flight line was transacted over the controlling counter.

The other two-thirds of his design housed eight separate offices: one for the commanding officer, one for the second in command, one for the designated maintenance officer, one for First Sergeant Foone, two for Platoon Sergeants Austeen and Towie, one for a conference room, and the eighth office was planned as the coffee room/break area. Cope's diligent attention to detail was evident everywhere.

There was little doubt Sergeant Carl Copelet had outdone himself in spearheading the essentials needed for making the 312th company area livable; respect and admiration continued to grow for him after completion of the 713th Transportation Company's maintenance office. His masterpiece, however, was the 312th's flight operations center.

Cope's heart went into that building, along with twenty years' worth of experience and the memories from two previous tours of duty in Vietnam. The result was the essence of what United States Army Aviation was all about.

The center was trisected to reflect the threefold purpose of flight operations: planning, monitoring, and recording any information about pilots, flight personnel, and helicopters.

Its hub was the middle third, where Copelet planned the section to meet the needs of an assault support chopper unit. The 20' x 30' room was the focus of the entire building. It was in this area that all flight crews would be assigned, every mission dispatched, and each flight would be monitored. Cope situated a radio in one corner of the room, and blocked any unnecessary access to it by building a hockey-stick-shaped counter, which also restricted entry into the record-keeping area comprised the second third of the operations center. Directly across from the counter, Cope displayed a huge map of the Third Corps Area of South Vietnam on the entire wall; he covered it with clear plastic, giving precise instructions that each mission would be plotted with erasable markers. The territory was the given responsibility of the 5th Division.

The remaining portion was the planning room. Plywood was used to form a conference table where mission planning would begin. The four walls were lined with metal gym lockers, which served as personal storage for pilot gear. Cope intended the room to serve as a debriefing place as well.

Although the 312th flight operations center was not any plaza or Ritz Hotel, it was designed to more than adequately fill the requirements for the assault helicopter company that it would serve.

"What do you think, Cooby?" Cope asked me on completion.

"Just want to know one thing, Cope."

"What's that?"

"Are you finished with bustin' my ass?"

"Nope!" he told me without blinking an eye.

"What's next?"

"Tomorrow morning, you, Boremba, Harsh, and me are going to Long Binh."

"Long Binh? What for?"

"The 25-K generator we need to power our corner of Bear Cat."

"Anybody told Colonel Ponderosa?"

"Men promoted to E-4, Specialist E-4 Coobat, have both rank and privilege to deliver good news to promoted PFCs. Mr. Harsh thinks the two of you deserve it."

# CHAPTER 11

## THE SAIGON CONNECTION

---

"What's this?" Boremba asked Sergeant Copelet. We were waiting near the deuce and a half scheduled to take Cope, Harsh, and the two of us to Long Binh.

"It's a rifle, Boremba; one of those weapons you trained with at basic."

"Not like this." Ponderosa looked perplexed.

"Isn't like what, Timmy?" I asked.

"This." Copelet tossed one to me.

The unfamiliar weapon was unlike anything I had seen. It had a long barrel, covered with a muffler-looking attachment. On the top of the unusual weapon was a long handle that apparently doubled as its sight, and it was complemented with a sturdy, lightweight plastic stock. I immediately imagined a space gun from a Flash Gordon movie.

"Sure looks neat, Cope; what's it called?"

"An M-16, and both of you will display one on the trip to Long Binh. I ain't hauling ass down any in-country road without some show of force," he cracked. "By the way, Cooby, where'd you learn to catch like that?"

"Brown Park ball field, in South Omaha."

"Don't either of you try to bullshit a lifer like me." Cope looked disgusted. "What was the weapon you trained on in basic, Boremba?"

"An M-1."

"You, Cooby?"

"None, but I did type the nomenclature M-1 a thousand times."

"Great, two guards who don't know how to shoot!" Cope cynically remarked just as the absent fourth party arrived.

"Ready to go tangle with the horse-trading brother?" Mr. Harsh was wearing a holstered pistol; when I saw it I noticed Cope was wearing one, too.

"Depends."

"Depends on what, Cope?"

"On whether you want to travel with two *shotguns* who have never used an M-16."

"They made it this far and we need the generator. Let's get underway."

"You heard the man, troops. Hop on."

Boremba and I did as ordered and jumped aboard. Whoever loaded it with the portable generators left enough room near the cab for two men to stand erect; the remaining portion of the truck bed was crammed with the booty, cleverly obscured with a tarpaulin.

Can't say the two reluctant guards wanted to be onboard the truck. Neither had strayed far away from the immediate 312th company area, and both had memories of arriving at Bear Cat. Hovering helicopters would not accompany this single vehicle.

Cope observed all rules and regulations while inside the Bear Cat compound; we passed by the yellow trailer house, the Bear Cat runway, and everything in between the 312th company area and the exiting gate. In comparison to our own exploding expansion, the 5th Division's home looked as though it hadn't changed one bit, and somehow not worthy of defense. I believe Tim sensed the same feeling, but the stripes and brass in the cab of the military vehicle outranked both of us.

On the other side of the gate, however, Sergeant Copelet goosed the six-wheeler to Olympic performance. We didn't just speed down the road, we flew down it, with a trail of dust that made us look like a spent arrow. There wasn't much left for Boremba and me to do but hang on for dear life. Almost one hour later, we entered the Long Binh complex and were met by a jeep that led us to a Quonset deep within its interior.

"Heard a lot about you, Mr. Harsh," Bob Copelet greeted the warrant. Cope's brother could have been his twin. Light ashen hair, steel blue eyes, ruddy complexion, Sergeant Bob Copelet, like his army counterpart relative, was about forty pounds overweight and stood every bit of six feet tall.

"Don't believe everything you hear from your brother," Mr. Harsh cautioned the wheeler-dealer.

"I don't, Sir," the air force sergeant quipped. "What I know about you comes from him." He pointed to another warrant sitting in a jeep parked alongside the Quonset.

"Filings!" Harsh recognized the CW3. "What the hell are you doing here?" Within seconds the two men shook hands.

"I'm stationed here, with a medevac unit. When the best *scrounge sergeant* in the war told me a brother was bringing another warrant to trade some goodies, I asked his name. He said, 'Harsh,' and I knew it was time for some days off."

"I'll be damned!" The surprised army pilot watched as ten of Bob Copelet's subordinates swiftly unloaded the cargo.

"Don't look so worried, Mr. Harsh," the sky cop/supply sergeant interrupted the repast. "Just be back here in two days, and you'll be set."

"Can I trust this man, Filings?" Harsh searched the eyes of his fellow flyer.

"Even with your sister, Jimmy," the other reunited pilot assured his friend. "Let's get out of here; we've got a lot of serious *catching up* to do." We watched the two flyboys drive away.

"Where they going, Cope?" I asked.

"Same place we're going, young specialist," Cope's twin joyfully remarked. "Saigon, boys, Saigon."

"Is that where we pick up the generator?" I asked.

"No, kid. It's where we generate a pick-up," he snickered. "My *moose* has been waiting for three weeks!"

"What's a *moose*?" Boremba looked confused; I was too.

"God, Carl. Were we ever that young?" Bob Copelet glared at his brother.

"Take it easy, Bob; this is their first time in country." Cope's quip stopped the sibling from saying anything more, but it did not prevent him from commandeering the military truck. Bob was an E-7, one rank higher than Carl.

"Let's beat feet, gentlemen," Bob Copelet ordered. Within minutes our truck was exiting the Long Binh gate.

It didn't take long for our truck to stop; when it did, we parked in front of a thatched structure not favoring in any way a bar or restaurant.

"I'm parched, little brother," Bob announced. "Let's get a drink."

Tim and I followed the NCOs into the thatched roof lean-to like scared little ducks afraid to stray from mom's close side. The place was no posh café; it wasn't even a dingy bar. Two wooden poles, mounted in a dirt floor, held up a thatched roof; in between them stood a lone, confiscated military desk surrounded by five irregular wooden chairs. A bamboo-looking curtain was hung across one side of the open room; there were no other walls to the structure itself. Surrounding it, was a roughly built masonry barricade topped with jagged glass. Bob Copelet had been there before.

"You'll get plenty of hooch in Saigon, but you won't get Vietnamese beer like they make it here; this brew will turn the hair on your chests into stumps," he bragged. "My moose's ma runs the joint, and I stop by when I'm on my way to visit Lele at our apartment in Saigon."

As soon as he finished talking, a small woman approached the one table. She bowed and screeched something. She wore a wrinkled black blouse that draped over her tiny shoulders and was girded at the waist. Covering her lower torso were baggy-looking pajama pants that stopped about five inches above the dirt floor exposing very bony ankles. The woman didn't wear shoes and her feet resembled rough leather. Her face was equally weathered and crowned with unwashed gray hair. She appeared to be in her mid-fifties, and when she spoke, the high-pitched sounds were similar to tones spawned from the Reuter pipe organ at my family church.

"Mamasan," Bob Copelet addressed her. "Bring some beer and glasses for my friends...and my usual."

She cackled, disappeared, and returned carrying a wooden tray with musty beer bottles, four dirty glasses, one chipped shot glass, and an old-fashioned fifth of Popov Vodka. Cope's brother did the honors, screeched something unintelligible to the woman, who vanished, then said, "Drink up, boys."

"Do you understand her language?" I asked the sergeant.

"Call me Bob." He poured himself a shot and followed it with a large gulp of beer. He repeated the scenario, and told me, "Enough to get along. Lele tries to teach me more, but I know her real language." He giggled as he said it.

"Is this stuff hot?" I cradled the beer in my hand.

"Around here, anything under 90 degrees is considered cold," he laughed.

Boremba and I both took a healthy swallow.

Tim gagged and immediately spit out the gulp.

I wasn't quite so smart; I ingested and tried to fake the rest.

"Good stuff, right?" The flyboy NCO stared.

"Paint remover tastes better," I responded, feeling the sounds of my voice scratch my throat like rough sandpaper. Poor Boremba was gasping for breath.

"It's either this or that shitty Lone Star from the LBJ Brewery." Bob took another hefty gulp. "Want to chase it with a little of this?" He pointed to the vodka.

"No thanks; the beer killed the only two hairs I had on my chest."

"How about you, PFC? Want a snort?"

"Wa-water." Boremba didn't need to say more.

"Don't drink the water here, kid!" Bob Copelet cautioned. "You'll wind up with a real good case of the shits."

"Leave 'em be, Bob," Cope admonished his brother. "What's your plans for the next two days?"

"We ditch the truck at my place and you hoof into Saigon; two days later, you come back and we aim for Long Binh. Topaz still runs the Grand, little brother," he added.

"It's been a few years, Bob; besides, you know we're just old friends."

"Hey, Carl," the ranking NCO told his sibling, "I've got a *moose...*'you' can do *whatever*."

Two of us watched Boremba recover, and the three of us waited for the air force sergeant to drink another shot of Popov chased with another beer. As soon as he was quenched, he yelled, "Mamasan...dong," and threw some funny looking coins upon the table. Within a few minutes, Bob Copelet was trucking down the same dirt road that brought us; this time, we were heading farther north, toward Saigon.

There wasn't much for Timmy and me to do in the back end of the truck but to fulfill the military definition of guard: "one who remains always on the alert and observes everything that takes place within sight and hearing." For two would-be shotgun pretenders, there was a lot to take in.

I instantly noticed an increase in traffic, and it was not coming from just military vehicles. Bicycles, old foreign cars, trucks, buses, and pedestrian traffic crowded the route that suddenly turned into asphalt. The strangest vehicle was a three-wheeled contraption looking much like the reverse of a tricycle. The unusual rickshaw was powered by a driver who was pedaling a bicycle. Hundreds were everywhere and not any one of them stood a chance against the brawn of a deuce and a half army truck. Nor did any bicycle, civilian, or foreign car; yet it was our truck that used its brakes every other minute or so to prevent collision. The expletives I heard shouted from the cab made it clear that Bob Copelet had traveled this way before, and somehow that knowledge made me feel a little bit more secure.

Standing in the back of the truck, Timmy and I had a bird's eye view of everything; both of us could tell some type of a bridge was directly ahead. It was some structure; outside of the military vehicles we passed, the bridge was the most modern thing we had seen. It was huge. It spanned the largest inland tributary I had ever seen. The sight it provided reminded me of several history classes I studied during high school and college. The Mekong was the visual lesson about the fertile Nile Valley that I somehow failed to grasp. Everything within sight seemed to be drawn like a magnet to it, on it, or toward it, with that everything including the most assaulting, sewer-like smell that made Timmy and I nearly choke. This river wasn't a boundary but more of a gigantic artery feeding the crowded, unfolding city we had entered. Old, or even *very* old, didn't come close to describing anything on either bank, or even floating on its filthy-looking water; ancient was more accurate.

Once on the other side, I was astounded at the number of people scurrying about, so much so I concluded crossing what resembled a street seemed to be the national pastime. Saigon was noisy beyond belief, saturated with all types of peddlers, appeared to be void of any planned trafficways, and had a lingering outhouse-like odor that didn't vanish. The people we saw were as plentiful as tassels in a July cornfield, and were dressed in the same way as the woman we encountered at the air force sergeant's drink stop.

I have no idea about how we got to where we did, but when Bob Copelet parked the military vehicle, we were in front of one of the monotonous two-story buildings we passed by thousands of times. Its bottom floor was vacant, boarded up, and imprisoned by rusty iron gates. The lower floors of the two adjacent buildings were the same, but clothing hanging out to dry appeared on the verandas of the upper level.

"Bobs," I heard a high-pitched voice anxiously shout. When I looked up, I saw a young Vietnamese girl waving from her second-story perch.

"Lele," Cope's brother acknowledged back, and in less time than it took for Timmy and me to get out from the back of the truck, she had gotten down from her perch, and had thrown herself onto the sergeant, gyrating up and down in some sort of frontal piggyback. "Lele wants boom-boom," she kept repeating while smothering his face with kisses.

"Later, Lele," Bob Copelet loosened the girl from her grip. "Later...right now I want you to meet my brother and his two army friends."

"No sees Bobs long time," the young girl pouted. Lele was no more than a teenager. Her black hair was cut short and resembled a pageboy style with bangs. Gaudy earrings, three inches long and made of stringed beads, dangled from her ears and matched the heavy lipstick on her face. Lele was not dressed like the other Vietnamese people. Leather boots covered her feet. She wore short black shorts with a five-inch similarly colored cloth band stretched around her not so well endowed upper torso. Her fingernails were painted red and she toyed with her necklace following the reprimand.

"Lele, this is my younger brother, Carl."

"Nicest to meets yous, Ka al," she stumbled. "Who's yous?" She recovered from her teenage pout and zoomed in on an unsuspecting Boremba.

"He's a soldier working with my brother, Lele," Bob Copelet interrupted.

"Theys stays with us, Bobs?" Lele suddenly ceased to pout.

"No," Cope stepped in. "We'll stay in a hotel tonight. All we need is a place to ditch our truck."

"Too bads for me," the teenager turned vixen cracked, "but very goods for other mooses. I could show *cherry boy* a really goods times."

"Stop teasing," Bob Copelet admonished the girl. "Go open the iron gates and lift up the *twirling door*." The door he referred to was a tin garage door that rolled up like a carpet with the assistance of a hanging chain. It appeared as though it was a makeshift replacement for a former window and door entryway either burned or bombed out of existence. "Give me those weapons, boys. The MPs arrest GIs carrying weapons after hours here in Saigon."

Bob Copelet drove the truck into the lower underside of the complex, unraveled the twirling door, locking it securely, closed the iron gates, and walked to where the three of us were standing. Lele trailed him like a hungry pup. "Show 'em Saigon, little brother, and have fun."

"We will, Bob." Cope shook his brother's hand. "We'll see you here in a couple of days." Our tour guide walked between us as he led us into the unknown.

"What's *moose*?" Boremba broke the temporary silence.

"A live-in companion, Tim," Cope struggled with the definition. "A concubine, if you will."

"And *boom-boom*?" Timmy persisted.

"Mating between human beings of the opposite sex," Cope responded. "In return for certain sexual favors, my brother pays Lele, and she uses the money for housing and food." I could sense Cope's discomfort; he was *fatherly,* however.

"Any more questions, Tim?"

"What's *cherry boy*?"

"A *cherry boy* is a man who has never been with a woman, Colonel." Cope's answer was as straight forward, and gentle as it could be; while we were both sweating from Saigon's intense heat, neither Tim nor I could hide the blush that suddenly appeared on our faces. "Any more questions?" Cope asked.

"No."

"How about you, Cooby?"

"None."

We walked silently for a few minutes, taking in the rush of people, the sights, and most of all, the lesson our tour guide had left us to consider. Suddenly, Copelet began a minor discourse.

"If the MPs stop us, let me do the talking; if we're separated for any reason, ask to be taken to the USO. Do the two of you understand?"

Timmy and I both nodded our heads.

"Good. I don't think it will happen, but you should know what to do if it does."

"Where we going, Cope?"

"To *The Street of the Flowers*, Cooby."

"What's that?" Boremba's face was still perspiring but the pink had disappeared; it had vanished from mine too.

"Now that's a good question, Colonel Ponderosa. The Street of the Flowers is one of the biggest market places in the Orient."

"Why that name, Sergeant Copelet?"

"Colonel, you can call me *Cope*, like Cooby does and in answer to your question, let me put it this way." Cope paused for a moment, then began, "Colonel, Saigon is not like Chicago. Even you can see it's older than dirt. There are very few indoor toilets. All garbage is dumped in the streets. I'm sure you've noticed the smell."

"Everything, Sergeant...I mean, Cope?"

"Everything!" he told us. "The merchants, however, in this ancient place, came up with beautification long ago, before Lady Bird Johnson was born. They brought in thousands of fragrant flowers to *deodorize* one entire street in the heart of the city. It's a tradition that has lasted.

"Fix it!" Ponderosa returned to one-lining.

"Has Chicago sandblasted the Wrigley Building, Colonel?" Cope quipped. These people have been living here for more centuries than you and I have fingers on one hand."

Two in our group of three gawked, gazed, and wondered; the city was filthy, crowded, and owned a matching stench. While we walked, we passed hundreds of Vietnamese, cackling in high-pitched voices, and scurrying about as if some fire was about to happen somewhere. The repetitive buildings we encountered were all old, in need of much repair, and were standing through the virtue of hope itself. At one point, I asked Cope, "Why so many containers of water every ten feet or so?"

"To hold fish," he told me. "Come over here, you two. Live action will show you why better than any explanations I could give." Cope led us to a spot near one wall, out of the line of heavy pedestrian traffic, and said, "Watch."

Within seconds, one Vietnamese stopped at one of the washtub-looking containers, handed some coins to another man squatting near it, reached inside, and pulled out some type of small fish. The buyer then bit the fish's head off, spat it into the street, and began to eat the remains of his purchase.

"It's barbaric to kill a fish with your teeth...then eat it alive."

"Really, Cooby. In most of the finer restaurants I've visited, raw fish is called 'sushi.' Follow me, I want to show you something else."

We followed, quietly, with our mouths open, but not too far open for an intake of the ever present smell. About five hundred feet later, two weaponless guards, closed their mouths, and opened their eyes and noses. We had arrived at The Street of the Flowers.

The fragrance was overwhelming; it completely negated the sewer-like stench where we had been walking. When I first sensed it, I felt as though I had entered some floral shop to pick out a corsage. I had to pinch myself to make sure I wasn't dreaming nor in some fantasy. I could tell by looking at Boremba's face that he was experiencing the same thing; the rare smile on Cope's indicated he was happy he had brought us.

The second unreal whammy was the sight of The Street of the Flowers. Garlands, bouquets, laurels, and sprays of blooming flowers covered everything. I had never seen such brilliant color in one place in all of my life. The singular street was divided by an elongated flowerbox in the middle; it was overflowing with even more resplendent arrays than on either side. The union of the pleasurable smell and the breathtaking sight made me think I had just entered a portal to heaven.

The marketplace was like an Oriental version of the Tournament of Roses Parade in Pasadena, with one slight variation. Here, flowers observed as floats of pedestrian traffic passed by. The place was spectacular.

We eased into the moving parade of people and walked a moment or two as we inhaled the sights, sounds, and smells. Timmy and I were awestruck and unaware that our tour guide was introducing us to a different type of civilization. Cope motioned for us to follow him, and he led us into one of the bedecked emporiums. The one he chose had a canopy of intertwining yellow hibiscus covering its lower interior. An entrance gate, blanketed with soft pink buttercups, blocked access. Inside, two men, backdropped by more pale yellow flowers, stood on opposite sides of a flat counter. They appeared to be waiters.

"Is that what I think it is?" I asked Cope when I saw what was for sale.

"Sure is!" he bluntly responded.

There were about ten, twenty-inch snakes, fastened at the neck to a stretched wire on the top of the counter. It was clear they were snakes. Directly behind them was a white cloth mirroring them. Most were rigid, but upon signs of any movement, one of the attendants would dip his hand into some lotion and rub the body of the snake, apparently drugging it into unconsciousness. While we were watching, an old woman entered the stand, pointed at one snake, and put some coins on the counter.

One waiter sprang into action. Using a sharp knife, he slit the reptile's skin from top to bottom, decapitated it, and sliced off a section of the lower tail. He removed the body from its container, placed it in a bowl, and offered it to the waiting customer, who began to eat it.

Cope did not need any encouragement in escorting us out of the place. All he said was, "Walking helps." The second we got outside, the powerful fragrance combined with what we had just seen, and the two of us bent over to gag. After one or two minutes, we regained our composure and began to walk. Cope followed us like a concerned father.

"That was horrible, Cope," I finally managed to speak.

"Depends on your point of view, Cooby."

"What's that mean?"

"Live food doesn't spoil in the heat; refrigerators aren't that plentiful here."

"Got any more surprises, Cope?"

"Just keep walking," he told us. I wanted to run, but didn't know where to go. We walked on, but both of the *greenhorns* were armed with a *previous experience* disposition and ready to say "no thanks" to another lesson in another culture. While we walked, I felt a repetitive tug on my fatigue shirt. When I turned around, I saw a small boy, barefoot and shabbily dressed, tailing us. His face, hands, and feet looked like they hadn't been washed in months.

"Hey, GI...my seester...five doll-er." The waif was talking to me.

"I don't know your sister...just how old are you?"

"Five doll-er... my seester," he repeated

"Go away, little kid." I tried to ignore him.

"Cooby, he's just a boy...take it easy," Cope tossed in a comment.

"Okay, Cooby...," the boy had picked up on my nickname, "four doller...my seester."

"Get away from me, kid; I don't want your *seester*."

Cope sensed my irritation and said, "Be polite, Cooby; he's just trying to make a few bucks."

"On his sister?"

"It's his country, not yours, Cooby. Try to remember he lives here."

I wanted to slap the boy's face but Cope's counsel won over and I told the kid, "No thanks." He flipped me the bird and stormed away. Watching his retreat, I became aware that anything was for sale.

"Ready for something to drink?" Cope asked.

"I am...as long as it's not Vietnamese beer nor served with raw fish or live snake."

"How about you, Colonel?"

"Coke."

"Follow me, fellas, but be prepared to buy Saigon Tea."

"What's that?" I inquired this time.

"Just tea," he matter-of-factly responded, adding, "the waitresses are required to encourage patrons to buy a drink for them as well as for yourself. The bar makes a killing on her drink and about 100% on yours. Once you've had a few too many, the waitress zooms in on a score."

"Only Coke," Boremba reiterated.

"Okay, Colonel, but the owner will only send another girl," Cope explained.

"One Coke," Boremba emphatically repeated as Cope led us into the lobby of the Saigon Grand Hotel, right in the middle of The Street of the Flowers.

I can't express the feeling I experienced when the three of us entered that lobby. I had never been there, yet I could sense something mysterious. Maybe it was the circular ceiling fans encouraging a gentle breeze to cool the obvious French furniture decorating its entrance. I'm not sure; I was expecting another *off the highway* dump.

"Did we just walk through a time zone?" I was mesmerized by a definite return to civilization.

"This was a special place to visit on my last tour," Cope shared. "Sure can tell the French have been in country, can't you? Ain't this place neat?"

"Lavish comes to mind, Cope," I commented, staring at the place in disbelief. Polished white marble mirrored the dark oak reception desk and accompanying wood trim. Boremba was speechless.

"May I serve you, gentlemen?" a maître d'hotel greeted us in impeccable English.

"The bar, please," Cope answered.

"This way, gentlemen." He guided us to two massive wood doors, opened them, and motioned for us to enter.

"Welcome to the Tiger's Den." Another crisply attired attendant met us. "Table for three?"

Cope nodded a "yes," then inquired, "Is Madame Topaz available?"

"The Madame has left for the day. If you so desire, I will dispatch a courier, Sir," he responded while seating us at a cloth-covered table centered in the ample room.

"Please tell Topaz that *Buddy* is in Saigon," he told the man, slipping two American dollars into his hand.

"As you wish." The waiter accepted the gift then left.

"Remember about Saigon Tea," Cope whispered. I am not so positive either of us paid any attention. We were both entranced by the glitter and sheer cleanliness of the den. This was not Bear Cat.

"Parlez vous Français?" a waitress asked.

"Very little," came an automatic response. Why I even answered I don't know. The last place I expected to be was in the Saigon Grand Hotel. When I looked to see who asked the question, I was reminded of Romy Schneider, playing a violin for a disenchanted priest, in a scene from the 1963 motion picture, *The Cardinal*.

"So, mon cheri, you do speak French." The girl spoke in the softest tones and was more beautiful than any dream I could imagine. "What can I obtain for the three of you?"

"Scotch on the rocks," Cope popped up.

"Only one Coke," Boremba remembered.

"And you?" She bent over to discreetly reveal an ever so bewitching bust line.

"Cubra Libra," I managed to tell her.

"With, or without lime?" she asked.

"With," I barely responded. The woman had disarmed me.

"Excellent! I'll return in a moment with your drinks." She bowed graciously, left the table, and went to the bar. I fixed my eyes on her every move, anxiously awaiting for her return.

"Your scotch on the rocks, your Coke, and your rum and Coke." She served the drinks. "I'll return when I see that your drinks require refreshing. Enjoy, gentlemen." I trailed her departure.

"Isn't she gorgeous?" I commented to my buddies.

"Who?" Cope played dumb.

"What is she doing at a bar?"

"Maybe she works here," Cope retorted; I didn't listen.

"She can't be Vietnamese, she don't look like the other women I've seen. Where's she from?"

"Probably mixed, Cooby," Cope observed. "The French have been in this country for some time, you know."

"Oriental," Boremba sneered.

"Geez! Am I the only guy at this table who can see how attractive the woman is? Just look at her face, that body, her shiny hair," I began to babble. "She has tempting eyes, fellas, speaks French and English, and smells better than the flowers outside."

"Waitress!" Timmy shot off a second scorning remark.

"So! I'm a Spec Four working for Elmer Fudd, Boremba," I fired back.

"Take it easy, Cooby," Cope intervened.

"I don't want to *take it easy*, Cope." I was smarting from the *Oriental waitress* crack Boremba made, but glued to any possible movement from Miss Saigon.

"In case you forgot, Cooby, we're here to swipe—I mean *trade* for a generator," Cope reminded me.

"Your brother told us to come back in two days."

"Exactly my point, Specialist. Are you planning on having Boremba and me watch you moon over a girl for 48 hours? We do eat, we do pee, and we do sleep!"

"Then let's stay here. The place looks terrific."

"You're right there, Cooby; it's a great place to stay. On my last tour, I spent a lot of time here. Met Professor Duc Hoh, an embassy worker, in this very room. His sister is the owner of the Saigon Grand. The three of us enjoyed a lot of great times in the Tiger Den," Cope reminisced. "You got any money? This is no free tent at Bear Cat."

"Will a hundred bucks buy me a room?"

"It'll buy several," Cope laughed. "This is not Chicago."

"Great! Let's stay; we can get separate rooms. I'd love to sprawl out on my own bed." I masked my dream.

"Hot bath?" Boremba sounded agreeable.

"There, Cope; it's settled."

"Between you and my brother, Cooby, I just can't figure who got hit in the ass harder by Cupid's arrow." He shrugged his shoulders. "Madilla's coming back to the table, so don't go creamin' your pants...I'll ask her to make arrangements."

"How do you know her name?"

"It's written on the nametag she wears, dummy!"

"M-A-D-I-L-L-A!" I spelled it out loud.

"Loosely translated from the combined French-Vietnamese, it means, *little flower*," Madilla softly whispered.

"It would have to." I couldn't say another word.

"Do you wish more to drink?" she inquired.

"Yes, but some information as well," Cope spoke up.

"And how may I help you, monsieur?"

"Has Topaz been told that Buddy is here?"

"Yes, monsieur; we expect her arrival momentarily."

"Thanks, Madilla. Can you arrange for three rooms? We'll be staying the night."

"You will?" I saw the glow in her dark eyes sparkle even brighter. "I will make all...." Madilla's sentence was cut off by the shout of the name, "Buddy!"

"Topaz!" Cope shouted back. He stood up, rushed to greet her, and escorted her to our table. "This is Topaz Hoh, owner of the Saigon Grand. Topaz, these are two of my friends from the 312th Helicopter Company, Specialist Dan Coobat and PFC Tim Boremba."

"My pleasure. Welcome to the Tiger Den." Cope offered the lady a seat, and sat down. "Madilla, refresh their drinks and bring me my usual. Now tell me, Buddy, what is my old horse-trading friend scrounging now?"

There were two things I noticed about Madame Hoh right from the beginning. The first was her flawless English. The second was her uncanny likeness to Madilla. Topaz looked to be about forty-five. She wore a light lavender frock that was sprayed with off-white floral designs. Pearl combs held a rolled bun in place and blended with salt and pepper hair tightly arranged over her head. An alabaster necklace made of shells hung around her thin neck and complemented a bracelet and earrings. There was a silver pearl ring on her right hand and it matched the color of her nail polish. Topaz had class.

"Two years hasn't dimmed the memory, Topaz; you know me well. The three of us are killing time while we wait for the delivery of a generator," Cope acknowledged the question.

"It's good to know the same span of time hasn't reduced your talents, Buddy."

"How's your brother, the professor?"

"You can see for yourself when he joins us for dinner. I made the arrangements as soon as the courier notified me of your arrival."

"My friends and I will be in good company," Cope told her.

"Madilla." Topaz snapped her fingers and she appeared in an instant. "See to it these two young men receive our best in hospitality and cuisine; Buddy and I will be in my private office."

"As you wish, Madame," Madilla bowed.

"This is their first time in Saigon," Cope explained.

"Live and let live, Buddy," Topaz counseled. "They'll be in good hands here at the hotel." In as an abrupt move as her entrance, Topaz stood up and motioned for Cope to follow her to the Tiger Den's entrance.

"Be in the lobby at 8:30 tomorrow," he told us, just as he left with the lavender lady.

Timmy and I watched the two disappear then listened as Madilla announced, "As soon as you have finished with your drinks, I will take you to the rooms; your dinners will be served there."

"Burgers?" Boremba instantly asked.

"We do serve the American food you call burger," she acknowledged Timmy's request. She turned to me and asked, "What do you desire?"

"I'll let you decide, Madilla." I was hungry, but not for food.

"As you wish." She departed and left us alone at the table. I traced her every step.

"Isn't she something else, Tim?"

"Better be good."

"Me?"

"No, the food."

"Wonder what she's thinking?"

"Better be burgers."

"Can't be married, Tim; I didn't see a ring."

"Can she cook?"

"Think she likes me, Tim?"

"Better like burgers."

"Did you see that, Timmy? I think she's looking at me."

"Better look at the menu."

"Is food all you think about, Tim?"

"I'm hungry."

I nervously gulped my Cubra Libra while Timmy sipped on his soda. My lifetime passed by in less than the two minutes before Madilla returned; Boremba merely waited for a dinner call. Neither of us needed encouragement when Madilla said, "Please follow me."

She played the perfect tour guide as she led us through the hotel, sharing little stories about the chandelier, the imported furniture, the oak woodworking, and the predominant French decor. "What the hotel lacks in size is rather minor when considering its quality and taste," she directed us up a grand staircase. "This will be your room," she pointed to Tim. I listened to her charming exchanges but didn't hear a word.

We both saw the huge canopied bed dominating his room as she opened the door. It was positioned between two lavishly draped windows overlooking The Street of the Flowers. There was a reclining chaise lounge and a writing desk on opposite sides of a door leading to a private bath. Against one wall was a chiffonier graced with a fresh bouquet of flowers.

The gleaming wooden floor was dimmed by scattered small carpets placed in appropriate spots.

"Enjoy your stay, Private," Madilla said. "The American burger you requested will arrive shortly. I have instructed the kitchen to include both French fries and your favorite cold drink."

Timmy smiled, walked into the room, and looked pleased. After Madilla closed the door I knew he'd aim straight for a warm bath. "I will now take you to your suite," she said.

Madilla led me two doors down the upstairs hallway to a corner room; when she opened the entryway, I saw the massive bed. Just as in Boremba's room, it was situated between the windows overlooking The Street of the Flowers. It too was canopied, but with one difference. Lace netting flowed from the top of the wood canopy to the floor, suggesting the bed to appear as though it belonged more in a bridal chamber than in a simple hotel room. Glass French doors exposed a fully mirrored bath area: one with a large porcelain basin, a crisp white stool, something I didn't know existed, a douche, and a claw-footed, milky-white bathtub, centered in the middle of the room. A third room, windowless, completed the suite. Like the bath area, this sitting room had glass French doors. A circular fan gently eased air downward to tease the two bouquets of flowers carefully put at opposite ends of a tempting love seat strewn with silk pillows. In front of it was a coffee table with magazines and newspapers. The room was a lovers' dream.

"I shall draw your bath." Madilla entered the suite and headed straight for the tub. I watched her turn on the water, test it with her wrist, and sprinkle the water with a bubble bath. A lot of thoughts rushed through my mind as I observed her but I was too timid and shy to act upon any of them; I found myself just lusting for her body. "Enjoy your stay; your dinner will arrive in about 15 minutes." She left the room and I wanted to scream; I hadn't made one advance.

I reluctantly began to remove my clothing, remembering Cope's admonishment about *creaming my pants* when I got to my civvies. I had and was forced to take the soiled shorts off rather carefully. What the hell is the matter with me? I asked myself.

As I lounged in the warm fragrant water, aching to kick myself for my less than aggressive male behavior, the door to the suite opened. Madilla came in. She was pushing a food cart which she wheeled into the parlor. She then entered the the bathroom.

Madilla had changed her clothes. She wore a tight-fitting salmon silk dress, slit at the thigh. The apparel accentuated every natural curve God gave her. She wore no jewelry. A pink flower had been pinned into her hair just above her left ear. Nothing could have improved her appearance. True to form, I submerged myself lower into the water in an effort to conceal chemical reactions overtaking my body.

She stooped over and picked up my pile of dirty clothing. The soiled shorts were on top and I turned blush red. I tried to sink deeper into the tub as she said, "I'll see to it they are cleaned." She smiled, bowed, and exited.

Several moments and a ton of self criticisms passed until she reentered the suite. Madilla locked the entrance and came into the private bath area.

She silently began to wash my hair; she soaped it and massaged it, rinsing it with water she carried in her cupped hands. When she had finished with my hair, she kissed it, and continued her oral stimulation with my neck and shoulders. I thought I'd died and went to heaven when her lips reached my neck. She continued with her magic by cleansing and loving my fingers, arms, legs, and toes. When she approached the groin area, she did not hesitate. Nor could I—erupting in a most pleasant orgasm assisted by her skillful manipulations. Mine was no premature ejaculation, and I felt no embarrassment at all."

"Not to worry, mon cheri," she softly told me. "We have all night. Let me help you dry off." She began to pat me with a towel and freely showered kisses on every part of my body she had dried. I couldn't resist the enchantment and became erect, feeling heavenly entrapped in my own naked confusion.

"You are hungry." She stopped her seduction, carefully wrapping my body in the cloth. If she had touched my groin I would have erupted one more time.

She directed me to the parlor and the food cart. I had not noticed the miniature lighted candles keeping the food warm but I was aware of the candle glow reflecting from her dark black eyes as she began to serve dinner. We began with delicious onion soup followed with a salad and croissants. For the main course, Madilla had chosen Steak Diane and was careful to watch my every bite.

"Do you approve?"

"Oh yes. Where did you learn to cook so well?" I wasn't lying, the food was excellent.

"In the Imperial City of Hue, from my mother and Topaz."

"Topaz? The lady in the Tiger Den?"

"Topaz is my aunt." She carefully placed the used dishes in the lowest portion of the food tray. "Coo-bee? Is that your first name?"

"Sergeant Copelet calls me, *Cooby*; Coobat is my last name."

"And your given name?"

"Danny."

"Dann-nee. I like that name." I hadn't given too much thought to it, but when the sound of my name eased from her lips, I felt as though I had heard fine crystal tinkle in a wind chime.

"Where is Hue, Madilla? I'm new to your country."

"North of Saigon, Dann-nee."

"Does your family live there?"

"Only mother. She remains in Hue to oversee what is left of my family's dwindling possessions."

"And your father?"

"Father was a French Army officer. He died during the unsuccessful occupation."

"I'm sorry, Madilla. I didn't know."

"I was but a child at the time, Dann-nee." She intoned my name again. "I really didn't know my father."

"Why don't you stay with your mother, Madilla?"

"Mother and Topaz feel my best interests are served by attending the university in Saigon. One day they hope for me to enroll in an appropriate school in France."

"And Madilla, what does she want?"

"Right now Madilla wants what is available, and what is available is Dann-nee, in this hotel, and at this moment in time." She fiddled with more dishes. "Tomorrow is uncertain; the future of my country is in question. Mother believes in one strong country; Topaz is inclined to accept independent countries. I abhor living in the middle. My place seems to be in studying French and I am taking some classes here at the university; my uncle, Professor Hoh, teaches there, but attendance is minimal. Most eligible males are required to serve in the military, and as I have pointed out, the final outcome is dubious, Dann-nee. Although I do not like it, I have little choice but to accept uncertainty while seeking to find some type of reality."

I hadn't given any thought to her perspective; I'd been sent to Vietnam; had to serve one year. I could leave after my tour. Madilla lived in Vietnam. I was speechless at the answer she gave, and I could see moisture welling up in her eyes. "I'm sorry for the conflict, Madilla; I had no choice in selecting it," I managed to feebly respond. "I wish all of it would go away...except for where I am, with you."

Madilla took a deep breath and sighed. "Enough of this political talk." She removed the towel wrapped about my body and began to entice and caress me in the way only her hands and lips could do. I didn't want to nor did I resist.

Somewhere during another excursion through the portals of heaven, I stopped Madilla's advances. "I want to make you feel as good as you make me feel, Madilla." I picked up her 95 pound body and carried her to the canopied bed. She didn't resist, even when I removed her off-pink silk dress.

Madilla's skin was the color of milk, and the breasts I lusted after were small but inviting. Her frame was small as well, without so much as an ounce of fat anywhere. I didn't know exactly what to do so I began by duplicating what she had done for me in the bathtub. I gently massaged her black hair then kissed it. I did the same for her neck, shoulders, arms, and fingers, watching her milky complexion cover itself with goose bumps. I heard her moan when I used my fingers as feathers to rub her slender legs. When I straddled her lithe body, I placed my arms around her tiny waist and I tried to squeeze myself into her as I rested my face against the midsection of her torso. I eased my face toward hers and kissed her, feeling the tantalizing spell of two erect nipples ever so slightly touch against my chest. I heard her gasp when I entered her body, but once inside, I felt her arms and legs surround me, as she too tried to squeeze me within her. We writhed in each other then both exploded in a communion of satisfying pleasure, holding each other as though we would never let go.

We remained locked in each other's arms, reveling in the afterglow of the lovemaking we had shared; I eased myself to her side, and she rested her black hair just under my chin. We did not speak. After thirty minutes, we started all over as if it were a first encounter. When I fell asleep, I knew how my own father felt for my mother.

I was awakened by a banging on the hotel door. Madilla was not lying next to me when I opened my eyes. I stumbled out of bed and onto a neatly folded layer of my clothes. On the very top was a pink flower. I stood up and went toward the nagging pounding, grabbing a towel to cover myself. When I opened the door, Cope and Timmy were standing in the entry.

"You were supposed to meet us in the lobby at 8:30 A.M.," Cope shouted at me.

"She didn't say good-bye." It was all I could think of.

"Get some damned clothes on," Sergeant Copelet yelled.

"She's gone."

"Goddamn it, Cooby, get your ass in gear! We've lots of scrounging to do."

I struggled to my stacked clothes, lost between a night to remember and an unforgiving morning. For a moment, I took sight of the unforgettable pink flower. Timmy came to where my clean fatigues were waiting and said, "Mine too."

"She's not here, Colonel," I reluctantly whispered.

Tim's blank stare didn't need a one-lining remark; he knew something special had taken place when he noticed the pink flower.

"Get the lead out," Cope blasted. "Don't have all day, loverboy."

I dressed as swiftly as I could, stunned by the morning after the night before. Tim led me out of the suite and to the staircase that had formerly been my gateway to paradise. We stopped at the reception desk where Cope discovered there was no payment due, announcing further, "Topaz has breakfast ready for us in the Tiger Den."

His words fueled my torch and I hoped that a tiny flower would serve it. Madilla was not there; nor was Topaz. Timmy and Cope relished their meal. I couldn't eat. I was crushed and felt very alone.

Both of my comrades enjoyed the meal, and following it, Cope stopped once again at the reception desk. "Tell Topaz *thanks* for her generous hospitality," he told the maitre d'hotel. As we stepped out into The Street of the Flowers, I could smell love and I knew I wanted Madilla forever.

The remaining portion of the day was spent walking from one pseudo military post to another. My mind was not on bartering but I did watch Cope beg, plead, and promise airlift to anyone who was capable of trading. His offers were for mainly civilian goods, such as coffee grounds, toilet tissue, and hard-to-get scotches and whiskeys; I was amazed at the number of takers and usually heard Cope say, "Trade is centuries old," following each encounter. No one doubted his abilities.

By six that night, Cope checked us into the USO Center. I wanted to stay another night at the Saigon Grand, but Cope casually informed me, "Topaz and Professor Hoh took Madilla back to Hue for a visit with her mother."

"Why didn't you tell me earlier?"

"I didn't dare. In case you haven't noticed, that is the first full sentence you've spoken since we left the hotel."

I couldn't argue with Cope's quip. All of the day was a blur and I had only Madilla on my mind. His revelation gave me at least a reason to explain her sudden disappearance.

"Let's chow down," Cope announced. Boremba's agreeing nod cinched the deal and we headed for the USO cafeteria. There was no French cuisine, and I wasn't about to luxuriate in a claw-foot bathtub nor sleep in a canopied bed. I wasn't hungry. I also shouldn't have acted so poorly at my friends who were merely trying to alleviate my pain. I simply felt as though a part of me had died and I was forever locked in merely remembering the most beautiful time I had ever known.

Cope fathered me at morning chow.

"If you're not going to eat, at least drink some damn coffee," he reprimanded me. I raised the cup and only took a sip, barely moistening my lips.

Boremba shoved his glass of orange juice next to my untouched tray of food and said, "Drink this."

I did take a gulp, but put it aside. "I'm just not all too hungry, guys."

"Suit yourself, Cooby," Cope said. "We have a few more stops to visit, then we head for Bob Copelet's apartment."

Lele was hanging clothing on the second-story veranda when we arrived at the dilapidated building. She descended to the lower level the instant she saw us. The girl opened the iron gates protecting the hideaway, cracking, "Saigon girls are number one, yes."

I tried to smile.

"For you too, cherry boy?" she addressed Timmy.

"We had a good time, Lele," Cope interceded. "Is my big brother ready?"

"Sure am, Carl." Bob Copelet raised the makeshift door concealing the hidden military vehicle. He backed the truck into the street, yelling, "Close the garage door, Lele, and bring those weapons down here."

Within ten minutes, Timmy and I were assuming shotgun positions in the back of the truck and waiting for the air force sergeant to say good-bye to a tearful Lele. Just as he was entering the military vehicle, to drive it away, he saw me and said, "What the hell happened to you? You look like you just lost your dog."

"Leave him alone, Bob; he got tangled with Madilla," the younger brother more than whispered to his older sibling.

"Madilla? Topaz's niece?" he damn near yelled. "He got lucky with Madilla? I've been trying to get into her pants for over a year!"

"Let it be, older brother!" Cope's second warning was clear, and I knew it to be a good thing for Bob Copelet to remain silent. I was ready to take the Flash Gordon weapon and ram it against the side of his face. I didn't get into Madilla's pants, as he so rudely implied; I invited Madilla into my heart.

When he assumed command of the 2½-ton truck, Bob Copelet repeated the challenge of attacking everything moving on the cluttered Saigon streets. Just as before, our powerful truck slammed on its brakes to avoid collision. I didn't hear the noisy sounds, smell the foul stench, or see any spectacular sights. I didn't notice any vessels on the Mekong or stifle any dust once the army truck left asphalt on its return trip to Long Binh.

CW3 Harsh and his pilot counterpart, Filings, were at the Quonset hut when our truck arrived. Bob Copelet backed the vehicle in the mini-warehouse and his underlings began to load it immediately.

"Have a good time in Saigon?" I overheard CW3 Harsh ask his flight operations sergeant. "Thanks to your brother, Mr. Filings and I had one hell of a great time."

"Sure did, Mr. Harsh. Even got to stay one night at the Saigon Grand, compliments of Topaz Hoh."

"Topaz? Didn't think she'd be around. On my last tour, she had a niece working for her that was a Eurasian beauty."

Cope didn't need a second invitation to pick up on the comment. "Can I speak to you privately, Mr. Harsh?" He led the warrant to a spot alongside the Quonset, out of earshot. Harsh turned to glance at me once during their conversation.

"Hey, Army!" Bob Copelet yelled. "Come and see what the U.S. Air Force is putting on your truck."

"Where'd you get a 30-K generator?" Harsh exclaimed as he eyeballed the nomenclature plate.

Liked the number, especially when I noticed there were 30 portable generators at the initial delivery. I *figured* it might better power those." He pointed to three small air conditioners.

"Where'd you get them?" a surprised warrant asked. "Are they mine?"

"Well," the Air Force E-7 fudged. "Only one is yours."

"Why'd I suspect there'd be a catch?"

"There's no catch...just a request."

"Which is?"

"One is for you; one for my brother. The third is for Major Frankel...We got a deal?"

"You got yourself a deal, Air Force."

"Nice doing business with the army," Bob Copelet shook Mr. Harsh's hand.

"Think we'll be doing more." The warrant watched as Bob Copelet's men covered his booty with a large tarpaulin.

"Better hurry, Sir. I retire to Des Moines in less than two months."

"Guard it, guys," he instructed his shotguns. As he got into the passenger side of the truck, he motioned for me to bend down. "If it'll make you feel better, Cooby, two years ago no one even got close to Topaz's niece," he whispered.

I thought about Mr. Harsh's comment a lot on the return trip to Bear Cat; his words soothed my head but did little for my aching heart. When our convoy of one arrived at the 312th company area, a detail of men was on hand to unload the truck, and the supply officer, Major Thurgode, present to spearhead its removal. I didn't know it, but the same detail had laid all the electrical lines and constructed a suitable building to house it.

"I know a clerk and an ex-infantryman who'll do anything to goldbrick out of three days' work," Frock greeted us. "See anything different about the place?"

"What?" Boremba acknowledged the crack.

"Not only are we ready for the generator, if you'll look around you won't see any more pitched tents...and it was done without any help from the two of you."

"Didn't need help," Timmy responded. For one moment, I escaped my doldrums and remembered how well Tim could sum up a scenario. The minor impact of two missing men in a company the size of the 312th wasn't relevant.

"So, give with some news, you guys. See something neat, do anything special?"

"Saigon," the colonel announced.

"You went to Saigon?" Frock was impressed. "Wow! What's it like, where'd you stay?"

"Saigon Grand Hotel."

"You stayed at a hotel! Was it neat, comfortable, and did you see anything special?" Frock was beside himself and anxious for anything less dull than Bear Cat.

"The Street of the Flowers."

"Cat got your tongue, Cooby?" Frock asked me. "I need details. Did you have a good time?"

"Yeah, Prez. I had a good time," I managed to speak a sentence. "I just can't get her out of my mind."

"Her? Who's her?"

"Topaz's niece," Boremba answered.

"Who's Topaz?"

"Hotel owner," Tim spoke for me again.

"You got lucky in Saigon?"

"It wasn't like that, Prez...I fell in love, just like you fell for Bunny."

"What's so bad about that?" Frock looked bewildered.

"She was gone the next morning, Prez," I shared. "She didn't even leave a note."

"Why, Cooby?"

"Don't know, Prez. All I know is I haven't been the same since."

"Can't imagine what I'd do if Bunny did that to me."

"I don't know what to do either."

"Write her," Boremba interrupted.

"Yeah, Cooby; write her."

"That's a great idea, fellas," I told them just before I went to the second tent in the second row of tents nearest the almost finished orderly room. I sat down on my bunk and wrote a brief note, sealing it in an envelope provided by my mother. I addressed it to:

MADILLA
c/o Saigon Grand Hotel
The Street of the Flowers
Saigon, South Vietnam

I lay back on my bunk, holding onto the letter, and collapsed from malnutrition and emotional exhaustion.

# Part Three

## *THE PACHYDERMS*

# CHAPTER 12

## THE PACHYDERMS

---

"Feeling better, Cooby?" Frock asked me the following morning in the mess hall. The ever shadowing Boremba came with him.

"I took the advice you both gave me, and wrote her a note. Sure hopes she gets it."

"She will, General," Frock reassured me. "You look much better than you did when you came in yesterday."

"I needed the rest."

"More than you know. After the two of you took off for Long Binh, Major Frankel enlisted the help of the Army Corps of Engineers and began the flight line, asphalting the whole area. Worked around the clock, three shifts a day."

"What's the big rush, Prez?"

"The helicopters come today."

"Who told you that?"

"Turtz. Said they're only an hour away; coming from the port city of Vung Tau."

I took a sip of iced tea and stared blankly at the dirty glass. Bosebaugh really does have our ass, I thought. Those troop-carrying, load-lifting helicopters were the reason we were at Bear Cat.

"It's starting." Boremba's observation was only somewhat true.

"No, Colonel, it's not." I was still staring at the iced tea. "It started at Benning; now we're finding out about the rest of the story."

"Well, at least the arriving pilots and crews will have a place to hang their clothes," Frock reminded us. "Remember when we got here?"

"Thank God for the little things." I got up, left, and headed for where I knew Sergeant Copelet was waiting.

The flight line building was two city blocks east of the company area, on the other side of an oiled road separating home plate from the aviation work area. Cope was standing at the counter fiddling with a brand spanking new coffeepot.

"From now on, by order of the current flight operations sergeant, the 312<sup>th</sup> operations office will have a coffeepot on duty 24 hours a day," he greeted me while he poured a cup for himself. "Cooby, I can't believe Thurgode got the power lines in place in so short of a time."

"And I can't believe I fell so hard in just one day. Am I entitled to a first, *second cup*?"

"Happens all the time." He poured me a cup. "I know; I fell for Reiko in just about the same way."

I took a sip and told him, "Same stuff as that good old Benning Brew...Will I ever get to Saigon again?"

"With the flying buses we got coming today, anything's possible...did you see what Major Frankel did while we were gone?"

"You mean all the asphalt? Big, isn't it?"

"Bet your ass it's big. No way Frankel would repeat the 'Benning bivouac blow away.' Remember?"

"As if I could forget."

"Looks as though the helicopters are coming in the nick of time, Cooby."

"Why is that, Cope?"

"A mind can't occupy two thoughts at the same time." He reminded me of a former lesson from Benning. "Didn't forget rule number one and rule number two, did you? When the big choppers land, my clerk won't have any time to think about somebody in Saigon; he'll be busy with a GI typewriter and a GI calculator."

"Infantrymen aren't issued typewriters and calculators."

"That's okay. Operations sergeants don't steal generators either."

His comeback made me laugh. Cope had a knack for making me see a forest in spite of the trees. "Must be true, Cope," I quipped back.

"What's that?"

"What you see, hear, read, or even expect isn't at all what you get."

"I'd use other words, Cooby, but your description seems close enough."

At 9 A.M., on the morning of April 10, 1967, the sergeant and I stood outside our operations building and watched the fourteen CH-47A helicopters swoop down from the Bear Cat sky like geese descending to find food and shelter. It was quite a sight. By 11 A.M., rules number one and two had kicked in as fourteen pilots, fourteen copilots, fourteen machine gunners, fourteen flight engineers, and fourteen crew chiefs swelled our complement of officers and enlisted by seventy. By 1 P.M., I was busy documenting everything, making certain I did it right the first time, or be forced to do it over.

By 4 P.M., on the afternoon of April 10, 1967, I became aware that someone else had watched the descent of the big helicopters as well. A jeep, flying a flag with two stars on its right front fender, parked at the 312th operations building. A courier delivered a sealed packet.

"What's in it?" I asked Sergeant Copelet.

"Bosebaugh's *ante up* call."

"I don't understand."

"You will, Cooby. Right now get into the jeep, go find Major Jones, Major Frankel, Captain Patton, and Mr. Harsh, and tell them the general has called in his markers, and we need to powwow at operations."

"Right now?"

"Right now."

I followed orders and returned with everyone but the CO of the 611th Transportation Company.

"Where's Frankel?" Cope asked.

"At the 5th; somebody's going to get him."

"As soon as he arrives, escort him into the conference room." Sergeant Copelet disappeared with the three officers behind the mapped wall and closed the door.

I seated myself at the console portion of the counter and waited. As I looked around I began to grasp what Cope had set up for the operations center. Cope was a genius, I thought. What a command headquarters, with even a third section of the building designed to tabulate and score any results.

Frankel arrived in five minutes, and I accompanied the major into the conference area.

"What's Bosebaugh want?" he immediately asked.

"Seven aircraft for seven combat missions...tomorrow," Captain Patton answered his question.

"No dice! The aircraft haven't been tested yet," Major Frankel responded. "Impossible."

"Sir," Patton spoke up again, "this order is signed by the general."

"Out of the question, Captain," Frankel reasserted.

"And what do I tell the general?" Major Jones, senior operations officer asked.

"I don't know, Major Jones. What I do know is what I do in tough cases like this."

"What's that, Frankel?" Jones asked.

"I seek advice from a 'bottom to the top' perspective. Sergeant Copelet, let's hear your thoughts. Any guesses?"

"Bosebaugh wants something," Cope answered.

"Seven aircraft tomorrow," Captain Patton fired away.

"Sir, with all due respect to rank in this room, there ain't a general alive who'd risk his career on a green unit whose pilots and whirlybirds just arrived in country."

"What do you suggest, Sergeant?" Frankel asked.

"Can't be positive, but I'd bet Bosebaugh is hinting for some handshake type agreement that provides him with airborne services back and forth from either Saigon or Long Binh...discreetly, of course."

"General Bosebaugh can do it now with any one of many UH-1D helicopters at his disposal," the captain objected.

"No, Sir, he can't," Cope replied. UH-1Ds just can't haul the bigger stuff, like redwood decking or new jeeps."

"I agree with Sergeant Copelet, gentlemen," *the man who could fly anything and make anything fly*, announced. "I'll go see what the general wants."

At 9 A.M., on the morning of April 11, 1967, I logged the 312th's first 'combat mission,' piloted by the CO of the 713th and copiloted by the operations officer of the 312th Assault Support Helicopter Company; sometime later that same day, General Bosebaugh stored refrigerated beef in his newly secured deep freeze, and Major Al Frankel ordered the immediate testing of all fourteen helicopters.

When April 15, 1967 came around, I was grateful for a congressional reprieve exempting an active Vietnam soldier from filing with the IRS; I didn't have time. Maintenance testing of the aircraft not only kept me busy with recordkeeping, it also unleashed the full strength of the sister company. Each aircraft took to flight at least five or six times every day and each pilot, copilot, crew chief, flight engineer, and machine gunner did the same. A pattern began to develop. At daybreak pilots reported to operations for scheduled flights; at dawn, they'd return with handwritten forms documenting assigned tasks. Calisthenics for a flight operations clerk became pushing a pencil, engaging a manual calculator, and stimulating an Underwood typewriter. Rules one, two, three, and four were alive and well and caused me to defer remembering about a night in Saigon.

The routine that emerged forced an increase of help at operations. Two air traffic controllers and two land-line communications experts swelled our operations staff to six. Bright and early, Cope and I, with three assistants, drove to the flight line. A rotating fourth stayed behind to do taxi service for flight personnel, duplicating the program at night. The flight operations sergeant and his operations specialist usually closed shop at 7 P.M.

A similar schedule materialized at the 713$^{th}$. After a first meal, a herd of maintenance men hoofed to the line, walked back at noon for a midday meal and again at night at day's end. When Cope and I left the line, duty guards had been in place for an hour.

Following two weeks of Frankel's "in-country" training, the routine generated a Benning-like monotony. Although the plentiful *Stars and Stripes* reported articles of "glory and combat," no one in the 312$^{th}$ or 713$^{th}$ underwent either real contact with the enemy or some reason for being where our company was. For all practical purposes, we just as well might have been back in Georgia.

"Hey, Cooby," Cope interrupted my frantic calculations one mid-April afternoon. "Let's go outside for a smoke."

"In a minute, Cope; I'm just about finished tabulating yesterday's flights."

"Now," he yelled, causing me to make a mistake.

"Shit. I'm going to have to do it again. Son-of-a-bitch."

"Good...now get your ass outside."

"What's so Goddamned important about being outside?" I angrily lit my cigarette.

"I need to talk about something fucking important, away from eavesdropping ears."

"So what don't you want the other operations personnel to hear?" I was pissed, and unaware that our vocabulary had picked up a lot of foul language.

"These Goddamned men."

"What Goddamned men?"

"The men of the 312$^{th}$ and 713$^{th}$, Cooby; I can feel the poor bastards are down."

"Let me guess why," I smart mouthed. "They're all away from home, in a foreign fucking country—one that's involved in a war in which they're not engaged—the food really sucks, the accommodations are shitty, it's hotter than hell, they all work their asses off, and on top of it all, they have a leader that even you call, *a flying dud.* I couldn't imagine a reason the poor bastards are down." I made no attempt to keep the sarcasm out of my voice. I was still pissed.

"These men need a boost in their morale."

"You're right—we do. Why tell *me*?"

"You're imaginative, Goddamn it."

"Cope, I'm the infantryman faking it as a clerk. I'm a guy who lost his heart in a hotel room. I'm the fellow who fucked up a 'totaling job.' Adding is my game; morale is not the same."

"That's it, Cooby!" Cope's face lit up. "I knew you'd come up with a solution."

"What fucking solution?" I was now more puzzled than I was pissed.

"Remember the limerick everybody hummed as they marched for presentation of the colors back at Benning?"

"Jesus Christ, Cope! I wrote it."

"Everyone remembered the best two lines."

"You mean: Led by Fang, with pumping hocks, and cadence caller, Sucker Tox?"

"That's the one, Cooby. We need another jingle like it; one the men can use to vent frustration."

"Boremba tells me Tox, our administration officer, is still looking for the shithead who wrote it." I wasn't about to double my chances to incur the captain's wrath.

"What'll Tox do, Cooby? Send you to Vietnam?"

I had used those very words with Boremba; yet as I looked at his genuinely concerned face, I understood he was just as demoralized as anyone. "I'd have to concentrate on something that applies to all of us, just like a fucking stupid parade, to capture the same meaning, Cope," I almost capitulated.

"Anything *fucking stupid* over here?"

"Everything."

"Any one biggee?" Cope began to pry open my imagination.

"Two stars and a *mellow yellow trailer house*."

"Pisses me off too. We suffer in the heat; he cools off in a pool."

"Every time I think about that bastard and his comforts, I hum a tune my sister used to play on our living room piano back home. Ever hear the song, 'Lola?'"

"'Whatever Lola wants, Lola gets?'"

"Paraphrased, it'd be: Whatever Bosebaugh wants, Bosebaugh gets. Pachyderms, General Bosebaugh wants you."

"Pachyderms!" Cope's formerly concerned face changed by 180 degrees. "Pachyderms! Who in the fuck leaked, Pachyderms?"

"I do work here, Cope."

"The code word is top secret!" He was serious. "I want to know who spilled the identity of the 312th and 713th!"

"What do you mean, who spilled the identity?"

"Who gave you the password for our company?"

"I did, Cope."

"What the hell does that mean—*you did?*"

"I invented the word."

"When?" he asked. His tone was clear.

"About four months ago."

"Why?" he persisted in grilling.

"Captain Patton asked me if I could come up with a word that had 10 different letters and described the 312$^{th}$ at the same time... It took a while, but one day I looked at one of our helicopters and saw an ugly, tough-skinned aircraft that could lift heavy objects. The *pachyderm* is an ugly, tough-skinned animal that can lift heavy objects. Since we had more than one, I made the word plural," I explained.

"Do you know why?" he continued cross-examining.

"My mother didn't raise dummies, Sergeant. P's 1, A's 2, C's 3..."

Mr. Harsh must have heard the exchange and came out to ask, "What's the ruckus?"

"Sir, do you know he's cracked our pachyderm code?"

"Cracked it?" Harsh smiled. "He's the one who came up with it, Cope...and anytime either one of you can help me move some files into the conference room, let me know."

"I will, Sir, but only after I tell you this whiz kid has composed a new poem." Another of Cope's natural gifts was to recover gracefully from an apparent embarrassment.

"Is it better than 'Pumping hocks and Sucker Tox?'"

"You know?" I thought only a few select knew about my limerick.

"Everybody but Fang and Tox knows who wrote it, Cooby. Who'd you immortalize this time? Better not be me."

"General Bosebaugh," Cope answered for me.

"Nothing like going right for the top, kid; what'd you write?"

"Whatever Bosebaugh wants, Bosebaugh gets. Pachyderms, General Bosebaugh wants you,"

Cope spilled my beans.

"Cooby, you're something else; it's perfect."

"I agree," Cope concurred.

# CHAPTER 13

## THE 312<sup>th</sup> ASSAULT SUPPORT HELICOPTER COMPANY

---

Although no one in the 312<sup>th</sup> and the 713<sup>th</sup> paid income taxes on April 15, 1967, we all found out there was a price to pay for being in the company. I found out my limerick was the hit of the outfit, and also found out what the price was.

Major General Bosebaugh did want the Pachyderms, and he called our bluff on April 23, 1967. He wanted seven aircraft, charging each with the responsibility of resupplying an area covering roughly a 150-mile radius of Bear Cat. Our initial combat mission of support included hauling food, ammunition, and supplies to various outlying sites of the 5<sup>th</sup> Division.

At the onset of giving the general what he wanted, names like Dong Tam, Rock Kien, Tan Tru, Ghia Rae, Phu Mi, and Long Thanh, were faraway places with strange sounding names — merely words I had to code on flight records. It took only one day of monitoring radio transmissions from our engaged aircraft, to realize the funny-sounding places were actual field sites with real soldiers, needing real food, and real ammunition to survive. Only a Chinook could deliver all of it from Bosebaugh's perpetual inventory.

Requests for more in the declining days of April became as endless as the saved supplies in the general's warehouse. Seven helicopters were labored daily with a periodic eighth; by mid-May, the Pachyderms defined that part of my limerick: What Bosebaugh gets, well, working ten or eleven aircraft a day.

Usually the night before, the 5<sup>th</sup> Division headquarters requested an emissary to pick up the combat missions for the next day. For seven aircraft, scheduling could be completed by midnight; for eleven, planning took much longer. Wake-up call for pilots and crews was 4:30 A.M.; takeoff, 6 A.M. With the help of our four new additions, Cope and I traded duty every other day, allowing one of us to sleep in. Our system worked but made for long 18-hour days.

As our Pachyderms flew support for the 5th, Pachyderm Operations monitored radio contact with the aircraft, and handled each problem as it occurred. Several of them were poorly thought-out division flight plans that directed the aircraft to wrong locations—a serious problem with weighty consequences. With seven or eight whirlybirds flying to as many drop zones in a single day, one miscalculated flight plan wreaked havoc on pilots sent to erroneous combat zones. Complaints to division headquarters were usually dismissed as trivial so Cope and I plotted our own missions based on previous experience with repetitive locations.

At the end of each day, either Cope or I would debrief the flight crews and commence the task of recording trivial information. "Why?" I asked Sergeant Copelet one May night.

"Why what?"

"Why do we report the same information every night? I mean, doesn't the Fifth's Battalion know it's 33 kilometers to Dong Tam, that an aircraft burns about fourteen gallons of fuel on the flight, and uses one pilot, one copilot, one machine gunner, one flight engineer, and one crew chief?" I was frustrated with the insatiable repetitive requirement for useless information, and I still hadn't heard anything from Saigon.

"There's a right way, a wrong way, and the army way," he reminded me of a previous lesson.

"Same shit, different day?" My smug quip didn't faze the 20-year lifer one bit.

"Afraid so...course you could rotate."

"*Rotate*? Let me guess; it's a new army invention."

"Nope, just the army way of keeping a unit together."

"You're shittin' me, Cope; you don't mean to tell me the army devised a way to keep a unit together?" I scoffed.

"Laugh if you want, but you must know that each of us has a one-year tour of duty...congressional law and all."

"Nice of the *trough dippers* to think of somebody else for a change."

"How many men came over with the 312th and 713th when we deployed, Cooby?"

"All of us?"

"How many will leave in February and March of 1968?"

I hadn't given any thought to a question like that, and it suddenly dawned on me that some in our unit might not go home. "I hope all of us."

"What happens if we all leave at the same time?"

"We wake up in Kansas from a bad dream!" Cope ignored my remark.

"Every three months, twenty-five percent of each outfit is rotated to another unit; the transfer creates a space for new arrivals but fills the opening for men heading home. In June, one-fourth of our outfit will be sent to other units."

"Who decides who goes and who stays?" I realized Cope, Frock, Boremba, and I could be separated.

"Big Mama 5th with recommendations from Fang, Frankel, Turtz, and Foone."

"Three-quarters of our company will finish their tour someplace else?" I wasn't a betting man but even I didn't like the odds.

"That's the system...on my first tour I went from Chu Chi to Vung Tau; my second tour had me in Long Binh for an entire year. That's when I met Professor Hoh." Cope was careful to avoid mentioning the Saigon Grand.

"How do I get four names on the recommendations list?"

"Kiss Fang's or Turtz's ass."

"Never."

"Then you're stuck in the waiting game, just like the rest of us, Cooby."

"Shit! I don't want any split-up." No information from Madilla was torture enough; now there was the conceivable break-up of my closest friends.

"Sorry, Cooby; it's the army way."

"Fuck the army, fuck Turtz, and fuck the big error in Colonel Fang's flight records," I erupted.

"What Goddamned error?"

"I found a computational mistake in Elmer Fudd's total flying time," I barked at Cope. "Screw him if he thinks I'll fix it. I don't give a shit—especially now."

"You better give a shit! If the dud's hours are shorted, your name will be on the top of the rotation list."

"Who cares if the son-of-a-bitch has been cheated out of 340 hours of fixed wing time?"

"You sure?"

"Positive. I checked it three times."

Cope remained silent for a time. Then he walked to our rudimentary landline communications network and picked up the telephone. "Colonel Fang, Sir, this is Sergeant Copelet from flight operations. An error has been discovered in your flight records, and I'd like to fix the problem as soon as possible." Cope then listened for about two minutes then said: "Sir, Flight Operations Specialist Coobat will be in your office shortly."

In a flash, Cope handed me the colonel's flight folder and escorted me to the Pachyderm jeep. "Think about *three to go* on the way up."

"What the hell does that mean?" He shoved me into the vehicle.

"You'll know when you come back; get going."

Boremba greeted me when I arrived at the new orderly room I was unwilling to visit. One-half of it was built to enthrone *the flying dud with two d's*. A demarcation wall clearly split the 20' x 40' building; in the center of it was a closed door. A sign read: Commanding Officer. Six desks were crowded into the front portion, three adjacent desks on opposite sides. Their placement created a natural aisle leading to the door plate. Boremba's, Frock's, and Turtz's were on the right; an empty desk, Captain Tox's, and the executive officers were on the left. The orderly room looked stuffy and almost foreboding.

"Knock and enter." Boremba's tone was gloomy.

I did, walked through the door, closed it, and approached something that belonged in an Omaha corporate office; Fang's desk came from someone's personal inventory. "Sir, Specialist Coobat reporting as ordered." He did not look up, nor did he acknowledge my formal greeting; I remained at stiff attention like the exhibited American flag behind him.

"What's this nonsense about incorrectly totaled hours on my flight records?" he snapped at me. "Give me that file."

I hesitated to step forward but had no choice; his flight records were in my left hand. I was maintaining the salute as I placed the folder on his desk and took one step backwards. Fang opened the records and looked at the top page. "It says I have 9660 total flight hours and no one will cheat me out of any of them," he declared.

"The figures are wrong, Sir," I managed to squeak out. The meet wasn't between a basic training sergeant and his recruit; this was commanding officer and a low-ranking subordinate.

"Who gives you the right to question previous expertise in flight records? As I understand it you're an infantryman subbing as a flight operations specialist," he blasted me.

"Sir, the records are inaccurate." I held ground.

"Nonsense, specialist."

"Sir, you have 10,000 total hours," I gambled.

"My records are not inaccurate," he pounded his hand on the desk. "I have every notion to bust you down to...did you say, *10,000 hours*?"

"Yes, Sir, I did." I watched the colonel page frantically through the inch-thick file, almost ripping through each page of documentation. "Which officer did this to me?"

"Sir, the error occurred about three years ago, when you were stationed in Germany." My voice had almost risen to one of normal pitch.

"Three years ago, and you found the error, here in South Vietnam?"

"Sir, I found it, but Sergeant Copelet helped me out in correcting it," I told him while still saluting.

"At ease...are you certain?" An amazed colonel remained skeptical.

"Sir," I finally dropped my arm, "three hundred forty hours of fixed wing hours were deleted from your total flight hours back in Hamburg. Why no one caught it, I don't know; the fact remains you have been cheated out of them. If you'd allow me, I'd like to show you where."

"Show me," he commanded.

I went to his side and showed him the DD 759 with the error. "It's a simple mistake in arithmetic, Sir; anyone could have made it."

"But someone did...my command would be better off if more were diligent in work performance. You are dismissed, Specialist. The request to improve my records is granted."

I took the folder, returned to the front of his desk, and saluted. He saluted back and I went out of the office and the orderly room, saying nothing to no one, blinking a good-bye to Boremba.

When I got back to operations, Cope greeted me with, "Thanks, Cooby."

"Thanks? For what?"

"Boremba called; we have been placed on the 'Retained Personnel List.'"

"Two down; two to go," I responded. "Now how do I get Timmy and Frock on it?"

"Don't think I'd be concerned about it, Cooby."

"Why do you say that? I am concerned."

"Considering what you've managed to accomplish in the last twenty minutes, there's no telling what'll you'll do in the next thirty days. First rotation won't happen until June 24 and it's only the middle of May. Besides, you don't have the time now; tomorrow's missions are here."

"Already?" I was surprised. Division hadn't altered the routine since Bosebaugh started to get what he wanted. Once the 5th added staying open 24 hours around the clock, as the orderly room did, the addition of another man at operations was compatible with Cope's and my devised plan. One day he'd come in late and stay late; the next I do the same. The method made for long work days, but I didn't care. After I returned from visiting the colonel, and the missions were planned, I'd be officially off duty until late the next morning after the aircraft took off. I went back to the company area to read any anticipated mail.

The regular had arrived, but there was none from Saigon. I penned another to Madilla but my frustration from not getting a reply to the first blocked me. I penned one home. God! Was my mother faithful. I had received one letter a day since I arrived in Vietnam; her correspondence was ever so important, but I ached for just one note from the girl in Saigon. I fell asleep about midnight.

About 3:30 A.M., an orderly room clerk was shaking me and shouting, "Coobat...Coobat. Wake up...Coobat. PFC Bokar from operations called. There's an important 'add-on mission.'"

"Call him back and tell him I'll be there shortly." I got up, hurriedly dressed, and went to the jeep provided for flight line operations. I arrived within five minutes.

"Hear any scuttlebutt about the add-on, Bokar?" I asked the charge of quarters.

"Nothing...just that there is one."

"Remember who called?"

"Mr. *Gung Ho* himself, Lieutenant Duffel."

"Go get it. Got any coffee?"

"Made a fresh pot right before the call."

"Good man! Any hunches, Roland?"

"Whatever Bosebaugh wants, Bosebaugh gets," he sang to me as he darted out the door.

I poured myself a cup of coffee and wondered whether a general would ever find out who rewrote the new lyrics to the Lola tune; before I finished with the eye-opening liquid, PFC Roland Bokar was back from Division HQ.

"Duffel say anything about the add-on, Roland?"

"He was out taking a leak; I got the sealed packet from his clerk." Bokar handed it to me.

I opened it and read the add-on.

"Where we sending our Pachyderm?"

"Not any place new; says we have to sortie something from Ghia Rae. Hell, we're going there anyway."

"What's *Mr. Gung Ho* want us to pick up?"

"Doesn't say, but I'm sure as shit going to find out why the son-of-a-bitch woke me up to add on another sortie at a spot we're already headed. We do it all the time." I reached for the landline telephone.

"Division S-3, Lieutenant Duffel speaking," his voice came across loud and clear.

"Sir, Coobat over at the 312th What we picking up? I need to plan for loading."

"That information is classified, Specialist."

"Do we carry it aboard or sling load it, Sir?"

"Just get the damn thing here, Coobat," he barked over the phone.

"Sir," I grew more pissed, "what do I tell the pilots and the crew to look for?"

"I will not divulge the contents of the add-on."

"Sir, without knowing what to tell the crews to look for, or whether they should take it aboard or prepare for a sling load, I must refuse to accept the add-on mission; if you wish, I can put you in contact with our operations officer."

"It's a crate full of steaks packed in dry ice," the lieutenant yelled into the phone. "A dumb shit head pilot accidentally dropped it at Ghia Rae. The steaks are for a party for the general. *Okay, Coobat?*"

"Sir, thanks for the classified info about the box of frozen steaks; I'll ask Major Jones if he wishes to accept it." I thought about my last meal; it was not USDA Prime.

"I'm throwing the party, Coobat; can we keep it on the QT?" Duffel asked in a more subdued tone.

"'Whatever Bosebaugh wants, Bosebaugh gets," I hummed. "I think we can work it in."

"Thanks, Coobat." I heard the phone click.

"All this crap for dry-iced steaks," Bokar cynically remarked. "I suppose we'll get another add-on to pick up a picnic table and benches."

I had to laugh at Bokar's crack, especially recalling the first Pachyderm combat mission. Bokar's humorous remark wasn't any different from negotiating for a K-30 generator or getting an air conditioner to make life more American in a Vietnamese war zone. I didn't say anything out loud but I started to wonder about the priorities of why I was where I was.

"Why don't you knock off a little earlier, Bokar; we'll be up and running in less than an hour," I told him.

"Sounds good to me, Cooby."

"Wake up Sergeant Copelet; tell him what's happened, then get some chow."

Bokar took off and I poured myself another cup while I waited for the crews to arrive. I chuckled when I remembered Duffel's definition of "classified information" and even some more when I thought about hearing my plagiarized version of "Lola." As I sat in reverie, Harsh and Patton came into operations. Prior to the general's getting whatever the general wanted, operations was their modus operandi; after the start-up of the 312th Assault Support Helicopter Company, their visits were qualified by morning flight preparations and late afternoon debriefings—so much so, Cope and I found ourselves forging their names on official documents.

"Hear this joint serves Benning Brew around the clock." Patton headed for the flight line coffeepot.

"Pachyderm Operations has a determined enlisted honcho who believes appliances, like the one you're using, should be written up as standard procedures in army manuals for flight lines." I watched him pour two cups.

Patton gave a cup to Harsh and carefully sipped from the one he took for himself, casually stating, "I also hear the bird we fly today is hauling everything but a kitchen sink."

"And from what I'm hearing, PFC Bokar has been assigned to the wrong MOS; advertising seems more appropriate."

"You authorize the steak lift?" the captain asked.

"Actually Harsh did, Sir; it wasn't too far back when he promised cargo space and 30 portable generators in return for a 30-K generator."

"Whatever Bosebaugh wants, Bosebaugh gets?" CW3 Harsh interrupted.

"Pretty much something similar, Sir."

"If the truth be known, I liked, 'pumping hocks and sucker Tox,' better," the CW3 laughed. "And since I'm talking about truth, we'd both like you to rotate with us to Long Binh."

"You two are rotating out of the 312th?"

"I've been offered Filing's old job at medevac, and he's coming along as a pilot, and information officer, for the 5th Division," Harsh listed a few details. "We requested it."

"Requested it?" I was surprised.

"Sure we did, Cooby," Harsh said. "If you had a choice between Bear Cat and Long Binh, which one would you pick?"

"Long Binh."

"Could be your choice too," the warrant announced.

"Rumor has it I'm on the 'retainee list.'"

"Rumor also has it that you've been promoted to E-5." He whipped on some charm—something I'd witnessed before at Fort Benning.

"What would I do at an evac unit?"

"First Air Medevac is also an aviation unit that's in need of a replacement for its rotating flight specialist," the glib officer baited me. "As the new flight operations officer, I can pick and choose a replacement. Any guesses who I'd select?" The man was a born salesman.

"That's quite a compliment, Mr. Harsh."

"This medevac pilot/information officer seconds the motion," Patton spoke up. "You could even help me edit a few published stories about the 5th."

"It means leaving Copelet, Frock, and Boremba, doesn't it?"

"Don't need a sergeant and two orderly room clerks," Harsh admitted. "We need one clerk/editor."

"Does sound like a great opportunity," I confessed.

"It is, Cooby, and the evac flies into Saigon daily." He saved his best argument, and shot it directly into my Achilles' heel.

"I sure could go back and see...the hotel," I caught myself.

"Maybe even someone who works there." His soft words ignited my passion and I was nearly convinced to concede when Sergeant Copelet entered operations.

"Why didn't you tell the CQ to wake me?" He automatically headed for the coffeepot. "You're supposed to sleep in."

"It was just an 'add-on.'"

"Well, you're relieved. I'll have someone wake you in three or four hours, Cooby."

I didn't need more encouragement. One early AM wake-up call, one wooden crate of classified steaks packed in dry ice, one offer I couldn't refuse, and one suggestion to catch some Z's were enough arguments to get my legs moving toward the second tent, in the second row of tents nearest the orderly room.

On the seven-minute walk back to the company area, I smelled The Street of the Flowers, visualized a canopied bed, and sensed the presence of Madilla. I must have had two wet dreams as I lay in my cot; I would have had three, but I fell asleep.

Five hours later an orderly room clerk woke me, and I dragged myself back to the flight line. When I entered the building, I found a somber-looking Copelet, and grim faces on the other men working in operations.

"On a leg of the Ghia Rae mission, the add-on portion, the one flown by Patton and Harsh, one well-placed sniper's bullet tore a hole in Mr. Harsh's neck," Cope reported. "He bled to death, Cooby...Patton is bringing the body back and will be landing on the pad shortly."

I became nauseous and could feel my knees beginning to cave in; I had to reach for the counter to prevent a fall. I started to shake and my breathing became labored. "I want to be there when Patton...lands." I couldn't say anything else.

"Take the jeep, Cooby," a shaken Sergeant Copelet told me.

I drove to the Pachyderm pad and waited for a Chinook helicopter, designated as *Pachyderm 107*, to land and taxi to a stop. Then I watched the butt-end ramp door open, and saw three crew members unload a black plastic bag from its belly. They put it alongside the aircraft, treating is as though it was just another piece of freight awaiting more handling. The crew reentered the helicopter and removed a soggy wooden crate which they placed next to the ugly bag.

I stared at the bag and the box as tears began to form in my eyes. The man inside the bag offered me a job today, I thought, while an uncontrollable urge started to rise from somewhere deep inside. I wanted to take the bag and the box to Lieutenant Duffel and tell him: "Here's the main course for your dinner...and here's the bill." I started to shake, overcome by grief and rage, when I heard the sound of the medevac helicopter.

The UH-1D landed near Pachyderm 107. Two men exited, came to the bag, and took it to the chopper. They returned to retrieve the wooden crate. Within a minute or two, Harsh was gone.

I had been frightened by then Specialist Copelet when he used the term, *deployable unit*; I was scared my first night at Bear Cat when 50 howitzers blasted reveille, and I knew I was in Vietnam. Nothing had more of an impact on me as watching two men take away the body bag covering the remains of a man I respected and admired. I was so shaken by the experience, I didn't notice Captain Patton standing next to the jeep.

"I'm going to miss him, Cooby," he choked as he told me. "We've been buddies for nearly five years."

The captain's flight suit was splattered with blood; his face was as ghostly white as bond paper. I could only guess at what he had been through. He remained silent as I drove him back to operations.

When we arrived, rule number one automatically showed its ugliest face. Either Cope or I had to debrief him and fulfill the insatiable need to *document everything*. The burden of asking a pilot about the details of watching his best friend die wasn't an easy task; I couldn't do it, but I listened as Patton spoke. "Once the box was aboard, and we were lifting off, I looked over at Harsh. There was a hole in his neck about the size of a tennis ball. His red blood was shooting from it like water from a garden hose. I had no choice but to fly the aircraft...I couldn't even reach over to touch him...my hands were on the controls. He slumped over before we reached 100 feet."

"I'll finish the report, Sir," Cope told him. "Right now, let's get you back to your hooch. You're in charge until I get back, Cooby." I felt the fear of God enter my soul when I watched Copelet escort the visibly shaken man to Pachyderm 3, the operations jeep.

Two hours later, Sergeant Copelet returned to a bleak operations center. He didn't look too good himself as we both stared at a suddenly ringing telephone that invaded our grief.

"Pachyderm Operations, Sergeant Copelet speaking," he answered.

I watched him listen intently for a few minutes, then heard him say, "Our tallies for the day are not finished, but we'll come and get the missions for tomorrow ASAP." He hung up the phone, pointed to the jeep, and said, "Go get the missions, Cooby."

"They're ready?" I was dumbfounded.

"Headquarters wants all fourteen aircraft; a big push is on for tomorrow."

"We've never used all of them," I told Cope.

"Go get the missions, Cooby; I'll notify Major Frankel, Major Jones, and Captain Patton."

"Patton? Can't the army leave him alone for at least a day?"

"More than anyone," the veteran flight operations NCO told me, "he needs to get involved."

Fifteen minutes went by until I handed Cope the sealed packet, and an hour later I was in the conference room with Major Jones, Major Frankel, and Captain Patton listening to Cope decipher "Headquarters' Big Push."

"The first six missions are same-o same-o," Cope began. "The seventh will take our remaining eight aircraft to what we know as Ghia Rae and Blackhorse, the twin peaks. The plan has the Pachyderms moving infantry to each peak, four Pachyderms to the base of each peak; we return here, reload with more infantry and in effect triple manpower at each of the field sites."

"Sounds like *king of the mountain*," Frankel observed.

"My guess too, Major Frankel," Cope concurred.

"Anything else, Sergeant Copelet?" Major Jones asked.

"Yes, Sir. We sling load sixteen howitzers to the same eight locations fortifying the troops with extra help."

"Any gun ship support?" a subdued Captain Patton asked.

"The $5^{th}$ will supply one UH-1D helicopter company with 14 Hueys, Captain."

"Bosebaugh must want the twin peaks," Jones commented. "Are we ready, Major Frankel?"

"As ready as we'll ever be, Major Jones."

"Meeting dismissed; see you in the morning, gentlemen," Jones told the assembled group.

"And make damn sure we have plenty of Benning Brew," Major Frankel suggested to Sergeant Copelet. "I have a feeling we are going to need it," he added as the officers left.

"Why didn't someone mention Mr. Harsh?" I asked Cope.

"It's the army way, Cooby."

"But it seems so cold."

"It is cold, and you're not going to feel warmer doing what you have to do now."

"What could possibly make me feel colder, Cope? We've had the first casualty, and he happens to have been both a close personal friend and our boss. Tomorrow we send eight Pachyderms to the same place where he was killed."

"Closing out Mr. Harsh's flight records," Cope somberly told me.

"Now?"

"Right now!"

"Why? What about a little time for grief?"

"We're at war, Cooby; there's no time for grief...It's the army way," he repeated the sickening two words.

"I hate the army way, Cope."

"And you'll hate rule number one too...after you finish Harsh's final DD 759."

Cope's impersonal comment sent shudders throughout my spine; I had never closed out the "bible" of an aviator's flying record. Cope's neutral conversation made me wonder if he was as dispassionate as he sounded. "So just how do I close out his records?" I inquired, faking impartiality.

"You fill out the regular one, whether or not it fills an entire page. You do another, and in place of recording information about flying time, you type in: Records Closed; Aviator Deceased. Get it done, Cooby," he ordered.

When I heard his words, I hated "the army way and rule number one" even more; when I finished with CW3 Harsh's DD 759, I hated Cope's orders to complete it.

"Finished?"

"Yes," I curtly answered.

"You fit for early shift tomorrow morning?"

"I don't like *the army way and rule number one*, Cope; and I didn't enjoy following your orders...One more thing. I have never heard anyone say, war is fun."

"Glad to hear it 'cause you're going to need that attitude tomorrow when 'Oscar Tango' happens."

"What's Oscar Tango?"

"Code name for 'Operation Take.' Now get out of here."

I left operations cast down; when I returned, Sergeant Copelet had already made a fresh pot of Benning Brew. "What you doing here?" I asked him.

"Reconsidered my 'lesson teaching' last night. Thought you could use a little support this morning...Want a cup?"

"Thanks, Cope; needed a reminder on the former and want the fix on the latter." It was on that day in May of 1967 I embraced the depth of my love for Carl Copelet. He was not only my teacher, he was my friend. It was also on the same day we didn't get to share a little downtime. As soon as we both sat down, fourteen crews arrived.

Within an hour, all of the 312th's Pachyderms were in the Bear Cat sky; everything went smoothly, including the return of eight birds that had come back to load more men, and continue with the second leg of Operation Take for the assault on Ghia Rae and Blackhorse.

"Pachyderm control, this is Pachyderm one-zero-seven, over," the first call on the second loading zone came over the radio. PFC Daryl Brechin, an air traffic controller assigned to flight operations, monitored the incoming call.

"Pachyderm one-zero-seven, this is Pachyderm control, over," he responded.

"Control, one-zero-seven. Sustaining heavy enemy gunfire on leg two of Oscar Tango. Three Pachyderms have suffered hits. Two known casualties. One 5th Huey is down. Landing zones are under attack. Do you copy? Advise, over."

"Copelet, Copelet," Brechin frantically screamed aloud for the sergeant. "What do I radio back?"

Cope took the microphone from the shaken Brechin and began to issue orders. "Pachyderm one-zero-seven, control. Fly over, abort mission. Do you copy, over?"

"Control, one-zero-seven. Aborting. Advising Oscar Tango to do the same, over," the pilot radioed.

"One-zero-seven, control. Has evac been contacted, over?"

"Control, this is...seven, over. Evac...Aborting...wounded birds..." the message was unintelligible.

"Pachyderm one-zero-seven, control," Cope returned a relay message. "Say again. You're breaking up. Say again, over."

"Con...seven...birds...abor..."

"Brechin, go get Major Frankel and bring him here ASAP," the sergeant ordered. Brechin ran from the only entrance to operations, yelling, "Major Frankel, Major Frankel." The CO of the maintenance arm of the 312th was inside operations in a few moments, time enough to hear more broken message from seven other Pachyderms flying the combined mission. He heard more of the same messages, as did everyone else in Pachyderm Operations.

Harsh didn't make it back...How many will there be this time?" I asked myself silently.

"I ordered the mission aborted, Major Frankel," Sergeant Copelet informed his former commanding officer.

"Good call, Cope; there's no sense in getting blown out of the sky," Frankel concurred.

"Learned the trick from *a man who can fly anything and make anything fly*," Cope acknowledged the compliment.

"Need three things, Cope," Major Frankel announced. "The first is to get those birds home; the second is a radio that will be installed in the maintenance building. The third one is a meeting with our communications officer. Have him in the building on the double...Cooby, drive me to the helipad."

While I was leaving with Major Frankel, I saw Cope pick up the phone and heard him tell the orderly room to find the communications officer and get him to operations ASAP. As I was leaving with the major, I listened to him order Brechin to have medics available at the flight line. What I saw most was Sergeant Copelet take command. "Any Pachyderm aircraft, Oscar Tango Pachyderm, this is control, over. Do you read? Over," he spoke into the microphone as Major Frankel and I left for the heliport.

We headed for the operations jeep, headed straight for the tarmac, and waited for a sound of rotary blades cutting through the Bear Cat sky. "Turn on the squawk box," Frankel ordered. "Let's listen as the professional I trained walks these scared birds home."

I jumped out of the jeep, and freed the arched antenna hovering over the jeep like a bent fishing rod. It stood up at attention as I turned on the transmitter. "When we move between aircraft, Cooby," the major cautioned, "do not let that standing antenna connect with rotary blades."

"Pachyderm control, Pachyderm one-zero-seven. Bear Cat in sight. Request permission to land, over," we monitored.

"One-zero-seven, control. Bring her home. Medics available, over." Cope's voice sounded reassuring.

"Roger, wilco, control. Be advised seven other aircraft will follow. One-zero-seven out."

The major and I sat in the jeep and listened as Copelet talked down all eight birds, one by one. Each one descended down like a crippled Pegasus using its hind legs as a brace for gliding in slowly. "They are damn good pilots," Frankel broke our silence when the last one cushioned touchdown. We watched them taxi to a berth and when they had all stopped, Major Frankel said, "Take me to one-zero-seven, Cooby." All I thought of was the same aircraft when I had watched the crew remove one body bag and one wooden crate.

"What happened, Daryl?" the major asked his counterpart pilot, Aircraft Commander Daryl Arrow, trailing his hand over the belly of the Pachyderm after exiting from its rear tailgate.

"We flew into a trap," the pilot told Frankel as he put a finger into one of many bullet holes that had invaded one side of the camouflaged Pachyderm 107.

"What kind of a trap, Daryl?" the CO of the 713th asked, as he too inspected the obvious indentations.

"First leg was great. The gunships flew over, we landed the troops, took off, and returned with the second load. Just as we were landing, gunfire came at us from everywhere. They couldn't have picked a better time or a bigger target...Some of the men inside didn't even know we were under attack. We were like sitting ducks," the major explained as he fingered into another bullet penetration. "Any one of these could have been in me."

"Why didn't the UH-1Ds spot the enemy?" a confused Major Frankel asked.

"Al, they grew right out of the landscape. One minute, no one; the next, they were crawling like ants."

"They're tunneled in, aren't they, Daryl?"

"You bet your ass they are," the aborted pilot concurred. "And if they're tunneled in at the base, they're *beehived* all over the top and middle of the twin peaks...Sure am sorry for the poor bastards we had to leave, but thank God, control had us abort...We'd be up there too!"

"The other aircraft sustain as much damage?"

"Al, we got our asses kicked."

"Stay here and help out, Daryl. I've got to get back to operations and have a little talk with headquarters...Let's head back, Cooby, and drive past the other Pachyderms."

I complied with the major's request and saw what he did not want to see. There were eight Pachyderms that sustained multiple enemy hits. By itself the sight was a grim reminder of what did happen when speeding metal contacted with a skin of a Pachyderm aircraft. What was uglier was watching as the wounded were assisted to awaiting medevac ambulances.

When we entered operations, Frankel assumed command.

"Who's on duty at headquarters?" was his first question.

"Lieutenant Duffel," Brechin answered.

"Get him on the horn, Private. I'm going to teach him a little bit about planning...Cope, have a map of the peaks?"

"Yes, Sir, I do."

"Get it, then locate Sergeant Foone and tell him we are on 24-hour, round-the-clock duty. I don't care how he does it as long as we have Pachyderms flying tomorrow morning. I won't abandon the men at Ghia Rae and Blackhorse."

"Sir," Brechin interrupted, "I have Lieutenant Duffel on the landline."

"Lieutenant Duffel," Major Frankel accepted the handset, "this is Major Frankel, CO of the 713$^{th}$. I have aborted your Ghia Rae/Blackhorse mission. If you have any questions, I'll be at Pachyderm Operations." He hung up the phone.

"Any guesses as to how long before he snitches to General Bosebaugh?" Cope asked.

"Long enough to attend the wounded and fix our aircraft. Have any luck with a radio for maintenance?"

"No spares; the only radio undergoing minimal use is the one in Colonel Fang's jeep."

"Requisition it; if the colonel can't be concerned while eight of his aircraft are shot out of the sky, he sure don't need a radio...Any luck finding the communications officer?"

"He'll be here within the hour, Sir," Cope formally addressed Frankel's rank.

"Good. I want him the minute he enters operations."

"Here's the map. Anything else?" Cope asked.

"I want to see the tallies of this aborted mission." He grabbed the map and a cup of coffee and went into the conference room.

"Back to work, gentlemen, we do have six missions to monitor," Cope announced to his crew, as the pilots from the miscarried mission arrived for debriefing.

All of them repeated what I heard Major Arrow report to Major Frankel. They were surprised, and as easy to hit as the broadside of a barn being swung at by a kid with a handful of cracked corn. Each delivered their documents and each added to the brutal score of an aborted mission. The session lasted for thirty minutes and I didn't notice the arrival of another officer.

I did become suspicious when I saw him come in and go out of the building several times. When he was outside, he gazed at the roof; when he was inside, he'd stare at Cope's wall map. I couldn't believe my eyes when I finally confronted him.

"Can I help you?" I asked the man with railroad tracks. The captain looked like the tin man from *The Wizard of Oz*; the only thing missing was an inverted funnel.

"Do you transmit radio signals from here, Specialist?" he asked.

"We try, Sir. Who wants to know?" I felt as though the rigid officer was in need of a good oiling.

"I'm Captain Eugene Femur, the communications officer. I was told to report here." Cope got up instantly and went into the conference room.

"Will you be hand delivering your flight records, Sir?"

"No, Specialist, I won't," the stiff man responded. "I'm not a pilot and am here to see Major Frankel."

"I'm Major Frankel," the commanding officer of the 713th announced.

"Captain Eugene Femur reporting as ordered, Sir."

"Femur, today eight of my aircraft were almost shot down and I couldn't communicate very well with any of them. What I need is an operating, reliable communications system."

"Hoist sails, Sir." The captain's response was similar to one Boremba might use.

"Riddles are not humorous, Captain," Major Frankel told him. "Today I've seen aircraft with enough holes in them to sink a ship; I can't guess how many men stopped the bullets. I can assure you, Captain, I am not amused."

"Sir, I apologize," Femur stiffened. "I did not mean to offend. I rotated in only yesterday."

"Apology accepted. Now what the hell does *hoist sails* mean?"

"Sir," the awkward man attempted to relax, "from what I have seen, you need to raise your antenna. By putting 15' or 20' between the antenna and the metal corrugated roof on the building, you will improve your transmitted signals as well as reception by nearly 50%," the tin man delivered his answer. "I might also add that I noticed electrical wiring and communications lines merely lying on the ground. Should there be any rains, Sir, your land-line connections will be literally *under the creek*."

"Sounds to me like you've got a full-time job, Femur," Frankel took little time in accepting the diagnosis. "Tell me what you need, Captain."

"I'll need a crew of men, Sir."

"Done; anything else?"

"Access to needed supplies, Sir."

"Cope, take this man to our supply sergeant; deliver my orders. Then take him to First Sergeant Foone and tell the first sergeant to allot six men to the captain...Will it be satisfactory, Captain?"

"Yes, Sir; when do I start?"

"Now, Captain!" Frankel's orders were clear. As Femur was leaving with Cope, I handed the major the report listing the devastating tallies for Operation Take. He looked at the totals, bluntly stating, "Christ, Major Arrow was right; we got our ass kicked today."

When he finished reading, a jeep flying two stars on its right front fender blocked the entry into operations. Colonel Fang shouted, "At-ten-hut," and opened the door for General Bosebaugh.

"At ease, men," the general announced. "Who aborted the mission Operation Take?" he asked.

"Three casualties, forty-one wounded, two downed UH-1Ds, and 250 bullet holes in Pachyderm aircraft aborted Operation Take, Sir," Major Frankel spoke up. "Would you care to visit the wounded, see the report, or inspect the aircraft?"

"I get your point, Major, but I can't leave those men at the base of the twin peaks."

"Then smoke 'em out, General." Frankel laid his cards on the table.

"Exactly what do you mean, Major?"

"If Mohammed can't fly to the mountain, Mohammad should remove the mountain," the veteran pilot suggested strategy.

"Air strikes?"

"They're tunneled in, Sir. Start at the top and go down. It's the only way to save the men at the bottom."

"When would you begin, Major?" Frankel's idea warranted the general's attention.

"Doctor Pepper time, Sir. Ten, two, and four...The line to headquarters is over there," Frankel pointed.

At 10 P.M. that same night, Bear Cat, and the rest of the 5th Division's Corps III area in South Vietnam, was brightened by a type of light that can only be provided by a night-time air strike. The entire countryside rocked as tons of air force might began the process to purge, by sheer explosive force, any living creatures hidden underground near the top of the twin peaks. For twenty minutes, the resulting bombing gave viewers a localized view of a mid-night sunrise. The same scenario repeated at 2 A.M. and at 4 A.M.; by 6 A.M., Frankel's repaired helicopters supplied the reinforcements required at the perimeter of the beleaguered field site.

By 10 A.M., the botched first attempt was over; Blackhorse and Ghia Rae were 5th Division property.

"Was it worth it?" I asked Cope after we tallied the final results of both missions. In total, there were four casualties, fifty-two wounded, 261 bullet holes, and two helicopters listed as combat losses.

"Was *what* worth it, Cooby?"

"Giving Bosebaugh what Bosebaugh wanted?"

Cope didn't answer right away. While I was waiting, I watched him fake the removal of tears from his eyes, seal the manila envelope with the tallies of the mission, place it on his desk, and stare at it blankly. My teacher looked at me and eventually said, "Was Harsh's death worth a box of fuckin' steaks?"

I didn't answer. I couldn't. I wanted to scream, "Hell no!" Somewhere inside, I ached to bury my face in Madilla's soft skin, and hide in the comfort of her love.

When I left operations and returned to the second tent, in the second row of tents nearest the orderly room, there were two letters resting on my cot. One was from home; the other had the return address of the Saigon Grand Hotel.

My heart pounded as I carefully opened it:

*My dear friend of Buddy:*

*Madilla has decided to remain in the Imperial City of Hue for a brief period. She has determined that my sister, her mother, requires her supportive help in caring for our family's dwindling possessions. I will give her your note when she returns.*

*Give my best to Buddy,*

*Topaz*

I felt hurt and simultaneously ecstatic. Madilla did not write back nor had she abandoned me.

I started for the tent's door, figuring I'd run down to operations and pump Cope for information about the Imperial City of Hue, and possibly more about the correct address. I realized he wouldn't know so I began a brief note to Topaz. I tore it up.

How I wanted my arms around her.

I didn't open the letter from home; rather I started another letter to Topaz, pleading that she contact Madilla for me. I tore it up, then scribbled a note to Professor Hoh, determined Cope knew his address in Saigon. I hoped he might be able to expedite my urgent message. I destroyed it too and collapsed from the anticipation of smelling The Street of the Flowers once again.

Wake up call was at 4:30 A.M., one full hour before the 5th Division blasted reveille. I had early shift.

# CHAPTER 14

## PACHYDERM MORALE

---

May 1, 1967 was a red-letter day for the Pachyderms, in spite of the loss of Mr. Harsh and the grim reality we had to face in securing Ghia Rae and Blackhorse. The real estate known as the twin peaks belonged to us, Bosebaugh had been placated, and I felt more secure in knowing I had a continuing contact with Saigon. Our company had undergone the rude awakening of discovering what Dulce et Decorum Est meant, and the terse reality exposed its ugly face down at operations each time an aircraft flew out of range, and we experienced poor communications.

At 8 A.M., Captain Femur and his crew of six men arrived. The valiant detail brought with them three 15-foot telephone poles, and two sets of metal clasps produced by the Corps of Engineers. The intent was to erect a 40-foot antenna-attached communications tower next to the flight operations building.

Hours of preparations resulted in a descending trench, culminating into a six-foot circular hole dug into the ground adjacent to the radio placement. The pole was rolled into place. Three men, atop the building, used rope to lift it up while three others similarly used fastened rope to coax it to an "attention" position. The doomed attempt failed so a deuce and a half replaced the ground men playing tug-of-war with the prone pole. The second try did lift the tower up, but pressure spawned one rope to snap, and this effort resulted in failure, causing some damage to the operations building.

"Hey, Phoebus," I yelled at one of the crew. I called him Phoebus because he hailed from Phoebus, Virginia.

"What the hell do you want?" the embarrassed private smarted back. The bulky man's name was Rassmussen, and we eventually nicknamed the hulk, "Ras of Phoebus." His sheer size rivaled that of Sergeant Turtz.

"The next time you want to obliterate operations, make sure you don't just cripple a corner; fix it so we all can have a week off," I cracked. A falling 45-foot telephone pole could have very easily crushed our hurriedly-built wooden operations center.

"You got a better idea, smart ass?"

"Yeah...Get a sky hook."

"Can't, you dummy. A whirlybird would huff and puff your whole house down," he quipped back.

"Wouldn't if you tried a real long sling load."

An onlooker, someone hellbent on fixing the missing communications between aircraft and Pachyderm Operations, shouted, "You got any more good suggestions, Cooby? Don't know why I didn't think of it myself."

"Only one," I yelled back to the unknown observer.

"I'm listening."

"Fasten the antenna before you sky hook the mother."

About an hour later, *the man who could fly anything and make anything fly*, piloted the Chinook. He used ten sling loads, putting 300 feet between his helicopter and the operations building. When Frankel finished, Femur handed operations a reliable communications system and I became certain *the man who could fly anything and make anything fly*, was capable of doing a lot more, especially with a tin man beside him who had no need to search for a brain.

Captain Femur and his crew began to bring the 312th and the 711th into the 20th century. His next priority was to use telephone poles to lift all power and communications lines from the ground. His placement of them patterned the design of any rural electrical cooperative that placed them effectively out of the way and parallel to roads and tents. When his detail finished with the second project, he began new ones.

One of them was the construction of boardwalks between tents and all other places where the men might travel between. At first this project met with heehaws and skepticism; few laughed much later when the monsoon season arrived and mud was six-inches deep. The "Oz look alike" even had jungle greenery brought in to provide relief from the camouflage coloring at Bear Cat.

Another was his crew's spearheading of a central post office, a needed service that relieved the orderly room of the onerous task of handling mail for 600 plus men. When it was completed, his "personal platoon of six," continued on until the company had laundry service, a functional barber shop, an interdenominational chapel, and access to movies shown in the company street. All of the men complained at the eighth showing of, *What's New, Pussycat*; we liked it when it was played backwards on its ninth screening. This team led by Femur and Phoebus clicked; no two men could've worked harder to offset the depressing atmosphere created by

Harsh's death and the blunder that occurred at the twin peaks. There was one other exception.

His name was Bob Follins; he was an E-4, a specialist in mechanics that rotated in about the same time the "tin man of Oz" and "Ras of Phoebus" embarked on building morale. Exactly why the orderly room assigned the motor pool expert to flight operations was a mystery, but his placement at operations did reawaken Cope's personal pet peeve with the army.

"Where'd you serve before you came here?" Cope asked the E-4 when he reported for duty.

"Dong Tam, then Chu Chi," the thin New York native told him. "Bear Cat will finish the last four months of my tour."

"What's your MOS, Follins?"

"Motor pool specialist."

"Served in Chu Chi myself, on my first tour." I watched as Cope's steel blue eyes became colder. "What'd you do?"

"Mostly was a gopher."

"What's a *gopher*?"

"Go for this, go for that...you know, drive trucks."

"Guess you'll fit right in," Cope cracked. "Got infantry playing clerk now; what the hell is one more...ever pull CQ duty, Follins?"

"You mean stay awake all night, sit on my ass, do as little as possible, then take the whole next day off? Sure, I've done that."

"That's good, Follins; you've got CQ duty tonight. When you're done with the mess hall, report here. He'll fill you in." Cope pointed to me.

"Don't do the mess hall thing, Sergeant," the E-4 told the E-6.

"Follins," Cope shot back, "I don't care if you drive a truck or don't, nor do I care if you eat or don't. Just make damn sure you're here." When Follins left, I understood the stern look on Cope's face and didn't make any comments.

Follins didn't just report for duty; he moved in. He brought with him a large box.

"What's that?" I inquired as he dragged the mysterious container into operations.

"I make my own food; won't eat the shit they serve."

"You cook your own food, Follins?"

"My ma sends me boxed pasta and dried cheese; sometimes she sends me one of these." He removed a twelve-inch salami.

"How do you cook the food?"

"On this." The specialist showed me a small grill. "Mom also sends charcoal, but dried wood works too."

"What do you make?"

"Mostly pasta, sometimes pizza, and every now and then, I fake it a little bit."

"Any good?"

"Kept me alive for three months in Dong Tam and three more in Chu Chi; it'll do the same for my last six in country."

"Go for it," I told him, realizing my time in country was double his. "Ever since the 5th took down the 'For Sale' sign at the twin peaks, the Pachyderms haven't been busy...What's your dinner going to be tonight?"

"Pizza."

"Who taught you how to make pizza on a grill?"

"My ma runs the best deli in New York City...Wait and judge for yourself." He removed a container of pepper, a jar of sauce, a miniature breadboard, and some other items I didn't recognize. Follins then went outside.

An hour later he shoved his breadboard at me. "Try it, I think you'll like it...Got more on the grill."

What I picked up smelled like pizza but didn't look like pizza. It looked more like ravioli; it tasted really great.

"Told you you'd like it...take the other piece."

I obliged him, and devoured the second serving. "You've got something great here, Follins."

"The secret is in my ma's sauce."

"You know Follins, you could make a killing over here, selling this stuff."

"You kidding? Who'd buy?"

"Any one of six hundred men who smelled and ate exactly what I ate."

"Maybe I'll experiment tomorrow...I do get the day off, don't I?"

"That's the rules," I responded as I departed for the company area.

"Chef-Boy-R-Follins" did not withdraw to his hooch the morning following his all night CQ duty; instead, the slick New Englander used his day off to scrounge the company area for "sticks and stones not intended to break bones." These essentials were his ingredients to form a basic pizza oven, fabricated behind the last tent, in the last row of tents, farthest from the orderly room. Even Boremba commented that night: "Nice smell."

In three short days, the 312th's *dynamic duo* assisted the new entrepreneur in forming a better oven; in two weeks, the Corps of Engineers had built a first rate, metal, pizza oven for the "Pachyderm Pizza" enterprise. By the middle of June, *Bosebaugh got what Bosebaugh wanted,* and Elmer Fudd overlooked standard operational procedures and any assigned Follins' duties. An added beer garden was totally a Follins' idea.

No one thanked him, nor did anyone thank Ras of Phoebus and Captain Femur.

When the monsoon season arrived at Bear Cat, the three men triple-handedly addressed the depression left over from our initiation into an assault support helicopter company. Deep scars were apparent in everyone. As rain and mud six inches deep weathered our unit to a halt, their attempts to bring a bit of America to Bear Cat, alleviated one hell of a lot of anger and frustration.

I ached to bottle up some of the rain and mud, and send it to the Paris peace talks. *Stars and Stripes*, and letters from home, were loaded with farcical reports. If simple rain could stop an entire company as easily as it could halt one ball game, why not sprinkle some on the bastards in France and give them something to think about.

The incessant downpours gushing from the Bear Cat sky were something I had never experienced. Every two hours or so, dark clouds formed from out of a blue horizon, dunking anything underneath. There was nowhere to go. As suddenly as the torrents began, a clear sky would reemerge and turn Bear Cat into a steam bath.

Flight became limited to time in between, restricting mission support for the 5th. Peeling off saturated clothing turned into a company pastime. Oftentimes I wondered about being out in the field. Quicksand mud was as near as a step off the Phoebus-Femur Boardwalk. High ground didn't exist. Pizza was a smell away.

I should have spent May, June, and July writing letters of commendation for Femur, Phoebus, and Follins. I didn't.

Instead, I waited, worried, and watched as twenty-five percent of my company rotated out.

# CHAPTER 15

## RELIABLE INFORMATION

---

Unlike the invasion of men crowding onto a vacant Fort Benning field during the beginning stages of the 312th, the rotation of 125 men was spread out over a three-week period. Although each new replacement didn't face building a place to live, the newly rotated men did have to face the weather provided by the tropical environment. I had often wondered why Cope erected his platformed tents on howitzer shells, concluding it was an old army custom. When rains from the monsoon created miniature lakes everywhere, I found out why the wooden floors were off the ground, and why we all took a quinine pill every Monday morning. Standing water became the womb for the incubating eggs of mosquitoes, the kind who inflict serious damage with one bite. It was unrealizable to treat each pond at Bear Cat, and doubly dangerous to attempt it outside the perimeter walls.

I guess I learned a little about myself in those first five months in country, and why soldiers like me greeted newly arrived men with catcalls. Misery loved company and that included anybody without four or five months experience. Cope wasn't there to admonish me when I saluted a truckload of green men with only my middle finger extended.

Prior to his own rotation to the 5th Division Information Office, Captain Patton had granted two days of personal leave to Cope. His brother, Bob, was not only departing Vietnam, he was retiring from active military life. How Cope boonswaggled a lift into Long Binh from a Division Huey, I'll never know; what I do know is how secure I felt when he returned. He was my "Snoopy blanket," although we never hugged.

"Brother get off okay?"

"Downed a whole case of Vietnamese beer before he wobbled aboard the 'Big Banana,'" he answered. Braniff Airlines had a contract with the U.S. Military to provide first-class flights home to any returning Vietnam Veteran. No one who served near Saigon or Long Binh could avoid seeing a brightly colored jet crisscross above the Vietnamese sky. They were known as "big bananas" because a number of them were painted an iridescent yellow.

"Lele cry at the terminal?"

"She wasn't there. She went to live with her parents a week before Bob left."

"What?" I was surprised; I had seen Bob and Lele play "pony ride" together. "Bob let her go a week before he left for home?"

"It's not like that, Cooby."

"Sounds like 'wham, bam, thank you, ma'am,' to me."

"Only because you think like an American."

"What's that mean?"

"Cooby, there ain't no 'Mom, apple pie, and Omaha, Nebraska' over here. Bob and Lele understood that."

"I sure don't!"

"You wouldn't; you've been taught American philosophy."

"You've lost me, teach...explain."

"Cooby, you didn't grow up in a poor country; Lele did. You can pick and choose from a dream-filled future; she don't have that option. If you want to comprehend, imagine living in a country that has undergone civil unrest for your whole lifetime. Maybe another way of explaining it is to point out a popular phrase: 'Eat, drink, and be merry; tomorrow never comes.' Over here it's, 'Eat, drink, and be merry; tomorrow probably won't come.'"

"I can't fathom a country under constant civil unrest."

"Exactly my point. Americans haven't 'walked a mile in another's shoes,'" he tried to explain. "Lele accepted the only improvement her life had to offer."

"And your brother, Bob?"

"My brother gave some girl a one year reprieve from a futureless life...Cooby, if you ain't got nothing, anything looks very attractive. Bob gave Lele that *anything*."

"He got paid, too."

"Hope so. Barter is indispensable to their way of life."

"Flesh is no means for barter, Cope."

"Tell that to the American Indian or to any Black man."

"Survival of the fittest?"

"Okay, listen to what my brother told me before he got on the Braniff jet. Lele told him about rumors spreading amongst her people...rumors so serious she was glad Bob would be out of country when they happened."

"What could a young girl know, Cope?"

Cope waited a minute before he reminded me of something. "Remember the experience you told me about when you arrived here?"

"Which one?"

"The one with Captain Clark...on your first day here."

"With that old woman on the Long Binh Road?"

"Yes, that one."

"What about it, Cope?"

"What did Clark tell you?"

"Never to underestimate any of these people."

"Well, Cooby...'when in Rome...' The people living here are like animals who have an innate sense to smell a forest fire or anticipate danger. Centuries of war had bred it in."

"And you believe a young girl...with rumors?"

"Would you believe Madilla?" he quipped back.

Cope struck a nerve, and seconds later the first sounds of an explosion were heard. The noise was unlike a howitzer sending out a reveille round. When the second one went off, we dove for the floor.

"What the hell was that?" I yelled.

"Stay down, Cooby. Everybody else, get on the floor," he ordered. Cope crawled to the radio in the corner of his operations center and stopped at the radio console.

Following two long minutes of prolonged quiet, Copelet picked up the mike. "Division control, Pachyderm control, over."

Silence.

He tried again. There was no response.

Fifteen minutes later, the radio squelched. "Pachyderm control, division control, over."

"Control, Pachyderm control. Advise, over," he responded to the transmission.

"Pachyderm control, division. Initial reports indicate two random incoming rockets. Source unknown. One confirmed strike on a UH-1D, Bear Cat runway. Some damage at Bear Cat One location. Red Alert in effect until outer perimeter is flown over by squadron of UH-1Ds, over."

"Pachyderm control, division control," Tox's voice was heard again. "Red Alert canceled. Two random incoming. Say again, Red Alert canceled, out."

When the message was over, Cope stood erect and walked to the entry to operations. I followed him much like Timmy always walked behind Frock. When we got outside, we could see two columns of smoke rising into the air. One was more noticeable than the other. It originated from the vicinity of the Bear Cat runway, and generated heavy billows of black smoke. The smaller one came from the center of Bear Cat.

"Isn't that near the mellow yellow trailer house?" I pointed toward the lesser smoke cloud.

"Bear Cat One *is* the mellow yellow trailer house."

"You mean one rocket hit the general's place? Captain Tox said they were random, Cope."

"Tox is greener than grass, Cooby, and no match at all for Charlie."

"Who's Charlie?" I asked my counselor.

"It's a term for the enemy we evicted from over at the twin peaks, Cooby. The two *random rockets* are personally delivered calling cards letting us know he's back, ready, and pissed."

"Great timing...we've got our hands tied with weather."

"Only brilliant American technology could prepare for everything but rain. Charlie has functioned in it for centuries."

"So what do we do now?"

"Not too much choice, Cooby. Those *smoke signals* are alerting the countryside of Lele's rumors."

Cope's candid remarks were accurate. The conflagration created by one direct hit conveyed a prolonged message over the 5th Division area of operations. As the day progressed, I began to understand what Cope had been saying. One by one, communiqué reached Pachyderm Operations:

Rock Kien and Tan Tru experienced rocket fire.

Dong Tam fired upon.

Long Binh hit.

Chu Chi had wounded.

Saigon Airport temporarily closed.

Each new report chronicled the severity of the surprise move.

Soc Trang overrun.

Heavy gunfire on the Mekong.

Landline communications severed.

Roads between field sites declared impassable.

One of the final reports confirmed the capitulation of the Imperial City, Hue. I was isolated, and Madilla was in a place overwhelmed by an enemy with a nickname.

Lele had been right. Cope's interpretation of her comments were right.

By twilight, Pachyderm Operations had planned missions for the 5th Division. Rain or shine, we had no choice. Soc Trang, Rock Kien, Tan

Tru, Dong Tam, and Chu Chi all needed food, ammunition, and more men. The field sites also needed to evacuate the wounded.

When the day ended, and the tally was forwarded to the insatiable information machine at division headquarters, I asked Cope, "Was it worth it?" Sixty had stopped lead; some were maimed for life. "This isn't a way to spend the eve of Independence Day, 1967."

"No, it ain't," he agreed.

Bear Cat didn't have to wait until dawn of July 4, 1967, to either retaliate or salute the misplaced holiday. Incoming rockets replaced the regular reveille call in a second daring announcement. There were two. One scored a direct hit on one more UH-1D; the second erased the entrance gate to the mellow yellow trailer house. The foreign firecrackers gave me a new definition for the American Holiday, and at day's end, tallies reminded me who had been in charge of the display.

All eight of our aircraft were greeted with noticeable, but unseen enemy. The casualties were light but unacceptable in spite of the weather which greatly modified our objective to support the 5th. Femur's radio tower offered the adequate communications, but improved radio transmissions didn't place an umbrella under the sky nor avert natural ambush sites. One landing Chinook was a very easy target.

The scenario repeated itself day after monotonous day in July and August of 1967. Eight or nine resupply missions met with the same inclement weather and the same no-win situation. Field areas could not be serviced effectively. The lesson was "Charlie had harnessed the environment."

Bear Cat remained in constant radio contact with division at Long Binh and Bosebaugh's perpetual inventories increased; yet all the supplies in the world didn't mean diddly shit to men who didn't have them in their hands. Each debriefing, at day's end, reported the same message: the enemy was tunneled in and using the monsoon season as a very effective asset. I hated it when I heard a pilot radio that an aircraft pushed needed supplies off the helicopter while flying over a zone, and I oftentimes recalled Captain Clark's initial warning to me: "Do not underestimate any of these people, Cooby."

We had underestimated the enemy in the Third Corps Area and published facts that didn't exactly reflect the whole picture. *Stars and Stripes* weekly reported such half-truths:

## *5<sup>TH</sup> DIVISION CHALKS UP IMPRESSIVE RECORDS*

### *by Captain Harold Patton*

> The 5<sup>th</sup>'s own 312<sup>th</sup> Assault Support Helicopter
> Company, the Pachyderms, total up some impressive
> flight tallies in its service to the division. In July 1967,
> the Pachyderms transported 9,000 tons of cargo, and
> airlifted 15,000 Fifth Division troops. The
> Pachyderms well deserve the title "The Leading
> Assault Support Helicopter Company," in Third Corps
> Area, South Vietnam.

I was proud to read about my outfit; I didn't know why there was no mention of body bags, number of casualties, or even the jettison of needed supplies at inaccessible landing areas. There was no indication of who was in charge of South Vietnam terrain. What made the news story more difficult to accept were letters from home echoing the patriotic efforts of my outfit. My mother was proud, and my sister wrote she'd name her unborn son after his distinguished uncle. While the written words were easy to read, my insides told me the only reliable information came from a young girl named Lele, who cautioned about "rumors." The landlord of the real estate I called home had a name.

That name was Charlie.

# CHAPTER 16

## "HOO-RAY"

---

By late August, 1967, newly assigned personnel through the army's rotation system, had acclimated as easily as it was to accept dry weather over wet. Flight operations down at the 312th successfully responded to the increase of ten aircraft per day seven days a week, and the Pachyderms had a new replacement for the rotated Captain Patton. Missions continued to be the standard "resupply" type and any news written in *Stars and Stripes* conveyed the fall of Charlie. While some truth hit newsprint, most of the uglier reality remained undisclosed.

One of the more than subtle realities, experienced but unheralded, was the explosion of two incoming rockets that occurred at Bear Cat every day since the reclaiming of the twin peaks. Not a man on the compound could ignore the repetitive and regular attacks. There were two each morning: they were well-aimed and well-placed, and each one chipped away at any newsprint indicating Charlie was washed up. The uncertain atmosphere was rarely spoken about; yet it was as evident as a rising smoke cloud coming from a hit target.

Nothing had a more positive influence on Bear Cat than the arrival of one Hollywood celebrity, who walked into the 312th operations center as if it were a California stage.

The VIP parked a jeep, one flying a red flag with two white stars, smack in front of the only operative entrance to Pachyderm control. She strolled in wearing khaki shorts and a blouse, and carried a small purse and an aviator's helmet.

She didn't say a word as she headed for the large wall map which she examined as though it was a script. When she finished with her scrutiny, she waltzed over to the flight line coffeepot, put her purse and helmet on top of the counter, and poured herself a cup.

She took a sip, winked once, and swallowed the Benning Brew. Still remaining silent, she took a second swig.

The USO veteran cocked her head, said, "Whew!," and meandered to where I was manning the radio console. She leaned over the counter, looked me straight in the eyes, and asked, "Don't they call you Pachy 3, big boy?"

I couldn't talk.

The comedienne flashed a smile making daylight look dim and asked, "Think you could give a lady a ride? Got the right equipment?" She pointed at the helmet.

I remained speechless. Martha Raye was in the flight line center.

"Bosebaugh Baby told me whatever Martha wants, Martha gets. Is that true, Pachy?"

"What's...Martha...wa-want?"

"Martha wants a ride on a real helicopter, with real soldiers, doing what real aviators do." She blinked an eye.

"Wa-what?"

"It's nice to know the brass, but I like action where the men are." Miss Raye blinked both eyes.

"Bu-but, Miss Raye, this is...a...com-combat zone."

"You saying you won't give me a lift, Pachy?"

"It's a bi-bit out of...the ordinary, Mis-miss, Raye."

"Get Bosebaugh Baby on that phone." She aimed a finger. "Martha is not getting what Martha wants." She looked irate and stared at the two stars flying on the jeep's flag.

"Na...no need, Mis..Miss Raye," I stalled. "When do you want to...fly?"

"Right now."

I didn't know what to do so I stared at the wall map she examined upon her arrival. I knew how she got to the center and I could guess who gave her the jeep. Suddenly I realized Pachyderm 105 was due to arrive for reloading and refueling before it continued with the Tan Tru/Rock Kien chow run mission.

I picked up the microphone and spoke: "Pachyderm one-zero-five, this is Pachyderm control, over."

"Control, one-zero-five, over."

"One-zero-five, control. What's ETA Bear Cat, over?" I sensed Martha Raye felt as though I knew what I was doing.

"Control, one-zero-five. ETA five minutes. What's up, Cooby, over?"

"One-zero-five, control. Have one PAX, over."

"Control, one-zero-five. Understood. Have PAX at pad. Over and out."

"Love ya, Pachy." Miss Raye blew me a kiss. "Don't fret; I found this place and I'll find the pad." Martha left, got into her jeep, and drove off. I sat dazed. The famous Martha Raye had been in my operations center and

I couldn't wait for everyone to return from the midday meal so I could spring the news.

No one believed my story.

They did four hours later when Martha Raye stopped by operations to "thank Pachy 3" for the ride.

I wasn't there.

I was in the company area preparing for Frock's and Timmy's promotion party. Cope accepted the thanks for me. He was invited to the bash but couldn't attend. He filled in for me and repaid his debt. I filled in for him when he went to Saigon to see his brother off. Although I would've loved to be a fly on the wall when Martha came by a second time, I had to help Frock rearrange the first tent, in the second row of tents nearest the orderly room. The general, the president, and Colonel Ponderosa all had the same rank and it was time for celebration.

We had folded all the cots and set up a poker table in the middle of the hooch. Half barrels, requisitioned from the motor pool, had been loaded with confiscated ice and stolen Lone Star beer. Invitations had been limited to the other six clerks in Frock's tent, Cope, and me. After we had finished setting up the tent, I looked at Frock and remarked, "See you're all dressed up for the gala." He was wearing a grimy jockstrap—the most comfortable piece of apparel to wear inside a tent at Bear Cat.

"It's all I intend to wear in this oven," he quipped back. "Want a beer?"

"Have one when I come back; want to grab a shower."

I left and went next door, to the second tent, in the second row of tents nearest the orderly room. I carefully peeled off the wet OD green t-shirt adhered to my upper torso, removed my combat boots and socks, and took off my fatigue pants and shorts, dropping them into a dingy pile alongside my cot. I grabbed my only towel, threw it over my shoulder, picked up the one bar of soap I owned, then headed for the Femur Boardwalk leading to the showers.

"Let there be water," I hoped.

When I released Cope's clip-on pet cock valve, no water used gravity to flow from the collection point above.

"Shit!"

I shouldn't have been surprised. Following the twin peaks experience, demand for water doubled. We not only had a full-time day crew, we had a full-time night crew. All water had to be trucked in.

I struck water in the third shower. The moist spray felt so luxuriating, I sucked it dry and had to head for a fourth. Liquid luckily gushed forth so I soaped myself, shutting the release off to conserve. When I opened it up, the water had run out.

Frustrated, I draped the towel over my shoulder, and went to the first tent in the second row of tents nearest the orderly room. I wanted the beer Frock offered earlier.

When I walked into Frock's hooch, eager to suck down some chilled Lone Star, Martha Raye was dealing cards.

"Pachy 3, don't be so bashful; come on in," she said as she dealt the deck in her hands. "I'd ask you to sit in on this game of strip poker, but I can see you ain't got much to lose." Martha stiffened as she attempted to restrain laughter.

I grabbed the towel from my shoulders and dropped it before I could cover myself. I stood there. I was naked, speechless, and embarrassed. Martha, Frock, Boremba, and the other invited guests roared.

"You must be why they call this place 'Bare Cat,'" she ad-libbed.

Frock fell off his stool overcome with laughter. He wound up on all fours with his butt aimed at Miss Raye.

Martha hurled the cards into the air and exclaimed: "Hell with strip poker; I'd rather watch the bare cats."

I finally cracked up, and in an impromptu way, Frock removed his jock strap, sling shot it at the poker table, and joined me in performing a Pachyderm cancan revue for Martha.

"Never got a script like this," the entertainer told us, as she got up from the makeshift stool and walked to a half-barrel. She picked up three beers, pitched two at the performers, and saved one for herself.

Two naked men and all the other semi-naked men then sat around and listened as Martha apologized for "staying with the brass but loving more being with the common ass." By the time she left, I had exceeded my two beer limit a number of times.

Somewhere near noon the next day, I crawled down to operations, unaware that Charlie awakened everybody else with his two-rocket reveille call at 5:30 A.M.

"Draggin' ass?" Cope took one look and surmised the rest.

"Think I drank a case of beer last night." I prayed I wouldn't hear one drop of the coffee he poured me crash into the cup.

"Drink." He gave me the mug. "You need to piss out the booze in your bloodstream."

"Smelling the coffee makes my head pound," I confessed as I rubbed my temple.

"Heard you lost at strip poker."

"Wasn't dealt a card," I whispered back.

"Quite a lady, isn't she, Cooby?"

"She could make Ho Chi Minh look lovable."

"She stay long?"

"Long enough."

"What'd you partygoers do when she left?"

"Got into a pissing contest."

"Got me there, Cooby. This is only my third tour."

"If you'll stop hollering at me, I'll fill you in."

"Okay," he spoke softly and masked a smile.

"We chugged beer. Then we went outside and stood on one side of the moat you had us dig around each tent. Whoever could piss the farthest, won."

"Wonder what your mother would think," he observed.

"Not funny, Cope." I took a healthy gulp of the brew. "Aren't you supposed to go to chow or something?"

"First, you need to promise that you won't cancan on your desk."

"Anything I should know before I kick your ass out?"

"Same-o, same-o, Mr. Sally Rand. Standard missions."

"If I had a fan right now, I know where I'd put it...Anything else, Cope?"

"Somebody is coming from the orderly room to talk to you about the R & R program."

"Secret code for repent and regret?"

"Rest and recuperation, Cooby. A Specialist Street will be telling you about how the army pays for air travel to spectacular places, and the soldier foots his vacation costs...Tell Street I want to go to Japan."

"Anything fucking else?"

"Yeah...Did you use your towel as a fan?"

I threw my coffee cup at the fleeing Sergeant Copelet, just missing him as he darted out the operations door. One hour and four cups of coffee later, Spec 4 Philip R. Street arrived.

"These are the designated places," he explained as he handed me a packet of brochures advertising Tokyo, Taipei, Bangkok, Singapore, Hong Kong, Kuala Lumpur, Penang, and several sites I didn't recognize. "Hawaii is reserved for married personnel and the continental United States is off-limits."

"Sergeant Copelet will go to Japan," I told him.

"Holy shit. He's my first."

"Put me down as your second, Street, and put Boremba and Frock down as three and four."

"You're not thinking about taking an R & R with the three of them, are you?"

"Bet your sweet ass, I am. The four of us go all the way back to Benning."

"Forget it, Coobat."

"What do you mean, *forget it*?"

"First Sergeant Turtz would never clear an R & R for all of you at the same time."

"Why not, Street?"

"Two of you run the orderly room and the other two run operations."

I felt like throwing something at Street but knew he was probably right. Without Frock and Boremba, the 312th's first sergeant was as useless as freshly clipped toenails on a corpse, and our new operations officer was too busy flying to boss record keeping. "I'll share the information with the flight operations personnel, Street; pretty sure you'll get some response."

"Hope so. Without evident activity, the 5th Division will withdraw the push on a company-to-company basis," he sadly reported.

"Got a deadline?"

"Sixty days...after three weeks on the assignment, I got four men who can't go together."

"Get Fang and Turtz involved," I suggested.

"Solving the Paris peace talks would be a lot easier; Fang's indifferent, and Turtz's flat ass don't give a shit."

"Want some help?"

"Sure. I can use anything...what you got in mind?"

"Someone who might make a difference."

"Who?"

"Trust me, Street; in the meantime, sign up Sergeant Copelet and me."

Street left to sell his incentive to the maintenance office, and I asked our communications operator to locate Martha Raye. I vaguely remembered her saying she'd spend the next three days "visiting with the common ass."

"Come on, Cooby," Private Bokar protested. "Where am I going to find Martha Raye? There's a whole division full of companies at Bear Cat...and if I do find her, what do I say...'Cooby wants to dance for you again?'"

"Pick up the damn phone, Bokar, and call every outfit on this base," I ordered the private. "And one more thing, I don't need to be reminded about last night."

In fifteen minutes, Bokar had located the star. "She's at the Corps of Engineers' mess hall, Cooby."

"Hold the fort, Bokar; I'm going to pay a visit." I got into the jeep and drove the half mile, determined to speak with Miss Martha Raye.

"I have an urgent message for Martha Raye from HQ," I lied to the massive sergeant blocking the entrance to the mess hall. "Tell Miss Raye the communiqué is *Pachyderms Dancing*."

The unsuspecting sergeant glanced at enlarged letters printed under the windshield of the jeep—Pachyderm 3—and swallowed my hoax. He returned with Miss Raye in less than five minutes.

"I'm sorry I interrupted your performance, Miss Raye," I blurted out, "but I didn't know a better way to get hold of you."

"So am I, Miss Raye." The military bouncer grabbed me by the collar. "He won't be bothering you again."

"Wait a minute, Sergeant," Miss Raye acknowledged me. "He danced for me last night; the least I can do is shut my big mouth and listen. What's up, Pachy?"

I explained my idea.

"I like it," she told me. "I'll be here for two days. If you can swing it, send the mellow yellow trailer house a message—maybe 'Dancing Pachyderms'—include a time frame like 10 A.M., and I'll be there."

"Thanks, Miss Raye." She gave me a big hug and yelled, "Good luck," as I drove back to Pachyderm Operations.

"Get me the 5th Division information office," I told Bokar.

"What the hell for?" Bokar wondered.

"I want to speak with Captain Harold Patton."

Bear Cat inter-communications were rather quick, thanks to Major Femur; inter-Vietnam communications didn't have his expertise. On the twelfth attempt, Bokar connected.

"Captain Patton, can you guess who this is?"

"Cooby." I heard his excitement. "Couldn't forget your voice."

"I couldn't forget my first operations officer."

"How's everybody at Bear Cat?"

"Whoever hasn't rotated out is doing great, Sir; how about you?"

"Doing fine myself; Long Binh is tame."

"New job suits you, huh?"

"Which one; pilot or reporter?"

"Read the stories; some are pretty good."

"Told you I could use the help of an English professor; offer still stands, you know. Come up and you'll become an E-6 the same day."

"Interested in a really great story?"

"With Charlie calling all the shots, I can't invent too much more. What you got, Cooby?"

"Martha Raye."

"Fill me in; I'm all ears."

"The lady with the big mouth has agreed to help the 5$^{th}$ Division kick off its R & R program. She'll be there as you photograph Colonel Fang signing up Sergeant Turtz. He'll be the first 312$^{th}$ participant. A picture in *Stars and Stripes* can't hurt in launching the morale-building plan down here."

"Couldn't hurt the 5$^{th}$ either."

"Timing is very important, Captain Patton. Miss Raye leaves Bear Cat in two days. Can you hop a wayward UH-1D and get here by 9 A.M. tomorrow?"

"Cooby, I'm a pilot, remember?"

"The men of the 5$^{th}$ will be forever grateful, Sir."

"Turtz going to Hawaii to visit his wife?"

"He don't know he's going anywhere yet."

"What...How do you expect him to sign?"

"If you really want a great story, Sir, you'll have to do a bit more than take a picture. Still interested?"

"Only if you tell me how to coerce Turtz."

"Sell Elmer Fudd on how top brass feels about morale, and amplify a bit on high-ranking enlisted participation. Your camera, the presence of Martha, and a follow-up story in *Stars and Stripes* will do the rest."

The captain paused with his quick retorts, and asked, "You sure you don't want to come up here?"

"And leave all this fun down here?"

"Be there at 9 A.M., Cooby...with notepad, camera, and a mouthful of magic."

"Thanks, Sir. That'll give ample time to, let's say, *establish a mood*. Probably won't see you, but I will be reading you." I smiled as I hung up the phone.

About a month later, in September, a small news article appeared in the middle of *Stars and Stripes*:

## 5$^{TH}$ DIVISION ADDRESSES MORALE

Miss Martha Raye watches First Sergeant Turtz as he signs as the initial participant in the 312$^{th}$'s Assault Support Helicopter Company's R & R program. Accepting the document is the Pachyderm Commander, Lieutenant Colonel Robert Fang, Jr. Turtz will be flown to Taipei, Taiwan, compliments of the United States Army, where he will enjoy five days of Rest and Recuperation. Miss Raye, touring with the 5$^{th}$ Division, was happy to appear as testament to the worthwhile program.

Written by: Captain Harold Patton

The story was printed underneath a picture capturing Colonel Fang, Sergeant Turtz, Specialist Philip R. Street, and Miss Martha Raye. Before the news became print and on the day it hit the newsstand at Bear Cat, Charlie never varied in waking up the compound with two rockets.

# CHAPTER 17

## MOLLY AND DUCKER

---

The ending of the monsoon season at Bear Cat created an upsurge in 5$^{th}$ Division activity. There was one reason why. Charlie was alive and well and somewhere on the other side of the walls surrounding the compound. There was an increase in support missions for the outlying 5$^{th}$ Division sites. He, meaning Charlie, was out there and nothing confirmed it more than the two incoming rockets, every day since the recapture of Blackhorse and Ghia Rae.

Major Frankel's order to remain open twenty-four hours a day stayed firm and there was little time for camaraderie between veteran Pachyderms. Most everyone in the 312$^{th}$ had a twelve-hour on and a twelve-hour off shift. Clerks like Frock, Boremba, and myself worked 14 to 18 hours per day.

By October of 1967, with normal tropical temperatures sweltering near 100 degrees, I was amazed at how often operations had to dispatch a courier to the mess hall to obtain more coffee grounds. Everybody took turns, but when mine came, I'd call either Frock or Boremba and set up some type of casual meet at the supply center.

"It's a pain in the ass for supply to always have coffee ready for so many crews, but I sure do like it when I can chew the shit with you guys," I told my Benning buddies when I met them at our prearranged spot.

"Don't envy the chore, Cooby, but Timmy and I like it a lot when you come up," Frock told me. "Seems to be the only time we can visit anymore."

"Run out faster," Boremba chimed in.

"What's the latest from the City of Al Capone?" I asked Tim about his home town of Calumet City, Illinois.

"No mail."

"How about you, Prez? Letters from Bunny keeping the night steamy?"

"I'm lucky if I get one a week," he responded. "Femur tells us most of the mail around here comes to you."

"Can't help it I was born the last of nine. With my brothers and sisters, my ma, and all her grandchildren, I won't ever catch up on writing back." The task of reading alone took up a lot of time.

"What's the latest from Omaha, Cooby?" Frock asked as he sipped on lukewarm salted tea. With nearly eight months of in-country service, Frock couldn't mask his dislike for the liquid.

"This," I removed an envelope from my pocket. I showed him a picture sent by my sister, Cecelia.

"Who's the baby boy?" Frock looked at the photo and gave it to Tim.

"My new nephew; my sister's ninth child."

"How many times are you called uncle?" Frock knew about my large family.

"Thirty two...but this one is special."

"Why so?"

"'Cause his name is Daniel Joseph. Last month, I became his godfather through proxy," I proudly informed them.

"I'll never be an uncle, Cooby; both Bunny and me are only children. Must make you feel good."

"Does, Prez." I took the picture back from Tim. "Could happen to you though. Your sister Bernadette might surprise you."

"Won't happen."

"I don't know, Timmy; she might."

"Won't marry."

After a small pause, Frock asked, "What's in all of the packages you get?"

"Last week it was cans of shoestring potatoes from my mom; this week boxes of Luden's Cherry Cough Drops from my sisters, along with a real surprise."

"What was it?"

"A box with twenty-five letters from the sixth grade class at my old elementary school...and they each want an answer."

"You don't have enough time to answer your relatives, Cooby. How you gonna reply to the kids?"

"With a little help from my Benning buds and some more from those two guys in my hooch, March and Molline."

"I suppose I could try one," Frock offered.

"Me too," Boremba surprised me.

"Cope said he'd do a few too...the letters are on the cot in my tent. Help yourselves. Better get these grounds down to the flight line. Pachyderm Operations doesn't run on aircraft fuel alone."

Later that night, four men in the first tent in the second row of tents nearest the orderly room were instructed by Frock and Boremba in composing letters; Cope had persuaded second shift operations personnel to do the same, and I was watching March and Molline undertake the task in the second tent in the second row of tents nearest the orderly room, as I penned my own reply to my niece, the sixth grade culprit.

Paul March was tall and Frank Molline short. Both men rotated into the $312^{th}$; both were allocated to flight line operations although their military specialty had little to do with aviation.

Six feet, three inches, March was one of the tallest men in the unit and had to duck each time he came into our tent. I nicknamed him, "Ducker"; some called him, "Stilts." Everyone living in the second tent, in the second row of tents nearest the orderly room, bumped into two feet that extended well over a regular government-issued cot. Paul's size forced second glances, yet no one complained. He was the weapons specialist for the $312^{th}$ and $713^{th}$ and arrived with an assistant.

Frank Molline hailed from New York City and spoke with the New England accent of his partner. What Ducker did for height and brawn, Molline did for small and puny. The man was a foot shorter than his comrade, had thick black hair, a swarthy Italian complexion, and resembled a perfect mix between Perry Como and Omar Sharif. Molline came with his own nickname: "Molly."

The two made quite a team; taking care of an arsenal in a tropical atmosphere was no mere challenge. By October of 1967, the two men's inseparable presence generated one more nickname for the pair: "MDs," machine-gun doctors.

Each morning, the MDs had a pile of weapons available for each mission; each night, the duo secured the returns. During the day, they worked at the ammo dump, a place they designed. Ducker envisioned a U-shaped pattern made from unused metal conex containers, the type that brought the $312^{th}$'s and $713^{th}$'s equipment to Vietnam, and also a type with a lockable door. In its center was a metal bathtub filled with solvent; directly in front of it, the counter where exchanges took place.

Molly, a dock-stevedore/welding-artist from the Big Apple, fashioned it all. Using careful rotation, the two ensured a reliable supply of effective weaponry.

I became very attached to the two; I called Paul by his nickname, Ducker, and I called Frank by the moniker he arrived with. Ducker addressed me as Cooby; Molly never did. He called me "Scooby."

Every other day, when I had early morning charge of flight line operations duty, Molly and Ducker would stop by prior to opening the ammo dump. Both wanted a cup of Benning Brew. Molly came in humming or whistling a song made famous by Frank Sinatra: "Strangers in the Night."

"Where's Ducker?" I inquired of the man humming "Scoo-be-do-be-do."

"Taking a leak; he'll be here in a flash...is your coffeepot ready for business?"

"Isn't fully perked yet."

"How many missions today, Scooby?"

"Cope logged ten last night."

"We had ten yesterday; think division will ever ease up?"

"Don't ever know what division will do, Molly. By the way, *thanks*."

"For what?"

"Taking the time to answer a few letters."

"Anytime, Scooby, anytime."

"Anytime for what?" Ducker came in and darted for the flight line pot.

"For the letters, Ducker. Thanks."

"Was kind of fun. Got any more?"

"Who knows what will arrive from Omaha," I answered as the light on the pot flashed on.

"Scooby, I'm sorry you can't go on R & R with your Fort Benning buds. You're stuck with me and Ducker."

"Couldn't be in better company, Molly, unless I hopped on a chopper to Hue to spend some time with Madilla."

"I'd rather meet my wife, Joanne, in Hawaii," Molly confessed.

"How about you, Ducker? What would you rather do?"

"I don't have anybody; I just want to get away from this place."

"That settles it, guys; let's plan a blast in Penang...ever been on an island, Molly?"

"Coney Island, but it's no paradise with hotels right on the beach."

"Street tells me we'll be the first three going on R & R since Turtz went to Taipei."

"Scooby, think $250 will get me by?" Molly asked.

"How much you got, Ducker?"

"Three hundred dollars."

"I got $375, and if $925 can't buy us a good time, we got a problem."

"The only problem we have, guys," Ducker remarked, "is waiting seven days before we take off."

"Then we'll kill the next seven days," Molly asserted just before the two left for the ammo dump.

None of us had to concern ourselves with any one of the 168 eager hours before R & R. Nor did the Pachyderms. The 5th Division cranked up and requested the use of all fourteen aircraft the week before we left. In spite of the stepped-up activity, Charlie continued with his incessant, two-each-morning rockets. By November 7, 1967, our outfit had achieved 40% of the record-breaking totals of sorties, men airlifted, and food and ammunition delivered to field sites as compared with October.

Not one single grueling tally concerned me on November 8, 1967. On that morning, near 9 A.M., three men, dressed in wrinkled summer khaki military uniforms, walked out of the second tent in the second row of tents nearest the orderly room, across the company area, and to a waiting jeep that would take them to a UH-1D flight patterned for Saigon. Fourteen Pachyderm helicopters headed off earlier that same morning, on fourteen combat missions, leaving few to see us off. Of those who did, all stared in envy.

The flight into Saigon was the first time any one of us saw Bear Cat from 2000 feet up. I thought it appeared much like farmland USA; everything looked arranged and orderly. When the twenty-minute flight ended, I ached to run to The Street of the Flowers, but a Branif Yellow Banana beckoned and I joined 299 other R & R bound men.

By 10 A.M., all passengers were buckled up and felt the power of the jet thrust itself upward and toward Malaysia. This bird was no Chinook or UH-1D: it was a clean, lighted, air-conditioned intercontinental jet with the wonderful smell of almost forgotten, real American food. Following takeoff, unlimited liquid refreshments were served and an hour into flight, the passengers were treated to an ample portion of filet mignon wrapped in bacon and complemented with baked potato, real butter, real cream, fresh bread, and crisp salad. During the four-hour flight, everybody imbibed, and everyone was given a nametag indicating a destination. Molly's, Ducker's, and mine read: Penang.

Upon touchdown, all passengers were tanked up, and no one heard the announcement broadcast over the plane's public address system. "Attention. Attention, please," went unnoticed four times as the big banana taxied to a halt. When it came to a complete stop, the pilot had no choice but to shut down all power, including interior lighting, to gain effectual attentiveness. The liquor had worked well to incite every soldier anxious for a little liberation.

"Attention. Attention, please," the fifth notice had reached ears forced to hear. "If your destination is the Island of Penang, deplane now; if your destination isn't Penang, remain aboard for continued flight."

I heard the groans of 250 men, and felt the glee of 49 others as we scrambled to the tailgate. Molly, Ducker, and I fought to stick together as the group was escorted to awaiting buses. "Is this Penang?" Ducker asked. I was not sure where we were, but on the fifteen-minute ride, I thought I was revisiting Saigon. Everything looked alike. The place was crowded with a sea of people darting everywhere and in between endless rows of low-story buildings.

The transportation led us to the Penang Information Center, where a United States Army sergeant directed us to enter an auditorium. Once inside, "hurry up and wait," presented itself. We were given an orientation on all the do's and don'ts of correct behavior in Malaysia, followed by two warnings: "You are visitors; if you break internal laws, the Malay Government will prosecute. In addition, if you are not present and accounted for at 8 A.M., here at the information center, five days from now, you will be held AWOL and a warrant issued for your arrest." Several hours later, fifty men were released on one dock on the Island of Penang.

Someone had notified the residents of our arrival; I saw at least 20 indigenous Malaysians standing near what appeared to be cabs. Molly zoomed in on one that could even capture the attention of a blind man.

He was tall, very thin, had a deep brown complexion, and when he parted his lips, his teeth radiated like the tubes of a fluorescent bathroom light fixture. He was poorly dressed, wearing worn shorts, sandals, and a sport shirt that had seen better days. He used broken English when he spoke, and he didn't look like a taxi driver at all.

Molly hired him on the spot.

"I take to tax-ee," he told the three as he pointed to a very used, diesel-powered Mercedes.

"What's your name?" Molly asked the man who resembled a boy who had been given a surprise birthday present.

"Nah-ame?"

"What do we call you?" Molly persisted.

"Ca...call you?"

Molly took his own finger, pointed it at his chest, and enunciated, "Molly." He repeated it again and duplicated the process for March and me, saying, "Ducker" and "Scooby."

A bright smile emerged on the Malaysian's face while he pointed to each of us and uttered, "Moll-ee, Duck-her, and Scoobee Captain, yes?"

We shook the frail man's hand, and then watched as he pointed to his own chest, saying, "Kalenda. Kalenda shows Penang to Moll-ee, Duck-her, and Scoobee Captain."

"Think he can find us some lodging, Molly?" I inquired of a New Yorker with his friendly arm around Kalenda.

"Lod-ging?" the happy employee attempted the new word. When the native spoke I understood the impediment created by knowing only one language.

"Yeah, Kalenda," Molly coached his newfound friend. "A place to stay...to sleep at night...rooms...a hotel."

"Hotel...yes, I take to *Fed-er-al-es*, Moll-ee." He opened the two rear doors of his vehicle, and then rushed for the front passenger door. "Scoobee Captain is here," he motioned.

"Why does he call me, *Scoobee Captain*, Molly?" I posed to our would-be interpreter.

"Must think you're a captain," he answered as he got into the backseat with Ducker. "Does not matter, anyway," he continued, "Ducker and me know you're not. Take us to the Fed-er-al-es, Kalenda."

I looked through a cracked rearview mirror when our taxi driver coaxed his bucket of bolts forward, and I saw black smoke belching from the car. I set aside cares once Kalenda steered the car to a crude road matching Penang's shoreline.

Coconut-laden palm trees arched forward everywhere, almost genuflecting at the blue sea they worshipped. The kneeling trees were as plentiful as fallen cones from an evergreen tree. In a natural return of adoration, the sea reciprocated by caressing the never-ending, sun-drenched beach with gentle splashes of return homage. The ongoing ritual captured many of my other senses. I could hear as the sea repaid her tribute, feel the ocean breeze soothe my skin, smell the continuous process, and survey colors as they exploded on abundant flowers. Each encounter was another taste to experience something engrossing. "Neat, wow, and oh!," became meaningless and trite exclamations; I imagined the beat-up old Mercedes to be a feather softly whisking me through the clouds.

Kalenda interrupted my reverie by stopping the taxi near one of many palm-covered cabanas intertwined over a landscape beyond belief. "Scooby Captain, want drink?"

"Yeah, Scooby Captain," Molly teased. "Let's toast our first day in paradise."

Ducker concurred and three of the four doors opened in anticipation. Kalenda remained inside the taxi behind his steering wheel.

"Come on, Kalenda," Molly encouraged our guide.

"Kalenda stays. For yous."

"For us." Molly dragged the resisting resident to a palm tree with a circular table built around it, and had to force the Malaysian to sit in one of four chairs whose legs were deeply implanted in pillows of immaculate sand. "For yous," he kept on persisting. "For yous."

Within a minute, a waiter, dressed in a casual shirt, shorts, and sandals asked, "What can I serve you?"

"What?" Molly shrugged at Kalenda, charading a rising bent elbow and a twisting wrist.

"Peen-yah-co-la-da," Kalenda smiled.

"Four piña colada?" the waiter asked.

"Four."

While we waited, Molly removed his summer khaki shirt, took off his shoes and socks, and cuffed up his pants to the knees. It wasn't very long before Ducker and I did the same, and when our refreshments arrived, we sat back and looked at something like the day after the seventh day of creation when God found a leftover and placed it where we were seated. Even the piña coladas came in authentic unshelled coconuts, severed at the top and garnished with a stick of pineapple.

"Fed-er-al-es, Scoobee Captain?" Kalenda interrupted the silent reverie.

"Fe-der-al-es," I answered him back.

"Is it on the beach?" Ducker popped up.

"No beach...in city. E & O onlyest hotel on beach...Cost much."

"*E & O?*" inquired the tall New Jersey native with his ankles buried in sand.

"The European and Oriental is a well-known hotel made famous by a writer, Ducker."

"Which one?"

"Somerset Maugham." *Of Human Bondage* was a classic, and required reading for a senior at Creighton University studying Twentieth Century Literature.

"Cost much, Scoobee Captain."

"The Fed-er-al-es, then." Ducker led the way back to the taxi, and once again, Kalenda rushed to open three doors, saving the front passenger side for Scooby Captain.

"Should we get private rooms, Molly?" Ducker wondered.

"Depends, Ducker."

"On what?"

"Girls, you dork."

"This place don't have call girls like New York and New Jersey, Molly. Does it, Kalenda?"

"Be-you-tif-ful gurles."

"We'll get three rooms," the one married man in the car announced. There weren't any objections and Kalenda smiled as we checked into rooms on the top floor of the Federal Hotel, the tallest building on the island. Each room set us back $7.50 per night. None of them were like the Saigon Grand; none of them were like the second tent in the second row of tents nearest the orderly room back at Bear Cat.

From that moment on, and for four days, three Bear Cat visitors convinced a native Malaysian to lead them to what they considered a soldier's dream. We frequented brothels, gulped gallons of beer or piña coladas, and pretended the time we were having was what we were seeking. We failed to see where we were and exhausted ourselves with inebriation and total abandon. Rest and recuperation became three B's: bars, broads, and booze. Our bodies capitulated after the third day. The three of us found ourselves sleeping it off most of the fourth day, with a pretty unanimous conclusion: "staying drunk and fucking anything wearing skirts was not a definition of manhood." I ached to hold Madilla's hand.

Frank Molline made a suggestion on the fifth day when Kalenda came to pick us up in the morning. "Why don't we do something different on our last day?"

"Like what?" Ducker, as well as me, became curious.

"Hey, Kalenda," he shouted at our taxi driver. "What do you do for entertainment?"

"An-ter-tain-ment?"

"Yeah. What do you do for fun?"

"What's fun?"

"Good times, happy times." Molly tried a few synonyms.

"Good times." He understood. "I go to special place."

"To watch the *gurles*?" Ducker smirked.

"No gurles...special place."

"Where, Kalenda?" Molly asked our friend.

"Other side of island...special place," he repeated.

"Scoobee Captain want to go?"

"Yes, Kalenda. Scooby Captain wants to go. Take us."

Within seconds, Kalenda coaxed the Mercedes to do an about face and aimed it in the opposite direction of the highly traveled beach and bar scene. After no time, lush growth turned into rocky terrain as our group headed for the eastern side of Penang. Our guide parked his taxi on a cliff and said, "Come, I show."

We could see and hear the ocean crashing into walls of rock some fifty feet below our perch, as Kalenda led us down the pathless precipice. We didn't know where we were going, and footing was scarce, but the three of us were determined to locate this *special place*.

About ten feet from the bottom, Kalenda executed an abrupt right turn, squeezing himself into an opening in the craggy wall. The crack in the cliff cut off all but upward vision, although we could smell the sea air and hear the pounding of waves. The crevice was thirty feet long. Once on the other side, Molly, Ducker, and I saw Kalenda's *special place*: a naturally-formed, isolated cove with one entrance.

A huge formation of rock blocked view of the sea. It cushioned a pounding surf before it smashed into a small sandy beach. The resulting private lagoon permitted only God to peek in from above.

Three of us sat down on the beach, overwhelmed with simple beauty; one of us removed his t-shirt and baggy shorts. With all of the modesty of a nudist proclaiming nature, Kalenda located a familiar spot and joined with the inviting water. "Come," he yelled.

Without a moment's hesitation, the guide's clientele stripped and joined Kalenda in the ocean, spending hours carousing as kids, skinny-dipping, playing water tag and king of the mountain. I rode Ducker's shoulders; Kalenda, Molly's. We were like schoolboys escaping to play hooky.

It wasn't until we all lay on the beach, worn out by our simple fun, that I realized a lesson of Penang. Four naked men were sprawled out on a beach. Three were half-breeds, tanned from the waist up; one was totally brown. Color didn't make a difference, and rule number four was true: "What you see is not what you get."

When our sunbathing ended, we helped each other dust off crusted sand; we joked about our water-soaked bodies and laughed, as only boys can, at our flaccid, shriveled penises. On the way back to the hotel, Ducker took a nap while Molly and I forced Kalenda to join us in a farewell dinner.

"For yous," he kept protesting.

"No way," Molly fought back. "Be there."

We dined at the hotel's restaurant, eating Kalenda's favorite: broiled shrimp. He enjoyed the meal and became humbled when we paid him the usual fee plus a large tip. "Is there something...a special gift we can give you to remember our time together?" Molly repeatedly asked.

"Friends e-nouf." He attempted to return the tip.

"There has to be something, Kalenda," Molly insisted.

"Is true...won't laugh?" a skeptical guide opened up.

"Is true...and we won't laugh," Molly reassured him.

"Kan-ud-dee doll-ur," he announced.

"You'd like a Kennedy half-dollar?"

"Yes, Scoobee Captain. A *Kan-ud-dee doll-ur*."

None of us had one; scrip or exchanged currency was all we were permitted. I promised I'd send him the gift, taking his full name and address, and writing it on a scrip, so I could follow up on my promise to Kalenda. That scrip actually became one of my Vietnam *souvenirs*.

I wrote a letter to my sister on the return flight to Saigon. She complied with my request to send a Kennedy half-dollar to Kalenda, but I never did find out if he received the present.

When the UH-1D arrived at Bear Cat, I immediately noticed one of several changes that had occurred in the week we were gone. Each berthing Pachyderm was encased in a 4-foot tall, U-shaped bunker with a similar sandbag bunker adjacent to it. Another was the M-45 holstered about the waist of the jeep driver sent to bring us to the company area. On the short ride, I noted armed men everywhere.

"Hope they clean 'em every night," Ducker commented as we got out of the jeep and walked to the second tent in the second row of tents nearest the orderly room.

None of us could avoid encountering a huge crater in the company street. The large gaping hole was five feet deep and twice as long. We sidestepped around it letting our curiosity guess at what happened, then heard a shout, "Get your three asses in the orderly room right now!" In less than ten seconds, Molly, Ducker, and I were standing at rigid attention in front of Master Sergeant Turtz.

"You shitheads have a good time?" Top eyeballed us.

"We had a great..." Ducker's response was shortened by a second verbal assault.

"Don't speak until I ask you a Goddamned question," Turtz barked. I felt Ducker's reaction and sensed my own; I didn't dare to even look at Molly.

"Visit the bars, drink a lot of booze, fuck all the broads wearing skirts?" he continued to insult us.

I wanted to yell back, "none of your damn business," but Ducker opened his mouth by repeating, "We had a good time."

"I didn't ask you if you had a good time," Sergeant Turtz yelled for everyone on the compound to hear, just as Major Frankel entered the orderly room. Ducker didn't utter another word; Molly and I kept our lips buttoned as Turtz continued. "You fucked up bad, you New Jersey punk." He slammed a forefinger into Ducker's chest. "Do you know what your fuck-up could have cost this outfit?"

"No, Sergeant Turtz, I don't."

"Don't play cute with me, smart mouth; I'll bust you down to nothing."

"Sergeant, I don't know what you're talking about."

"Shut the fuck up," Turtz screamed. "I told you not to speak until I asked you a Goddamned question."

"What's the trouble?" Major Frankel intervened.

"No trouble, Sir. Just some old-fashioned discipline for a soldier who screwed up royally."

"At ease," Frankel ordered. We relaxed but remained tense. "Sergeant, have you informed these men why they're here?"

"I shouldn't have to, Sir."

"Then tell *me* why they are here."

"Because he locked up our weapons in the metal conex containers at your flight line, Sir, and this assistant didn't have the presence of mind to remind him, and this operations clerk, who oversees both, forgot about a small thing like the key." Turtz plunged his finger into each of our chests for added effect.

Major Frankel looked at March and asked, "Did you lock up the weapons before you went on R & R?"

"Yes, Sir, I did."

"And did you take the Goddamned keys with you when you left?" Turtz exploded in another outrage.

"Calm down, Sergeant; that's an order," Frankel told Top. He looked at March and asked, "Why?"

"Sir, I was ordered by Sergeant Foone to secure all weapons during any absence from my duty post."

"Did you take the key with you on R & R?"

"No, Sir. I hung the key on the post beside the front door of the orderly room. It's where I have logged it 'in and out' since I've been at Bear Cat." March pointed and Frankel went to examine.

"The log is initialed 'PD,' and dated 11/7; the key is hanging on a nail, Sergeant Turtz."

"Your help in clearing this matter up is appreciated, Major Frankel, Sir," an embarrassed First Sergeant Turtz awkwardly retreated and without so much as an "I'm sorry" or "Glad you had a good time," he announced, "Dismissed."

Molly, Ducker, and I wasted no time in exiting, and as we scurried to our tent, I recalled a time when Turtz intimidated me. This time the man humiliated one of my friends, and I vowed there'd be no third. Our startling return became worse when we observed another crater in the company street between rows two and three.

I snapped out of depression when I saw eight letters and two packages on my bunk. Nine had the return address of Omaha; one rose colored communiqué, came from the Grand Saigon Hotel.

I silently held the one letter in my hand, afraid to open it. I imagined The Street of the Flowers and I could smell Madilla.

A pressed pink flower fell to the floor as I opened the folded page inside the envelope. I had seen the live version of that flower twice: once on top of a pile of my freshly cleaned clothes; a second time, in Madilla's hair. The note was brief and said everything I wanted to hear:

Danny—Come to Saigon—Madilla

I didn't open either of the packages nor did I read any mail from home. I lay back on my cot and fell asleep, bonding with a folded note holding a pressed pink flower from the Saigon Grand Hotel.

I was awakened by the charge of quarters at 4:30 A.M.; Cope had covered for me for a whole week, and I was back at Bear Cat.

Molly was humming "Strangers In The Night" when he came into operations. "How many today?"

"Thirteen, Molly. Where's Ducker?"

"Out taking a pee...coffee ready?"

"Help yourself, Molly."

"You okay, Scooby?"

"Never felt better...better take two cups; knowing Ducker, he's already started to inspect all the weapons."

Molly left whistling my tune just as the first load of pilots came. God, I'm glad to have Cope, I thought. He'd not only double timed for me for a whole week, but made sure that my first day back would go easy. And it did. By 7 A.M. all thirteen birds took off without a hitch, the CQ of operations had been relieved, and I began to bury myself in the backlog of paperwork.

"Look who's back." Cope startled me at 7:30.

"What the hell are you doing here?"

"Yesterday I would have answered that question with 'watch your mouth, E-4'; today, on the other hand, I have to be careful how I address an E-5."

"You shouldn't be here...what happened while I was...what did you say?"

"Congratulations, Specialist Fifth Class...and I came here for one reason, and it wasn't to find out if you had a good time in Penang." Cope walked over to his desk. "I came here to give you these." He had removed a small box; in it were two tarnished E-5 rank plates. "I wore these a lot of years, and I want you to have them." My eyes fixed on his E-6 emblems as he replaced mine with his old ones. "I know you'll wear them well."

I was speechless.

"My name didn't make it to the promotion board." He read my thoughts. "Yours did." He took a step backwards, and did something I rarely saw him do. He saluted me.

"It's not fair, Cope."

"Cooby, my agreement was to come over, get promoted to E-6 with the possibility of E-7. I got promoted."

"It's still not fair. I have a rank it took fifteen years for you to get."

"You're forgetting your own rule four: 'What you see or hear is not what you get.' If that doesn't appease a logical mind like yours, try, 'The right way, the wrong way, and the army way.'"

"But why me, Cope?"

"You found the bonus error in Elmer Fudd's records. A colonel doesn't forget something like that."

"I didn't kiss his ass."

"What makes your promotion so sweet is he thinks you did."

"I'll never understand the army way, Cope."

"Doesn't matter...now tell me about Penang."

"Think the army should rename R & R."

"To what?"

"The 'Three B's.'"

"What's that stand for?"

"Bars, booze, and broads."

"Cooby! What would your mother say if she asked you that question?"

"I won't be sharing that with her, Cope." Somehow I knew he wouldn't ask her the question either. "What happened while I was gone?"

"A day after you left we got hit by twenty rockets. Two hit the company area."

"I saw the holes."

"Turtz panicked and ordered the men to be armed for the impending invasion...personally led the charge to the weapons containment section during the Red Alert. When he got there, it was locked and he lost it."

"Holy cow!"

"He came busting in here demanding I get the Corps of Engineers to break open March's containers. The idiot kept shouting, 'I want everybody armed tonight'...as if an M-16 could shoot down an incoming rocket."

"The corps come?"

"Yeah, but it was too late...the excited men broke the containers open. Turtz handed out the weapons himself. From now on, everyone must carry a weapon." He showed me an M-45 strapped around his waist. "Yours is in the safe."

"What?"

"That's the poop."

"What good will an M-45 do me if a rocket lands on the building?"

"Beats the shit out of me, but you'll be wearing one if it does."

"It's stupid."

"No, Cooby, it's the army way."

"Twenty rockets, huh? Bear Cat get a lot of damage?"

"Not too much...I think Charlie wanted to scare us."

"Sounds like he succeeded."

"Scared Turtz, I know. Even Bosebaugh got on the radio and ordered the howitzers to pound everything on the other side of the berm. Wake up call around here is like a cap popping in a toy gun compared to the tons of explosives they dumped...and that was just the start."

"The start?"

"Bosebaugh ordered air strikes for the entire area outside the perimeter of the compound...I felt like the submerged part of a wick in a burning candle...God! The other side of the berm was brighter than sunshine."

"Holy shit, Cope."

"Security's been doubled, fortifications built around military equipment, and all leaves canceled."

"Guess it's not a good time to ask for a couple days off...I got a letter from Madilla; she invited me to come to Saigon."

"Cooby, as I see it, there are three things you can do. One is to become invisible; two would be to turn airborne and parachute into Saigon. The third fluke you have is to join Martha Raye's USO tour... but she's long gone. Even the Bear Cat gate has been closed.

"Damn it."

"Hey, E-5. I'm stuck here too."

"You didn't get a letter from Saigon."

"Sorry, Cooby. Only helicopters will be leaving Bear Cat, and I'm not too sure all of them will return."

"Don't sound good, Cope."

"Neither did the twenty incoming...and Charlie's new way of greeting us every morning."

"You're starting to scare me, Cope. What new way?"

"Pecking away at us with two morning rockets worked like a dripping faucet in a bathroom; twenty rockets at a time is Charlie's way of flushing a toilet. Charlie's going to increase the water flow."

"In what manner, Cope?"

"Don't know; wish I did. What I know is I need sleep. See you later this afternoon."

After Cope left, I realized I didn't thank him for his way of saying congratulations; I also noticed an M-16 standing at attention near the radio operator. I strapped up with my newly assigned hardware and strangely felt the metal gun radiate cold next to my thigh. I will send her a note explaining everything, I thought, while I began to bury myself in the backlog of paperwork.

# CHAPTER 18

## CHANGES

---

I was on duty for ten plus hours the first day after I returned from Penang when Cope reappeared later in the afternoon. When he showed up, he brought someone along.

"Cooby, want you to meet Specialist 4th Class Thomas Bealy, the finance clerk for the 312th and 713th. Bealy's the guy you've been sending all those pay requests to."

"So you're the clerk who refuses to authorize flight pay." I shook his hand.

"In person, and right from Georgia's heart. Nice to meet ya."

Bealy was my height and matched my weight; his arched eyebrows outlined two deeply set brown eyes while pointing the direction to more than a nose. His skin was very light and somehow defied the tropical climate of Bear Cat. When he opened his thin lips to speak, he showed a smile empty of one front tooth. Like Boremba, his fatigues mantled on a slender frame.

"Where do I park my paperwork?" He referred to files in the back of Pachyderm 3, our operations jeep.

"Check him in next to you, Cooby," Cope ordered.

"Okay, Bealy, follow me." I led the man into the third section of operations and showed him a desk butted next to mine.

"Plenty of room here," he approved.

"Need some help unloading?"

"*Sons of Dixie* don't refuse help." Bealy's drawl was unmistakable.

"Can I ask you a question, Bealy?"

"Sure enough."

"Why do you keep rejecting the 'Request For Flight Pay' forms that I send to finance every month?"

"No documentation, no pay," he answered. "Even an E-5 like you should know the army way."

"Sucks, doesn't it?" The Georgian caught me off guard.

"More than little piglets on a Southern farm," the man agreed. "Might have an old-fashioned remedy though; sent a few inquiries. If they're the right ones, there's gonna be be a big bunch of enlisted flyboys with stacks of scrip on next payday."

"Good luck."

"Between you and me, one of us will get the men paid." The tone in his voice was positive and reassuring.

"Why don't I move the jeep to the back door? We won't have to lug your files so far."

"Good thinking, I'll wait here."

I went outside and drove the jeep to the rarely opened door. Bealy propped it open, and we began to move his files inside. "You do have a lot of them, Bealy."

"Paying 800 men each month takes a lot of regional pine trees. Thanks for the help," he added after the last box was stacked.

"Welcome to the 312th, Bealy."

"Shucks. I don't need a welcome to an outfit I've been with since day one."

"Since day one?"

"Fifth Division lassoed my behind right after I finished finance school and attached me to the 176th at Benning. Yours was my second set of pay files. Mine were the first."

"Before Colonel Fang's?"

"Yes, Suh!"

"I don't remember seeing you at Benning."

"Wasn't around the company area."

"Where were you?"

"In the day, I was at battalion finance; at night, my wife Rita and I lived in allotted housing."

"Where were you when the 312th arrived here?"

"Turtz sent me directly to 5th Division finance...been there making 'the Eagle shit' until upper command ruled to expand the S-3 section. Most finance clerks in the 5th have been booted back to company level."

"Got a hooch yet, Bealy?"

"First tent in the second row of tents."

"Second tent; same row."

"Kiss my dick...we're neighbors."

"What do you like to be called?" I asked the man with a gap in his smile.

"The guys at finance call me, 'Ma.' They say I watch my pay records like a hen watches her chicks...and speaking of records, I better get my ass in gear. Headquarters wants three sets of records returned ASAP. First priority for men transferring out is pay files and when those personnel are officers, the army wants them yesterday."

"We have officers transferring out?"

"Fang, Jones, and Tyndal," he casually remarked while searching for the files.

"Elmer Fudd is transferring out?"

"Who's Elmer Fudd?"

"Our own *flying dud*, Ma. Know who's replacing him?"

"All I know is I have to get his, Jones's, and Tyndal's records back to finance and that I'll be getting six more. Once I get that done, I can start thinking about the next problem."

"What's your next problem, Ma?" I used his handle for the second time.

"Turtz assigned me to operations and made me, 'Awards and Decorations' clerk. I can't scratch out a lousy letter to Rita let alone write some fancy stuff for an award."

"Maybe I can help you, Ma. My major in college, just before I enlisted, was English."

"Kiss my dick! Is this my day or what? That's plain neighborly."

"Can't promise much, but I can try."

"Told ya. *Sons of Dixie* never refuse..."

Bealy's words were cut off by an explosion happening close to the operations building. The accompanying flash made daytime look dull and thunder sound more like a lady finger firecracker. No one noticed the smoke that poured into the building; we hit the floor instantly. Within ten seconds, another explosion shook operations. Cope yelled, "Get to the bunker," and everyone inside crawled toward the doorway next to the radio station. A bunker had been recently built, designed to hold six men. The eight foot sandbag bunker was parallel to operations and one of its ends was near a trap door concealing the radio set. Cope was the last one in and positioned himself near that trap door. We heard two more explosions; neither were as close as the initial ones.

After a tense few minutes, Cope opened the trap door and secured the hand mike. "Any Pachyderm aircraft, this is Pachyderm control. Bravo Charlie (Bear Cat), undergoing mortar attack. Do not attempt landing. I say again..." he repeated the transmission three times. Moments later, the compound's sirens blasted Red Alert.

Cope ordered everyone to "keep calm and stay put"; I didn't obey and cautiously peeked out the other entrance. When I looked toward the Pachyderm heliport, I viewed two Chinook aircraft aflame; in their backdrop, closer to the edge of the landing area, bursts of fire were reaching to touch the sky.

"Cope," I shouted, "two Chinooks have been hit and I think the refueling dump as well. One side of the runway in on fire."

"Keep your head down, Cooby," he shouted as a fifth rocket rocked Bear Cat. "Pachyderm 6, this is Pachyderm control, over. Pachyderm 6, Pachyderm control, over," he repeated into the hand-held mike.

"Pachyderm control, this is Pachyderm one-zero-niner, over."

"Pachyderm one-zero-niner, control. Fly over Bravo Charlie. Do not land. I say again, do not land. Under mortar attack. Relay to other Pachyderms. Over."

"Control, one-zero-niner. Understood. Roger. Wilco, out."

"Break. Break. Pachyderm 6, Pachyderm control, over," Cope attempted another call.

"Who's Pachyderm 6?" Bealy asked me.

"Colonel Fang, Ma," I answered then remembered we had confiscated the radio in his jeep. "Cope, Fang don't have a radio. We took it for Frankel, remember?"

"Major Femur fixed that problem a week ago, Cooby," he notified me. "Pachyderm 6, control, over." He tried again.

The radio remained uncomfortably silent as two more incoming rockets hit Bear Cat. The surprise attack used up forty-five unforgettable minutes, and when the "all clear" sounded, we sheepishly exited the bunker to see armed men rushing to the berm. Moments later a squadron of utility helicopters, heading in the exact direction, overflew Pachyderm Operations. As I listened to the pop of aircraft gunfire, I realized the significance of the cold M-45 leaning against my thigh. Army way, or not, the metal felt reassuring.

"Where was Fang?" I asked Sergeant Copelet. Before he could respond, Major Frankel was inside operations issuing out orders.

"Get some ambulances to the pad, form a crew to help out, and stay glued to the radio, Cope. I'm going to the heliport. Get Pachyderm 3, Cooby," he ordered.

I raced to the jeep parked by the back door where I had left it and drove to the front of operations. When I got there, I saw the cavity caused by the first rocket. I maneuvered around it and waited for the major. I clutched heavy on the four banger, dug a little asphalt, and darted to the Pachyderm pad.

What neither of us could avoid was a creek of fire. Flying debris punctured a corner of the rubber container holding aircraft fuel, forcing it to gush forth into the drainage ditch paralleling the entire runway. It and the manmade ravine were aflame.

"Thank God the fuel supply ruptured in that corner," Frankel observed. "If it had been anywhere else we would be driving on flaming tar."

"Look at the height of those flames, Sir."

"Charlie won't have difficulty finding more aircraft, if he decides to hit us again...not a damn thing we can do either," he commented. Refueling personnel were helplessly staring at the singeing sight. "Go to the first Chinook."

I steered the jeep to Pachyderm 107; it had sustained a direct hit. One incoming landed between the two sets of rotary blades effectively splitting the aircraft in half. Dark smoke was rising from a jagged hole blasted into the roof of its belly.

"Pachyderm one-zero-seven is no more, Cooby...fuselage has been blown apart." We gawked in disbelief as two men emerged from the bunker built alongside it. They were helping a wounded man. They were able but shaken; the victim was groaning in pain. His upper torso had been torched; the exposed flesh on his arms looked like burnt plastic. Frankel got on the radio and requested ambulance assistance.

"Bennie's inside, Sir; he wouldn't leave," the victim managed to tell the major. "He ain't moving."

I followed Major Frankel to the charred remains of the helicopter. When we looked inside the tailgate, we saw the lifeless body. He was lying face down on the floor. His body had been scorched an ashen black. The introductory smell of burned human flesh was an unforgettable experience.

"Let's get him out of there, Cooby!" Frankel ordered. Without a moment's hesitation, he put his hands under the man's arms and motioned for me to grab his feet. We placed the remains on the tarmac. Within minutes, two medics from an ambulance had sealed PFC Bennie Zirch in a body bag. I didn't need an explanation for the face masks they wore.

"Take me to the other one." Frankel ignored the same urge to vomit that I was trying to hold back.

The rear end of 101 had been rocketed and was ablaze when we arrived. A mortar landed in the center of the helicopter's tail rotary blades. They were reposing on the ground, disconnected by impact. The blast can opened the aircraft's ass end breaching the fuel tanks. The fire was melting Pachyderm 101 before our eyes.

"Hope they got off," Frankel whispered to himself. I overheard his prayer and couldn't hold back gagging. When my reactions subsided, I asked the major, "Why, Sir?"

"Cooby, Charlie just showed us who is 'king of their mountain.'"

Looking around, I could tell he was right. Bear Cat had been hit in vulnerable places. The brief excursion to our flight line left unmistakable marks. I could count one body bag, a burn victim, two destroyed helicopters, a demolished refueling depot, and a wall of flame making my interpretation of Dante's Inferno look like a minor brush fire.

"What happens now, Major Frankel?"

"Depends on Wesley Right, Cooby."

"Who, Sir?"

"The 312<sup>th</sup>'s new commanding officer."

I had forgotten about the replanted finance clerk and his need to expedite three sets of pay records; one of the records belonged to Lieutenant Colonel Fang. "I know I am an enlisted man, Sir, but may I ask you a question?"

"Fire away, Cooby."

"Is it prudent to rotate our commanding officer, his executive officer, and your XO, all in one fell swoop? I've been told Fang, Jones, and Tyndal are rotating."

"It's the army way, Cooby." Like Cope, Major Frankel had been around a lot longer than me.

"These three men are 75% of our top command, Sir."

The skipper of the 713<sup>th</sup> didn't reply; while heading back to operations, three vehicles approached. The lead truck was a half-ton pickup with four armed guards. So was the third. The middle vehicle was the jeep issued to Pachyderm 6, Lieutenant Colonel Robert Fang. We stopped and so did the column of three.

"Major Frankel, I've decided to vacate my post early; you are in command until Right arrives," Elmer announced, then motioned for the driver to proceed. I watched Major Frankel salute the exiting Fang, using his middle finger, right hand pointing upward.

"Ever piss in the wind, Cooby?"

"Once or twice, Sir; never at a rat leaving a ship."

"Sums it up pretty well, Cooby, but I'm more worried about casualties...Those bastards always seem to know how and where to strike."

I didn't comment; I hurried Pachyderm 3 along. There wasn't much more to say. When we arrived, Cope was loaded with chiming telephones, incoming radio transmissions, and one relocated finance clerk who was frantically searching through files strewn over the floor.

"I'm temporary CO, Cope; you're in charge here," the major announced.

"Fang stopped here on his escape path," Cope guessed.

"What'd the son-of-a-bitch want?"

"His pay records, and an assured recommendation for the Legion of Merit Award."

"He ask you?"

"No, Sir; went directly to the finance clerk."

"What's his name, Cope?"

"Specialist 4th Class Tom Bealy."

"Specialist Bealy." There was no interpretation needed from the tone of the major's voice.

"Yes, Sir." Bealy appeared front and center.

"I'm your CO now, son, and I'm ordering you to do two things. First, if anyone requests Fang's records, send the person to me. Second, forget any awards or decorations for the former commander. Do you understand?"

"Yes, Sir." Bealy appeared relieved.

"Cope," Frankel turned to Sergeant Copelet. "Keep our birds from roosting for as long as you can. I'll be up at the orderly room assuming command and having serious talks with Division Intelligence."

After Frankel departed, Cope did what came natural to him. He took control, and he began by putting everybody in operations to work. "The mind can't occupy two thoughts at the same time," he announced, "so go find something to do." The philosophy worked just as it had at Benning. It worked throughout the resultant strafing, scorching any twig that dared to move on the outside of Bear Cat's perimeter. The combined efforts of army and air force made anyone living inside Bear Cat feel as though they were in the middle of a forest fire yet safely surrounded by a moat of dirt called, the berm.

The hurried retaliation was labeled "Operation Clean Out"; when it ended, Bealy read my "Summary For the Day's Activities Report."

"Kiss my dick," he remarked. "One body bag, one burn victim, two destroyed Chinooks, and a fuel dump; where's the poop on the enemy?"

"Isn't any, Bealy."

"That don't seem right; why not?"

"For all we know Bear Cat fired on an invisible enemy who got in his licks then disappeared."

"Somebody set off those five rockets...and he can't be somebody who disappears, Cooby."

"What I do know, Bealy, is from now on everyone at Bear Cat will be either in or near a bunker and with eyes open."

"This Georgia ass will be in one...bet on it."

I couldn't agree with any remark more completely. When I heard it, I began plotting the next day's missions, and I wasn't in the debriefing room. I was near the radio console next to the bunker that spared my behind from flying debris. When it came time for me to return to the second tent in the second row of tents, I lingered, staying with the charge of quarters, who like me, resisted wandering far from the safe proximity to a sandbag shelter.

Hours later, I was back in the company area, and inside a crowded bunker adjacent to a vacant hooch. Sleep became impossible; vivid recollections of Zirch's body bag stayed in my open eyes. I was kept awake by the memorable stench of burnt human flesh. Only the good Lord knows how I ached to get into Pachyderm 3 and escape to Saigon. I needed the soothing comfort of Madilla. She was only fifty miles away but it might just as well have been 5,000.

No mortar rained on Bear Cat that night; many internal rockets exploded within me. As the light of early dawn did its best to allay the dark night of uncertainty, I rushed from my sandbag bed, and to flight operations. I did not want any more ugly memories.

Cope sensed my turmoil and didn't admonish the early arrival. He also put me back to work. "Our new CO arrives at the division pad shortly, and you're picking him up."

"Kiss my dick," I borrowed Bealy's expression. "Why me?"

"I'm the boss, remember."

I couldn't argue; Cope was the boss. I also needed a diversion and accepted driving the Pachyderm jeep to the 5th's heliport. After the UH-1D landed, I saw the biggest man I had ever seen bend to exit the aircraft. Ducker and Turtz were like munchkins from Oz compared to Major Wesley Right II, the 312th's new commanding officer. He ignored my military greeting and gingerly jumped into the jeep's passenger seat, dwarfing it into oblivion. Major Wesley Right II, was blacker than Platoon Sergeant Towie.

We silently waited for a mustached Major Cris Moel, his new executive officer, to load gear and get aboard. Nothing was said on the short ride to the company area. When we arrived, Major Frankel greeted the new CO.

"Welcome to the new command, Sir," Frankel saluted.

"Thank you, Major Frankel," Right acknowledged the greeting with a formal return gesture. "Word has it *you can fly anything and make anything fly.*"

"Don't believe everything you hear, Sir."

"Normally don't...until scuttlebutt repeats it over and over. This is Major Chris Moel, the new XO."

Frankel saluted the bearded man and shook his hand. "May I show the two of you to your quarters?"

"Major Moel can store our gear; right now I'd prefer to see my command."

"Where first, Sir?"

"Operations...everything in an aviation unit happens at flight operations first...Is Colonel Fang flying on a mission?"

"No, Sir. He left Bear Cat yesterday."

"Wasn't Bear Cat hit yesterday?"

"Five incoming; three direct hits," Frankel told it as it was.

"Fang bugged out, correct?"

"Colonel Fang left after the attack."

"Temporary CO?"

"Was," the major who could fly anything replied.

"What's our aircraft strength?"

"Twelve Chinooks, Sir."

"I was told the Pachyderms boasted sixteen, Major."

"Tactical Operational & Equipment (TO & E) authorized fourteen, Sir. Two bit the dirt yesterday; two replacements are available in Vung Tau."

"Casualty rate?"

"Too many body bags; too many wounded." Frankel pursued his honest approach to the interrogation.

"Like your direct responses, Major; we'll work together well," the new CO remarked as I parked Pachyderm 3 parallel to the crater formed the previous day.

"Ah-ten-hut," Frankel credited rank as Wesley Right II entered Pachyderm Operations.

"At ease," he softly responded as he began his own tour of the facility. He began with the oversized acetate wall map which he silently scrutinized. The new CO briefly looked into Cope's conference area, checked out the radio console and telephone networking system, inspected the wall safe, and glanced into the back third of Pachyderm Operations. When his self-guided tour was over, he headed straight for the flight line coffeepot. "Is this for anybody?" he asked.

"Twenty-four hours a day, Sir," Cope spoke up.

The new CO poured a cup, took a sip, and winced a bit. "This will do well, Major Frankel." Right's eyes traversed the room in approval. "Now take me to maintenance."

I followed the two majors on Cope's diversion, acting as the official driver. We took in the helipad, the company area, and ended up at Follin's Pizza Parlor. "When can I fly as your copilot, Frankel?" I overheard the black CO ask.

"You say when, and Cooby will schedule it, Sir."

"Cooby," Right addressed me. "Set it up tomorrow and don't take it easy on the old man...why the handle?"

"Flight Operations Sergeant Copelet gave me the name, Sir. It's his version of *Coobat*."

"Promise not to take it easy, Cooby," he cautioned as I dropped the two majors at the orderly room.

I didn't have to try. Later the same day 5$^{th}$ Division requested all twelve aircraft. Co-commander Right's flight included Dong Tam, Chu Chi, Phu Mi, Lo Duc, and a probable add-on to the twin peaks, Ghia Rae, and Blackhorse. The new commander surprised me by showing up at operations to go over the pre-flight plans hours before takeoff.

"Didn't take it easy on you, Sir." I eyed him studying my scheduling work. "You'll have to push the pedal."

"What's the *probable add-on*?"

"Twin peaks, Sir," I automatically answered.

"Pretty quick response, Specialist...what makes you so certain?"

"Common sense, Sir."

"How so?"

"Sir, most of our trouble comes from those two hills, and even I know it's easier to hole in a big pile of rocks than in a flat burned-out jungle."

"I'll take that as good advice, Specialist. Anything else I should know?"

"S-3 advises our replacement Chinooks are available."

"Where are they?"

"Vung Tau, Sir."

"See to it they are here tomorrow," he ordered. With that comment he abruptly departed, leaving the charge of quarters, Ma Bealy, and me alone.

"In my nine months here, no pilot has checked on the mission the night before," I admitted.

"In mine, I've never been a charge of quarters." He didn't have to say any more.

Memories of the daytime surprise attack were as stark as the blown-up breach in front of Pachyderm Operations. I understood his helpless feeling; anything could rain down on Bear Cat.

"Want to know something, Ma?"

"What's that, Cooby?"

"The Fifth Division, with all its weaponry, aircraft, manpower, and superior technology, can't give us the one thing we need the most."

"What we need the most, Cooby?"

"A *Snoopy blanket* to shut out the sky."

"You're right, Nebraska; air power ain't nothing when you can't find the target."

"Mind if I hang around for a while? Not ready to shut my eyes yet, Georgia."

"My eyes...and my ears...are gonna be open all night."

I lingered until 3 A.M. exchanging my fears with Bealy's. I told him of Madilla, my one night with her, the responses I'd received from Saigon, and the need I had to escape into the comfort of her waiting arms. He told me of Rita, and of his life with her in rural Georgia. How I envied what he spoke about; Bealy was married and had a better plan.

I walked back to the company area praying no surprise would fall from the sky. I went to the bunker next to the second tent in the second row of tents, and crawled inside the opening hoping my eyes wouldn't close. I expected more incoming and realized that no matter how hard we tried to locate Charlie, he had no difficulty in finding Bear Cat. None came that night and I was lulled into unconsciousness by the awesome silence.

Frock found me at 9 A.M. "Copelet needs you down at the flight line."

"Whatever Bosebaugh wants, Bosebaugh gets," Sergeant Copelet recited my limerick.

"What's Bosebaugh want?"

"Four more Chinooks."

"Division says there's only two, Cope."

"Division forgot Bosebaugh gets what Bosebaugh wants."

"Why two more than authorized strength?"

"Eight for Blackhorse, eight for Ghia Rae...tomorrow."

"All four at Vung Tau, Cope?"

"Ready and waiting."

"How do we get them here? All our flyboy officers are flying or on duty."

"Cooby, you didn't get three stripes, and I didn't get four because Captain Patton thought they'd look good on our fatigue shirts."

"Right and Frankel know?"

"Found out myself twenty minutes ago."

I went to the radio transmitter knowing the Pachyderms had two crews, made available by the recent destruction of two aircraft. I picked up the mike and hailed, "Pachyderm one-zero-one, Pachyderm control, over."

"Control, one-zero-one, over."

"One-zero-one, control. Got four, I say again, got four, great big elephants that need a place to call home real soon. Do you copy, over?"

"Control, one-zero-one. How soon, over?"

"One-zero-one, control. Elephants are homesick now, over."

"Control, one-zero-one. Go get 'em, out." Major Right's orders were clear and distinct.

"Okay, professor, what do we do now? Two crews don't add up to four," Cope told me when the radio went silent.

"Why not split the crews in half?"

"Doesn't jive with the army way, Cooby."

"Does having twelve aircraft when we need sixteen?"

"Nope!"

"Then as I see it we have only one problem, Cope."

"I'll bite...what is it?"

"Getting the crews to Vung Tau."

"You get your crews; I'll hum a few bars of 'Lola' to division command and snatch a lift to Vung Tau. If it is true 'Whatever Bosebaugh wants Bosebaugh gets,' Bosebaugh will have to give a little too."

Four hours later the Pachyderms had sixteen aircraft available; at 7 P.M., the same night, Right, Frankel, Moel, Towie, Foone, Copelet, and I were examining mission plans for the 5th Division assault on Blackhorse and Ghia Rae.

The bold plan involved the joint efforts of the air force, the 5th Division, and army aviation. Initially, a strafing by air force fighter jets was aimed to surprise the site with several repeated attacks. This assault was to be followed by a concentrated bombardment of the 5th's howitzers supplemented by two columns of flame throwers and army tanks. All sixteen Chinooks would be utilized to transport troops once the firepower ceased. This forward plan had two purposes. The first was to confirm suspected enemy; the second was to remove the threat.

The operation went off like clockwork. The air force softened the site, division damn near shrank the peaks to piles of rocks, and army aviation flew in the mop-up crew to inspect and secure the two heavily battered zones. Charlie's hiding place was unearthed and a vast supply of arms and ammunition. What wasn't found was Charlie, who signaled his invisible presence by sending two rockets to Bear Cat the night following Operation Take Over. Seven days later, and fourteen incoming later, *Stars and Stripes* published the following article:

### FIFTH DIVISION SEEKS, FINDS, AND DESTROYS

Major General Bosebaugh's Fifth Division has found and destroyed one of the largest caches of Viet Cong arms and ammunition in the history of the Corps III Operations in the Southeastern Asia Theater of War.

"Hats off" to the combined efforts of Air Force, 5th Division, and U.S. Army Aviation.

By Captain Harold Patton

The print captioned an aerial photograph of Blackhorse Mountain, taken moments after detonation destroyed weapons and ammunition found at the site. There was no mention of statistics for either side. There was no contact made with the enemy.

# CHAPTER 19

## THANKSGIVING AND CHRISTMAS 1967

---

I didn't have any difficulty with my ears during the traditional end-of-the-year American holidays. Charlie made sure everyone at Bear Cat knew he was present on the other side of the berm. His playful two-a-morning rockets continued without fail following the assault on the peaks; each was deadly, without a known source, and aimed with a precision that made residents feel as though Charlie knew more about Bear Cat than division insiders. His incessant taunting was not without effect. Each new incoming forced speculation about what would be hit next.

I did have problems with my eyes on November 25, 1967, when I was seated in a decorated mess hall with Frock and Boremba staring at a turkey dinner with all the trimmings.

"Can you believe this, Prez?" I asked the Georgian.

"I heard Major Right flew the aircraft into Saigon to get all the fixings." Frock was ready to eat.

"He did, Prez; I pre-planned the flight," I told him as my fork bottomed out into whipped potatoes and gravy.

"'Pumpin' Hocks' would never do anything like this," Frock managed a crack between mouthfuls.

"Cope told me Right helped cook the food."

"Tastes great," an appeased Boremba agreed.

"So is the company," Frock interjected. "You know, you guys, we've been together for nearly a year-and-a-half."

"Remember when we arrived, Timmy? Everyone flipped us the bird and called us *green*."

"Not *green* now."

"We're *short-timers*." Frock cleaned his drumstick to the bone. "I got less than 100 days left in country, and then it's back to Georgia and more good meals like this."

"This meal might not be all we can thank Major Right for, Prez. Cope tells me the CO is trying hard to get the Bob Hope Christmas Show to stop at Bear Cat...wouldn't that be something?"

"Think he can pull it off, Cooby?" At the news, Frock stopped eating and Boremba dropped his fork.

"He got us the turkey, didn't he?"

"Copelet say when? Who's on the tour?" Frock fired a few rapid questions at me.

"Raquel Welch, Barbara McNair, the Gold Diggers, Miss World, sports figures, Les Brown, and maybe even Delores Hope."

"Did Cope tell you when, Cooby?"

"Said it might be Christmas Eve, but..."

"Christmas Eve! Bob Hope will be here Christmas Eve?" Frock's loud reaction forced a number of eyes to glance at our table.

"Prez, you didn't let me finish," I whispered. "It all depends."

"Depends on what?" he shot back.

"Incoming rockets." Boremba surmised the situation.

"We kicked ass at the peaks...saw the *Stars and Stripes* story, Timmy!" Frock yelled at his clerk buddy..

"Prez, we found a large cache of weapons at the peaks."

"I know we did...we also destroyed the weapons...isn't that what we were supposed to do?"

"Only half, Prez."

"*Stars and Stripes* didn't report the other half."

"Figure the rest out, Prez. We missed something."

"Jesus Christ, Cooby. We blew the top off the hideout. What the hell did we miss?"

"Charlie," Boremba one-lined.

"Not one round was fired back during the assault," I informed the Georgian.

"Not even one?" a misplaced pilgrim asked. "Where'd Charlie go?"

The entire Fifth Division asked the simple question posed by Prez: "Where the hell did Charlie go?" Missions on Thanksgiving Day were three and they consisted of resupply flights. Everyone knew Charlie was out there, and everyone heard his calling cards on Thanksgiving morning. One demolished the Follins Pizza Company; although Spec 4 Follins had rotated out, the blast polished off two of his pizza ovens. The second put an end to a UH-1D in the Bosebaugh $5^{th}$ Division perpetual inventory. Later on that Thanksgiving evening, a lone incoming rocket landed on a $5^{th}$ Division beer garden. There were no casualties but it was evident Charlie was alive, well, and toying with the Fifth Division.

The sporadic attacks continued regularly after the holiday and throughout December. No one knew from where they originated yet all knew they were meant to badger, and weren't restricted to military targets, but increasingly areas such as latrines, showers, and anything representing a soldier's daily routine. When the water supply was targeted, Bear Cat residents understood the meaning behind "sweat."

In defiance, the men on the compound created a wagering pool, a Bear Cat Calcutta. For one scrip buck, printed with a name, a target, and a date, any 5th Division soldier could gamble on the growing pot. One Corps of Engineers serviceman won $500 by guessing December 10 and the Bear Cat PX; his lucky win was meaningless without a place to spend winnings. A few days before Christmas, the jug of dough grew to $2500.

"You in the pool, Cope?"

"Some pool, Cooby; everybody has picked December 24, and the stage for the Bob Hope Show."

"You have any better guesses?"

"No, Cooby, I don't. Whatever it is, you can bet your ass it'll be something near and dear, and an object no one else has suspected."

On December 24, 1967, at two in the afternoon, Mr. Bob Hope took center stage. Over 7500 men encircled the raised platform built in the middle of the Bear Cat runway. All of us stood up and applauded for five minutes as the main man appeared. Hope wore khaki knee-length shorts, a bold shirt, and a safari hat. He had an unlaced combat boot on one foot and a white sneaker on the other. Loud plaid socks covered his skinny lower legs. The comedian swung a golf club with the ease of a division infantryman parading an M-16.

"Hello, Advisors," Hope announced to the counselors of the undeclared peace action, while glaring with his famous half grin/half smile. Everyone stood up and broke into another spontaneous ovation; no one sat down again.

"Tell me..." Hope tried to calm the applause. "Tell me, fellas, if you guys are the advisors, how come I was not *advised* I'd be standing in the middle of the Bear Cat pool?" He crossed his eyes, stared at his ski-nose, and looked blankly at the crowd.

Pandemonium broke loose and 7500 GI-issued ball caps took flight; the accompanying noise diminished the blast of weapons destruction at Ghia Rae Mountain.

Hope's monologue lasted ten minutes; laughter another twenty. Robert McNamara and President Johnson topped his list of favorite victims, followed closely by Lady Bird and the "two semi-beautiful" daughters.

"And speaking of beautiful, right here, Miss Barbara McNair," he stepped into the next segment.

The gorgeous black entertainer flashed one smile and began to sing; no one in the audience doubted her version of "I Am Woman, W-O-M-A-N."

Sultan Hope and a harem of Gold Diggers followed with a dumb skit loaded with superb scenery; when sultry Raquel Welch came out to sing and dance, not one soldier could hear a word of her song. What every red-blooded man saw was the reason everyone wanted to go home. Her alluring fishnet blouse was intoxicating, and her dance was the sexiest performance anyone had seen in a long time. She was some sight, as was Miss World who embodied elegance as equally as Raquel embraced eroticism.

Hope continued the entertainment by ad-libbing with several popular sports personalities and "Les Brown and his band of renown" backed up the entire show. When the show came to an end, Hope had saved the best for last.

The veteran actor asked Barbara McNair to sing the first chorus of "Silent Night," harmonized with her on the second, and invited the audience to close the program by singing along. There wasn't a dry eye on stage and there wasn't a dry eye in the audience.

Bob Hope, and his wonderful 1967 Tour, was history at 4:30 P.M., December 24, 1967.

The 6:30 P.M. rocket dashing Bear Cat back to reality, landed on the Red Cross radio station. Known as MARS (Military Armed Forces Radio Station) the system provided emergency two-way radio communications with the States.

At 8:30 P.M., Christmas Eve, two hours after Charlie's Yuletide present, I called the orderly room from my post back at operations.

"Hi, Timmy; it's Cooby. Please inform Major Right the Red Alert has been canceled. There was just one rocket."

"Who won?"

"We'll never know, Timmy. The blast took out the MARS Station where the pot was kept, along with the two guards who were on duty."

"Oh my God!" Timmy sighed into the phone.

"Timmy, also tell Major Right, Battalion advises of a Christmas Truce. It's in effect, as of 9:00 P.M."

After I hung up the phone, I remembered Cope's earlier prediction: "You can bet your ass it will be something near and dear to us, and an object no one suspects." It was then I began to formulate my own philosophy about the difference between "Occident and Orient." I was part of an army trained to power through any obstacle; Charlie, my adversary, used a subtle, more effective approach, one based on an erosion of the will to continue.

# CHAPTER 20

## TRUCE

---

Couldn't describe the mixed feelings I had at 10:30 P.M., Christmas Eve, 1967. I had been informed by division that a Christmas truce was in effect. There would be no missions.

"Couldn't pick a better day myself," Cope told me after I notified the orderly room and hung up the telephone. "Sorry the luck of the draw has you on duty, Bokar," he sympathized with the charge of quarters.

"No big thing, Sarge," the PFC responded. "Santa isn't coming here tonight."

"Wouldn't say that, Bokar; Cooby's getting a present."

"Already got mine, the Bob Hope Christmas Show."

"You're getting another."

"I am?"

"You've got Christmas Day off...but only if you agree I get the day after Christmas off. Deal?"

"Deal."

We both felt guilty leaving Bokar and walked up to the company area.

"Really believe there's a truce, Cope?" I asked on the short jaunt back.

"If there ain't, we'll be the first notified...now go celebrate. Merry Christmas, Cooby."

"Merry Christmas, Cope," I told him, aching to head to a traditional midnight mass. The longing wasn't conceivable; Bear Cat's one-size-fits-all tent/chapel had taken a direct hit from one of Charlie's indelible incoming rockets.

I went to the second tent in the second row of tents. Molly and Ducker were celebrating the Christmas truce, and were guarding three presents that had arrived for me from home.

"Open them," a tipsy Molly instructed me.

"We know you'll share," Ducker belched.

I unwrapped the first care package. Inside was a small artificial tree. Molly began to assemble it immediately. Several plastic ornaments were in the second package and Ducker used them to trim the holiday symbol. In the last box was a Christmas tin filled with gently-wrapped, homemade kolache and a note from my ma which read: "Wish you were here to enjoy these with me." By the time I thought of sharing my special goodies, my friends had crawled to their cots and were asleep. "Merry Christmas, anyway," I whispered as I freed one treat and enjoyed the delicate pastry memory from Omaha.

Christmas Eve 1967 was unforgettable. I wasn't home, yet I could taste it. I had been entertained by Bob Hope but depressed by the undeniable havoc from an incoming. I was in the midst of a police action during the middle of a truce. I sang "Silent Night" and wondered whether it would be. I was a soldier in the United States Army who failed to locate an elusive enemy.

I fell asleep taking turns staring at an artificial tree and reading another daily letter from home. When I awoke, I did so automatically at 5 A.M., and not because a retaliating howitzer reveille or incoming rocket severed the silence. Eighty percent of Bear Cat was asleep; I found slumber disquieting. As I lay there on early Christmas morning, I glanced at the well-intentioned Yuletide tree sent by my mother. Close to its base, sitting alongside one another, was the tin container from home and my army-issued M-45. I remained in the confused state for hours until an idea crept from my subconscious mind, one implanted there by Carl Copelet: "A mind can't occupy two thoughts at the same time."

I got up and headed for the shower; with the country at truce, I prayed the watery experience would unburden my unstable state of mind. The temporary reprieve worked.

Timmy was seated outside his hooch when I returned.

"Merry Christmas, Ponderosa. Care to join me in an ethnic holiday breakfast?"

"What?"

"My mom sent me some homemade kolache."

"Ko-latt-chee?"

"Kolache are Bohemian pastries, Tim. Interested?"

"Sure."

I went into my own tent. Molly and Ducker were sound asleep. I carefully removed the special tin and rejoined Boremba. "They're really nothing but baked dough filled with a flavorful center—sort of like a donut without a hole. Got prune, poppy seed, or apricot." I showed Timmy the opened tin.

"Apricot." He reached in, picked the orange one, and took a bite. I selected a prune, my favorite.

"Good, isn't it?"

"Yes."

"Want another?"

Boremba didn't answer. He got up, and went into his hooch. When he came out, he was holding what looked like a wrapped Christmas present. He opened the box and showed off its contents.

"What is it?"

"Oplatki."

"What's *oh-plat-key*?"

"Blessed bread."

"Who blessed it, Tim?"

"Ma's priest."

"Why?"

"Polish custom."

I took a piece. It looked and tasted like a communion host. Boremba grabbed another kolache as Frock emerged. He was dressed in the most suitable garb for the climate.

"Geez, Prez, you didn't have to put on your jockstrap for us," I told the nearly naked man.

"A guy never knows when Martha Raye will show up," he quipped back. Frock sat on the steps leading into the tent and automatically reached inside my tin. "Hey, this tastes great."

"And your roving hands make my ma proud, Prez. Say, who's minding the store?"

"Major Right. Gave all the clerks the day off. Cope do that for you?"

"He gets tomorrow off."

"What do you think, General? This truce gonna last?"

"Nothing's over 'til the fat lady sings."

"Only two women I'm interested in. One's Bunny; the other is the gal on my short-time calendar. Neither one is fat," he noted. "That reminds me, guys. I have a gift for each of you."

Frock got up and went into the hooch. As he came out, he handed Timmy and me a rolled-up scroll. I unraveled my gift and looked at a sketch of a naked female body, drawn like a puzzle into ninety numbered parts. Digit three was her left breast, two was her right breast, and one, her groin. "Merry Christmas," he told us. "As of today, you can each pencil in number ninety. I'm at 66," he bragged. Prez came over with the advance party in late February 1967; Boremba and I landed in March.

"Short-Timer's Calendar...what a neat present, Prez."

"Thought you'd like it." He stole another kolache.

"I didn't think about presents, Prez." I felt bested.

"My Benning buds are the best present any guy could get on Christmas," Frock told us, adding, "I'm gonna go inside, bring out three Cokes, and we can honor the day with a toast to our friendships."

I didn't disagree and Timmy nodded his approval.

When Prez returned, carrying the sodas, I felt more embarrassed; the feeling changed to laughter when Frock planted his bare behind on the wooden step and slid into a jagged one-inch sliver. He shot straight up and tried to locate the invader. "I can't see the damn thing. Will one of you guys pull it out?" Frock executed a full 180-degree turn and backed his butt into my face, just as PFC Bokar from operations passed by on his way to the showers.

"Hope Cope never finds out about the kinky stuff you do on days off," Christmas Eve's operations CQ cracked.

"You don't understand, Bokar," Frock attempted some explanation.

"Write those words on my next 'slip' to the division medics after I return from a three-day pass and require permission for a shot in my ass." Everybody in the 312th knew the good-looking private from Peoria was a frequent visitor to the aid station.

"It's only a damn sliver, Bokar," Frock yelled back.

"Looks kinky to me...don't worry, Frock, the medics won't have any problem finding that big ass."

"Pull the son-of-a-bitch out, Cooby," Frock pleaded with me. As if I had any choice. The wounded reveler was practically straddling my face.

I yanked the harpoon out, and Frock sat down. "Don't give me any of your one-liners, Boremba," he attempted to regain composure. The glare he flashed would have halted a rocket.

"Now we're even, Prez; only a real pal gives a gift like I gave to you." I couldn't resist but another stare indicated laughter was over.

"I need a beer," Frock announced. Boremba and I hid muffled laughter as we watched the big Georgian rub his butt while reentering the hooch.

"Who's the fat lady?" Prez asked when he reappeared. The almost "ramblin wreck from Georgia Tech" brought out three beers with him.

"It's just an expression, Frock." I caught one when he tossed a Lone Star to me.

"Come on, Cooby. We're Benning Buds; you can confide in us."

"Oh, it's something that keeps appearing in the *Omaha World-Herald* my ma sends me weekly."

"What keeps appearing?" Frock chugged his beer.

"Articles about Henry Fonda's daughter."

"Jane Fonda." Frock's stance changed from embarrassed to anger instantly. "I heard about that bitch in *Stars and Stripes*. She ain't fat and she can't sing."

"*Tribune* too." Mrs. Boremba forwarded a weekly to her son from Chicago just like mine did from Omaha.

"She shoots her big mouth off with words like, 'immoral, brainwashed, baby killer,' and she's talking about me. If I spoke that way, I'd be shot as a traitor. I plain ass don't like the broad," Frock vented.

"I don't like the cracks, either, guys. What I know is something keeps putting her in the newspapers, and it makes me wonder whether the tune isn't fat with meaning."

"My ass would feel better if I never heard that name again. I'm here defending her right to dissent and I don't get the same privilege." Frock crushed his empty beer can.

"And if you had the same privilege, what would you say?"

"Give me sixty-six safe days and get me the hell out of here."

"Why, Prez? You're as red blooded as any of us."

"All we do is blast away at their real estate, only to find them slowly but surely coming back." Frock left to get another beer.

"And you, Ponderosa?"

"Can't win."

"Why not, Tim?"

"Wrong approach."

"What's the right approach?"

"Don't know."

I couldn't fault Ponderosa; I didn't know what the right approach was either. I did realize that a temporary Christmas truce would not remedy the problem. How could it? The entire 5th Division hadn't been able to locate Charlie in nine months.

Bealy, Ducker, and Molly joined the Christmas repast. We spent most of Christmas Day 1967, drinking Lone Star beer and bullshitting the time away.

The truce held.

There were no surprising rockets the next morning nor did the 5th retaliate with a Bear Cat reveille. Outside of a few test maintenance missions, and the regular chow runs to outlying sites, for all practical purposes flight line operations were closed and Bear Cat on hold. The remaining days of 1967 became same-o, same-o. Cope and I exchanged duty days but neither of us stayed later than 5 P.M.

By the time New Year's Eve arrived, the whole compound anticipated its arrival, along with the apparent cessation of the war.

What a celebration it was.

All of my previous Fourth of July's and New Year's Eve celebrations combined couldn't rival what occurred at Bear Cat, South Vietnam, midnight, December 31, 1967.

Every M-16 rifle on the base saluted 1968 by expending phosphorus tracer bullets into the Bear Cat sky. Over 7,000 singular weapons pooled together to create a gossamer work of upward-rising, orange-shooting stars, intertwining with one another to present a florescent blanket. Ponderosa, who was standing between the prez and the general, put one arm around each of our shoulders. "Best friends," he said. Boy was he right; better friends didn't exist anywhere on the planet.

Ten minutes after the beer ran dry and the 1968 salute fizzled, the orderly room charge of quarters located me and said, "Coobat, report to Pachyderm Operations immediately."

"Call Captain Tox at S-3 right away," the flight line's CQ announced as I entered operations. His words impacted me like a bucket of cold water. I can't explain why the comment was sobering. I picked up the landline and telephoned Tox.

"Sir, this is Coobat at Pachyderm Operations."

"The truce is off; division needs fourteen aircraft for missions tomorrow morning," he reported.

"What?"

"While the Fifth played, Charlie delayed. He hit Chu Chi, Dong Tam, Rock Kien, and Tan Tru. The highway to the City of Saigon is closed; so is the road to Long Binh. We are off temporary R & R, Cooby, and right back where we started."

The news shattered any idea of truce and I was forced to request the unfortunate CQ, on duty New Year's Day, to drive to Battalion S-3 to pick up mission orders from the Fifth Division. When he left, I called the orderly room.

"PFC Devlon, 312th orderly room," the man who interrupted my 1968 holiday celebration answered. The new rotatee was as green as I was when I arrived at Bear Cat.

"Devlon, this is Coobat from operations. I want you to go to the first tent, in the second row of tents, and wake up Specialist Boremba. His is the first bed to the left as you enter the hooch. Get him to the orderly room and have him call operations. Is that clear?"

"Yes, Specialist," the newcomer responded.

Three minutes later, Timmy phoned Pachyderm Operations.

"Need your help, Tim. The truce is off. Tell Devlon to locate Right and Frankel, find Towie and Austen, the platoon sergeants, and notify Sergeant Copelet. The 312th is flying tomorrow and we have only hours to prepare."

"Okay, Cooby; I'll get on..." Boremba's voice was cut off by the shattering sound of an explosion. Its impact was felt three blocks away at operations.

"Timmy, Timmy," I screamed into the landline. "Are you okay?"

There was no answer. The deadly silence scared me just as another explosion rocked the operations complex. "Kiss my dick." Bealy dove through the door. "That one came real close to having my name on it."

"Get to the bunker, Ma," I shouted.

Bealy wasted no time and I was right behind him. When we were secure, Red Alert procedures doused all the lighting at Bear Cat. We huddled next to each other inside our protective bunker frightened by more rockets exploding on Bear Cat. One hundred years passed in the thirty minutes we silently crouched together.

Both of us resisted the urge to move as the "all clear" siren wailed. Reluctantly, we peered out to see the damage.

"Charlie hit the refueling dump at the Fifth," he choked. The smell of burning oil was as thick as fog.

"That ain't all, Ma; Look around." I had attended a few night baseball games back in Omaha. Our pad was as bright as it had been the night Major Frankel and I witnessed a direct hit on our own gas pumping station.

"Pachyderm control, this is Bear Cat control, over," we heard the radio squelch as electrical power returned.

"Pachyderm control, Bear Cat control, over."

I ran inside operations and acknowledged: "Bear Cat control, Pachyderm control, over."

"Pachyderm control, Bear Cat control. All missions for tomorrow are scrapped. Do you copy, over?"

"Bear Cat control, Pachyderm control. Affirmative. Understood, out."

"Why they canceling the missions?" a confused Bealy asked.

"Can't refuel aircraft with burning gasoline, Ma. I better let the CO know. Pachyderm 6, Pachyderm control, over." Why I felt Major Right would be near the radio, I don't know. I was correct.

"Pachyderm control, Pachyderm 6. Monitored message. Unable to transmit to Bear Cat HQ. Control must relay, do you copy, over?"

"Pachyderm 6, Pachyderm control. Wilco, out."

"What's that all mean, Cooby?"

"The antenna here allows me to transmit to the twin peaks, Ma; the little wire on the CO's radio limits him to short range. He can hear Bear Cat control but can't talk back because of the distance."

"Why doesn't he come here, Cooby?"

"Suspect he's got his hands full handling the damage up at the company area, Ma."

"Was it hit?"

"Don't know, Ma; I was talking to Boremba and the line went dead."

"Was Timmy hurt?"

"I don't know; communications have been severed."

"After the celebration I went back to my hooch; Timmy told me they called you down here. Thought I'd come see if you needed help. Heard the first explosion and started to run; when the second one hit, I dove through the door. Where is the CQ?"

"Sent him to get the missions they canceled. Should be back soon. Sure hope nothing happened to him."

"Me too."

"Hey, Bealy?"

"What, Cooby?"

"Remind me to never read *War and Peace*."

"What's *War and Peace*?"

"A book by a Russian author who talks about the conduct of man during a continental war."

"Shucks, Cooby. You don't need to read that."

"Why not, Bealy?"

"'Cause we made it through a truce during the middle of a police action."

How cleverly the Georgian summed up my feelings. When dawn arrived and sunlight replaced flame, reports filtered into operations. Two body bags, seventeen wounded, a fuel depot, and three aircraft filled the awaiting area on the "Summary for the Day's Activities Report" filed daily with headquarters. There was no mention of the lone mortar that hit the swimming pool at the mellow yellow trailer house. Bealy relieved the frightened CQ and remained with me down at operations for the rest of the night.

The surprise attack was the largest that ever hit Bear Cat. Eleven rockets encored the 140,000 phosphorous tracer bullets. The counterstroke caught Bear Cat completely off guard and taught the truce-lulled compound which adversary led in the ongoing debate over ownership of terrain.

Most of the subsequent chaos subsided by 7 A.M. when a radio transmission squawked: "Pachyderm control, this is Bear Cat control, over."

"Bear Cat control, Pachyderm control, over."

"Pachyderm control, Bear Cat control. Have missions. Do you copy, over?"

"Bear Cat control, Pachyderm control. Understood, out." I had no choice but to send Bealy; we hadn't been relieved. When Bealy returned, Cope was with him.

"Where the hell were you?" I barked at Cope.

"Drunk on my ass like everybody else," he fired back. He said nothing more; he didn't have to.

"Much damage at the company area?"

"Orderly room took a hit and there's another hole in the company street. No one was hurt. Would have been here earlier but Major Right needed someone to detail a clean-up."

"What do you think headquarters wants?"

"Only one way to find out."

"We stared at the requests for five Chinooks. All of them were required to transport wounded and dead. Nothing was asked to be brought in. There were two trips each to Dong Tam, Rock Kien, Chu Chi, Tan Tru, and Ghia Rae.

When January 1, 1968 came to an end, the Pachyderms had flown eight body bags to the Saigon morgue and had transported eighty-eight wounded to medical facilities.

"Cope, I thought we scared Charlie out when we blew the lid off at the twin peaks."

"What happens to an ant hole when you step on it?" Cope asked me back.

"The ants rebuild."

"Charlie's been doing that for a lot of years."

"Where? Nobody's reported sightings."

"Everywhere, Cooby; everywhere underground."

# CHAPTER 21

## LEMANS OF HONG KONG

---

Everyone in the 5<sup>th</sup> wondered *where* underground.

Once Charlie's New Year's Day salute was finished, the present but elusive enemy disappeared. The 312<sup>th</sup> continued to resupply outlying field sites with ammunition and food, but only an occasional incoming mortar reminded Bear Cat of the invisible threat. The first day of 1968, was unforgettable; the following three weeks confirmed no enemy sightings. The Pachyderms rarely exceeded the use of six aircraft per day.

The truce-like lull worked in my favor.

The R & R program, designed to foster morale, had not expanded, in spite of the *Stars and Stripes* front page news article and the unsung efforts of Specialist Street. Less than 1% of the Pachyderms partook in the special benefit, and by January 1, 1968 the 312<sup>th</sup> and 713<sup>th</sup> were forewarned with removal of the program. The sister units were allotted 25 men per month, but in January only 5 signed up. Boremba and Copelet opted for Japan; Frock, PFC Castro, the soldier who sat with Timmy and me on the initial flight to Vietnam, and I, scheduled ourselves for an R & R to Hong Kong.

I felt a little guilty about a second R & R. The little resistance I received from Street encouraged me to go for it, although I had some thoughts about my real intentions.

I didn't have too much difficulty in recognizing the difference between trying to get a few days off to sneak to Saigon and the relative ease of signing up for a seven day R & R to some exotic army-approved resort. Without saying anything, I planned to vanish at the Saigon terminal, spend several glorious days with Madilla, and reappear on the day of my supposed return. I anticipated Frock's help.

"Does Madilla know?" he asked when I sprang the plan at the terminal.

"Not yet," I confided, "but she will when we find the telephone." We found one and Frock improvised an emergency so well the unsuspecting attendant dialed the phone for us.

"Topaz please," Frock spoke into the old-fashioned cast iron phone.

I felt excited when he handed the heavy device to me.

"Topaz, this is Buddy's friend, Danny. Remember?"

"Yes, I do, Danny. I gave Madilla all of your letters."

"Thanks, Topaz. May I speak with her?"

"Madilla is back in the Imperial City of Hue; she will not return until the end of this month," she announced. "Is Buddy doing well?"

I felt crushed but managed to say, "Buddy is fine."

"I'm glad, Danny. Where are you? Are you coming to the hotel?"

"No, Topaz," I stuttered. "I'm at the airport about to depart and I just wanted to hear...say hello to Madilla."

"I will inform Madilla of your call and please give my regards to Buddy."

"Thanks, Topaz." I hung up the phone. The look on my face was explanation enough for Frock.

"Come on, Cooby. Let's go to Hong Kong." The Georgian put his arm on my shoulder and led me to the Braniff jet. He gave no advice and remained silent until the aircraft took flight. "The first thing I'm going to do is get the biggest bed in the best hotel and sleep until noon," Frock announced to Castro and me. We had managed to snag a trio of seats; I got the window.

"And I'm going to find some Hong Kong chick and sleep with her until noon," Castro bragged. "What about you?" he asked me.

"I'll play it by ear, Castro," I advised him, spotting the stewardess starting to serve drinks. "I'd like a double scotch."

"Drinks are on me," Frock informed us.

"Thanks, Frock; you're okay," Castro replied, coming back with, "Can you get her to sit on my lap?"

"I can pay for the drinks, Castro; the rest is up to you. But I'd take note of the guard up front and the one in the rear of this jet. Neither one looks like a girl scout."

When the Braniff stewardess gave me my double, I gulped it down in one swallow.

"Take it easy, Cooby," Frock warned me. "We got all of R & R for that."

"I'll get the next round." I motioned to the hostess.

"I'll have one of his," Castro notified her.

"I'm fine," Frock said.

I poured the second double down my throat, closed my eyes, and tried to imagine the repast I might have had. I could smell The Street of the Flowers and the pull on my heartstrings damn near made me cry. Damn it, I thought.

Castro elbowed me back to reality with the offer of a third drink. By the time the stewardess returned to serve it, I had passed out from disappointment and the sudden intake of four ounces of Johnny Walker Red Label.

Several hours later, Frock woke me. We had landed in Hong Kong. Touchdown rivaled Bear Cat reveille. I didn't feel any better when we deplaned. The Hong Kong Airport had been built in the harbor, and like Saigon, Hong Kong hadn't any use for a modern sewer system. Frock became the crutch I needed; he led me to the usual army bus and supported me throughout the regular orientation. His help eased me to a taxi, and he darn near carried me into the Hong Kong Hilton.

We got three adjoining rooms on the eleventh floor. Our rooms were pure splendor compared to the Federales in Penang. Frock eased me into a plush chair overlooking the harbor. The view was breathtaking.

Hong Kong was an island. It was crowded beyond belief. The only room for expansion was upward. Up to that moment, the only knowledge I had of the oriental city was limited to the words, "Made in Hong Kong," on the back of a pack of firecrackers.

All three of us kept our stated first plans. President Frock slept until noon in a big bed, Castro found his chick, and I played it by ear. In all truth, I should say by eye. From my eleventh story perch, the ongoing entertainment happening in the harbor was mesmerizing. Seaway traffic had a heartbeat of its own accompanied by a hypnotizing color. Everything was live and in technicolor. Nighttime Hong Kong was like a gigantic blinking Christmas tree. I fell asleep in the chair overcome by the overdose of too much liquor and the spectacular show aflame in front of my eyes.

Somewhere near noon the next day, Castro had dragged Frock into my room. "You guys have to try this." He poured some of his liquid into three glasses.

"Tastes like fresh orange juice; haven't had any since Georgia," Frock guzzled.

I did the same.

"Got any more, Castro?" the president asked.

"This plus the stash in my room." Castro emptied what was left.

"What is this stuff, Castro?" the Georgian wondered.

"A Hilton Hit. Want more?"

"Sure do."

"Castro left and returned with another quart. As he filled our awaiting glasses, Frock asked, "What's in it? I know they don't grow oranges here."

"One-half vodka, one-half tangerine/mango. Wait 'til I show you my next surprise." Castro left the room. When he returned he brought his conquest from the previous night. The girl was Asian, probably somewhere near eighteen, if that much, was dark skinned with black hair and eyes. Her body was very slender, her breasts were small and looked as though they hadn't fully developed, and she wore only a sheer negligee. Castro removed it and began to fondle the girl placing Frock and me in a front seat live sex show. "She'll do anything I tell her; she's mine. Want some?"

Initially the audience was stunned; fifteen minutes later, both the Georgian and the Nebraskan found out how willing the spirit was and how weak the flesh. The Hilton Hits we drank certainly didn't discourage us, and by 2 P.M., three vacationers from Bear Cat were involved in an orgy. At one point, Castro invited the eleventh floor attendant to take photographs with his Polaroid. By 3 P.M., even the attendant was naked and involved in a four-way gangbang.

Our version of Sodom and Gomorrah didn't end. Castro insured there were plenty of the Hilton Hits, and we took our party to Hong Kong itself, where sex was clearly for sale everywhere. It didn't matter if it was a taxi, on a street, in a restaurant, or inside the trolley car taking visitors to the highest point on the island. For a price, if the imagination could envision it, decadence became a reality.

No one forced Frock and me to participate, but boy did we indulge. Castro imagined having a young boy give him a blowjob, while he was eating lobster on the Aberdeen, the world's most famous floating restaurant. He got it, we watched, and consumed even more booze. The reveler induced us to join him at a "naked party" in the Cherry Bomb Bar, a nightclub not far from the Hilton. Frock and I willingly contributed the $25 per person entrance fee, and watched as he serviced two women at one time.

We escaped the brawl that erupted, and when we dragged our butts back to the Hilton, Castro had his conquest plus two more Hong Kong call girls waiting with enough liquor to flood the harbor. The bacchanalian binge survived well into early morning hours and was but a faint memory around noon the next day, when the eleventh floor supervisor knocked on the door. His tapping sounded like early morning wake-up at Bear Cat; the man was delivering snapshots of the orgy held in our adjoining rooms.

"Wait 'til you see these." Castro accepted the telling photographs. "I'm a *Latino Stud*, and I ain't alone."

I carefully eased myself into an upright position using my hands to cover the penetrating power of natural daylight; I glanced at the photos. Frock tried to ease his headache by trying to gently rub his temples.

"My mother would never go to church if she saw these." I was aghast at the explicit scenes.

"If Bunny sees these, my ass is cooked!" Prez was also shocked at the behavior captured on film.

"Burn them, Castro," I told the Latin lover as I viewed one lurid scene after another.

"They're mine; I paid for them." He grabbed the damning proof and crawled back to his room.

Frock and I were in no shape to even attempt trying to convince him otherwise, but he did agree not to show any of the pictures at Bear Cat. We needed time to recover spending the next 24 hours sleeping it off. Both of us agreed never to take a Hilton Hit again. Castro continued to party.

On our last full day, we revisited the Aberdeen. The memory of the fresh lobster sounded appealing. While there, Castro persuaded the prez and me to at least try a different drink, a Singapore Sling. The grenadine tasted great; three of them later, the old warning about *spirit and flesh* bit the dust, and the three of us were having manual stimulation of the sexual kind from young boys hidden under our table.

I slept the entire flight back to Vietnam; I'm sure my fellow R & R vacationers did too. They, like me had beat their bodies to a pulp. "Fasten your seat belts," awakened me just before our purple Big Banana outmaneuvered the potholes on the Saigon runway. Within two hours, Frock, Castro, and I were walking to the first, second, and third tent, in the second row of tents nearest the orderly room.

"Look at that one!" Frock noticed a crater from a mortar. "Two clicks to the right and we wouldn't be coming back to a tent." There was more than just one.

"With these holes, and the ones we walked into on our R & R, I think I'm qualified for the Le Mans speed race, Prez."

"Interesting remark, Cooby. Mom's maiden name is Lemans. It's what the 'L' means in Hubert L. Frock."

"Welcome back," Boremba greeted us.

"Hi, Ponderosa. Good to see you." I felt good just looking at his face.

"Good time?" he inquired.

"Take it from *Lemans of Hong Kong*; a good time had us, Timmy...looks like Charlie sent more 'calling cards.'"

"Same-o, same-o," the third part of the Fort Benning trio responded.

"Anything new we should know about, Timmy?"

"New pool."

"What's everybody betting on now?" Frock asked.

"Charlie."

"Big pot?"

"Three thousand dollars."

"Where's division holding the stash?"

"HQ S-3."

"What's the wager, Timmy?"

"One buck; one date."

'You bet, Colonel?"

"Yes."

"What date you pick?"

"April first."

"You won't be here in April; none of us will."

"I know."

"Hey, you guys. I get to scratch off a whole week on my short-time calendar."

"Me too, Prez. How many days do we have left, Timmy?"

"Sixty-two."

"That means I have thirty-seven." Frock was elated.

"Thirty-eight, Prez. This is a leap year," I relayed the bad news.

"Leave it to the army to cheat a guy out of one day," Frock snorted, entering his hooch to unpack.

"Rule four sucks," Boremba summed it up.

I headed for the second tent dragging my gear, thinking about Boremba's crack. Frock left Fort Benning on February 28, 1967. As with all Vietnam Veterans, the army insisted on a one-year tour of duty, and it wouldn't define the term as 365 days. Boremba and I got stuck with an extra day too. I thought about "What you hear in the army is not what you get" as I entered my tent and saw a new man sitting on Ducker's bunk.

"Paul March know you're using his cot?" I asked.

"Who?" the soldier replied.

"Specialist Fourth Grade Paul March, that's who."

"March rotated four days ago," he informed me.

I instinctively glanced at Molly's vacated bunk and asked, "Molly gone too?" I sat down in shock.

"Who's Molly?"

"Specialist Molline, the weapons man," I whispered. The sudden news was overwhelming. "You the replacement?"

"No, I'm a flight operations clerk."

"Know where Molly and Ducker—March and Molline—went?"

"I was told Chu Chi."

"Chu Chi! I didn't even get to say good-bye." I felt as though I wanted to hit something.

"How come you're not at work?" I lashed out at him.

"I report for CQ duty tonight."

"Is that so?"

"Sergeant Copelet told me to settle in first and then report at 5 P.M.."

When the newcomer mentioned Cope's name, I realized he was not the target for my anger. "I'm sorry, I didn't even ask your name...It's been a long week."

"That's okay. I'd feel bad if I found out my bunkmates were gone," he consoled me. "I'm Nick Ciatkin, from Ohio."

"I'm Cooby...I mean, Scooby...I mean Coobat." I fought with my own handle. "Call me anything but, *specialist*."

"You can call me, Nick."

"Any water left in the showers, Ciat...Nick?"

"Plenty. Just got back myself. Copelet said you went on R & R to Hong Kong. Have a good time?"

"Not really, Nick, and your news just made a bad trip worse."

"I'm sorry; guess I'm pretty green."

"Has nothing to do with you, Nick," I told him. "Maybe a good long shower will help me perk up."

I unpacked, stripped, grabbed a towel, and headed for the nearest water supply. An army resupply water truck was pulling away from the stall as I approached. As I turned on Cope's inventive valve, the cool liquid poured freely and I luxuriated in the precious steady stream. All the water in the world won't thin the booze in my system nor flush away the guilt I have for my animal behavior in Hong Kong. Molly and Ducker are gone...God, Madilla, I hate myself for cheating on you, I mulled over in my mind. I didn't feel any better when I remembered the "Leap Year Bennie" compliments of the U.S. Army, either. Rule four does suck!

When I got back to my tent, Nick asked me, "Shower do any good?"

"Not really, Nick."

"Why don't you take a walk down to operations...maybe that'll help."

I dressed and headed for the flight line.

Bealy, Bokar, and another newcomer, Brechin, wanted to hear about Hong Kong. Cope didn't.

"You'll have plenty of time to chew the shit once your R & R is officially over and mine begins. Get your ass into the jeep," he ordered me. "Move it!"

"See you fellas in the morning," I told everybody. "Fill you in tomorrow."

"Expect you to drive me and Boremba to the Huey when we take off for R & R, Cooby," he said on the short ride back.

"Deal, Cope."

"Sow too many oats, Cooby?"

"Far too many."

"You'll live."

"But I feel so bad."

"You'll get over it," he reassured me.

"You bet on the new pool, Cope?"

"Sure did."

"What day did you pick?"

"February first."

"You'll be on R & R with Boremba; why that day?"

"It's the beginning of the Chinese New Year," he said as he dropped me off.

# CHAPTER 22

## PRE-TET, TET, AND POST-TET

---

I slept until 5:30 A.M. the next morning and didn't go to operations until 6, damn near waking the greenhorn who gave me the cold news about Molly and Ducker. Cope's wall map had two missions plotted on it; both were maintenance flights. Boremba's one lining, "same-o, same-o," was just as accurate as any of his comments. Nothing was happening.

"What time did Cope leave last night, Nick?" I asked the Vietnam recruit.

"About 10 P.M., after he called S-3. The phone has been quiet since."

"These missions aren't scheduled until 8; why don't you knock off early, Nick?"

"You sure?"

"Take the jeep."

"Thanks, Spec...I mean, Cooby."

As soon as Nick left, I rechecked the two maintenance missions and went to my desk expecting to find a full week of backlogged paperwork. There was none. Every file was up to date and new file tags had been replaced. When I went to the flight line coffeepot, I noticed that it had been cleaned, polished, and filled.

I poured myself a cup and waited for the operations personnel to report for work. A man would have been bored performing the work covering two flights on January 25, 1968; by 9 P.M., I couldn't figure how I burned up fifteen hours. Headquarters didn't call during the day, and when I checked before my shift was over, I reconfirmed the one and only planned mission for the Pachyderms on January 26, 1968. It was a company planned flight to Saigon, carrying two R & R bound passengers.

At 8:30 A.M., on that day, I drove Pachyderm 3 to the orderly room to fulfill a promise.

"Colonel, I haven't seen you in Class A's since Fort Benning...and I've never seen you in them, Cope."

"Even I don't mind dressing up to see Japan," Copelet quipped. "Ready, Colonel Ponderosa?"

"Ready."

"You two get first-class treatment; we're flying you to Saigon in a Chinook."

"As it should be," Cope smiled.

"Have fun, you two; wish I were going with you."

"I do too, Cooby," Cope commented as we parked next to the awaiting CH-47A.

I got out of the jeep and saluted the two boarding men. Boremba waved. In a rare moment, Carl Copelet stood tall and straight, and from the tailgate of the helicopter saluted me back. I watched the chopper fly away wondering if I could fill Cope's shoes in his seven-day absence; I was now the official NCOIC of Pachyderm Operations.

I allowed myself to believe I was doing a great job during the remaining days of January; the reality of doing nothing was closer to the truth. Ending January, 1968 was like the proverbial March "going out like a lamb." Just as I was about to shut off my 15-watt piano lamp at 11:30 P.M. on January 31, 1968, the CQ from the orderly room notified me to report to operations ASAP.

I arrived in ten minutes and began to help Bealy with an overabundance of incoming landline telephone calls. None of them came from headquarters; all originated from neighboring companies and within the 312th itself. "What time do the Pachyderms take off tomorrow morning? Twelve aircraft or all fourteen? Why aren't we flying tomorrow?"

"Headquarters hasn't called, have they, Ma?" I asked my CQ.

"No," he told me.

"What's going on...why all these calls from inside the compound?"

"The guys must know something headquarters doesn't."

Bealy was all so correct. At 1 P.M., on the morning of February 1, 1968, headquarters called: "Bear Cat, the 5th Division, and the whole country of South Vietnam is on Red Alert! There will be no missions for tomorrow."

Major General Bosebaugh broadcast orders to his command moments later: "All soldiers will be armed and equipped with steel helmets and flak vests. Bear Cat's berm guard is to be doubled. Movement in or out of Bear Cat is suspended, leaves are canceled."

When Bosebaugh's transmission ended with a terse, "out," I realized Charlie wasn't hiding anymore. I notified Major Right and ordered Bealy to go to the company area and come back with one more man, three helmets, three vests, and all the ammunition two men could carry. When he left I opened the trap door to the radio, switched to auxiliary power, and monitored incoming radio transmissions. Dong Tam, Rock Kien, Tan Tru, Chu Chi, Ghia Rae, Long Binh, and Saigon reported countless throngs of armed men who sprang from out of nowhere.

While I waited for Bealy, the S-3 line rang: "Intelligence has confirmed a battalion of men outside the perimeter of Bear Cat." Major Tox's message was clear and concise.

I relayed the information to Major Right just as Bealy arrived with Nick Ciatkin. The three of us moved inside the bunker simultaneously as all artificial lighting over the compound was doused.

We couldn't see anything inside the darkened bunker, but I did feel my heart pound against my chest. The first sounds I heard were explosions created by tripped claymore and land mines. These were followed by heavy machine-gun fire. The operations bunker was fifty meters from the Bear Cat berm and I could hear flying metal impact all around. The noise of 140,000 phosphorous bullets on New Year's Eve was a minor pop in comparison. I know I prayed, thanking God for the eight inches of sun-parched sandbags between me and that flying metal.

A horrible silence followed what I perceived to be the attack by the confirmed battalion. The explosions quit and the machine-gun fire subsided and I thought the charge had been repelled. As I crouched with my two comrades, I both loved and hated the awesome silence.

"Pachyderm control, Bear Cat control, over," the radio squelched through the interim calm.

I crawled away from the security of my friends, nabbed the radio handset, and acknowledged the broadcast.

"Bear Cat control, this is Pachyderm control, over."

"Pachyderm control, Bear Cat control. In ten minutes, every UH-1D at Bear Cat will encircle our perimeter. Advise your command, over." Major Tox's message was ominous.

"Bear Cat control, Pachyderm control. Wilco. Break. Pachyderm 6, Pachyderm control, over."

"Control, Pachyderm 6. Monitored, out."

I dropped the microphone and eased back to the safety three frightened men could provide to themselves. I leaned on them and the bunker wall. "The poor bastards will find out what hell is like," I told my buddies.

"The poor bastards!" Bealy exploded. "Whose side are you on?"

"Mine, you son-of-a-bitch. A charging man carrying a rifle ain't no match for a mini-gun firing 600 rounds per minute. With our squadrons, somewhere near 300,000 rounds of hot lead is going to shower down on anything moving on the other side of the berm...and that don't include firepower from howitzers."

The ten minutes seemed like ten years. When it began, I watched the reflections of the firepower sparkle at me on the sweat pouring down my buddies' faces. My own sweat saturated my fatigue shirt. The three of us fought peeking outside, but on the rare occasions that I did, I saw Hueys plummet toward the ground, swirling downward in blazes of light, and winding up as huge fireballs. I had read of "no atheists in foxholes"; the sudden repetitive rushes of adrenaline confirmed that I was a true believer and could easily understand the word, *expendable*. I begged God for a cessation.

When it came, silence momentarily engulfed Bear Cat. It was short lived. The entire 5$^{th}$ Division ensemble of howitzers unleashed more wrath than any resident of Bear Cat had ever experienced. Literal tons of explosives hit every square inch immediately in front of the berm. This massive display of might was encored by air force jets. Bear Cat was an oasis in the largest conflagration I had ever seen in my life. I had smelled burnt flesh; on February 1, 1968, I was overwhelmed by it.

As daylight brightened the sky, everyone concentrated on statistics: casualties, wounded, destroyed aircraft. No one bothered to estimate any figures about the other side. Whatever was left on the outside of the berm, was chalked up to "another inch of ash." Bear Cat had defended itself.

Incoming radio signals portrayed a different picture to the III Corps Area of South Vietnam. Dong Tam, Phu Mi, Soc Trang, Rock Kien, Ghia Rae, Long Thanh, Long Binh, and Saigon reported continuing contact. The surprise offensive closed the Saigon Airport. The old Imperial City of Hue was captured.

When Major Tox called from headquarters, I didn't want to hear, but asked, "How bad is it, Sir?"

"Charlie surprised the whole division and the entire country. Even the embassy in Saigon was attacked."

"Headquarters have any initial reports, Sir?"

"Not everything has been tallied, Cooby; from what I have seen there's been too much, too often, and too many. Advise Sergeant Copelet the three of us will be burning a lot of midnight oil for some time."

"Sir, Copelet's on R & R." After I spoke the words, I felt the sudden impact of being the NCOIC of operations. "Any instructions, Sir?"

"Stay near the landline and keep the radio on. Send someone to pick up these reports for your CO."

I knew the reports he spoke of were crucial to Major Right. I had three choices. I could go myself and leave a finance clerk and a *greenhorn* in charge. I could route the new guy, Nick Ciatkin, or I could send Bealy. I knew anything might rain down on Bear Cat at any moment.

Luckily, Bealy volunteered. He broke a world record traversing the one mile distance between the two sites.

When I read the report, I phoned Major Right.

"Read it to me, I can't leave the company area," the CO ordered.

"Forty-seven casualties: twelve officers, thirty-five enlisted, 192 wounded," I began. "Seven UH-1Ds destroyed. Several field sites under seige. Long Binh remains closed. The embassy has been attacked. South Vietnam is under Red Alert."

"Headquarters request Pachyderm support?"

"Sir, Major Tox, S-3, has informed me that only radio signals will enter and exit Bear Cat."

"I hope he's correct; I wouldn't send my dog to the other side of our berm...Headquarters label the uprising?"

"The Tet Offensive, Sir."

"Keep me informed, Coobat." He hung up the landline.

Both majors were wrong.

Ten incoming rockets violated S-3's orders following sunset. Four creamed helicopters, one polished off a jeep, two destroyed mess halls, and three removed latrines. When daylight gave natural lighting to another devasting scene, I understood the frustration a hungry dog experienced in a butcher shop. The 5$^{th}$ could handle an opponent it could see above ground but was ineffectual in dealing with the skill, the will, and the tenacious ability of Charlie who operated beneath it.

Three frightening days passed. Division persisted with its policy to allow only radio signals to enter or exit the compound. The self-imposed quarantine initially resembled security; it didn't take long for the directive to commute down to day-to-day life. Mail stopped; water trucks failed to come in; food became in short supply. Headquarters kept confirming no enemy sightings; Charlie continued to spray us with mortar shells. I didn't have to be an intelligence officer to reason that Charlie was coiled somewhere under that jungle floor, and ready to strike again.

I wondered about the infantryman outside the perimeter of Bear Cat, and I surely worried about Cope and Boremba. By February 6, 1968, both men were AWOL (absent without official leave) and carried as "missing" on the company roster.

Division's *wait and see* policy changed on February 7. Headquarters authorized one UH-1D to transport dispatches from Long Binh. The singular Huey would also be bringing two passengers. I knew who they were and parked alongside the headquarters jeep when the helicopter arrived.

Cope and Timmy jumped from the UH-1D and scurried to the Pachyderm 3 jeep. "Where the hell have you guys been? You know you're officially AWOL," I admonished both as I sped away.

"Stop the jeep, Cooby," Cope announced.

"We can talk later, Cope. Is the airport closed? You know Bear Cat is quarantined, don't you?" I rattled away, glad the two of them were safe within my company.

"Stop the fucking jeep, Cooby," Cope shouted from the passenger side.

"Stop, General," Boremba said as he gently placed a hand on my shoulder.

I brought the jeep to a halt, looked at Copelet, and asked, "Okay, you guys in some type of trouble? Where in the hell have you been?"

"At the Grand Saigon Hotel," Cope told me.

"At the Grand! How is Madi...I mean why there?"

"No one notified our pilot the airport was closed by the military; after we landed, all hell broke loose. When the gunfire started, Boremba and I hightailed out of the terminal, made it to a back street, and finally to the Saigon Grand. Watched our Big Banana being torched as we left."

"Holy shit."

"Topaz hid us in her suite; no one is safe in Saigon. Was even an attempt on the life of Elsworth Bunker."

"The ambassador?"

"The attack wasn't successful, but that isn't why I asked you to stop the jeep." Cope stopped talking, took a deep breath, and somberly said, "Madilla led the attack on the embassy. She's dead."

I couldn't believe what I had heard and fell against the steering wheel. No words could have pierced my heart more effectively. "There has to be some mistake, Cope," I pleaded. "Tell me you're wrong."

"There's no mistake; Topaz identified her body."

"You're wrong. You didn't know Madilla. She sent me a note to come visit her. You're wrong, Cope," I screamed at him.

"I'll drive, Boremba; make sure he gets to his tent."

I wanted to cry.

I couldn't speak.

Boremba pushed me into the passenger seat.

I was dazed, frightened, and numb.

How Boremba inched me to the second tent in the second row of tents, I do not remember. When I got there, I began to drink myself into oblivion, and when I collapsed, I did so hating rule number four.

I didn't budge from my cot the following morning when Charlie replaced reveille with incoming mortar. I listened but cared less. Two hours later, I told Timmy to "fuck off" when he urged me to eat. Frock showed up at 9 A.M. carrying a cup of coffee. I yelled at him to "get out of my face." I wanted to die.

Somewhere near 11 A.M., Cope entered my hooch and sat on my footlocker. He didn't say a word.

"I don't give a damn," I broke the silence. The pain in my heart paralleled the pounding in my head.

"Remember the night in Saigon, Cooby?"

"Remember! How in the hell could I forget?"

"Topaz told me to *live and let live*."

"Woop-de-do. Me, you, and Topaz are alive."

"She was teaching us something, Cooby."

"Seems like she left her niece out."

"No, she didn't, my teacher friend. Sometimes the grade 'C' is misinterpreted in anticipation of an 'A.' Topaz knew she couldn't force her values on her sister's child, a girl who had the right to choose."

"That some of the 'Cope-Style' Topaz-Madilla oriental philosophy?"

"Cooby, you could no more be a Communist living in Vietnam than Madilla could be an American caged in the United States. Topaz allowed Madilla to choose."

"Who cares, Cope? Madilla is dead."

"She did. Madilla cared enough to follow through."

"Was she right? She led the attack on the embassy."

"She thought so; she got killed trying."

"I hate this place, Cope."

"I'm not too fond of it myself."

"You said you thought Madilla was right."

"No, I didn't, Cooby. I told you Madilla believed she was right. Would you risk your life to protect the street in front of your mother's house?" he asked.

"Sure I would."

"That's exactly what Madilla did."

"But she's dead; Madilla is gone."

"Cooby, I'm sorry for you, but there are hundreds of men and women who didn't ask to be in this fight. They died too. In five thousand years of recorded history, no one has quite learned how to *live and let live*."

"It's not fair, Cope."

"War never is...see you in a couple of hours."

Sergeant Copelet left without saying anything more; I remained in my cot with a lot to think about. An hour and a half later, Ma Bealy was in my tent.

"Cope send you too?"

"Yes."

"I don't care."

"Kiss my dick, I do," Bealy exploded.

"I ain't moving."

"Then I'll just plunk my ass down on your footlocker and wait."

"Don't waste your time, Bealy."

"Waste my time! Kiss my dick, Cooby. Did you waste time when we were in the bunker the night Charlie tried to overrun Bear Cat?"

"What the hell you talking about?"

"I don't have fancy words like you; I'm a plain hick...but that was me leaning against you inside the bunker," he said. "I was scared real bad and you were there for me. If I have to, I'll sit right here for as long as it takes."

Bealy's straight language triggered emotions within me I didn't know I had. I got up from my cot, grabbed him, and sobbed on his shoulder.

"Cope told me about Madilla," he whispered. "I know how I'd feel if I lost Rita."

Bealy's heartfelt words made me realize how blessed I was to have friends like Boremba, Frock, Cope, and Bealy. One tried to feed me, the second hoped some coffee would ease a hangover, the third did his level best to relieve a troubled mind, and the fourth appealed to my heart. "Ma, thanks," I told him. "I think I care a little bit now."

"You sure? Want me to stay a little longer?"

"No. I need a shower and then I'll come to the line. Thanks again, Ma."

When I arrived, Cope and his working crew were busy scheduling thirteen aircraft for late afternoon missions. Every landing zone was the same.

"Why we sending all the Chinooks to Long Binh? Does HQ think they'll be safer there?" I asked.

"Nope...We need supplies."

"Cope, if Charlie can pinpoint a latrine, those birds will be easy picking."

"Not if the mission is commanded by the man *who can fly anything and make anything fly.*"

"What's Major Frankel got in mind?"

"A power torque straight up and out of reach."

"How about when they return?"

"None of them will land as usual. Frankel's picked thirteen different landing sites on the compound."

"Think it'll work?"

"I'd bet every one of the $3000 I won on the 'where's Charlie pool' on it, Cooby. In forty-five minutes, thirteen Chinooks will suck air as every howitzer at Bear Cat pounds the outside of our perimeter."

"God, it sounds risky, Cope."

"We got more to lose without supplies and the major's plan uses Charlie's strategy."

"In what way?"

"Charlie knows where we are. We don't know where he is. If Charlie didn't know where some of us were, maybe he'd be as confused as us."

The daring plan worked, and it worked three times in a row. Each time the helicopters returned, Charlie mortared a vacant Pachyderm pad. We repeated the diversionary plan two more times the next day. We had learned to disperse and hide like Charlie, and we had re-supplied Bosebaugh's warehouse with the all the essentials that had been depleted during and following the surprise siege.

"You okay, Cooby?" Cope asked the second night after we reinvented the *Berlin airlift*.

"Nope. I feel like a pregnant woman who's been informed she's carrying a dead baby."

"Give it time. I'm not as educated as you, but even I know 'it's better to have loved and lost than never to have loved at all.'"

"I can tell you about the *loved and lost* part; I'm not too certain about the *better* part, Cope."

"Did your ma ever tell you about 'idleness and the workshop of the devil?'"

"Once a day."

"Good. I need help plotting the missions for tomorrow."

"What's Bosebaugh want?"

"A need to share our supplies with those poor division fuckers outside Bear Cat who can't live without them."

"A need to share" barely described the monumental task of safely distributing supplies to outlying field sites. A landing twin rotary Chinook was a very easy target; Frankel understood it and insisted on minimal time unloading all of the *live or die* supplies.

As with his other plan, all thirteen aircraft took off simultaneously; unlike his previous plan, our aircraft had UH-1D helicopter support. During the initial takeoff, the safest place to be was the Pachyderm pad; Charlie had wised up and randomly sprayed Bear Cat. Still, Frankel's daring freed the hold on our compound. His scheme ended only radio signals entering and exiting Bear Cat.

At 4 P.M., the plan was labeled a success. The Pachyderms had flown twenty-six helicopter loads of men, ammunition, medical supplies, and C-rations. By 8 P.M., following the debriefings, Cope and I sealed up the "Summary of the Day's Activity Report," and dispatched it to headquarters. The data contained on it testified to the price tag paid for by the Fifth Division.

Two men died, forty had been wounded. Three UH-1Ds were combat lost and thirteen Chinooks had sustained too many contacts with flying metal.

"I hate this place, Cope."

"I do too," he concurred.

I hated it more at midnight when the invisible Charlie commenced a mortar-every-half-hour-assault that lasted 'til dawn. At about 3 A.M., the 5th had enough of the teasing; it responded with volley after volley of howitzer firings. The flashes alone made me feel as though I were in the center of a candled birthday cake; the thuds made Bear Cat shake as though it were undergoing an earthquake. Lord, I wanted to scream and run away, but there was nowhere to go. Each blast forecast another shovel of dirt heaped on a coffin.

The quiet of the dead ensued at daybreak. Short-lived, it was replaced by the thunder of fighter jets that almost kissed the top of Pachyderm Operations on their way to set Bear Cat's perimeter ablaze. The air force used up an hour torching and scorching and I believe microwave technology was born on that morning. Bear Cat again repelled another assault, but it wasn't that way for the Fifth.

Incoming radio transmissions relayed the opposite for outlying field sites. One reported another attempt on the embassy in Saigon. The ambassador fled to safety on board an aircraft carrier in the Gulf of Tonkin. When noon came it was evident Charlie encored February 1, 1968. Contrary to recent *Stars and Stripes* news articles, the Asian War in Vietnam was nowhere near *winding down*.

I had the jitters the rest of the day. Nothing came into Bear Cat and nothing went out.

"Shame on us," Cope remarked. "They fooled us twice."

The mood deepened when Charlie ceased firing incoming mortar. Two days later, the apparent lull allowed the 5th to request the use of seven Chinooks. "Think it's safe?" I asked Cope.

"Doesn't matter," he answered. "The missions are not resupply. We're hauling out wounded and dead."

As the totals were added up, Bear Cat's Pachyderms played hearse for 22 and transported 77 men to adequate medical facilities. Reports did not include contact with the enemy. Charlie had again become one with the terrain.

Bear Cat remained on Red Alert for the duration of February, 1968; the berm guard was kept at a maximum. It was the same for the entire 5$^{th}$ Division. Only authorized missions left the compound and all were under orders to climb to 4000 feet before attempting forward motion. Support for the 5$^{th}$ shrunk to four per day; the atmosphere changed to eerie. Everyone felt as I did; all expected a "third time" to be "the charm." Nowhere was the dread more apparent than in the behavior of my Benning Buddy, President Hubert Lemans Frock. He had vacated his tent on February 20 and had taken up residence in the bunker between his hooch and mine.

"How many days left now, President Short-Timer?" I asked him the night he moved into the bunker.

"Nine more fucking days in this hell hole and Cope and me are out of here," he answered. "I know the story; I'm not taking any chances." Frock referred to what any seasoned Vietnam soldier understood. An unpublished part of rule number four, and 22 body bags forwarded to the Saigon morgue after the second assault, gave meaningful credence to it: "If you do buy it during your tour, it will most likely occur during your first green 30 days, or your last careless month."

"If you have nine, I have thirty-three, Prez."

"You better move into a bunker; those bastards will attack again."

"Talk to Cope lately?" I changed the subject.

"Not since we made plans to tie on a big one in San Francisco when we leave this stink hole."

"Think his plans have changed, Prez."

"What do you mean *they've changed*?"

"Told me he's extending and taking advantage of the 'Early Out Program.'" It was a little-known subparagraph of rule number four. If a soldier serving in Vietnam had six months or less remaining service time following his tour of duty, he could extend his tour by thirty days and be released from further military commitment. Cope could shorten his military career by several months.

"Cope extended?"

"You'd do the same, Prez. Out of me, you, Boremba, and Bealy, he's the only one of us five to outfox the army. We get cheated out of one day because of leap year, and he extends for thirty and is given months. I think it's the perfect touch to his twenty-two year army career."

"I wouldn't extend for one more minute in this damn place; I'm praying I last the last nine days."

"You'll be fine, Prez...and remember, I want to drive you to the chopper that takes you out of here and back on the way home to Bunny and Georgia. Deal?"

"Deal."

On the February 29, 1968 no one could find Frock at 8 A.M., the time for me to drive him to the helicopter. He was not in the first tent in the second row of tents, he was not in his bunker, and no one remembered seeing him. I was frantic when I drove First Sergeants Foone and Turtz to the awaiting aircraft. I hope he didn't do anything stupid, I prayed.

As I watched Turtz and Foone board their ticket home, I saw Frock scramble from the bunker alongside the helicopter. He was running and dragging his duffel bag behind him. "Good-bye," I shouted; my voice went unheard. Bunny will make it all better, I thought, watching the UH-1D disappear in the Bear Cat horizon.

I went back to operations and checked the missions for the day. I was miffed over Frock's unusual send-off. Three missions were scheduled for February 29. All three were chow runs to Dong Tam, Rock Kien, and Tan Tru. There would also be the other half of a fourth. The first portion took Foone, Turtz, and Frock; the second half brought in their replacements: Sergeant Mound for Turtz, Sergeant Kist for Foone, and PFC Kenny for Frock. There was one more passenger. His name was PFC McDowal; he was my replacement.

There were no debriefings following any of the day's workload. Leap year 1968 officially ended at noon. There were no hits, no runs, no errors, and no Charlie. After I forwarded the dull "Summary for the Day's Activities Report," I reflected on February 29, 1968.

Would March be a lion or a lamb?

Would the Fifth find Charlie?

Would I make it to my last day?

Would Frock be okay?

Would there be a third assault?

Are you watching, Madilla...?

March 1 turned out to be an exact duplicate. Three Chinooks, three resupply missions, and one dual-purposed flight into Long Binh. The newly promoted Major Tox plus two sergeants, Austen and Towie, were rotating out. All of them had been cheated of another day due to a paper SNAFU. I snippily felt elated they had to endure another day, but none of my feelings showed in their faces as they left. I returned an hour later to pick up replacements. It was then I realized there'd be an infinite supply of new trooops to replace or even swell the large number of American military men in Vietnam. PFC Kenny was Hubert Frock and PFC McDowal was Daniel Coobat. Something else I realized as I drove the men to the company area: I was watching myself.

I shared my insights with Cope when I returned back to the flight line.

"It's the army way, Cooby," he told me again for the hundredth time. "Now I have something to share with you." He removed some documents from an envelope and read me his official orders from the U.S. Department of Defense. Copelet was assigned to headquarters as air traffic controller for his extended thirty days.

"When do you report?" I tried to hide my regret.

"While I'm attached to the 312$^{th}$, my new duties will be at headquarters until April 1, 1968."

"Any suggestions about who I can lean on?"

"You've been very special to me too, Flight Operations Sergeant Coobat."

"What did you say?" he astounded me again.

"You forgot about rule four. New orders assigning me to another duty post automatically grants me a thirty-day leave. Technically, you are my boss until you leave. How does it feel to be the non-commissioned officer in charge?"

"Shitty."

"Want to hear what's on the rest of these orders?"

"No, I think I heard more than I can handle."

"You'll recognize all the names," he persisted: "Specialist E-5 Bealy is assigned to four years duty, inactive reserve, Georgia, effective 24 March 1968." Bealy had been drafted for two years. "Specialist Timothy Boremba is reassigned to Finance Headquarters, Fort Knox, Kentucky, effective on or before 10 May 1968." Timmy had enlisted in the army for four years. "Specialist E-5 Hubert L. Frock is reassigned for two years active, two years inactive service with the Georgia National Guard, effective 1 April 1968."

"Kiss my dick. Bealy will love it, Boremba deserves it, and Prez will at least be home in Georgia." Frock had enlisted for six years.

"There's one more name; it appears three times," Cope continued.

"General Bosebaugh's?"

"No. Although the guy's a general, he don't wear any stars," Cope commented then added, "Specialist E-5 Daniel Coobat is promoted to E-6; Specialist Coobat is granted an MOS change from 11 B 10, Infantryman, to 71 P 20, Flight Operations Specialist; Specialist E-5 Coobat is assigned to one year inactive reserve with the Nebraska Guard." I had enlisted for three years.

I was speechless.

"Say something, Cooby, even if it's wrong."

"All I can think of is Mr. Harsh. He pushed for that MOS change...I often wonder what would have happened had Mr. Harsh lived and I joined him and Captain Patton up at Long Binh."

"Two things, Cooby. *Stars and Stripes* would have much better news stories and you'd been promoted to E-7 or E-8, and outrank me."

I faked a laugh at the remark but blurted out, "You're the one that should have been promoted, Cope. It's unfair."

"One last time, Cooby. There's a right way, a wrong way, and the army way. Forty-five days from now, when we're both home, it won't make any difference."

"It makes a difference to me."

"I know it does; right now you have the responsibility of training a new man...and officially...I am *in-between* assignments."

"Who am I going to lean on when you leave, Cope?"

"I'll always be there for you to lean on, Cooby; now it's your turn to lean on yourself. This is your desk."

Cope got up and walked out of the Pachyderm Operations building, which he had built.

# CHAPTER 23

## BEAR CAT'S TWENTY-ONE GUN SALUTE

---

The first part of March was lonely without Copelet. Although it was pretty much uneventful, it was also very spooky. Charlie kept hidden, to himself, and didn't fire one rocket on the camp. Forthcoming intelligence reports were minimal at best, and I was certain the Fifth didn't know too much about either his strength or whereabouts. I loathed the army logic implied in the sudden reassignment of Cope. Most of all, I took up resenting Specialist Fourth Class Patrick McDowal.

McDowal arrived in Vietnam as an operations clerk. He was trained in proper radio procedure and schooled for all of the tedious paperwork army aviation could dish out. He was a 71 P 10, and he eased into my job as naturally as a creek empties into a larger body of water. What pissed me off the most about him was his ability to swallow my not-so-well-disguised narrow-mindedness.

After about a week-and-a-half alone with McDowal, Cope made an unscheduled appearance, saying something like, "I sure do miss the Bear Cat brew."

"Look who's at Pachyderm Operations, Specialist Coobat," McDowal announced his arrival. When I looked up to see Cope I resented McDowal even more. Not only had he acknowledged my former boss first, he also called me, *specialist.*

"Got a cup of coffee for a nomad?" Cope asked. "How's it going, Cooby?"

"So so," I whispered. The silence that followed could have been shattered by the crash of a snowflake hitting cement. Bealy, Bokar, and Ciatkin all pretended to be busy as Cope poured himself a cup.

"Any truth to the latest rumors about Bosebaugh?" the new Spec Four pierced the awesome quiet.

"Which one, McDowal? There's so many," Cope responded.

"The one about him leaving Bear Cat on March 9."

"If he came on March 9, 1967, he'll be leaving on March 10; leap year applies to generals too," Cope enlightened my replacement, casually sipping the brew he made infamous.

"Who started the jingle, Sergeant Copelet? You know the one about *Whatever Bosebaugh wants, Bosebaugh gets.*"

Cope glanced at me and asked, "Care to answer?"

"Nobody knows, McDowal," I lied. "'Whatever Bosebaugh wants, Bosebaugh gets' is like 'Remember the Maine.' It's an anonymous verse." Silence thickened; Cope muffled some disapproval.

"Have you seen the *decals* painted on our Pachyderms, Sergeant Copelet?" the glib McDowal tried another save. "My favorite is 'Bitchin' Betty,' on Pachyderm one-zero-niner."

"One of the reasons I'm here," Cope played along. "How about it, Cooby? Care to show me some Pachyderm artwork?"

"Sure Cope," I faked less than a snarl. The spec four had just reminded me that I hadn't leaned on someone in a week or so, and I hated the reflective mirror.

We escaped into Pachyderm 3 and I slowly drove to the Pachyderm pad. "McDowal reminds me of a young kid I met." He began a conversation.

"*Kid* is a good word."

"The guy I'm talking about had the smarts of a general and president combined; watching him made me feel dumb."

"You dumb, Cope?" I jockeyed Pachyderm 3 into viewing range of the berthing Chinooks. "Some sight, right?"

"Sure is...just like what I saw in that *kid*. When I watched him, I felt like I was witnessing a rebirth."

"You never spoke about Korea...and I never wanted to pry."

"The *kid* I'm talking about reported to me in July of 1966, at Fort Benning...and I hated him as much as you hate McDowal."

I stopped the jeep and momentarily stared at Cope. "Is it that obvious?"

"Yes."

"How'd you hide it so well?"

"I had Major Frankel to lean on."

"You're not there...who do I lean on?"

"Cooby, you lean on understanding," he began. "McDowal has never been in a bunker during incoming mortar, has never pulled a burned body from a Chinook, didn't return from R & R only to find his buddies rotated, and has yet to be hailed by rule number four. As far as I know, McDowal did not lose a Madilla, and only has talent, like you in July of 1966. Live and let live."

"More *Topaz-Cope* philosophy?"

"Plain common sense."

I thought about his succinct appraisal; he was right as usual. I was treating McDowal like shit. "How about if I do something I haven't done, Cope?"

"What's that?"

"I cross the company area tonight with some beers, go to your tent, and 'lean' on you for a while. I got tonight off."

"Bring more than some beers."

"Can I ask you another question, Cope?"

"Fire away."

"Who told you I was hard on McDowal?"

"Nobody did; I figured since I trained you, you'd do the same thing to your replacement."

"Guess I knew you didn't come to see the decals on our Pachyderms."

"Take me back, Cooby; don't want to feel dumb like I did back at Benning."

I drove Cope back to the company area and returned to the flight line. When I walked in, McDowal asked, "Sergeant Copelet like the decals?"

"McDowal, it's *Cope*, and from now on call me, *Cooby*."

"It's a deal if you call me, Mac."

"Deal."

McDowal waited a moment then ventured, "Cooby, before you and Cope tie one on, would you help me with a DD 759 I'm having trouble with?"

"How'd you know we're getting together, Mac?"

"I don't have a close friend like Cope, but it don't mean I can't envy what you two have."

As soon as McDowal made the statement, I saw myself in front of Specialist Copelet back at Benning. I was by myself and didn't have a friend. "What's the problem with the DD 759?" I opened up.

"How do you fill in columns when there are no errors, no runs, no hits, and no Charlie?" he asked.

"With *zero*; it's the same figure we've been placing on the 'Summary for the Day's Activity Report' for the last few weeks."

"I thought I'd leave it blank."

"Rule number one, Mac." I began to sound like Cope. "Document everything. Rule number two, no documentation, no pay."

"Got ya...now why don't you get your butt out of here and go have those beers?"

I didn't need more encouragement.

I left operations and went to my hooch. I stripped and headed for the showers. I wrote one letter home, skipped chow, scrounged two six-packs of Lone Star from my tent's community supply, and scurried to Cope's hooch. "Too soon old, too late smart." I tossed a Lone Star to Cope when I entered his tent.

"And that, Cooby, is not *the army way*." He caught it.

"Thanks for today, Cope." I saluted the sergeant.

"Sit down," he reprimanded me. "Tell me about home."

"You first, Cope."

Five beers later an incoming rocket exploded. Cope hit the floor and pulled me down with him. Upon impact of the second, Cope and I hustled to the bunker near his tent. He sobered up instantly; I didn't until the third mortar hit. Red Alert sounded and all electrical power was cut. Three more incoming landed on Bear Cat as we huddled together in that bunker.

"I better get my butt down to operations, Cope."

"Live and let live, Cooby." He grabbed my arm.

"McDowal needs my help."

"The best help you could give is to let him deal with what he'll have to handle when you're gone." He tightened his grip.

"Cope, he's green."

"He won't be after tonight; if he needs you, he'll put out the word."

"He won't, Cope."

"He sounds like a kid I met at Fort Benning."

I didn't agree with Cope but remained with him in the bunker, smoking one cigarette after another, until the all-clear siren wailed.

"You're going to operations, aren't you, Cooby?"

"No."

"Liar."

"Okay, so I'm going."

"I'd probably go too, but I can tell you what you're going to find."

"I did come to lean on you, remember?"

"You'll find a frightened soldier, scared, but capable and effective. When I found my replacement, his nametag read, *Coobat*. I've been harping about 'a right way, the wrong way, and an army way,' Cooby. In an hour or so, you will understand that rule four also teaches 'the way that it is.'"

In spite of Cope's prediction, I was not prepared to face what I had to witness.

McDowal had assumed command. The CO had been notified. The emergency radio was up and operating. The "Summary for the Day's Activities Report" was sealed and ready to send. Even the coffeepot was readied. I expected chaos. Timidly I ventured, "Got everything under control?"

"Everything but my pissed-in fatigues."

I didn't say anything at first, but when I did I knew my attitude toward him had taken a full 180-degree turn. "Did it myself, Mac; second and third time as well."

"I hate this place, Cooby."

"Nobody likes this place, Mac...any damage reports?"

"Headquarters confirmed six incoming; three landed at the mellow yellow trailer house."

"Casualties?"

"One of the general's aides and one security guard..How'd Charlie know Bosebaugh was leaving?"

"Mac, when I first came here, a captain introduced me to an old Vietnamese woman who was carrying a tree branch on her shoulders. She balanced two tied bags on each side. I failed a dare to lift the woman's load, but I remembered the captain's advice: 'Never underestimate these people.' His words hold true tonight." I told the story. "Any news on the general?"

"One mission tomorrow is to fly him to Long Binh."

"Then he is leaving."

"After a brief change of command ceremony at the pad. Major Right has been ordered to attend...needs someone to drive him. Care to play taxi, Cooby?"

"And miss out on 'Bear Cat Believing While Bosebaugh Was Leaving?'"

"Another *anonymous* verse, Cooby?"

"Author's 'non-de-plume' is 'Scoobee-do.'"

"Sure it ain't 'Scoobee-don't?'"

"Just sign me up, Mac. What time do you need the taxi driver?"

"Nine A.M...if Charlie doesn't interrupt the occasion with his version of a twenty-one-gun salute."

"I'd go anyway, Mac."

"Get out of here, Cooby; see you tomorrow after the bon voyage."

I picked up Major Right in the morning; I parked the jeep next to three other vehicles most likely ordered to be at the sendoff. When I shut the engine off, the Chinook revved up. Seconds later a caravan of seven vehicles raced to the awaiting Pachyderm.

Six were deuce and a halfs carrying armed guards. The middle vehicle was a jeep flying a flag bearing two stars. When the column halted, sixty men scrambled to create some type of gauntlet of protection, forming two parallel lines of men leading from the jeep to the helicopter. Bosebaugh, wearing a flak vest and steel helmet, sported an M-45. He hurried through the human phalanx and disappeared.

I watched Pachyderm 109 fade into Bear Cat's horizon; so did Major Right and all of the assembled men. I watched Major Right toss his ball cap into the Bear Cat sky at the departure and joined with the other assembled men in doing the same thing.

Charlie remained elusive and didn't fire any twenty-one-rocket salute; if he had, no one at Bear Cat would've heard. The entire compound erupted in a farewell yell of relief that rivaled the Bob Hope Christmas Tour.

A lone UH-1D landed at the Pachyderm heliport after the base-wide cheering subsided. A tall figure jumped out of the bird. He caught his own duffel bag and walked to the jeep flying two red stars. With a gesture of an umpire signaling a man out at first base, the new commandant of Bear Car thumbed away the caravan of six trucks. Before boarding, he removed the two-star flag and motioned for the driver to park in front of the remaining dignitaries.

"I'm Brigadier General Norman L. Pot. Follow my jeep."

Everyone trailed, eventually winding up at the site of the mellow yellow trailer house. We stared at the charred results of three incoming rockets. Nothing was yellow. I was stunned at what I saw next.

General Pot stood upright in his jeep and removed his personal side arm. He fired a symbolic shot at the debris.

"Remove the blemish...dismissed," he announced. The general motioned for his driver to advance and I knew the much needed "Lion of March" had arrived.

I didn't change my opinion on March 15 when *Stars and Stripes* headlined:

### *AMBASSADOR BUNKER AWARDS BOSEBAUGH A THIRD STAR*

Ambassador Bunker pins the Legion of Merit Award on Lt. General Bosebaugh. Following a thirty-day leave between assignments, the newly promoted 3-Star will assume duties at the Pentagon. In brief comments at the ceremony, General Bosebaugh accredited success to the men of the Fifth Division.

# Part Four

## *GOING HOME*

# CHAPTER 24

## THE LAST DAYS

Charlie continued to perfect *elusive* during my final days at Bear Cat; so did work for the Fifth Division and the Pachyderms. On March 23, 1968, a day before my 26th birthday, I reported to assume my duties as NCOIC of the 312th Assault Support Helicopter Company for the last time.

"Get out of here," McDowal barked at me when I entered operations. "Nobody works on their last day in country, and tell it to Bealy as well."

"Can't I even have one sip of Benning Brew?"

"No! Get your coffee at the mess hall," he yelled.

I didn't want to leave; I didn't have to. PFC McDowal was my subordinate. Reluctantly, when I did, I realized the 312th's flight operations center was in very good hands. As I walked back for the last time, I looked at two buildings that were a part of my life, especially one with an antenna standing on top of its roof like a straight arrow. It sure did make a lot of missions easier, I thought. Didn't dare to think about whether the missions had been as effective. I unconsciously counted Femur's telephone poles; they sort of reminded me of old Burma Shave signposts, a little bit of civilization in a no man's land. When I arrived at the company area, I met Bealy and Boremba.

"You won't hold it against Bealy and me if two jobless soldiers share a coffee break with you, will you, Timmy?"

"Jobless?" Bealy asked.

"The new NCOIC of Pachyderm Operations fired us today; his exact words were, 'Nobody works on the last day at Bear Cat.'"

"Me too," Boremba informed us.

"Major Right order you to clear out, Tim?"

"No, Street."

"Well, 'soon-to-be-Vietnam-Vets,' let's go toast each other with coffee."

"Water," Timmy got in a one-liner.

The three of us went to the mess hall; we found Cope there; he was alone in the NCO section. Chow ended hours earlier.

"Big day for the three of you tomorrow," he greeted us.

"Your big day ain't too far away, Cope," I told him.

"April Fool's Day, 1968. And this year I get to cheat Uncle Sam out of undue taxes and Momma Army out of about six months of commitment." He saluted himself with a sip of coffee. "Too bad Frock isn't here to join the original Benning Five...anyone hear from Georgia?"

No one answered the rhetorical question. I broke the uncomfortable silence with, "Married men on honeymoons do not have letter writing on their minds."

"Kiss my dick," Bealy exploded. "Frock did say Bunny wouldn't tie the knot until the old boy came home."

I had no idea why Frock left without saying a word; none of us did. I didn't know if he had married; I hadn't received any letter. I did feel good vibrations when Bealy lit up like a Christmas tree at the suggestion. I even saw a tiny smile of approval on Boremba's face.

"You guys packed?" Cope asked. "Better be prepared by six tonight," he added.

"Why six, Cope? We got all night."

"At six P.M. tonight, Pachyderm Operations is hosting a farewell party for its own Ma, its own colonel, and its own general. Major Right set it up, ordering Street to fire one butt in the orderly room and McDowal to fire two butts down at operations...he's piloting the mission to Saigon to bring back fifty pounds of steak...It's the only mission we have for March 23, 1968...wear civilian."

I did wear civilian; so did Bealy and Boremba. They were the only ones we had. We were also given a four-hour party, the best pre-birthday party I ever had in my life.

At 6 A.M., on the morning of March 24, 1968, Cope came to the second tent in the second row of tents nearest the orderly room. He was dressed in a rumpled Class A uniform. It didn't matter; mine was too. "I'll carry the duffel bag," he said. "I'm also driving the jeep."

"I wish I could do the same for you," I nearly broke out in tears.

"My pleasure." He grabbed my duffel bag, motioned for me to get my ass moving, and yelled at Boremba and Bealy as we passed the first tent in the second row. I turned and took one last look at my hooch. An ache in my stomach told me I couldn't lie about missing it.

Cope drove past operations on the way to the helipad. McDowal, Bokar, Breckin, and Ciatkin were outside. Every one of them were saluting the passing Pachyderm 3 jeep in traditional Bear Cat fashion. The "fuck-you" finger had a very special meaning this time.

When we got to the awaiting Chinook, Cope hastened to the front of Pachyderm 3 and announced, "Front and center, Cooby."

I followed his last order to me.

"I'm not as good with words as you are, so I'll steal them from a favorite movie, *Going My Way*. 'I'm certain the right thing to say will occur to me after you've gone.' In the meantime, wear these." Sergeant Copelet removed his own rank plates and pinned them on me. He then took a step back and saluted me.

"Not good enough, Cope." I embraced Sergeant Copelet in a long hug, engrossed in a feeling *brothers in war* share. My eyes were too wet to confirm seeing a tear in his but my ears heard his voice crack when he said, "Good-bye, Cooby."

I entered the Chinook, sat down, and reflected about the entire last year in the short thirty minute flight to Saigon. I was floored when the big Braniff Banana disproved Cope's Army Way *to hurry up and wait*, and took off on time shortly after 9 A.M. I participated in the deafening uproar on board as it did; eighteen hours later, on March 24, 1968, the purple aircraft screeched its tires to a halt on American soil, in California. It was a second birthday present in one 27-hour day. Bealy so noted it with "Kiss my dick; two presents in one day"; Boremba told me, "Happy Birthday."

"All I want to do is get off this purple machine and kiss some American soil," I told them both. I had to wait. Rule number four showed its ugly head once again and the aircraft took a long time to taxi to a halt. When it did, we were at an edge of the military airport.

California spring smelled terrific and I noticed it the instant the side door of the Braniff opened. When my turn came to deplane, I saw a big sign saying, "Returnee Station" about 300 feet in front of my exiting ramp. Leading to it was a painted runway with double lines. On one side of the not-so-red welcoming carpet, a military band played "Happy Days Are Here Again." On the other side was a chain-link fence, about ten foot high, a boundary between the military installation where the plane taxied and civilian California. A group of fifty or so people were assembled near it and they were chanting "Hell No We Won't Go."

I didn't get the chance to kiss American soil. All of the returning Vietnam Veterans were scurried through the resulting gauntlet of sound. Coming back home to America became a stereophonic experience I will never forget, and I understood at that moment, how impossible it would have been to "redress any grievances." I was then reintroduced to subparagraph B, rule number four: hurry up and wait.

All returning military personnel underwent a twelve-hour ordeal. All of us were searched, stripped, and showered. We were inoculated, prodded, probed, counseled, examined, reexamined, redressed, rechecked, re-counseled, paid, and released to the country we all believed we had so proudly defended. The only redeeming part of reentry was the announcement making 300 "charge free" telephones available.

"Ma, it's me, Danny," I cried into the phone.

"Is this a joke?" my mother answered with the softest sounds I had heard since Madilla.

"No, Ma. It's me. I just landed in California."

"Is it really you, Danny?"

"Yes, Ma; it's really me. I'll call you as soon as I know what flight will bring me..." The announcement had failed to let anyone know there was a one-minute limit. My chagrin reflected on Bealy's and Boremba's faces.

"I can't believe this," Bealy remarked.

"I can't believe it either, Bealy. The sooner we get out of here, the sooner we'll be home."

I saw the fleet of taxis at the exiting end of the "Returnee Station" somewhere near San Francisco.

# CHAPTER 25

## 1968 AMERICA

My scratched Timex told me it was about midnight, on March 24, 1968, when the cab driver asked, "Where to, you war mongers?" I wanted to deck the bearded son-of-a-bitch. I was exhausted. The eighteen hour flight back to America, the stereophonic welcome, and the trying cross examination of mustering out had combined to push me to a limit. Bealy and Boremba soothed my anger but had to literally restrain me when he persisted with a rude, "Let me guess, grunts? Is it San Francisco International? Ten bucks...each...and up front."

The quiet ride toward the airport in the darkened city didn't ease the tension. My fellow veterans did. Although I never appreciated the color green, I began to hate, loathe, despise, and abominate it that night, in that cab. Military summer dress uniforms were green.

"What's the matter, Army? Not enough booty in the war chest to tip a poor taxi driver?" He insulted us again as we arrived at the terminal.

"You've been paid," Bealy told the rude man as Boremba dragged me from a tryst that would not have been pretty.

"United Airlines," Ponderosa told us and we followed. I was in no position to offer advice to anyone.

There was one flight leaving at 4 A.M., bound for Omaha and Chicago. The news was great for me and Tim. Bealy was Atlanta bound.

"Any connecting flights from Chicago to Atlanta?" he asked the agent.

"Don't know, Army; I live in Frisco."

"Did United cease flying from Chicago to Atlanta?" I interrupted. I remembered flying from Atlanta to Chicago to Omaha back during my Fort Benning days.

"Don't know, Army; told your buddy I live in Frisco."

"Where's the military assistance desk?" I politely inquired.

"Beats me," the ticket agent answered. "Have two first-class tickets left on the 4 A.M. flight. Take them or leave them."

"You guys go ahead," Bealy offered. "I'll find another way home."

"We're going together; now let's go find the military assistance desk."

"Suit yourselves, Army. Makes no difference to me," he commented as we left to search the terminal.

I didn't like the "I don't knows" we heard, but more shrugs and continued indifference appeared to be accepted behavior. I began to feel like a *green thumb* with clones. My suspicions became confirmed when the three of us found the military assistance desk, well veiled behind a row of phone booths.

"Ma'am?" I caught the attention of the female officer behind the desk. "We've just returned from Vietnam and we'd like to fly home together. Can you help us?" The armband she wore indicated military police.

"Where's home, Specialist?"

"Omaha, Chicago, and Atlanta, Ma'am."

The black lieutenant instantly picked up the phone on her desk. "Three returning vets bound for Omaha, Chicago, and Atlanta. Anything?" While waiting for an answer, the lieutenant placed the speaker part of her phone under her chin and said, "Welcome home."

"Thanks, Ma'am," I told her. Bealy winked and Boremba smiled.

"United Airlines...Flight 646...4 A.M. departure, with stops in Denver, Omaha, Chicago, and a connecting flight to Cleveland and Atlanta...$229...$299...and $340...first class...half-fare for military standby...plenty of room...Thanks, Al." She hung up the phone and asked, "Can you come up with $877; I don't recommend military standby."

I had $375 of mustering out pay; Boremba, $325, and Bealy, $300. Boremba and I gave Bealy the needed $50 and handed it to the lieutenant. She left and came back with three first-class tickets for Flight 646.

"Thanks again, Ma'am...Can I ask you a question?"

"Yes, Specialist, you can."

"Why didn't you recommend military standby?"

"'Cause you'd rot waiting to board the plane."

"Why?"

"Your uniform. The only *green* that folks want to see today is on a dollar bill. Good luck to the three of you."

Boremba said one word as we departed, "Hamburger."

Neither Bealy nor I could disagree with the one-liner. The last time we had eaten was somewhere over Hawaii; even the army, at the returnee station, had covered everything, but food.

We stopped at an airport concession stand; we waited at the counter for fifteen minutes. Two waitresses ignored our *green* presence until an airport security guard just happened to pass by.

"I must have been busy," the woman told us. "What can I get you?"

"One hamburger, two hot dogs, three Cokes," I said.

Twenty minutes later she placed three Cokes and three hot dogs on the counter.

"The dog tastes raw and the bun feels like cardboard," I told my buddies after one bite.

"Not Coke," Boremba put his drink down.

"At least the food at Bear Cat was cooked," Ma Bealy noted.

Hungry, we found Gate 27, the boarding area for Flight 426. It was close to 3:45 AM. There weren't too many people waiting to board. When we sat down to wait for the boarding announcement, those who were sitting near there went to sit elsewhere. At 3:55 AM, the airport PA announced boarding. We shot up and went to the entrance. What we heard was, "All Military are Standby." The attendant did not ask for tickets. When I showed him my First-Class Tickets, he repeated, "All Military are Standby."

At 3:58, the flight attendant allowed the three of us to enter an empty First-Class Section of Flight 646. Before I sat down, I glanced into tourist and noticed the aircraft was close to sixty per cent vacant. Neither Boremba, Bealy, or I was visited by a stewardess on the two-hour flight to Denver.

"Let's stretch our legs," I told my buddies when the United Airlines Jet touched down at Stapelton. "We have a forty-five minute layover, and I'd like a cup of coffee."

"Coke," Boremba one lined.

"We deplaned and entered the terminal. What we found was more blank, indifferent stares to simple questions as, "Is there a food counter in the terminal. We doubled-timed our search and found one.

"I'd like one black coffee and two Cokes," I told the fast food waiter.

"That cost money; you got ten bucks?" he responded.

I reached into my green uniform and produced one of the five ten-dollar bills I had left. I placed it on the food counter, rested my hand on it, and defiantly said, "I got the ten bucks, buddy, do you have the coffee and the Cokes? After what I've been through in Vietnam, you look like a minor skirmish." I had had it up the ass with with poster-waving dissenters, wisecracking cab drivers, rude ticket agents, poor customer service representatives, absent stewardesses, and discourteous waiters.

At that precise moment, two military policemen passed by the concession stand. I don't know what tipped them off, and I probably never will, but one arm-banded guard asked, "Anything wrong, Army?"

"The counter seems to be out of inexpensive coffee and Coke." Both MPs were buck sergeants making me the highest ranking man in the group.

"Pot looks full to me." One guard glanced behind the counter. He then added, "Walker, you keep harassing these returnees and I'll have your stand closed...Get them their drinks!"

"United Airlines, Flight 646, for Omaha and Chicago, is boarding at Gate Four. Last Call for Flight 646," the Stapelton Public Address announced.

One guard pointed directions to Gate Four, and the three of us beat feet. We left without coffee, Coke, and my ten bucks.

Once again, three *green* men were detained at the boarding area with, "All Military Are Standby." When we were allowed to enter first class, a new flight crew had been scheduled for the flight and two first-class passengers came aboard. "At least I'll be able to ask for a cup of coffee," I thought to myself during takeoff.

I was wrong.

Once the aircraft leveled off, both passengers left to the tourist section; the stewardess closed the curtain separating tourist from first class. I relished being in the best company a man could have on the fifty-minute air flight to Omaha, and I burned up each second promising to write, call, and stay in touch. I hugged them both before I deplaned in Omaha.

I greeted my mother, my sister, and one niece at the Eppley Air Field Terminal. I held the woman who had sent one letter a day to me for a whole year, and hugged both my sister and my niece. On the way through the terminal, I saw more stares of disgust, and as I walked through its front entrance, heard, in my own hometown, a yelled-out catcall: "Baby Killer."

"Hi, Bernie," I greeted my oldest brother who had been waiting in my mother's home. "Good to see you."

"What the hell is the matter with this peacenik army?" he greeted me. "Are all you guys on drugs? It wasn't that way when I was a corporal back in 1946."

I was crushed by his remark. Although I hadn't eaten, I stopped being hungry and grabbed the first chair to sit in.

"I'm so happy you're home, Danny," my mother tried to ease the pain she knew I felt.

"Ma, I've been up for a long time. I think I'll just lie down and sleep."

I slept for twenty hours.

Sergeant Copelet's letter arrived a few days later.

# EPILOGUE

---

*March 28, 1968*

*Dear Cooby:*

*It's been a few days since you left Bear Cat. A lot has happened. The news is not great.*

*The 312$^{th}$ was deployed to the First Corps Area about a day after you left. I'm told it's somewhere near the DMZ around Pleiku. The company we helped build is now vacant.*

*I have even worse news. The very morning of the move, Ciatkin committed suicide behind an officers' latrine. The first sergeant asked me to identify the body.*

*Only have a few days left and I'll spend it as an air traffic controller for the Fifth. It sure is spooky being the only resident of the former 312$^{th}$.*

*I miss you, professor.*

*I'll call as soon as I get home.*

*Hope all is well,*

*Cope*

*PS: Sorry you had to find out something else about rule number four the hard way. Being in an unpopular war makes it difficult to return home. It was the same after Korea.*

# THE ARMY WAY

---

RULE NUMBER ONE:

*Document everything.*

RULE NUMBER TWO:

*No documentation, no pay.*

RULE NUMBER THREE:

*Do it right, or do it over.*

RULE NUMBER FOUR:

*a) What the soldier sees, hears, or reads, is not what the soldier gets.*

*b) Hurry up and wait.*

# Book Review for PACHYDERMS

**Written for Military Writers Society of America
By Father Ron Moses Camarda**

*Pachyderms* is a diamond in the rough. The book reads like a screenplay of a movie with substance… but better. The characters come alive, albeit complex, simple and surprisingly likeable through the mind of a very gifted and unknown author. St. Augustine's Confessions came to my mind as I finished this book. Danny looks deeply into his own heart and soul and recognizes his own faulty judgments and foibles. The book is raw and demands that you feel, think about, and experience and observe the fears, terror, boredom, and blunt force of an illogical war encountered by a young new recruit who was overwhelmed by the inevitable deployment to an unpopular, seductive, and perplexing Vietnam War that blasted the body, mind, and soul of the people who encountered it.

If you dare to take the journey of this book, you will require a good dose of courage for the self-reflection. The author forced this Iraq combat veteran chaplain to re-evaluate some of my false assumptions of Vietnam Veterans and all combat veterans for that matter. Humbling.

To me, the book is more than real. It explores the depths of the heart and soul of young unsuspecting kids thrown into a cauldron of invisible enemies, confusion, lust, virtue, immorality, poor leadership, superb leadership, terror, friendship, passion, fickleness, greed, death, red tape, the Army way, and love.

The story is compelling and resonates with life on many levels and dimensions. The book is connected and comes full circle in most cases. Some of the "unresolved" issues are just that, irresolvable. How could anyone understand suicide, returning soldiers treated like criminals, inept commanders receiving awards for causing so much misery, or a scared friend not saying good-bye?

The story, which more resembles a memoir, is complicated. Vietnam Veterans are complicated. This story really got under my skin. I almost gave up on giving the book serious consideration. That would have been a grave mistake. Any American history teacher or scholar would discover that *Pachyderms* is a hidden treasure, to use a Scriptural analogy.

Before I read about the deployment of Cooby, I was so intolerant and skeptical of Vietnam Vets in general. I was blind to the plight of the enlisted. When I read in shock about the R & R trysts of the soldiers to places like Hong Kong and Penang with the merciless debauchery, lust, and the animalistic behavior, I was really angry with the soldiers. But I still really loved them unconditionally and I understood that they were not thinking with their brains, but only with their broken hearts. I forgave them and read on as difficult as it was. I am filled with gratitude for these men who suffered and were tormented by even their own family members upon return. Danny allowed me the privilege of comparing the return from the war in Vietnam to the war in Iraq. I am not sure I would have survived. In war, "Charlie" (code for the silent and invisible enemy), can never hurt us other than physically. Only friends and loved ones can inflict the wounds of the heart and soul. And that is very clear to me, what all of us Americans did to our returning Vietnam Veterans. For some of them, death was a more humane or compassionate choice compared to returning to a hostile America of the time. It just is. Vietnam Vets are not innocent nor without sins, but they do deserve to be forgiven for their own sins. They do not need to take the responsibility of those politicians and lousy leaders who sent them there without true support for the troops. My own sins are a plethora. Who are we to judge?

Danny Buoy, like his sergeant who went from feared boss to endearing friend, mentored me through this book. Just as his former sergeant corrected Danny Coobat, when he failed to mentor his replacement, in a very subtle way, Danny encourages those who dare to listen to his story.

"The reader" has never been in a bunker during incoming mortar, has never pulled a burned body from a Chinook, and didn't return from R & R only to find his buddies rotated. At 17-years-old, I entered into the world of the military complex. Danny touches on many of those highs, lows, and real life in between in navigating the torturous journey of becoming, not just a modern warrior...but a decent and mature human being capable of honest and humbling self-criticism. He also shares with us the ability to love and to be loved.

The story is ordinary, gut-wrenching, and extremely thought-provoking, monumental and profound. The journey will be impossible if done alone. The 312th Company that lives only in our memories is the best teacher, with no bull.

Thank you, Sergeant Coobat (and your friends both living and dead). Welcome Home!

"Not good enough, Danny." I wish I could embrace you, Sergeant Coobat, in a long hug, engrossed in a feeling "brothers in war" share. My eyes are too wet to confirm seeing a tear in yours, but my ears heard your voice crack when you said, "Good-bye, Reader."

# ABOUT THE AUTHOR

Danny Buoy is the pseudonym of a real soldier who served in the Vietnam War. Danny was born, reared, and educated in Omaha, Nebraska. In 1966, the only college graduate in a family of nine, Danny found himself without a draft deferment. He decided to enlist rather than wait for his draft notice, and one year later his home was a tent in South Vietnam. Quite to his surprise, he had become a Flight Operations Specialist for a U.S. Army Chinook Helicopter Company, a rather unusual job for a soldier who had trained for the Infantry.

When Danny arrived home in Nebraska, he discovered a nation that was unwilling to acknowledge his service in the very war they had sent him to fight. *Pachyderms*, his first novel, is his attempt to show a side of the Vietnam war that few Americans have ever seen.

www.ingramcontent.com/pod-product-compliance
Lightning Source LLC
Chambersburg PA
CBHW050029180626
46810CB00002B/635